The Proud Liberal

A Novel
by Mark Mathabane

New Millennium Books
Portland, Oregon

Produced in the United States of America

New Millennium Books release: August 2010

Mathabane, Mark
The Proud Liberal: a novel / Mark Mathabane
ISBN 0-9672333-4-8
ISBN 978-0-9672333-4-5

To order books, email books@mathabane.com or visit www.mathabane.com

To David Ernsberger, Edward "Ned" Chase, and Fifi Oscard, dear friends who passed away in 2005. Your character as proud liberals, and your fearless championing, at home and abroad, of free speech, equal rights, equal justice, and equal opportunity, which are the hallmark of humane societies and progressive democracies, inspired this book.

Other books by Mark Mathabane that are available
as printed books or e-books at www.mathabane.com

Kaffir Boy

Kaffir Boy in America

Love in Black and White

African Women: Three Generations

Miriam's Song

Ubuntu

Author's Note

This story was inspired by my conviction that liberalism is one of the best ideologies in human history but has been so maligned by conservatives in America that it is now considered one of the worst. It is my hope that liberals everywhere will proudly defend their creed, and use it to create a better world for all, regardless of color, nationality, race, religion, social class, gender or sexual orientation.

"The strongest man in the world is he who has the courage to stand alone."
– Henrik Ibsen

"It has been the one song of those who thirst after absolute power that the interest of the state requires that its affairs should be conducted in secret...But the more such arguments disguise themselves under the mask of public welfare, the more oppressive is the slavery to which they will lead. ...Better that right counsels be known to enemies than that the evil secrets of tyrants should be concealed from the citizens. They who can treat secretly of the affairs of a nation have it absolutely under their authority, and as they plot against the enemy in time of war, so they do against the citizens in time of peace."
– Baruch Spinoza

"Without Head Start, Higher Education loans and scholarships, the Fair Housing Act, Medicare, Medicaid, clear air and water, and civil rights, life would be nastier, more brutish, and shorter for millions of Americans."
– Joseph Califano Jr.,
the Secretary of Health, Education and Welfare
under President Jimmy Carter, describing
liberalism's important contributions
to American life

"We (Democrats) cannot win by being Republican lite."
– Howard Dean

Part I

Chapter 1

Sunday, August 6, 2003

Mustafa's callused hands tightly gripped the vibrating steering wheel of the semi truck as it crossed the Louisiana border into Mississippi. It was 7:30 a.m. The grey overcast sky threatened rain and Mustafa's bloodshot eyes battled sleep. He had been on interstate highway I-20 since leaving Texas shortly after midnight. Only the nagging fear of being stopped by state troopers, and the back of the truck searched, prodded him to stay awake.

Mustafa had reason to dread a search. Hidden inside crates marked FURNITURE: HANDLE WITH CARE in the back of the truck were AK-47 assault rifles, gas masks, police scanners, tear gas, camouflage netting, fake UN and Department of Defense identity cards, fake social security cards and birth certificates, and ten carefully sealed containers packed with ingredients for producing enough weapons of mass destruction to wipe out half the population of the United States. The cache of WMD included military grade cyanide and radioactive isotopes for making dirty bombs.

Mustafa, a member of a clandestine group known as al-Qaeda *in America*, had picked up the arsenal at a remote refinery located about 30 miles northeast of Midland, Texas, which belonged to the American subsidiary of Phoenix, Inc., a foreign-owned oil company with headquarters in Saudi Arabia and offices in more than 80 countries.

Al Qaeda in America's mission was to ignite *Operation Saladin*, the deadliest and most sophisticated terrorist plot ever launched against the United States since 9/11.

The financier of Operation Saladin, and owner of Phoenix, Inc., was one of the richest men in the world, and also one of the most reclusive. According to *Forbes* magazine, his net worth was estimated at $30 billion. He had made most of his fortune in the oil business, including arranging ingenious ways for Iraqi dictator Saddam Hussein, following the first Gulf War, to siphon billions from the UN Oil-for-Food program. Known to his shadowy accomplices in al-Qaeda in America by the code name Aziz, he owned two private islands, one in the Caribbean and another in the Persian Gulf, a fleet of luxury jets and yachts, professional sports teams, a publishing and broadcasting empire, and more than two dozen palatial homes scattered across the globe.

Sporting a salt and pepper Van Dyke, and resplendently attired in the flowing, gold-trimmed robes and headdress of an Arab Sheik, the 73-year-old Aziz sat on a leather executive chair behind an antique mahogany desk inside his favorite plane, a custom-built 747 he had bought for $250 million from Boeing and spent an additional $20 million retrofitting to suit his extravagant taste. The jumbo jet – which had a dining area with a fully stocked bar, a movie theatre, a gold-plated bathroom with a Jacuzzi, a game room, and a 400 square-foot master bedroom with giant curtains mimicking the shifting sands of the Arabian desert – was cruising at an altitude of 37,000 feet over the Arabian Sea, headed for Aziz's heavily guarded Persian Gulf private island.

Twenty-four hours ago, Aziz had presided over a top-secret meeting held inside the ornate study of one of his sumptuous homes, a fortress-like, fifty-room, Mughal-Gothic mansion in Lahore, the second largest city in Pakistan. Attending the meeting were half a dozen emissaries from al-Qaeda's leader, Osama bin Laden.

Aziz grabbed a gold-plated cordless phone in the middle of the shiny desk and made an encrypted long distance call to North Carolina.

"This is Aziz speaking," he said in a thick foreign accent. "Last night I met with bin Laden's representatives. They are eager to know the latest on Operation Saladin."

"Tell them I've already recruited, vetted, and armed all the fifty cells we need," came the excited reply from Aziz's right-hand man, whose cryptonym was Ghazi. "And because of its proximity to Washington, DC, I've chosen the North Carolina cell to launch the military phase. A short while ago its leader Abdul informed me his driver Mustafa picked up the shipment of weapons from Texas early this morning."

"Does it include ingredients for making WMD?"

"Yes. And the cell's bunker is already equipped with a lab."

"Excellent. What about the political phase?"

"That's also proceeding according to plan. The marriage between Alison Ramsey and Eliot Whitaker III, without which Operation Saladin cannot succeed, will take place at precisely 1:30 P.M. EST. I'm personally attending to make sure nothing goes wrong."

"Enjoy yourself."

"Don't forget to watch it," said Ghazi. "It's live on CNN."

"I sure will," said Aziz, then hung up. His large face, bloated by years of a hedonistic lifestyle, broke into a Cheshire grin. He lit a Havana cigar. After several puffs, he grabbed a bottle of his favorite brandy, a Rémy Martin Louis XIII Diamond Cognac worth $6900, in a silver cooler on the desk next to leather-bound copies of his two favorite books, the *Kama Sutra* and *The Rubaiyat of Omar Khayyam.*

Aziz carefully uncorked the bottle and slowly poured its contents into a pear-shaped crystal snifter. He cradled the cognac in his neatly manicured hands for about a minute or so to release its delicious bouquet, then rang a bell. Instantly, from behind the giant silk curtains, appeared six gorgeously attired belly dancers.

"You called, master?" the tallest of the six, a blonde, asked demurely.

"Yes," said Aziz. "Omar Khayyam says the bird of life has but a little way to flutter, my slaves, and the bird is already on the wing. So let's have fun."

As erotic music filtered through the plane's hi-fi speakers, the women danced. Afterwards, they stripped and pleasured each other and then Aziz on a king-size bed whose carved headboard was decorated with images of frolicking nymphs and satyrs.

Shortly before 1:30 p.m., EST, a satiated Aziz dismissed his harem, grabbed a gold-plated remote control, and turned on the 42-inch plasma TV in the center of the mahogany entertainment unit. He settled into a comfortable position on the damasked chaise lounge and, between sips of cognac, watched as the wedding on which hinged the success of Operation Saladin unfolded live before millions of CNN viewers worldwide.

Alison Ramsey couldn't have chosen a more perfect day on which to get married – except that it was to the wrong man. The cloudless autumn sky above the Piedmont was a soft robin's egg blue, a chorus of birds sang among the dappled leaves of the towering oak and elm trees surrounding Duke University Chapel and, after a torrid summer capped by Hurricane Isabel, temperatures frolicked in the upper 60s and a gentle breeze blew.

Oh my God, what have I done? Alison, her heart pounding a mile a minute, moaned in silence as she and her bridesmaids bustled about one of the Chapel's backrooms, making last minute checks of their looks and pinning on their delicate corsages. *What was I thinking when I agreed to marry Eliot when the man I really love is Myron?*

It was too late for Alison to back out of a wedding that had cost a million dollars, and had been paid for by her wealthy godfather, Reginald Hunter, or Uncle Reggie as she fondly called him. Already, inside the cavernous Gothic chapel, reminiscent of Britain's Canterbury Cathedral and whose seventy-two exquisitely detailed stained glass windows depicted the life of Christ and Old Testament stories, the choir sang the processional by Frederick Handel, her favorite composer, to the sonorous accompaniment of the Flentrop organ mounted above the entrance doors. Three hundred spiffily dressed invitees – including scores of celebrities – packed the ornately carved mahogany pews.

Journalists from the nation's top TV networks, newspapers, and magazines jostled each other outside the chapel's majestic entrance, eagerly awaiting the appearance of the wedding party. The intense media spotlight – there were even representatives from *People, Southern Bride,* and the *National Enquirer* – only increased Alison's jitters. Her small hands trembled as she tried fastening the clasp of her necklace of white pearls.

How did I get myself into such a fucking mess? Anxiously, Alison watched her four bridesmaids scurry about the cool room, oblivious to her secret torment: Chanel Moore, her best friend from their days at Wellington Academy, a prestigious North Carolina boarding school, was an anchor for News 8, the top-rated news program in the Piedmont Triad; Karen Briggs Meriwether, a born-again Christian she had befriended during Outward Bound her junior year in high school, was vice-president for a major Southern bank; Vicky Thompson, her buddy from the Columbia Graduate School of Journalism, was CEO of a dot-com based in Research Triangle Park; and Linda Mitchell, her roommate at UNC Chapel Hill, was an environmental lawyer in Washington, DC. All of Alison's bridesmaids, who ranged in age from twenty-five to twenty-eight, looked absolutely gorgeous in matching lavender House of Bianchi bridesmaid dresses.

"Here, lemme help you," said Chanel, her maid of honor, grabbing the necklace.

"Thanks," Alison sighed as she absently stroked the folds of white satin flowing around her. She looked stunning in a Shantung gown with an illusion neckline and sleeves covered in delicate Alençon lace. A mock satin overskirt lent a petal effect to the full skirt underneath. The chapel train had lace appliqués and bow detailing. Her shiny dark hair was piled and sprayed into a flawless chignon and a twenty-five foot veil was carefully pinned around it. Chanel remarked that she resembled a princess in a fairy tale.

Alison thought otherwise. *This is no fairytale. It's a fucking nightmare. And there's no way I'm going to marry a man I know in my heart I don't love.*

Suddenly, Alison heard the heavy wooden door creak open. Her mother peered in. At fifty-two Darlene, an award-winning furniture designer, was in terrific shape, thanks to playing tennis at the local Country Club and doing Pilates several times a week. Five foot eight, she was elegance and sophistication personified in a meadow pink silk dress with matching pearl earrings. Her thick chestnut hair was swept up in a loose bun, and her soft brown eyes were enhanced by naturally arching eyebrows.

"Five more minutes, girls!" Smiling radiantly at Alison, Darlene added, "You look absolutely lovely, darling." She blew her a kiss then disappeared again.

"Oh my God, why can't I stop shaking?" Alison groaned. "My nerves are shot. Look – even my bouquet is vibrating!" The yellow, red, orange, and pink roses, cradled in wispy baby's breath, were indeed jiggling wildly in her white-gloved right hand.

"It's normal," Karen said in a reassuring tone. "I had the jitters so bad before my wedding people thought I was an epileptic. I almost had to be carried down the aisle strapped on a stretcher." After saying this, the petite Karen hurried off to the other side of the room to help Linda and Vicky with their corsages. Chanel and Alison were left alone.

Alison looked pleadingly into the glittering brown eyes of the statuesque African-American woman who was as close to her as a twin sister, and who was privy to the secrets of her love life. "Chanel, am I crazy?" she said in a desperate whisper. "I'm about to walk down the aisle and marry Eliot, yet all I can think about is Myron."

"Shit, I knew this would happen. You're still in love with him, aren't you?"

"Yes. I mean, no. Oh, I don't know," Alison said, frustrated. "Chanel, I trust your judgment. Please tell me the truth. Am I making a mistake by marrying Eliot?"

Chanel hesitated, and then slowly nodded. Alison grew pale.

"Like I told you before, girl," Chanel said, "I think you've rushed into this whole thing without thinking things through. It's bizarre, to say the least, to marry someone you clearly don't love a month after breaking up with someone you were madly in love with."

"You forget that Myron jilted me."

"But that's no reason for you to act crazy. If you think you can bury the pain of what Myron has done by rushing into a marriage with Eliot, you're making a big, big mistake. This marriage is for real, girl, not make believe."

Alison reflected for a while. Yes, Chanel was right. It had been her fury at Myron that had propelled her into a rebound marriage with Eliot when he had proposed. The fact that she and Eliot had briefly dated in high school wasn't enough reason for marrying. She should have taken time to heal, to reflect. Why had she acted so impetuously?

Before she could answer her own question, the door flew open and Darlene rushed in. "Okay, girls," she said excitedly. "This is it.

Remember to walk slowly, just like you did last night at rehearsal." Karen, Vicky, and Linda headed for the door.

"Well, come on, dear," Darlene said, looking at Alison, who lingered behind in a sunlit corner of the low-ceilinged room, Chanel by her side. "What are you waiting for?"

Alison didn't budge. Instead, her marine-blue eyes filled with tears. She turned away from the door and stared out the window. "I'm not coming," she mumbled.

"What did you say?" Darlene asked, moving closer.

Alison turned and faced her mother. "I'm not coming," she repeated.

Darlene gasped. Her face turned snow white. In an instant she was at Alison's side. "What the hell do you mean you're not coming?" She grabbed and shook her.

Alison looked at her mother through tear-filled eyes. "I still love Myron, Mom. And I'm convinced that if I walk out of here and marry Eliot I'll never be happy."

As she spoke, tears rolled down Alison's cheeks, leaving black mascara trails. Chanel crumpled a Kleenex and handed it to Alison.

"Now what should we do?" Darlene asked, a helpless look on her face.

Alison heard the processional song, Handel's *Music for the Royal Fireworks*, soar toward its soul-stirring crescendo. She pondered the consequences of not walking down that aisle and marrying the man she didn't love. Eliot's father, Theodore Whitaker, III, was one of the most powerful and influential conservatives in American politics. His backing was crucial to her father's efforts to cast himself as a conservative Democrat in his bid to win North Carolina's open gubernatorial seat at a time when, with President Bush's approval rating above 75 percent following the U.S. invasion of Iraq, running openly as a liberal, especially in the South, was considered by the pundits to be political suicide.

With his temper, stubborn pride, and jealously guarded pedigree, Theodore would be absolutely livid at seeing his only child humiliated in front of the world. There was no telling what such a man, whose ruthless business and political tactics were legendary, might do to exact his revenge. What was supposed to be the wedding of the decade would turn into the scandal of the century – especially if word leaked out that Myron, the man she truly loved, was black.

Knowing the South's racial history, and the role race had played in recent elections across the region, Alison had no doubt that her father's candidacy, on which rested the hopes of millions, would be utterly ruined.

Alison was torn. *I'm damned if I do and I'm damned if don't.*

While Alison was wrestling with the biggest crisis of her life, the man who had precipitated that crisis by unexpectedly calling off their wedding less than two months ago was leaving an important meeting of a newly founded liberal political action committee called Let's Unite for a Progressive America or LUPA. The meeting was held in the paneled conference room of LUPA's two-story offices on K Street, the major thoroughfare in Washington, DC dubbed "the Wall Street of influence peddling," that was home to numerous think tanks, advocacy groups, and lobbyists who shaped America's destiny.

The agenda for the meeting was finding ways to combat conservative propaganda about liberalism, and to invigorate it as a political force, at a time when the Democratic and Republican Parties were waging a titanic battle to see whose ideology would shape American society in the 21st century. It was a battle the Democratic Party was clearly, and badly, losing. This was shown by the fact that the GOP now controlled the presidency and both Houses of Congress, and had adroitly succeeded in transforming the word "liberal," one of the most resplendent in the lexicon of American democracy, into a politically toxic shibboleth, almost akin to being called a child molester.

Participants at the closed-door meeting, which lasted three hours and included several wealthy liberal donors who were fed up with the cowardice of many leaders of the Democratic Party and their willingness to prostitute the party's core principles for ephemeral political gain, had agreed that LUPA should adopt a two-pronged approach if liberalism was to stage a political comeback. First, LUPA should devise strategies for effectively branding what the Democratic Party stood for, and for reminding the American people that most of the priceless freedoms and rights they enjoyed as citizens, and which were now under siege by conservative ideologues, had been achieved under liberal administrations. Second, LUPA should comb the country seeking candidates with the courage to defend liberalism's sterling record in public service with as much conviction and passion as conservatives were crowing over the paltry and specious achievements of their bankrupt and effete ideology.

These proud liberals would be given all the help they needed – political, financial, and strategic – to wage effective and savvy campaigns. And Myron, as LUPA's chief strategist, was charged with finding such candidates and convincing them to run. Myron was ideal for the job. Aside from having worked on the campaigns of various liberals, among them Edward Kennedy and Howard Dean, he had recently published a bestselling book called *One Nation: How Liberalism Can Unite America.* But given how dreaded the liberal label was by politicians, Myron knew that his quest was more difficult than that of Jason's for the Golden Fleece. He also knew the stakes – for the future of American Democracy – if liberalism were to become extinct as a political force.

An avid cyclist, Myron rode his K-2 bike to his one-bedroom apartment at the Kennedy Warren on 3133 Connecticut Avenue, where he had been living since relocating from Harlem in early August to work for LUPA. Despite having landed a liberal's dream job, Myron felt utterly miserable. The painful breakup with Alison, his best friend and political soul mate, had left him depressed and riddled with guilt.

I shouldn't have let Mama pressure me not to marry the woman I truly love simply because of her skin color, he thought as he stopped at a red light and glanced up at a news helicopter flying low across the blue sky. *I was being a hypocrite and a coward.*

Only immersion in his work kept Myron sane, and the furies of depression at bay.

I wonder how Alison's wedding went, he thought ruefully as he biked past the National Zoo, whose entrance teemed with visitors, many of them lured there by the presence of two celebrity giant pandas from China, Mei Xiang and Tian Tian.

After locking up his bike, Myron hurriedly made his way to the elevator across the Kennedy Warren's 20-foot-high lobby with its painted Aztec beamed ceiling, aluminum balustrades, staircase railings, and fluted and rounded marble-faced pilasters. Reaching his apartment on the fifth floor, he tossed his fat backpack on a futon couch crowded with books, newspapers, and magazines. He walked over to the rattan accent table and pressed the blinking message light on his digital answering machine.

There were three messages. The first was from the alumni office at his alma mater, Columbia University, soliciting a donation to the annual fund. The second was from his mother, saying she was back home in New York City after visiting relatives in Greensboro, North Carolina. The third was from Isaac Driessen, his roommate from Yale Law School. "Congratulations," Isaac said in the message. "I just read in *The Times* that you've been hired to lead a liberal PAC. I'm now back home and have a job with the Southern Poverty Law Center. I specialize in representing death row inmates. I hope we can catch up next time I'm in DC, or you are in Montgomery."

Myron smiled. He recalled how Isaac, a proud liberal like himself, had, after Al Gore's controversial loss in the 2000 presidential election, become so disillusioned with American politics that he had decided to travel abroad, first to South America and later to South Africa and Egypt, to work as a human rights lawyer for Amnesty International. Myron jotted down in his BlackBerry the cell phone number and e-mail address Isaac had left on the answering machine. "I too should have gone abroad," he thought, stepping into the brightly lit kitchen with maple cabinets and a marble countertop. Myron had had an opportunity to go work for an AIDS non-profit in South Africa, but had declined the offer because his mother had just undergone ovarian cancer surgery.

After brewing a mug of Tension Tamer herbal tea, Myron, a former collegiate tennis player who had won the NCAA double championship, kicked off his size eleven Stan Smith tennis shoes, which he wore even with business suits because they felt comfortable. He then sank into a navy-blue leather recliner, flicked on the 27-inch color TV perched atop an oak stand with tempered glass doors, to catch up on the day's news.

Myron couldn't believe what he saw on CNN. There were Alison and Eliot being declared man and wife by a pudgy white-robed Baptist minister inside the Duke University Chapel. The camera zoomed in on Alison's oval face with its prominent cheekbones. For some unknown reason Myron suddenly recalled what a fortune teller had told Alison three months ago after studying her face. Myron and Alison had just become engaged and were strolling down a busy street in New York City's Chinatown following lunch at their favorite restaurant. "You have a fire face which is typical of outdoorsy, fast-paced, and adventurous people who sometimes take crazy risks," the wizened fortune teller had said. "When you're happy, there's a glitter in your eyes."

Myron noticed that the glitter in Alison's marine blue eyes, into which he had gazed with affection countless times, was gone. It had been replaced by a melancholy sadness, for which he blamed himself. Myron could no longer hold back the emotions he had kept bottled up since their painful breakup.

"My God, what have I done to the woman I love'?" he wailed, burying his head in his hands. "Why did I force her to marry Eliot?"

Twenty-six-year-old Eliot beamed and felt as if he had just won the lottery. While standing in the middle of the upper nave, gazing into Alison's eyes and pledging to love her forever, in sickness and in health, he still couldn't believe that she was about to become his lawfully wedded wife. Eliot was convinced that such a miracle couldn't have occurred had it not been for the intervention of a man he called his "guardian angel."

After the pudgy-faced and silver-haired minister finished pronouncing Eliot and Alison man and wife, and Eliot had kissed the bride, he cast a furtive glance in the direction where his guardian angel was sitting in the middle of a row of wooden chairs reserved for honored guests. The chairs had replaced the original front pews that were destroyed by a fire in the nave during the 1970s. When their eyes met, Eliot's guardian angel – a short man with a slight limp in his left foot, a broad forehead and pomaded gray hair slightly parted in the middle – smiled broadly and winked.

Eliot's guardian Angel was none other than Ghazi.

Mustafa didn't see the roadblock until it was too late. Several police cars were ranged across the four-lane highway. At first Mustafa was under the impression that there had been an accident, but to his horror, he noticed that the state troopers were searching vehicles, and that they seemed to be focusing their search on trucks like his.

Mustafa began sweating bullets. Had the police been tipped off about the cargo he was transporting? In a panic, he thought of fleeing, but he knew that would be folly. He would be instantly shot. As he eyed a serious-looking state trooper with a holstered gun dangling by his side coming toward him, Mustafa anxiously awaited his fate.

"Your driver's license please?" said the state trooper.

"Sure," Mustafa said, trying hard to prevent his hand from shaking as he gave the state trooper his driver's license. "Here it is, sir."

"Your name is Buck McGuire?" asked the state trooper, looking carefully at the face on the driver's license and then back at Mustafa.

"Yes, sir," said Mustafa.

"And you live in High Point, North Carolina?"

"Yes, sir."

"And you work for New South Fine Furniture Gallery?"

"Yes, sir. May I ask what the roadblock is about?"

"Sure," said the state trooper. "We are looking for a group of five men of Middle Eastern descent. A waitress at a diner along the highway reported that she overheard them cracking jokes about 9/11 and President Bush. They then made suspicious comments in a strange language. She said the men were driving a semi."

Mustafa breathed a big sigh of relief. He couldn't believe his luck. "I'm a patriotic American," he said with eagerness. "I fought in Operation Desert Storm as a Green Beret and was awarded the Congressional Medal of Honor." He pulled out from behind his denim shirt a gold star surrounded by a wreath, topped by an eagle on a bar inscribed with the word "Valor." He showed the gleaming medal to the state trooper.

"I'm honored to make the acquaintance of a real American hero," the state trooper said deferentially, admiring the medal. "Truly honored, sir."

"Thank you," said Mustafa. "I hope you catch them terrorists."

"Don't worry, sir, we will. We know what they look like. Drive safely now."

The state trooper handed Mustafa his driver's license and returned to his colleagues. Soon thereafter, Mustafa's semi, packed with WMD destined for al-Qaeda in America's cell in Asheville, North Carolina, was waved through the road block.

Following the wedding ceremony, Alison and Eliot rode in a silver Rolls Royce to a private reception at the historic Carolina Inn on the campus of UNC Chapel Hill. On the way there, Eliot kept babbling about what a wonderful honeymoon awaited them in Bermuda. Pretending to be listening and happy, Alison was pondering how to undo the biggest mistake of her life: marrying the man she didn't love for political reasons.

As the Rolls pulled into the crowded parking lot of the Carolina Inn, the solution finally occurred to her. *I'll sue for divorce as soon as dad's campaign is over. In the meantime, I must do everything to avoid becoming pregnant with Eliot's baby."*

Chapter 2

High Point, North Carolina, May 10, 2004

Alison struggled to find a more comfortable position on the king-size poster bed in the middle of the hotel suite. "This baby is too big," she complained. A week overdue, her midsection was so gargantuan that Alison was having a hard time even lying down.

Eliot reached over and helped her turn. "It's because it's a Whitaker, honey," he said, gently stroking her eggplant belly. "My father came in at ten pounds six ounces. I was nine pounds. And my grandfather was the biggest at eleven pounds."

Eliot, this may not be your baby. Oh, God, how am I ever going to explain to him – to the world for that matter – if this turns out to be Myron's child? Alison was convinced that the baby she was carrying was Myron's baby because, forced by political realities to marry Eliot nine months ago, she had done everything to insure she didn't become pregnant by him. She had worn a diaphragm with spermicidal lubrication during the few times they had made love, and on all those occasions she had insisted that he wear a condom. But despite such elaborate precautions she had become pregnant. Since she didn't believe in abortion, though she was a passionate supporter of a woman's right to choose, she had carried the fetus to term, and let everyone believe it was Eliot's baby.

In an attempt to distract herself from the nightmarish scenario of what would happen to her father's gubernatorial campaign if the baby everyone expected to be white turned out black, Alison reached for a small leather-bound volume of poetry whose cover bore the letter *A* in calligraphy. A gift from her godfather, the anthology lay open on the nightstand next to Eliot's Diet Coke. She tried reading one of her favorite poems, "How Do I Love Thee," by Elizabeth Barrett Browning, but she abandoned the effort half-way when the sonnet brought back memories of Myron, and the countless evenings they had spent reading poems to each other while sipping red wine or herbal tea in his Harlem Brownstone apartment overlooking the Hudson River.

"I wish we'd stayed home," Alison said.

Dumbfounded, Eliot stared at her. "On election night! Come on, honey."

"Don't you care about how I feel?" Alison retorted peevishly.

"Of course I do."

Eliot and Alison were in Suite 1229 of the Sheraton Greensboro Four Seasons Hotel, the largest convention center between Washington, DC and Atlanta, Georgia. For the past half an hour they had been agonizing over election returns in what was turning out to be the closest race in North Carolina primary history. The adjoining suite, reachable through a connecting door in the middle of the pastel-colored wall, had the funereal atmosphere of a wake as Alison's father, mother, in-laws and several of her father's key advisors solemnly monitored election returns. Alison had excused herself from their company on the pretext of wanting to lie down to relieve her aching back. But the main reason she wanted to be alone was that, realizing that the baby was due any moment, she was obsessed by a single thought: *Who is my baby's father?*

Her anxiety increased as the race tightened. It had been a cliffhanger all evening, despite the lowest voter turnout in North Carolina primary history. The lead had seesawed more than a dozen times between her father and his opponent, a multimillionaire hog farmer named Stephen Douglas, who was more conservative than Jesse Helms. Most traditional Democratic voters had stayed away from the polls despite the balmy weather – the day had seen record temperatures in the mid-70s – apparently disgusted and dismayed at having to choose between two candidates who, throughout a mean-spirited and expensive primary campaign, had tried mightily to out-conservative each other rather than proudly articulating core Democratic Party principles.

"I think your Dad will pull it off," Eliot said, sipping a diet Coke.

"Even if he does," Alison said indifferently, "I doubt very much he'll win in November. Voters don't like politicians who keep reinventing themselves."

"Of course he'll win," Eliot said. "He's now a bona fide conservative. You should have heard his speech last week at the Family Values Convention in Winston-Salem. Absolutely no trace of liberalism in it. And he received a ten-minute standing ovation. Longer than that which they gave their hero, Jesse Helms."

Alison's limbs tightened in muted anger. *Eliot, I don't want to start arguing with you over politics, okay. My back is killing me.* "Can you please help me up?" Alison said, as she attempted to roll over to the left side of the bed. "I need to go to the bathroom."

"Maybe you should've agreed to induce," Eliot said, assisting Alison to her feet.

"No," Alison said vehemently. "I don't want any strange chemicals in my fucking body, okay. I want to deliver my baby naturally." She waddled like a penguin to the bathroom. When she came back, she said wearily, "We can go join the others now."

Upon entering the adjoining suite, Alison and Eliot found everyone riveted to the 27-inch color TV screen. They sat down on a burgundy loveseat behind everyone else.

"Hi, Sweetie," Darlene said with a weak smile. "Feeling better?"

"I'm okay." Alison glanced at her father. Ramsey was slumped in a high-backed chair by a cherry writing table, nervously twirling a Mount Blanc fountain pen. Two of his advisors hung aimlessly about. On the table were a multi-channel speaker phone, a lamp, and copies of two speeches: one to be delivered if he won and the other if he lost.

Alison was convinced that her father was headed for certain defeat. She was equally convinced that had he not, in his desperation to flee from his liberal record, alienated his base of traditional Democrats by flip-flopping on a host of issues they deeply cared about – the Iraq war, civil rights, the environment, workers' rights, public education, and abortion rights – the results would have been entirely different.

He'd have waltzed away with the fucking nomination, Alison thought with traces of bitterness. *Now he's in the political fight of his life.*

As Alison shifted positions in an effort to relieve the mounting strain on her lower back, she heard Chanel, who was co-anchoring election night for News-8, say:

"The race between Lawrence Ramsey and Steven Douglas is still too close to call. With 95 percent of the precincts reporting, Douglas is ahead by a mere 500 votes. If his slim lead holds, the political neophyte who a few months ago had absolutely no name recognition, was thirty-five points behind, and was dismissed as unelectable by pundits because of his conservative politics, will have pulled off one of the biggest upsets of the political season. When we come back from a commercial break, we'll go live to our reporters at each campaign headquarters for an assessment of the mood in what is turning out to be the closest election in the history of North Carolina."

While most Tar Heels were glued to their TV sets, eager to see if Douglas would prevail in the hotly contested Democratic gubernatorial primary, thirty-eight-year-old Nancy McGuire had her 27-inch RCA color TV turned off. Sitting on a faded brown sleeper sofa in the living room of a clapboard farmhouse with a wraparound porch, situated on the outskirts of High Point, Nancy was busy rehearsing a plan about how she was going to steal a newborn baby before her husband Buck returned from his latest trucking trip.

I must have the baby by the time he gets back tomorrow, Nancy thought as she went over details of the elaborate scheme she had concocted approximately seven months ago, following her third miscarriage while Buck was away delivering furniture in Texas. She hadn't divulged the miscarriage to him or anyone else. Instead, she had continued wearing maternity clothes, gaining weight, and pretending to have morning sickness.

Nancy stared at the paraphernalia arrayed about the faded rectangular Queen Anne coffee table in front of her. They included a blonde wig, blue contact lenses, a nursing uniform, her old hospital ID, and a note on which she had scribbled, "Call Buck."

Nancy picked up the phone and dialed Buck's cell phone number.

"Hi, honey," she said, trying hard to keep her voice from trembling.

*****

Mustafa had just finished tumbling a hooker with long red hair on the sagging king size mattress of a seedy motel room in Little Rock, Arkansas when his cell phone rang. He answered on the third ring and was startled to hear his wife's cheery voice.

"Hi, love," he said as the prostitute stroked his back. "Has the baby arrived yet?"

"Yes. Buck Junior came this morning. But my water broke before I could get to the hospital. So I delivered him all by myself. Right here at home."

Buck was stunned and impressed. "Wow. Is he okay?"

"Sure. Remember I used to work as a nurse."

"Of course," Mustafa said. "And you, hon, how you feeling?"

"Fine. Just a little tired."

"I can't wait to hold Buck Junior in my arms. Is he feeding well?"

"He's got your appetite, hon."

Mustafa laughed.

"When will you be home?" Nancy asked.

"Tomorrow night like I told you," Mustafa said. "I'll drive like the wind."

"Don't rush. I don't want you to get into an accident."

"I won't, honey," Mustafa said. "And I'm very proud of you."

"Thanks," Nancy said. "I love you, Buck."

"I love you too, honey," Mustafa said, and then hung up.

"So you're a father, huh?" said the prostitute, kissing him on the neck.

"Yeah," Mustafa said proudly.

"That's nice," said the prostitute. "Does that mean you'll no longer need me?"

"Hell no," Mustafa said.

Mustafa turned around and picked up right where he had left off.

Long abuse had created in Nancy a sixth sense that told her that there had been a woman in the room with Buck while they were talking. As she mournfully replaced the cordless phone in its cradle and walked back to the coffee table, tears trickled down her face.

Only a baby can stop Buck's sleeping around, she thought as she resumed putting on her disguise. *And he said he wanted a boy, an heir.*

Nancy also hoped that if she gave Buck the son he badly wanted, he might even stop hanging out with those strange men with Muslim names like "Abdul" and "Ghazi" who, whenever they called, referred to him as Mustafa instead of Buck. Nancy remembered that when she had timidly asked him who the strange men were, Buck had said that they were part of a covert counter-terrorism unit organized by the Department of Homeland Security to track down domestic terrorists affiliated with al-Qaeda, and that the Muslim names were code names designed to provide them deep cover.

"This is highly classified, honey," Buck had said. "So don't tell anyone or millions of people will die. The Muslim terrorists we are after are plotting to carry out an attack bigger than 9/11. Nothing short of America's future is at stake."

Nancy didn't want to be blamed for causing an attack bigger than 9/11 so, like a good American patriot, she had believed Buck, just as she had believed the lies he always told her whenever he was late returning from trucking trips. Little was Nancy aware that the man she had married out of desperation twelve years ago belonged to an organization that was in cahoots with America's number one and deadliest enemy, Osama bin Laden.

Chapter 3

Buck's journey to becoming an ardent disciple of Bin Laden was very different from that undertaken by John Walker Lindh and Adam Gadahn, two white Americans who had gained notoriety as Jihadists. Lindh, twenty-four, grew up in an affluent California community before making his way to an al-Qaeda training camp in Afghanistan, where he personally met with bin Laden and was mesmerized by his ideology of terror and calls for a Jihad against America. The son of a government lawyer and a health care aid-worker, Lindh, who was raised Catholic, told FBI interrogators after his capture while fighting for the Taliban during the U.S. invasion of Afghanistan in 2001, that he had first become interested in Islam at age twelve after watching the movie, *Malcolm X*.

Gadahn's journey to becoming an al-Qaeda operative and spokesman was not that much different. According to the FBI, Gadahn, who had several aliases – Abu-Suhayb Al-Amriki, Abu Suhayb, and Adam Pearlman – was raised on a goat farm in California and home schooled until the age of fifteen. After converting from Judaism to Christianity his father, a musician, had changed the family name from Pearlman to Gadahn, which is derived from the Biblical name Gideon. The young Gadahn, who had been fond of heavy metal music and listening to fundamentalist Christian radio before converting to Islam, had joined al-Qaeda after moving to Pakistan in 1998.

Buck, on the other hand, came from an impoverished family in Western North Carolina that had little time for organized religion because survival was a daily and desperate struggle. His illiterate parents had eked out a living as sharecroppers on a tobacco farm. Buck was their only surviving child – his three siblings had died in infancy from preventable diseases – and he had grown up in a two-room shack without running water or electricity. His playmates were mostly the children of black sharecroppers. When there was not enough to eat at home, his playmates would invite him to share their scanty meals. He used to get angry whenever he heard some of his white friends use the word "nigger." He would call them "white trash" and dare to fight them.

Buck's attitude toward blacks started to change after he was laid off during the spring of 1997, when the textile factory where he worked relocated to Mexico. Finding another job proved impossible, due to his problem with PTSD and lack of a college degree. He began drinking heavily, became abusive, and started cheating on Nancy. Soon, he was hanging out in sleazy bars patronized by rednecks who, influenced by right-wing talk radio and its relentless liberal bashing, blamed their lack of jobs not on globalization, but on liberal programs they claimed coddled lazy and immoral minorities.

These men started telling Buck about white supremacists around the state who were dedicated to protecting white people's rights, and to fighting for a whites-only homeland, through any means necessary. One of these was Johnny Chandler, a former Army cryptographer whose father had been a rabid segregationist during the Civil Rights Movement. Enraged by the growing number of interracial couples in the U.S. military, Chandler had single-handedly established more than a dozen Klan dens on bases across the South during the 1980s. When the top brass clamped down on them, following the conviction in 1986 of Klan recruiter John A. Walker as a Soviet spy, Chandler had quit the army so he could continue his white supremacist activities unmolested.

These activities included establishing a Klan paramilitary group called "Saviors of the White Race," whose goal was to ignite a "Great Revolution." The blueprint for the Great Revolution was *The Turner Diaries*, a bestselling apocalyptic novel that luridly details how a white private guerilla army violently overthrows a liberal federal government (euphemistically called Zionist Occupation Government or ZOG) for legislating miscegenation and multiculturalism. The guerilla army then blows up FBI headquarters and the U.S. Capitol, and obliterates New York City and the state of Israel with nuclear bombs seized from Vandenberg Air Force Base in California. After victory is achieved, the guerilla army transforms America into a fascist Aryan Republic through the mass-executions of all non-whites, along with Jews, gays, feminists, and "race traitors": liberal white politicians and white women married to blacks and Jews.

Before being accepted as a member of Saviors of the White Race, Buck, because of his previous relationship with blacks, was subjected to a lie detector and stress test by Chandler, to insure his absolute loyalty to the cause of white supremacy. Buck had passed the tests with flying colors. One fact that made Buck a prized recruit was his job as a long-distance trucker for New South Fine Furniture Gallery. At the time Chandler was scouring the nation for weapons with which to arm his militia for the Great Revolution.

Three weeks after the U.S. invaded Iraq in 2003, Chandler struck gold when he was invited to attend the inaugural meeting of al-Qaeda in America, held at a heavily guarded country chateau in Blue Ridge Mountains of North Carolina. At the meeting, which was attended by more than two dozen leaders of white supremacist militias from across the country, Chandler had met the mastermind behind Operation Saladin, whose code name was Ghazi, and its financier, whose code name was Aziz. Chandler was stunned when Ghazi, after learning of his quest for weapons, offered him and his men much more than they needed. Ghazi's offer included an arsenal of biological, chemical, and radiological weapons; money to construct an underground bunker equipped with a laboratory for manufacturing sophisticated dirty bombs; and the distinction, after undergoing rigorous training, of launching the military phase of Operation Saladin.

Chandler had accepted the offer with alacrity. What particularly pleased him about it was Ghazi's revelation of an ingenious way he had devised to prevent Lawrence Ramsey, Chandler's number one enemy, from being elected governor of North Carolina.

Chapter 4

The mood was very tense as Ramsey and his entourage waited for a Viagra commercial to end so they could find out if Douglas would hold on to his slender lead and pull off a stunning come-from-behind victory. Alison didn't know what would be better, for her father to lose, or for him to eke out a win only to have his campaign for the general election destroyed by revelations that her baby was black. Her mind became so overwrought from wrestling with this dilemma that she gradually drifted off to sleep. She dreamt that the baby had been born, and that her fears had proved unfounded. The baby, blond, blue-eyed, and with alabaster skin, was clearly Eliot's. His birth brought mother and father closer together, despite their political differences. The baby became such a big hit with voters on the campaign trail that Ramsey ended up winning the governorship by a landslide and, four years later, was elected President of the United States.

Alison was awakened from her pleasant dream by the jarring ring of the telephone. Heart pounding, her eyes flew open just in time to see her father lunge for the phone and press the speaker button. She heard the jubilant voice of his campaign manager, Hunter, cry, "We did it, Lawrence! We did it, my friend! We've won!"

The suite instantly erupted into loud cheers. Champagne bottles popped. Theodore, grinning broadly, embraced Mary-Lou. Eliot, also grinning broadly, gave Alison a squeeze that almost took her breath away. Ramsey, a dazed look on his high-browed face, turned and planted a solid kiss on Darlene's flushed and upturned face, then hugged her tight. Ramsey's pollster and speechwriter gave each other stunned looks.

"Has Douglas conceded?" Ramsey asked with bated breath, hovering over the speakerphone, his arm around Darlene, who had tears in her soft brown eyes.

"He sure has," Hunter said. "His campaign manager just called a minute ago."

"Boy, that was close," Ramsey said, heaving a sigh of relief.

In one of the most breathtaking reversals in North Carolina political history,-Ramsey had won by a mere one hundred votes, 268,354 to Douglas's 268,254.

"A victory's a victory despite the margin," Hunter said. "But it sure was a squeaker. And early exit polls show that the black vote turned things around."

"Good thing I spoke at the NAACP convention last week."

"Yeah."

"So what's next?" Ramsey said in a voice that had regained its usual confidence.

"You and the family can come on down now," Hunter said, in a loud voice that sought to rise above the ballroom din. "An acceptance speech is in order."

As his entourage spruced up, Ramsey and his advisors quickly went over the acceptance speech Hunter had prepared for him. Within ten minutes they were all crammed inside the paneled elevator and headed for the Guilford ballroom on the first floor. Hunter met them in the lobby. "Ah, there's my dear Alison," he beamed, coming over to her, arms outstretched. He gave her a huge bear hug. "I won our bet, didn't I?"

"You're amazing, Uncle Reggie," said Alison with admiration. "I was convinced Dad was going to lose. I guess I was wrong to disagree with your strategy." Alison had insisted that her father not distance himself from his liberal record, while Hunter had countered that doing so was the only way Ramsey could win.

"You meant well, dear," Hunter said with a smile that creased his prominent forehead and showed off his small, glistening white teeth.

"I know what a proud liberal you are." Hunter scrutinized Alison's face. "But you look a trifle sad, my dear. How can you be blue on such a joyful occasion? Surely it's not because you lost the bet."

Alison flashed a weak smile. "No. It's the baby, Uncle Reggie."

Hunter's eyes widened. "The baby? You don't mean –"

"No. I'm not about to go into labor yet. And that's the problem."

"Be patient, my dear. It'll be over soon. And the baby will make you and Eliot so proud that you'll look back on the experience as having been well worth it."

But, Uncle Reggie, what if it's not Eliot's baby? Alison thought as she watched Hunter embrace the rest of Ramsey's retinue. *Maybe I should finally tell him about my fears so he can advise me what to do. On second thought, he might not understand. Who would? I'm married to a white man and my baby is black. Oh, God. . . .*

Hunter led the Ramsey party into the 40,000 square feet column-free ballroom, which was noisy and packed with the candidate's jubilant supporters. Cameras flashed and a multitude of hands reached out to shake Ramsey's as he made his way to a stage festooned with American flags. Red, white, and blue balloons and confetti rained from the high ceiling as "God Bless America" blared from the speakers. A huge blue and white banner draped behind the dais read, "RAMSEY: A NEW DEMOCRAT."

Alison stood directly behind her mother, anxious to hide her immense belly from the roving news cameras. Her dress was cut from dark fabric rich in jewel tones. For a maternity dress, it was quite attractive, but she was convinced it made her resemble a pig on a spit. She had gained nearly forty pounds during the pregnancy, and almost all of it was packed in her mid-section. Eliot proudly wrapped his arm possessively around her waist. Behind them stood his parents, smiling and waving at the jubilant crowd. Outwardly, they were the perfect American family.

Ramsey, his body-language miraculously transformed by a narrow victory gained at the expense of his principles, confidently leaned into the cluster of microphones sprouting over the podium like so many antennae. He smiled and waved at the adoring crowd. The brown hair at the back of his head was starting to thin, but he looked much younger than his fifty-eight years thanks to regular jogging, even while on the campaign trail. His marine-blue eyes, lined with fine wrinkles, were deep-set and thoughtful. He wore a conservative navy blue suit, a white monogrammed cotton shirt, and a red tie, courtesy of the clothing specialists and image makers from Hunter's consulting firm, who had completely refurbished his wardrobe, which was considered too liberal, to conform to his image as a conservative Democrat. Darlene stood next to him, looking up at him proudly.

"Ladies and Gentlemen," Ramsey began in a smooth, even baritone that had made him a popular singer of the Glee club during his days at his alma mater, Guilford College. "My opponent, Stephen Douglas, has finally conceded."

A roar of cheers filled the ballroom. Blue and white "Ramsey for Governor" and "A Leader We Can Trust" signs bobbed all over the place.

"I'd like to congratulate him on a hard-fought race. He's promised me his complete support in the general election, and I thank him for that."

"Ramsey! Ramsey! Ramsey!" the crowd chanted.

When most of the chanting had died down, Ramsey continued reading verbatim the speech Hunter had written for him. "My victory is proof that, despite what happened during the 2002 mid-term election, Democrats can still win in the South. But to win we must abandon discredited liberal policies and embrace mainstream conservative values."

The crowd applauded. Ramsey proceeded to recite a litany of promises of what he would do if elected governor. Goaded by his desperation to distance himself from his liberal record, he promised to support President Bush's senseless Iraq war, his unnecessary tax cuts for the rich, and his discriminatory call for a constitutional amendment banning gay marriages. Ramsey's timeserving speech was greeted with loud and enthusiastic cheers from an audience of conservative Democrats Hunter's consulting firm had carefully selected to give the appearance that Ramsey was no longer a liberal. Even the hard-to-please Theodore couldn't stop clapping, especially when Ramsey promised to support Bush's tax cuts for the rich. Theodore turned to Eliot and, nudging him by the elbow, whispered, "Your father-in-law is now a true conservative, son. No doubt about that. All what's left is for you to make sure Alison becomes one."

"I will, dad," said, Eliot in a voice of someone eager to please an authority figure.

Hunter discreetly handed Ramsey a handwritten note. He quickly read it, then leaned into the microphone and said, "The networks have just declared Clarence Lynch winner of the Republican gubernatorial primary."

The crowd booed.

"I look forward to running against him in the general election," Ramsey said with a confident smile. "Ours will be a race to prove whose brand of conservatism represents the true values and interests of the people of the state of North Carolina."

The crowd applauded and cried, "Ramsey's! Ramsey's! Ramsey's!"

Alison felt like puking at the spectacle of her father's unabashed co-opting of the Republican agenda in his desperation to get elected. She found it hard to believe that a man once considered the standard-bearer of the liberal movement in the South, a man carved in the mold of some of North Carolina's most progressive leaders – the Aycocks, the Sanfords, the Grahams, and the Hunts – a man who in the 1960s and 1970s had crusaded against the Klan, supported integration and lost an election rather than prostitute his liberal soul for political gain – now sounded more conservative than Jesse Helms.

As she listened to her father pander to white prejudices, ignorance, and fear, Alison couldn't take it anymore. She discreetly left the stage. Eliot followed behind.

"What's wrong, honey?" he asked.

"My back is killing me. I wanna go home."

"I'll come along."

On the way to the parking lot, Alison wondered what would happen to his father's conservative masquerade if the baby she was carrying turned out to have been fathered by a black man. Alison thought back to the 2000 U.S. Presidential primaries, during which Arizona Senator John McCain, who had the big "Mo" after trouncing George W. Bush in the New Hampshire Republican primary by 19 points, was defeated in the South Carolina primary, partly because anonymous push pollsters had told voters that he had fathered an illegitimate black child and was therefore too liberal. In reality, McCain and his wife Cindy had adopted a girl from a Mother Theresa orphanage in India.

If the baby is Myron's, Alison thought with a shudder as Eliot pulled out of the crowded parking, *the Lynch camp won't have to resort to any anonymous push polling. The fact of a black baby will be out there for the entire world to see.*

"Are you cold, honey?" Eliot asked.

"Yes," Alison said, even though she wasn't.

Eliot closed the windows. "Do you mind if I turned on the radio?" he asked as they left the crowded parking lot. "I don't want to miss Lynch's acceptance speech."

"Go ahead."

Chapter 5

Tall, tan, and trim, with blow-dried blonde hair and the kind of sparkling blue eyes one usually associated with a matinee idol, Clarence Lynch stood before the podium like a conquering hero. Flashing a megawatt smile he had perfected for the cameras, he waved at his sea of admirers, all of them white, except for a sprinkling of nervous-looking black faces induced by bribes to attend and who stuck out like sore thumbs.

They adore me, Lynch thought as he blew kisses this way and that and pumped his right fist in the air. Despite his huge ego, Lynch, who had a law degree to go along with one in drama, was smart enough to know that good looks, image, and money were often more important than ideas, principles, and veracity in the pursuit of high political office in America. As he surveyed the delirious right-wing crowd packed inside the ballroom of the North Raleigh Hilton and Convention Center, he also knew that he was, without a doubt, their beloved Messiah, having run the most conservative campaign in the history of North Carolina. Because of that, pundits had dismissed him as being incapable of winning. These same pundits, despite being repeatedly wrong, were still consulted around election time by cable TV news as if they were Delphian Oracles. Not only had Lynch proven the talking heads wrong by capturing the Republican nomination – he had done so by a landslide.

Out of a field of four candidates, Lynch had garnered sixty percent of the vote. Randy Smith, a turncoat two-term Democratic congressman who had been leading in the polls, and who had been backed by the Republican Party establishment as a reward for his perfidy, signalized by his calling George W. Bush "the greatest president since Lincoln," was a distant third, with only twenty-eight percent of the vote. According to exit polls, low voter turnout, along with a sophisticated voter-turnout drive unrivalled in the history of modern politics, had played a decisive role in Lynch's upset victory.

"We did it, my silent army! We did it!" Lynch shouted into a cluster of microphones. "We confounded the skeptics, the naysayers, and the pundits! They kept insisting that I was unelectable. They kept calling me an extremist. But apparently pundits forgot one thing, my friends. They forgot that North Carolina is no bastion of liberalism. This is the home of Jesse Helms! This is conservative country!"

The crowd erupted in thunderous applause.

"We want Lynch! We want Lynch! We want Lynch!" the crowd chanted.

"You've got him!" Lynch roared into the mikes. "And he's a genuine conservative! Unlike that counterfeit, Lawrence Ramsey! You know what? The American people don't like counterfeit money! They don't like counterfeit fur! They don't like counterfeit diamonds! And they sure don't like counterfeit conservatives!"

Signs bobbed frenziedly all over the ballroom, held high so that TV cameras could capture their in-your-face messages: "The Iraq War is Holy!" "Affirmative Action is Reverse Racism!" "NC Needs More Prisons!" "Abortion Is Murder!" "Deport All Illegal Aliens!" "Build a Berlin Wall Along the Rio Grande!" "Mandatory Prayer in Public Schools!" "Liberalism Equals Socialism!" "Guns Don't Kill, People Do!" "Marriage = One Man, One Woman," and "Let's Take Back Our Country!"

On the stage with Lynch were his slim, blonde wife, Mary Ann, their two blonde and blue-eyed daughters, family members, and a half a dozen close aides and advisors. The stage was festooned with American flags. One huge banner was draped across the back of the speaker's platform. It read: "Lynch: The True Conservative."

Lynch waved his long arms for silence. He began his acceptance speech by graciously thanking his primary opponents. "It's morning again in America, my friends," Lynch said in soft cadences, breaking into a smile as he read verbatim the speech that Ghazi had personally crafted for him. "After floundering for decades in a morass of liberalism, the nation God gave to us to love, honor, and defend has finally found its political moorings. Conservatism is now the New American Order. Everywhere Democrats are feverishly repudiating liberalism and becoming our clones."

He paused for several seconds for dramatic effect, and then said, "But who, in their right mind, would want a clone when they can have the real thing!"

"Down with clones!" someone shouted.

"Down with all phony conservatives!" yelled another.

Several signs bobbed up and down reading, "Liberals can run, but they can't hide!" and "2004: Liberals meet their Waterloo."

"Lately, I've found myself cheering for a lot of liberal Democrats," Lynch said. "You know why? Because most of them sound more conservative than I do."

The crowd burst into laughter.

"Seriously, now. Liberal Democrats are saying precisely what we conservatives have been saying for years about welfare, crime, affirmative action, illegal immigration, national security, and traditional family values. And the funny thing is that, back in 1980, when Ronald Reagan predicted a conservative revolution that would realign politics in America, liberals scoffed at him. They derisively dismissed the slayer of communism as an underrated actor whose best performance, deserving of an Oscar, was playing the role of President of the United States. Well, let me tell you something." Lynch wagged his right finger in mock chastisement. "Liberals are the actors. No one knows what they stand for – or believe in. After the wallop we gave them in 2002, they're now fleeing from the liberal label as fast as their unwieldy big-government legs can carry them."

Widespread laughter.

"And you know what?" Lynch said. "Liberals have even purloined our conservative script and are feverishly memorizing its lines for 2004. But the problem, my friends, is that liberals are very bad actors. And I should know, having, like the Gipper, once graced the silver screen myself. They can't even follow simple directions."

More laughter.

"They don't know whether to turn left or right or remain in the center. I say it's about time those disoriented liberal clowns were hooted off the political stage."

The ballroom erupted into wild laughter, applause, and cheering. Lynch waited patiently for the hubbub to die down. He was clearly enjoying this.

"I predict that after Election Day, liberalism will be extinct as a political force in America," Lynch declared gleefully as he adjusted one of the microphones. "It will be buried in the same ignominious grave as communism, feminism, socialism, welfarism, homosexualism, multiculturalism, and all the other -isms of the left. And that shameless fraud Ramsey, who's trying desperately to pass himself off as a born-again conservative, will be buried along with his favorite dogmas. Better still, as the last liberal in the South, we should fossilize him. We should place him in the Museum of Natural History in Washington, DC, to remind posterity of what the hideous liberal monsters looked like who once roamed our beloved America and tried to ruin it with their social engineering."

This line provoked the biggest laughter.

"Tar Heels aren't fooled by his radical political cosmetic surgery," Lynch said. "He's nothing but North Carolina's Ted Kennedy. Yank away the conservative façade and underneath you'll find the same old wrinkled, bloated, hideous liberal with an incurable addiction to tax-and-spend big government and counter-culture social engineering – the political equivalent of crack cocaine. I say, once a liberal, always a liberal. Thank you, my friends, and God bless our beloved United States of America."

Lynch, followed by his family and entourage, exited the stage. The delirious audience, on cue, burst into an ear-splitting rendition of *The Battle Hymn of the Republic*, skillfully bastardized by the Lynch camp to hide its liberal origins as an abolitionist hymn. The new version went this way

Mine eyes have seen the glory of the coming of Clarence Lynch;
He is trampling out the liberals so beating them will be a cinch;
He hath loosed his fateful sword and he'll never budge an inch;
His truth is marching on.

Chapter 6

The traffic lights glowed red and green on the rain-drenched streets as Alison and Eliot drove home from the Sheraton Greensboro Hotel. Eliot's dark-blue Jaguar passed through open fields redolent with the scent of spring blossoms on its way toward the Whitaker Estate, a sprawling 30-room mansion with stables, an indoor swimming pool, and a tennis court. While Eliot guffawed at Clarence Lynch's zingers against liberalism, Alison gazed vacantly out the window, still deeply disturbed by what she considered her father's betrayal of her deepest beliefs and convictions in his acceptance speech.

"Can you please turn off the radio?" said Alison, feeling another dull cramp in her abdomen. "I can't stand listening to that right-wing demagogue."

"Okay, honey," said Eliot. "But what Lynch is saying is true. Liberals have ruined America. Even your dad has finally realized that. That's why he's running as a conservative this time around. And I bet you he'll win in November."

"I've known my father all my life, okay," Alison said curtly, turning to face Eliot. "He has compassion for the poor. He supports civil rights. He's always fought for the underdog. And I can't believe he would want to build more jails," Alison added as the Jaguar exited

Highway 68 and turned left. "The U.S. jail population is the highest in the Western World. But that still hasn't made a dent on crime."

"Prison sentences haven't been tough enough because of liberal judges."

It's frightful the power Eliot's father now has on him, Alison thought, clenching her teeth as another intense cramp hit her. *I can't believe he's the same person I dated in high school, who worked in homeless shelters, marched against the Klan and for gay rights, and proudly wore 'Jesus is a liberal' buttons, despite his father's threats to disinherit him. I wonder what happened to change him into a reactionary demagogue.*

When the cramp was over, Alison said, "Eliot, don't you know that when we simply lock people up instead of rehabilitating them, we're turning them into hardened criminals?" Alison, who had covered the courts while working as a journalist in New York City, was well aware of the inequities inherent in the criminal justice system. "All at taxpayer expense, mind you. How many of those kids who are glutting our jails could have been successes in life if they'd had the same opportunities we've had? We should be educating them and giving them hope. Not locking them up and throwing away the key."

Like most people who tended to fiercely defend views they held uncritically and had gained second-hand, rather than arriving at them through the exercise of their own reason, Eliot was unyielding. "But you're forgetting one thing – they're criminals!" he said, almost yelling. "And criminals must be punished, not pampered!"

"Most wouldn't *be* criminals if they'd had a choice."

Eliot was clearly incensed. Tension lines formed around his small mouth. The grip of his chubby hands on the black leather steering wheel tightened.

"You liberal do-gooders are naive, you know that," he snapped. "Are you telling me that all those black thugs who sell drugs and murder people in cold blood are really sweet little angels who just need more liberal indulgences?"

"Why do you say 'black' thugs? Whites commit crimes, too."

Traffic started to slow due to an accident at the corner of Johnson and Eastchester Ridge Drive. A light truck had collided with a white Toyota Celica, and two police cars, a fire-truck and an ambulance with flashing lights were at the scene. A white cop in a yellow rain-coat stood the middle of the street, directing traffic.

"Look at the statistics!" Eliot said, bringing the Jaguar to a halt behind a Food Lion delivery truck. "Only fifteen percent of the people in this country are black, but blacks make up sixty percent of the prison population."

"Mainly because of racism," said Alison. "Think, Eliot. We brought them here in chains. We systematically broke up their families and denied them basic human rights for generations. We refuse to acknowledge our latent fear of them, which makes us confine them in inner city ghettoes and do everything we can to keep them down."

"That's fucking bullshit!" Eliot shot back. "I've never owned any slave. I've never oppressed anyone. So don't try to dump all that liberal guilt shit on me, okay?"

This time I won't allow you to browbeat me, Eliot, Alison thought, even as she felt another bout of pain coming on. *I won't back down. I have convictions like you do and I'll defend them, whatever the cost.* "How would you like to be looked down upon simply because of the color of your skin?" she asked. "How would you feel if you were constantly a victim of racial profiling by the police? How would you feel if people who've never met you automatically assumed you were uneducated, lazy, foolish, immoral, and oversexed simply because of the color of your skin?"

The white cop signaled for traffic to move and Eliot let go of the brake pedal. "Tell me something, Alison," he said, trying to calm down, "Do people look down on Oprah? On Bill Cosby? On Will Smith,? On Eddie Murphy? On Barack Obama? On Collin Powell! On Condoleeza Rice! On Tiger Woods! NO! They adore them. For your information, Michael Jordan is the most popular hero among white kids."

"But those are exceptions, Eliot. Most blacks aren't professional athletes, entertainers, or politicians. They're ordinary people who want to do their best for their families. Yet they're constantly being reminded that they're second-class citizens."

"Bullshit. A lot of blacks are lazy and want something for nothing. Blacks like Chanel, who never complain, who get an education, and who work hard and play by the rules, are the exceptions. That's what I found so admirable about Chanel when we were students at Wellington Academy. She didn't play the race card or portray herself as a victim. Instead she worked hard and was willing to lift herself by her bootstraps."

"That's a stereotype. Most blacks work just as hard, if not harder, than whites," Alison said. "And like Chanel, they value education. They don't want handouts or pity. And they need boots before they can lift themselves up by their own bootstraps."

"How would you know? You're not black!"

"Because I used to go to Chanel's church – until your father said it wasn't proper for a Whitaker to be seen at what he called a 'Negro church.'"

"Do you think it's normal for someone who's white to always be going to black churches?" Eliot shot back. "What's wrong with white churches?"

"Why are there black and white churches in the first place?"

"Because we worship differently. Whites sing hymns and have nice, organized services for just one hour a day. But not blacks. They shout and holler all day long. Church is supposed to be a solemn occasion, not entertainment."

"So you mean to tell me there's a white God and a black God, is that it? No wonder eleven o'clock Sunday morning is the most segregated hour in America."

"Let's just stop this, okay? I'm sick of arguing."

The dull cramps were getting more intense and more regular now, but Alison wouldn't relent. Once she had worked herself into a passion over something she cared deeply about, it took a while for her to calm down. And she hated to lose an argument, especially a political one and when she was convinced she was right.

"Have you ever tried," she said, as the Jaguar made another left turn, "really tried, to put yourself in an African-American's shoes for just a minute?"

"Why the hell should I do that?"

"Because it would change your perspective on race."

"I doubt it."

"Remember Rodney King?"

"Yeah. What about him?"

"What if you had been in his shoes? What if racist white cops had pounced on you and clubbed the shit out of you? How would that have made you feel?"

"Why was he running away from the cops if he wasn't guilty?"

"Because he was afraid of them."

"I'm not."

"But you aren't African-American, Eliot."

"Are you?"

"No."

"Then what makes you such a damn expert on blacks?" Eliot said as the Jaguar drove along a narrow, serpentine road lined with giant trees, at the end of which lay the Whitaker estate, valued at $15 million and considered the second largest private home in North Carolina, behind the famed Biltmore Estate in Asheville.

"I'm a human being, Eliot. I can empathize with their plight. And as a woman I know firsthand what it feels like to be discriminated against. Not to be taken seriously. I know what it feels like to fight three times as hard and get only half as far."

"That's a bunch of liberal crap," Eliot said. "Discrimination has never prevented blacks from making it America. You should read *Ebony* sometimes. You'll be amazed at how successful blacks are. For instance, did you know that minority women in law firms make on average $10,000 more per year than white women?"

"I do read *Ebony*. It's mainly a feel-good magazine. But I went to Harlem and the South Bronx while I was studying journalism at Columbia University. I know what life is like for the millions of African-Americans who are trapped there. I've written stories about welfare mothers, drug addicts, AIDS orphans, gang members, and black-on-black violence. And those stories aren't known to most white people, that's why they can afford to stereotype blacks, and to support right-wing solutions to their problems."

Eliot was livid. "If you're so in love with black people," he said, almost shouting, "then why the hell didn't you marry one and move to a fucking ghetto?"

The remark jolted Alison. *If I'd married Myron, I wouldn't be having this silly debate about whether racism exists in America,* she thought as they rode the rest of the way home in angry silence. Alison had been planning to tell Eliot for weeks that there was a possibility the baby in her womb might be a black man's, but the time was never right. In the back of her mind a small voice always stopped her by whispering, "Wait until the baby comes. If it's white, there will be no reason to tell Eliot about Myron."

She suddenly felt a strong urge to blurt out about her year-long relationship with Myron, and about their secret engagement, regardless of the Pandora's box such a revelation would open. She was about to say something when the dull cramps in her pelvic region turned into a series of sharp pains that coiled around her lower back like a boa constrictor. As the Jaguar reached the white ante-bellum mansion's cobbled circular driveway, Alison let out a short scream as the baby twisted inside her and then dropped into her pelvis. Suddenly, the car seat became soaked with warm liquid. "My water just broke," she cried as the pains became sharper. "Take me to the hospital. Hurry!"

As the Jaguar was racing toward Triad Regional Hospital, and Alison panted through each contraction, she kept wondering, *what if this is Myron's son?*

Chapter 7

Myron had tried watching Ramsey's acceptance speech as an objective political analyst. But he couldn't long remain emotionally aloof. Seeing a pregnant Alison on the stage with Eliot had brought back painful memories that led him to angrily turn off the TV.

If I hadn't jilted her, Myron thought, rising from the floral sleeper sofa, *it would be my child that she's carrying.* Fighting back tears, Myron slowly walked across the thick rug to the tiled bathroom, where he gazed into the oval mirror. He was stunned by how much he had aged since breaking up with Alison. Not only had he lost weight, but his short dark hair was now speckled with gray, his cheeks were sunken like a ghost's without a place to haunt, and his once playful brown eyes had a melancholy tinge.

I look like Methuselah, Myron thought as he peed. *And yet I'm only twenty-seven.* After washing his hands, Myron walked over to the carved mantle above the cold fire-place, where several photos were arranged in a neat row. For a long while he stared at the silver-framed one in the middle. It showed Alison leaning against a smooth rock at the summit of Mount Jefferson in New Hampshire. He had taken it the day after he had proposed to her around the campfire during their long weekend hiking trip in the White Mountains. He also remembered the passionate love they had made that night under a canopy of stars, and his mother's reaction when he had told her that he and Alison were engaged.

I was a fool to let her pressure me to break up with my soul mate, Myron thought, biting his lower lip. Myron wondered why his mother had put so much pressure on him in the first place. It wasn't like her to meddle in his private life. Stranger still, she had been reluctant to give him reasons for her vehement opposition to the marriage, except to say, "Someday I'll tell you, son, and you'll understand why calling off the wedding, painful as it was for you, was the right thing to do. Trust me."

Only the truth can ease the terrible guilt I feel at having forced Alison to marry a man she didn't love, Myron thought as he brewed another cup of tea. *She clearly was hurt and humiliated. According to Chanel, that's why she rushed into a marriage with Eliot. Even then, she had second thoughts, and has never been happy throughout her marriage.*

Despite his breakup with Alison, Myron still kept in touch with Chanel, whom he had met at Alison's graduation from the Columbia Graduate School of Journalism.

Recalling that in about a week he planned to be in New York to attend his mother's 50th birthday, Myron decided he would confront her then. *Unless she's a closet racist, she has to tell me why she was against my marrying Alison, the only woman I've ever loved.*

As she plodded around the maternity ward – she believed that being on one's feet would speed up labor – clutching Eliot's hand for support, Alison wished that that hand had belonged to Myron, the man she truly loved. *I'll never forgive him for dumping me*, Alison thought as she grimaced through another long and vicious contraction.

Seeing Alison in pain, Eliot felt guilty at having argued with her about race, and sought to make up by saying, "Please forgive me for all the bad things I said in the car, honey. I honestly didn't mean them. You know that I'm not a bigot."

"Of course I know that," Alison said, recalling that when the two of them were students at Wellington Academy, Eliot had been very liberal. It was only after his mother Laura died from breast cancer two years ago, and a grief-stricken Eliot had come under his father's domineering influence, that he had begun to parrot his right-wing beliefs.

Alison paused to let a contraction pass. She did the pant-pant-blow method she had learned in a Lamaze natural childbirth class. She had been in labor nearly ten hours and there seemed no end in sight. The strain was starting to show on her face.

"Are you sure you don't want an epidural, honey?" Eliot asked, a concerned look on his chubby face. "I hate to see you in such pain. The nurse said ninety-five percent of mothers who deliver here take something for the pain. Why don't you?"

"There's a good reason for this pain," Alison replied, grimacing as another contraction, longer than the previous one, slowly began. "It's productive pain. I want to be in that rare five percent of women who experience natural childbirth."

Alison stopped and, leaning heavily on Eliot's shoulder, panted until the pain subsided. Then she was free to plod and talk for the next two or three minutes until the next contraction. "My mother was knocked out cold when she had me," she said. "She has no idea what it feels like to bring a baby into this world."

"But we've already paid more than three grand to Dr. Meyer. Why not take his advice? He said that the drugs they give women during childbirth are quite safe."

"We wouldn't have had to pay that much if I'd used a midwife."

"That's primitive."

"Eliot, there are women in this world who don't have the luxury of childbirth suites or drugs. And they do just fine." An excruciating wave of pain washed over her. It was her strongest contraction yet. She screamed and clung to Eliot. She furiously did the pant-pant-blow. The pain seemed to be winning. Her face contorted in agony.

I won't be weak. Pant-pant-blow.

"Help!" Eliot cried, eyes wild with terror as he tried to hold up Alison. "Somebody, help!" A nurse and Dr. Meyer ran to assist Eliot in getting Alison to the delivery room and up on the table. Within minutes her feet were mounted in the stirrups.

"Ten centimeters dilated," Dr. Meyer said after examining her. "She's ready to push." Alison saw sheets flying over her, creating a breeze as they settled onto her bare legs and stomach. Medical assistants and nurses rushed in and out of the room. Dr. Meyer pulled on his latex gloves with a snap and tied a mask over his face.

"Push, gal, push!" cried a slightly overweight nurse named Betty, whose brown hair was cut in a bob that made her already round face resemble a perfect circle.

Alison pushed and hollered without being in the least self-conscious because hollering somehow eased the pain as the baby made its way through the birth canal.

"It's crowning," Dr. Meyer said. "That's the baby's head."

"Oh, my God," Eliot stammered.

"Come on, push, gal, push!" Betty chanted. "Push! You can do it! Push!"

After one more push and a loud scream, the pain was over. Alison felt as if she had just finished running the New York City Marathon – twice.

"It's a boy!" Betty cried. Everyone's attention immediately shifted from Alison to the tiny purplish hunk of flesh Dr. Meyer was cradling in his gloved hands.

"I have a son," Eliot muttered in disbelief. "I have a son."

"What will you name him?" Betty asked.

"Dylan Andrew Whitaker."

"Has a nice ring to it," said Dr. Meyer. "Here, you do the honors." He handed Eliot a pair of scissors. With unsteady hands Eliot cut the umbilical cord. A spank on the baby's tiny buns brought forth that first lusty cry that seemed to say to all the world, 'I'm alive," a cry that so deeply touched Alison she instinctively reached for her child. She held the baby near her face, marveling at the miracle of creation, scrutinizing its features. This was the moment she had been waiting for all these months. *Now I'll finally know if Myron or Eliot is my child's father.*

Chapter 8

The morning after his razor-thin victory in the Democratic Party's gubernatorial primary, a beaming Ramsey strode into campaign headquarters in downtown High Point. He shook hands with bleary-eyed staffers, most of them liberal college students who, though secretly disappointed by his distancing himself from their favorite creed, still regarded him as their best hope for a better future. If the truth be told, they really had no choice. During an election year when, because of Bush's dizzying popularity following his invasion of Iraq and relentless liberal-bashing by the GOP, progressive Democrats across the South were tripping over each other to be newly baptized as conservatives.

"You're all doing a terrific job," Ramsey said with a smile. Feeling slightly warm, he loosened the blue silk tie that matched the dark suit the clothing specialists from Hunter's political consulting firm had recommended he wear in order to look more conservative. "Keep up the good work and we'll win in November."

Ramsey spotted Hunter standing by the corner, cell phone in hand. "Can I speak to you in private for a minute?" he said, walking briskly toward him.

"Sure." Hunter put away the cell phone and followed Ramsey into the back room. It had a long wooden desk in the middle, three folding metal chairs, a faded brown couch, a metal bookshelf filled with political books and an assortment of magazines, a desktop computer and a Panasonic combination fax, scanner, and phone.

"I really appreciate your hard work," Ramsey said in a low and pleasant baritone. "I couldn't have won the nomination if I hadn't followed your strategy."

"The credit belongs to Alison," Hunter said, pulling up a chair. "She sacrificed a great deal to help you win, Larry. First, she agreed to marry Eliot soon after breaking up with Myron to give your flagging campaign a timely boost. And then she barnstormed the state urging students, women's groups, and minorities to vote for you, despite her strong disagreement with the tactic of running a conservative campaign. You ought to be very proud of her."

"I am," Ramsey said, sitting down near a dispenser of bottled spring water. "That's why I wish she were happy in her marriage to Eliot."

"I thought she was." Hunter filled a paper cup with purified water.

"I did too. But Darlene doesn't think so."

"I'm very sorry to hear that. Hopefully the baby will bring her and Eliot together."

"That's what I told Darlene."

"What did she say?" Hunter asked, sitting down.

"She's skeptical. She thinks Alison's still very much in love with Myron."

"So what does she want Alison to do? Divorce Eliot and marry Myron?"

Ramsey flashed an awkward smile. "Funny, I asked her the same question."

Hunter poured himself a cup of water. "I hope you won't mind my saying this to you as a friend, Larry," he said after a sip. "But I think Darlene's in denial. I know how much she wanted Myron as a son-in-law. She thought the world of him. So did you. And so did I. But we couldn't well force him to marry Alison if he didn't want to."

"I told her that."

"And the truth of the matter is that if the two had married, you'd have been trounced in the primary. Douglas wouldn't even have had to campaign. Remember those focus groups and polls I did after Alison told us of her secret engagement to Myron?"

Ramsey nodded glumly as Hunter put the plastic water cup on

the desk.

"The polls had you losing by as much as thirty points if Alison had married a black man," Hunter said with emphasis. "Thirty points. This is still the South, Larry, not New York City. And a politician would be foolish to forget that."

Ramsey sighed. "I know it's still the South, but surely attitudes have changed some. After all, the Supreme Court abolished anti-miscegenation laws in 1967 – almost thirty years ago. And when I was in the state legislature I personally sponsored the bill to have North Carolina repeal its statutes in 1977."

"Of course, things have changed," Hunter said, "And thank God for that. But you yourself know that changing laws hasn't changed most people's attitudes."

He's right, Ramsey thought as he doodled with his Mount Blanc fountain pen.

"It's one thing to ask conservative whites to vote for someone with a record as liberal as yours," Hunter said, leaning forward. "It's quite another to ask them to vote for a man who let his only daughter marry a black man. It's a fact that most white people still consider interracial couples freaks – just like gays. And here in the Bible belt many even consider them sinners. I still remember one old lady calling into a Raleigh radio station during the O. J. Simpson trial and saying that God had created the races separate and placed them on different continents. She added that race-mixing was as bizarre as birds mating with chimpanzees because blacks and whites are two different species."

Ramsey screwed his forehead with its receding hairline. "She really said that?"

Hunter nodded. "Yes, those were her exact words. And the old lady isn't alone in her views," he added, his eyes narrowing as he spoke. "No, not by a long shot. The only difference today is that such views aren't openly expressed. But believe me, they influence how people vote more than a candidate's stance on the issues. That's one reason why I recommended that you distance yourself from liberalism. Many white Southerners equate liberalism with the Civil Rights movement and integration. And they have never forgiven the Democratic Party for championing both."

Ramsey shook his head despondently. *He's right.* He recalled how many an election across the South had turned on the issue of race, and how the GOP, by adroitly using code words like States' Rights, crime, welfare, and school choice, had repeatedly exploited the issue on its way to gaining ascendancy in the region. "I wish Darlene would understand how strong and widespread prejudice still is," he said, letting out a heavy sigh.

"Well, I'm afraid that, as a Northerner, she's still caught up in the optimism of the Civil Rights movement," Hunter said. "And I don't blame her. If anything, I share her optimism. That's why I'm trying to do everything in my power to help you win so you can provide real leadership on the racial issue. No one is doing that right now."

"I told her that."

Hunter looked keenly at Ramsey. "And what did she say?"

"Oh, she thinks that I've given you too much control over the campaign."

"Jesus Christ," Hunter said in exasperation, throwing his arms wide open. "How can she say that? I always consult you before any important decisions are made, don't I?"

"Of course you do."

"And you approve of the staff I brought with me from the firm?"

"Sure. They're a first class bunch."

Agitated, Hunter rose. "So what does she want? Does she want me to burden you with the minutiae of a campaign? Does she know how distracting that can be to a candidate? Especially one with an image problem as bad as the one you have?"

"I told her that she's wrong in her criticism of you."

"She'll thank me for running a tight ship come Election Day. But there's a long way to go yet, especially considering these latest internal polling results."

"What do they show?" Ramsey said eagerly.

Hunter spread several computer printouts on the desk. Ramsey scooted his chair for a closer look. Hunter pointed to the most significant results with a thin finger.

"Your support among independents has slipped by fifteen percentage points in two weeks," Hunter said. "Your support among your base is also eroding. So if the election were held today, Lynch would beat you by as many as twenty points."

"Shit!" Ramsey said, indignant. "What accounts for such a wide margin when only three weeks ago Lynch and I were in a statistical dead heat?"

"Like I said, you continue to have a serious image problem," Hunter said calmly. "Voters still don't know what you stand for. They don't know if you're a liberal or a conservative. So they don't trust you. The staff and I make sure you sound like a true conservative in campaign literature and commercials but in front of a microphone or camera you revert to your old liberal self or at best you straddle the fence. You remember what the papers were calling you in the days leading up to election night?"

"Of course I do," Ramsey said with a snarl. He rubbed his temples, fighting off an incipient headache. He recalled descriptions of himself in the media as "too slick," a "fence-straddler," "wishy-washy, "wanting to have it both ways," "flip-flopper," "chameleon," "unprincipled," and "lacking a core." The last two really hurt. "I'm not an actor, Reggie," Ramsey said in a voice tinged with self-pity. "You can't just give me a script and expect me to perform like some monkey. For instance, I felt very awkward delivering that acceptance speech you wrote for me. That wasn't me at all. Maybe the best thing for me to do, now that I've won the primary, is to stand up for what I believe – to stop being ashamed to be called a liberal if that's what I truly am."

Hunter shook his head. "I wouldn't do that if I were you. It would be a fatal mistake. There's no way you can win wearing that label. The state is too conservative."

"But labels don't mean anything," Ramsey said, in a voice that carried little conviction, "as long as voters know where I stand on the issues. Yes, I'm a liberal on some issues and a conservative on others, just like a lot of politicians."

"Don't kid yourself, Larry," Hunter said. "In politics labels are *everything*. The South is now GOP country largely because Republicans have successfully painted Democrats, including centrists like yourself, as nothing but big government, tax-and-spend, counter-culture liberals. And they're doing it again this election year. And this time, unlike in 1994, they have Fox News backing them up."

"Then the liberal media should expose their lies and propaganda."

Hunter laughed. "The liberal media? Are you kidding me? I know you used to be a philosophy professor, Larry, but we aren't living in Plato's Republic. The liberal media is nothing but a myth. Fox News and right wing talk shows are the media now. And the day

Rush Limbaugh, Sean Hannity and Glenn Beck kill the goose that lays their golden eggs by exposing the canard of a liberal media is the day the Martians will land on planet Earth."

He's right, Ramsey frowned.

"Voters want their politics simple, Larry," Hunter went on with growing intensity. "They want the issues presented in black and white, in thirty-second sound bites. Labels like 'conservative' and 'liberal,' even when they're inaccurate, make it easy for them. They simply don't have the time nor the inclination to ponder complex issues. And as a former philosophy professor, you surely know that the American people, though most believe in Christianity and reason, don't want their politicians to behave like Christ or Socrates. They want them to be pragmatists, and to do what is expedient."

Much as I hate to admit it, Reggie is right, Ramsey thought with bitterness.

Hunter pressed his fingertips together. He gazed thoughtfully over Ramsey's shoulders at the photo of Ramsey with former U.S. Senator Terry Sanford, which was pinned next to a poster reading: "Ramsey: A Leader You Can Trust."

"You know, you have a lot in common with Terry Sanford. He too was a liberal Democrat and deeply committed to racial justice when he ran for governor in 1960. Yet to win the Democratic primary against Beverly Lake he ran as a segregationist. But that didn't mean he *was* one. He turned out to have been one of the most progressive governors the state ever had. And he did the most to empower blacks, combat poverty, improve race relations, and diminish the influence of the Klan, which, as you well know, at one time had its largest following in the South right here in North Carolina."

Ramsey recalled that Sanford was his primary inspiration for going into politics. He was eager to continue Sanford's legacy, which had led a Harvard Study to rank him as one of the 20th century's most creative and effective governors. But Ramsey also recalled that Sanford, whenever his integrity was on the line, stuck to his principles, even when he knew that doing so would cost him important votes.

The best example of this was when Sanford incurred the wrath of the Klan, who called him "a liberal scalawag," when he was one of the few Southern politicians to endorse "Red Kennedy," as the Catholic and pro Civil Rights Massachusetts Senator was called when he ran for President in 1960. Ramsey regarded Sanford as a true profile in courage, and himself as nothing but a time-server. But these were different times, Ramsey said to himself in an effort to pacify his outraged conscience. The end more than justified the means, and prostituting one's principles was the norm in politics.

"But I can't win if I'm perceived as a fake conservative," said Ramsey.

"I'm not done repackaging you," Hunter insisted. "And remaking your image, if you cooperate, won't be that difficult. You're already a moderate on a lot of issues, just like Sanford was. You've never been a flaming liberal like Ted Kennedy or Mario Cuomo. They would have to be reincarnated rather than repackaged."

Ramsey smiled faintly. "What about those dismal polling results?" he pointed.

"Forget these." Hunter crumpled the sheets and tossed them in a metal wastepaper basket. "At this early stage in the game, they're basically meaningless. But if you switch courses now, the label of flip-flopper will definitely stick."

"So what more do I need to do?" Ramsey said, plaintively. "I'm trying hard to sound like a conservative. Obviously, it doesn't come easy."

"No one said it would. But with Theodore Whitaker now backing you because of Alison's marriage to his son, your image with conservative voters is bound to improve. Also, if I can convince Kessler at our meeting this afternoon that you've indeed repudiated liberalism, he might take you off the list of politicians his PAC has targeted for defeat this fall. Who knows, if I do a good job of burnishing your conservative credentials he might even agree to bankroll your campaign."

Richard Kessler was considered one of the most influential people in American politics. Through his political action committee, American Renewal through Strength and Values, or ARTSAV, which was considered a 527 under the Internal Revenue Code regulating campaign contributions, Kessler, a billionaire, annually spent tens of millions of dollars of his personal fortune to influence the defeat of politicians of either party he considered too liberal, and the election of those who openly repudiated or distanced themselves from liberalism, which he described as a "cancer that was destroying America morally, culturally, spiritually, economically, and militarily."

"If you can convince Kessler to back me, it will be a miracle," Ramsey said.

"It's a long shot but I'll do my best," Hunter said, grabbing his black leather briefcase. "By the way, are you still planning to see Alison and the baby this afternoon?"

"Yes. After I pick up Darlene from the showroom."

"Don't forget to give Alison my love," Hunter said.

"I will."

"You know," Hunter said at the door, "I can't wait to use photos of you holding Alison's baby. With traditional family values one of the hot-button issues this year, such ads will reap us a bonanza with social conservatives. Who knows, it might even make them forget that you were once a strong supporter of a woman's right to choose."

"I still am," Ramsey said.

"Of course I know," said Hunter. "But voters shouldn't. At least not until after they elect you governor. Then you can become your old liberal self and use your progressive accomplishments as governor to launch a White House bid in 2012."

Ramsey and Hunter had on several occasions discussed the idea of his possibly running for President after serving two terms as governor, but being slightly superstitious, Ramsey was coy about openly embracing it. "Let's not get too far ahead of ourselves, Reggie," he said. "I still have a very tough election to win."

"And you shall, Larry," Hunter said. "All I ask is that you trust me and my unorthodox strategy for running this campaign. If you do, I promise you'll be the only liberal in the South who'll survive what I predict will be another Republic rout."

"I completely trust you, Reggie," Ramsey said. "You're my political Svengali. Bush has his Karl Rove and Clinton his Dick Morris. You combine the best of both."

"Thanks for your trust," Hunter said. "I promise you'll never regret it."

Hunter exited the door. After Hunter left, Ramsey began calling prospective donors to beg for money – something he loathed as akin to prostituting himself.

I pray Reggie convinces Kessler to bankroll my campaign so I won't have to do any more of this groveling, Ramsey thought. The calls over, around 2.20 p.m., he climbed into his black Lexus LS 430 and drove to the headquarters of his furniture company to pick up Darlene, so they could go visit Alison and the baby at the hospital.

Despite going to bed late because he had spent the night monitoring election results from across the country, Myron awoke, as usual, around 6:30 a.m. He went for a five-mile jog through Rock Creek Park, and then stopped by a bakery across the Woodley Park metro station, where he purchased the Sunday editions of the *Post* and the *Times,* along with three freshly baked cinnamon raisin bagels. He was glad that he didn't have to go to work. All he had to do was to attend a late afternoon meeting at the LUPA offices, where he was to report on how many liberals had made it beyond the primary, and what kind of help they deserved in the general election in order to withstand a tsunami of Republican attacks aimed at defeating any Democrat with the temerity to run as a liberal.

Back in his apartment, Myron showered and made breakfast. While sitting at a small round oak table eating a vegetable omelet with a toasted bagel, he turned on the TV to watch C-Span's *Washington Journal.* The African-American host and his guest, the *Raleigh News & Observer's* Washington correspondent, were discussing North Carolina's election returns, with a particular emphasis on Lawrence Ramsey's narrow victory in the Democratic primary, despite his having distanced himself from liberalism, and Clarence Lynch's stunning landslide victory in the Republican primary, largely because of his unabashed embrace of the conservative fever currently gripping the nation.

Ramsey shouldn't have distanced himself from liberalism, Myron thought. *By so doing he alienated his base. Unless he finds a way to energize it in the general election, he'll lose. There's no way he can out-conservative Lynch.*

Myron had just brewed a cup of green tea when the phone rang. He was surprised to hear Isaac's mellifluous voice, calling from Montgomery, Alabama.

"How are you doing, buddy?" asked Isaac.

"Okay," said Myron in a flat voice. "And you?"

"Very busy," Isaac said. "I just found out that there's a client on death row who might know a thing or two about who murdered my Mom and her assistant twenty years ago. He's scheduled to be executed in a couple weeks. I'm working like mad to see if the

Supreme Court can issue a stay of execution so I can interview him."

"What's his name?"

"Tommy Cone. He's an unrepentant Klansman."

"Good luck getting him to talk."

"What about you?" said Isaac. "What's keeping you busy these days?"

"Well, I'll be visiting several states where a few Democrats squeaked through their primaries by running progressive campaigns," Myron said. "Given Bush's stratospheric popularity in the polls, they definitely face an uphill battle in November. But LUPA is determined to help them come up with strategies to win."

"It's a shame that your ex's dad isn't one of them," Isaac said. "He'd have made a formidable candidate in the general election had he run as a proud liberal."

Myron had told Isaac about Alison, their engagement, and subsequent breakup.

"I agree," Myron said, stirring honey into his tea. "There's no way he can out-conservative Lynch. The guy is a master at manipulating white fears, insecurities, and prejudices. And he's got a limitless war chest. I heard on C-Span that his net worth is more than $300 million. And he's pledged to spend whatever it takes to win."

"Do you think there's a chance that Ramsey, now that he's the Democratic nominee, will pivot and run as a proud liberal?" Isaac asked. "After all, his liberalism has never been that radical. Like former governors Hunt and Sanford, he's a fiscal conservative and in the past he's proven he can appeal to independents voters."

"There's always a chance," Myron said. "That's why LUPA wants me to stop in North Carolina during my trip South and talk to him and his campaign manager."

"Does that mean you might bump into Alison?"

"That's possible."

"Well, that will be some reunion," said Isaac. "You know, I'm still puzzled as to why your Mom pressured the two of you to break up and wouldn't give any reason."

Myron sipped his tea. "I too am puzzled," he said. "And I'm determined to confront her about it. I'm flying to New York tomorrow to celebrate her 50th birthday. I need to know the truth, Isaac. Otherwise I'll never get over the guilt I feel at having made Alison miserable by forcing her to marry a man she clearly doesn't love."

Chapter 9

With bated breath, Alison held and studied her baby's features. Still purple from being confined in the womb, he was growing paler with each lung-full of air. Thick white mucous covered most of his tiny, wrinkled body. With a jolt, she noticed that his hair, though straight, was black. *Is he Myron's?* But she recalled that her own hair was also black. Frantically, she tried to get a look at the baby's eyes, but they were clamped shut so she couldn't tell their color. Alison was still pondering what feature to scrutinize next when Betty took the baby, wrapped it in a white blanket, and whisked it to the nursery to be bathed and examined by a pediatrician. Eliot followed her, apparently more interested in his son than in Alison. On his way out, he effusively thanked Dr. Meyer.

The doctor, a neighbor of Alison's parents, pulled off his pale green mask and smiled at Eliot. He was a tall man with slicked-back, auburn-gray hair, a heavy Southern accent and a jovial demeanor. "It was a privilege to deliver the first grandchild of North Carolina's next governor," said Dr. Meyer with a smile.

A nurse wheeled Alison down the hall to the recovery room. Alison couldn't wait for Dylan to be brought to her after being washed, so she could determine once and for all his racial identity. *Oh, Myron, why weren't you by my side? What if Dylan is your baby?* she thought as she lay on a narrow, adjustable hospital bed with cold metallic rails.

Minutes later, Eliot opened the door and walked in, all smiles. "Dr. Meyer says Dylan's one heck of a big baby," he said proudly. "I wonder how much he weighs."

"Betty should be back in a little while," Alison said distractedly. "You can ask her." She was too exhausted to say more. For some strange reason, she missed the feeling of being pregnant. She had felt a sense of loss the moment Eliot had cut the umbilical cord. She missed the sensation of the baby rolling and turning lazily inside her, the way astronauts do in the weightlessness of space. She missed his warmth, the light fluttering of his fingertips against her, the light kick of a tiny heel somewhere deep inside her womb. The nice round mound between her breasts and pelvis, the warm belly she had stroked, talked to and read poems to, was now flat and flaccid, like a dead jelly fish.

Minutes later Betty knocked boldly and entered the room, beaming.

"Dylan is a big boy," she said. "He came in at nine pounds five ounces."

"Nine pounds five ounces!" Alison exclaimed. "No wonder I felt like a Walrus."

"I told you he was a Whitaker," Eliot said joyfully.

"When can I see him?" asked Alison, eager to ascertain the baby's race.

"He's asleep now," Betty said. "He's exhausted too, you know. The poor little thing had to help its Mama in the delivery. But I'll see what I can do."

"I can't believe I have a son," Eliot said, clapping his hands together in triumph. "I called Dad and Mary-Lou at the family's villa in the Cayman Islands. They're both ecstatic. They're cutting their vacation short and will be home this evening."

Betty glanced at her watch. It was 2:10 p.m. She said, "The pediatrician will be examining Dylan shortly. We've had a record number of deliveries, so it may be a while before I can bring him to you. I suggest you get some rest. You did a wonderful job, honey. And you're the first woman in this hospital to deliver without the help of drugs."

Alison flashed a proud smile. *It wasn't easy, but I did it.*

"Just put on your call light if you need anything," said Betty.

A minute after she left the room, Eliot said, "I'm hungry. I think I'll go to the cafeteria and get something. Can I bring you anything, honey?"

"No, thanks, I don't have much of an appetite."

Eliot grabbed his jacket and headed for the door. As soon as Eliot was out the door, the phone rang. It was Darlene calling to tell Alison that she was proud of her and that she and Lawrence were on their way to the hospital to see the baby. When Alison hung up, her heart was pounding. *Oh, my God,* she thought with a shudder, *I'd better make sure of the baby's race before they get here.* Alison immediately picked up the phone and dialed the nursery extension. Trying hard to suppress the anxiety in her voice, she asked Betty to bring Dylan over as soon as possible so she could breastfeed him.

After calling Alison to tell her that she and Ramsey were on their way to the hospital, Darlene put away her cell phone and turned to Ramsey, who was driving after picking her up at the showroom for New South Fine Furniture on Martin Luther King, Jr. Drive.

"So how did the meeting with Reggie go?" she asked.

"Oh, fine," Ramsey said in a lackluster voice. "We discussed the latest polls."

"How do they look?"

Ramsey let out a deep sigh. "Not too good. I'm thirty points behind Lynch. Apparently my acceptance speech didn't go down well with voters."

"I'm not surprised," Darlene said. She retrieved her lipstick and a small mirror from her purse. "You sounded fake when you pretended to be a conservative. Voters don't trust politicians who keep reinventing themselves."

She's right, Ramsey thought as the Lexus came to a stop at a red light in a neighborhood with a mixture of modest homes and housing projects, where most of the workers at New South Furniture Gallery – black, Hispanic, and white – lived.

"I know you're probably tired of hearing me say this," Darlene said, glossing her thin lips before the small mirror, "but I still think you should run as yourself. It's a mistake to try and repudiate your record simply because you're afraid of being called a liberal. After all, everyone knows you fought for affordable health care for all, civil rights, women's rights, gay rights, workers' rights, and for a safer and cleaner environment. Those are things to be proud of, honey. They show you care about people."

"It's not that simple, honey," Ramsey said, with evident frustration. "Reggie says that if I run openly as a liberal this year, I'll be committing political suicide."

"I don't like the power Reggie has over you," Darlene said, putting the lipstick and mirror back in her purse. "He's turned you into a Republican clone."

Ramsey glared at Darlene. "I'm not a Republican clone, dammit. I couldn't ask for a better campaign manager in Reggie. His strategy is working. I wouldn't have won the nomination without him. And he'll bring me victory in November, despite the odds."

The traffic light turned green and Ramsey and Darlene continued in tense silence past the Leonard Street Park, which was filled with families enjoying the balmy afternoon weather. The park was next to the St. Stephen AME Zion Church, where Reverend William Blair, John Coltrane's maternal grandfather, had been minister.

Ramsey, a jazz fan and a strong advocate for safeguarding historical landmarks, had fought hard to preserve the Coltrane's legacy in High Point. Coltrane, the most revolutionary and widely imitated saxophonist in Jazz after Charlie Parker, had attended the church, and Leonard Street Elementary School.

"So you're willing to hurt our only daughter in order to win a damn election, is that it?" Darlene said presently, her anger rising.

Ramsey's eyes blazed. "What the hell do you mean by that?"

Darlene stood her ground. "Haven't you noticed that Alison is very unhappy as Eliot's wife? And do you think you'd have opposed her marriage to Myron – the man she really loved – if Reggie hadn't convinced you to run as a Republican clone?"

"Don't be naïve, Darlene," Ramsey said. "Color matters to more people than you think. It even matters to African-Americans. That's why the Afro-Purist movement is gaining followers. And you remember, don't you, how viciously its leader attacked me because of my support for integration? The attacks almost cost me the primary."

Ramsey was alluding to a series of scathing editorials in *The Motherland*, the Afro-Purist mouthpiece, accusing him of advocating liberal policies such as abortion rights, integration, and gay rights, which the separatist group considered inimical to the long-term survival of the black family and community.

"What almost cost you the election is your waffling, Larry," Darlene said as Ramsey made a slight right onto East English Road. "Voters don't know what you stand for, or believe in. The only reason blacks stuck with you is because of that speech I convinced you to give before the NAACP, despite Reggie's opposition. It reminded them of the old Ramsey who was proud to be called a liberal, who defied Klan death threats, and who was unwilling to pander to white bigotry in order to win an election."

"But voters today hate liberals. Just look at the polls."

"You know why," Darlene said as Ramsey turned left into a tree-lined street. "It's because most liberal politicians these days are weak-kneed and spineless. They haven't fought back when attacked. They've let conservatives define what liberalism is. And, predictably, conservatives have done so to suit their own ends, just as they always do during elections. There's nothing to be ashamed of in being a liberal, honey. Absolutely nothing. Where would America be without Head Start, Social Security, Pell Grants, the Fair Housing Act, Medicare, Medicaid, clean air and water, and civil rights?"

"I'm not ashamed of being a liberal. Just wait until I'm elected governor."

Darlene let out a mocking laugh. "So your liberalism is for summer weather only, is that it? When the going gets tough, you prevaricate, you run, and you hide."

Ramsey shook his head. "You forget what this election means, Darlene," he said. "The future of North Carolina is at stake, along with its reputation as a progressive state," Ramsey said. "If I win, I can fight to preserve the environment. I can protect civil rights. I can improve the education system. I can help create good jobs. I can provide universal health care. I can help the Democratic Party make a comeback in the South. Most important, I can provide leadership on the race issue, something few politicians today are doing. It doesn't matter how I get to the governor's mansion, as long as I do the right thing once I'm there. Even Alison will surely understand that."

"I doubt that very much," Darlene said.

Am I being this defensive because deep down I know that Darlene is right? Ramsey wondered as he stopped at a red light, about a block away from the hospital.

Before Ramsey could answer his own question, the car phone rang. He picked it up. After listening for several moments, he put it back in its cradle between the front seats. Face beaming, he turned to Darlene and said, "What did I tell you?"

"What happened?"

"That was Reggie."

"What did he say to make you so happy?"

"He's a miracle worker. He pulled off a political coup."

"What did he do?"

"He's just convinced Kessler, of all people, to back my campaign," Ramsey said. Do you what that means, honey? It means that I'll be able to raise enough money to compete against Lynch, who already has a $30 million war chest."

"It's not money you need, Lawrence," Darlene said as the Lexus pulled into the parking lot of Triad Regional. "It's political courage. Wasn't it you who once said that a politician without principles is like a body without a soul?"

Ramsey, the one-time philosophy professor who had admonished students at Guilford College to heed the example of Socrates, who chose to drink the hemlock rather than to do what was expedient to save his life, didn't have an adequate reply when his wife reminded him that more than political office was at stake.

All Ramsey could do, as he and Darlene exited the Lexus, was mumble, "Wait until I'm elected governor and you'll see how liberal I am." Ramsey parked the car next to a brown station wagon belonging to none other than Nancy, Buck's wife.

Chapter 10

If Ramsey had known how high the stakes really were that election year, he probably – no he most certainly – would have acted differently. But, alas, he didn't know. Nor did he know that his entire conversation with Darlene was being recorded by two men, one tall and lean and the other short and stocky, from a small room adjacent to a large one filled with technicians manning television monitors, phones, and computers. The two men, Dawoud and Fadi, were in charge of surveillance for al-Qaeda in America, and the room they were hunkered down in had walls of triple steel and was buried two hundred feet beneath an ante-bellum mansion located on a private five-acre property outside Winston-Salem.

The building was one of two command centers for the execution of the political phase of Operation Saladin. The second command center, also an ante-bellum mansion, was located in Arlington, Virginia, about twenty-five minutes from the White House.

"They've finally reached the hospital," said Fadi, removing a pair of AKG headphones as he sat on a leather swivel chair before an L-shaped console decked out with TV monitors and computers used to carry out sophisticated surveillance.

"Did you get everything?" asked Dawoud, swiveling his chair and facing Fadi.

Fadi checked the input levels on the hard disk. They were working perfectly, and had picked up every word of the thirty-minute conversation, thanks to an Infiniti bug wired directly under the dashboard of Ramsey's Lexus, between the driver's and the passenger seats. Ghazi had similar bugs strategically planted around Ramsey's campaign headquarters, his company office, and his red-bricked home in the upper-class suburb of Emerywood. Ghazi had also ordered that Alison's bedroom be wired, so that her intimate conversations with Eliot could be closely monitored.

"Yeah," Fadi said. "I got every word."

"Great," said Dawoud. E-mail the audio file to Ghazi immediately."

"Where is he?"

"He's on his way to the chateau for his meeting with Aziz."

Ghazi was riding in the back of a bullet-proof Mercedes Benz S500 with tinted windows, on his way to Boone for an important strategy session with Aziz, who had just flown in from his Lahore mansion, where he had conferred with bin Laden's emissaries.

About half an hour from his destination, Ghazi retrieved from his black leather briefcase, in which he kept the blueprint for Operation Saladin, a thick leather-bound volume of the collected works of William Shakespeare. Between leisurely martini sips from the limo's well-stocked mini bar, Ghazi reread his favorite play, *Othello*.

It would be an understatement to say that Ghazi adored Shakespeare. He had read several times over every one of the Bard's 37 plays, 150 sonnets, and three non-dramatic long poems; and he had also perused more than a score of biographies of arguably the greatest English writer in history. His favorite Shakespearean character was the ruthless and cunning Iago, whom he had flawlessly represented in more than a dozen performances of *Othello* during his college days in the 1950s.

And while teaching a course on English Literature at the American University in Cairo in the early '70s, Ghazi had written several esoteric yet influential articles on the bard. They included one that laid to rest, at least among serious scholars, the claim by two professors at Palermo University that Shakespeare was not an Englishman born in Stratford in 1654, but a Sicilian named Michelangelo Florio Crollalanza, whose parents had fled the Holy Roman Inquisition because their Calvinistic beliefs were considered heretical, and had settled in London, where Signora Crollalanza had a cousin in Stratford.

After reading *Othello*, Ghazi retrieved a small black notebook from his briefcase. Using a fine-tipped Mount Blanc Fountain pen, he jotted down several insights he had gained from his latest study of the play's climactic scene in which Othello, baited and goaded by the vengeful Iago, becomes so insanely jealous that, on the basis of a mere handkerchief, he strangles his chaste and faithful wife Desdemona, believing her to be a strumpet.

Ghazi then cross-referenced the insights with those he had gained from his reading of other books he had relied upon for ideas in the formulation of a strategy for the execution of the political phase of Operation Saladin. The books included Sun Tzu's *The Art of War*, Hitler's *Mein Kampf*, Plato's *Republic*, Nietzsche's *The Will To Power*, John Stuart Mill's *On Liberty*, George Orwell's *1984*, Etienne de la Boetie's *Discourse on Voluntary Servitude*, Kevin Phillips' *American Theocracy*, William Shirer's *The Rise and Fall of the Third Reich*, and David Goldfield's *Still Fighting the Civil War*.

On the first page of his small black book Ghazi had succinctly outlined his modus operandi. It was based on the one skillfully used by Joseph Goebbels, Hitler's club-footed and brilliant propaganda minister, to rally the German people behind Nazism:

The seekers of absolute power must always remember that fear, ignorance and prejudice are their greatest allies. Carefully cultivated and ruthlessly exploited, the three can undermine any government, no matter how Democratic or powerful. Furthermore, the seekers of absolute power must never admit a fault or wrong; never concede that there may be some good in their enemies; never leave room for alternatives; never accept any blame; concentrate on one enemy at a time and blame him for everything that goes wrong; and never forget that the masses will sooner believe a big lie than a little one. P.S. A true leader never apologizes for anything. It's a sign of weakness. Hitler never did.

Ghazi had augmented this strategy with a diligent analysis of the psychological profiles of nine people central to the success of the political phase of Operation Saladin. These were Alison, her father, her mother, her former boyfriend, her husband, her best friend Chanel, Myron's mother Ruth, Queen Nefertari, leader of a black separatist movement called the Afro-Purists, and Rayvon Turlington, the popular host of an Afrocentric talk show on cable TV. Each individual had a separate and voluminous entry in the black notebook in which Ghazi, who had a PhD in Psychology on top of his master's in literature, had recorded every detail his investigations had unearthed about their lives, their habits, their idiosyncrasies, and, most important, their strengths and weaknesses.

Ghazi had just put away his notebook when his car phone rang. The call was from Fadi. "Ramsey and Darlene just arrived at the hospital, sir," he said.

"Did you tape their conversation?"

"Yes, sir. I just e-mailed you the audio file."

"Excellent. I'll share it with Aziz."

Chapter 11

Aziz was eager for Ghazi to arrive for their most important strategy meeting since Operation Saladin was launched a year ago. To mark the special occasion, he waited in his favorite room on the west wing of a German style chateau about ten miles north of Boone. The room was large, ornate, and had floors of imported Italian marble and a breathtaking view of the misty Blue Ridge Mountains. Its walls were festooned with gilt-framed rare paintings costing millions of dollars, and its vaulted ceiling was decorated with frescoes similar to those Michelangelo had painted in the Vatican's Sistine Chapel.

Sitting behind a hand-carved mahogany desk across from a huge marble fireplace, Aziz recalled the genesis of Operation Saladin at a meeting on November 3, 2001, a week after President Bush signed into law the U.S. Patriot Act, which Congress had overwhelmingly approved in response to 9/11, despite strong warnings from civil liberties groups that the act undermined the Constitution and personal freedoms.

The meeting took place at Aziz's primary residence, a heavily guarded 40-room Italian-style Renaissance Palazzo in Egypt, overlooking the Mediterranean Sea. The palazzo had its own private beach, helipad, 18-hole professional golf course, floodlit tennis courts, and an amusement park with a golden Ferris Wheel.

This Xanadu was one of more than two dozen palatial homes that Aziz owned. They included a mansion on Hilton Head Island, South Carolina; another one in Beverly Hills, California; a penthouse apartment overlooking Central Park; a mansion in Cape Town, South Africa; an apartment in London, England; a dacha outside St. Petersburg, Russia; a duplex townhouse in Georgetown, Washington, DC; a condominium in West Berlin; a villa in Istanbul; a mansion in Lahore, Pakistan; and a castle in Munich, Germany.

The meeting was between Aziz and Ebenezer Bickley, a former Klan grand wizard who during the 1960s had headed The Fiery Cross, one of the most violent white supremacist groups of the civil rights era. The group was responsible for the firebombing of scores of black churches and businesses belonging to liberal white Southerners, and for the abduction and killing of more than a dozen civil rights activists.

Aziz had bankrolled the Fiery Cross's agenda of terror, and in the fall of 1968 facilitated Bickley's escape, first to South Africa, and later on to Egypt, after he was implicated in the bombing of the offices of a pro-civil rights newspaper in Montgomery, Alabama, during which two people were killed.

During his exile, Bickley had acquired a different name and undergone elaborate plastic surgery. Upon his return to the U.S. following Bill Clinton's election as president in 1992, Bickley was stunned by the racial progress America had made because of the courageous and unapologetic activism of liberals: countless schools had been desegregated, previously white neighborhoods had been integrated, there were a record number of black office holders across the South, and interracial families were a common fixture in states where, before the liberal Warren Court in 1967 struck down anti-miscegenation laws, it was considered a felony for blacks and whites to marry.

But Bickley, an astute analyst of the subtext underlying America's intractable race problem, had quickly realized that despite all this obvious racial progress, liberals had not completely triumphed. Though racist laws had been abolished in both the North and South, the attitudes which had spawned them were still very much alive. The most visible sign of the staying power of bigotry in the South came when former Klan Grand Wizard David Duke was elected to the Louisiana state legislature. Duke ran for President twice, and in 1990 ran for governor of Louisiana, winning the majority of the white vote but losing the election to former governor Edwin Edwards, whose victory was attributed to the black vote. Up North in Boston, once considered the citadel of liberalism, school busing was subjected to some of the most virulent white opposition in the country.

And across the rest of the country Bickley saw politicians continue to play the race card shamelessly and adroitly. He had been particularly impressed when Ronald Reagan invoked States Rights during a speech at the launching of his 1980 presidential bid from Neshoba County, where three civil rights workers – Andrew Goodman, James Chaney, and Michael Schwerner – were murdered by the Klan in 1964. Bickley had been among the Klansmen who had taken part in the triple homicide.

The persistence of racism in America, and its shrewd exploitation by politicians of both parties during elections, had led Bickley to devise a different strategy in the pursuit of his white supremacist agenda. Central to the strategy was the recruitment of scores of Klansmen and Neo-Nazis whose membership in hate groups was unknown to law enforcement, and training them to infiltrate the American political system in order to carry out their nefarious agenda of systematically destroying liberalism as a political force, and of removing the checks and balances undergirding American Democracy as a prelude to erecting a fascist government akin to that outlined in the Turner Diaries.

Bickley was in the process of recruiting his army of fifth columnists when 9/11 galvanized the nation behind a common, external enemy in the form of al-Qaeda. Recalling Winston Churchill's maxim that "the enemy of my enemy is my friend," Bickley decided to adapt his strategy to a post 9/11 world by seeking ways to work with al-Qaeda. It was at this time that he learned, through one of his former students at the University of Cairo who had recently joined al-Qaeda, that Aziz, his one-time benefactor, was actually the group's principal backer, providing the bulk of the funding for its worldwide operations, which the CIA estimated cost about $30 million a year.

Two weeks after learning this crucial fact Bickley, who had secretly applauded the 9/11 attacks, had flown to Egypt, where he shared with Aziz a top secret plan he had drawn up on how bin Laden and his fellow Jihadists could join forces with white supremacists in the U.S. to achieve their mutual goals. These included the destruction of liberalism as a political force and the election of a white supremacist president and Congress, who would radically alter U.S. foreign policy in the Middle East by ending America's support of pro-western Arab regimes in countries like Egypt and Saudi Arabia. Most important, a white supremacist president and Congress would end America's unconditional support for Israel, and secretly provide her enemies with the weapons – biological, chemical, and nuclear – they needed to finally wipe the Zionist state off the face of the map.

Dazzled by the brilliance of Bickley's plan, Aziz had instantly embraced it, particularly because it meshed perfectly with a secret mission his dying father had entrusted to him. Two days later, Aziz had flown to Pakistan in his private jet, and from his mansion in Lahore was able to discreetly forward Bickley's plan to bin Laden through trusted intermediaries who were rogue members of the Pakistani Intelligence Service known as ISI. At the time, the al-Qaeda leader, now a hunted fugitive, was hiding in a cave deep in the mountains of Tora Bora on the Afghan-Pakistani border.

The plan's sheer audacity took bin Laden's breath away. It made 9/11 look like the work of an amateur. And bin Laden was no amateur. He knew that he couldn't defeat the United States militarily, and that the Bush administration was determined to spread "democracy" throughout the Middle East, the biggest threat to his dream of establishing an Islamic Caliphate stretching from Saudi Arabia to the Sudan. Most importantly, bin Laden was aware of the strategic advantages of using proxies to achieve his goals, particularly given the fact that he was now a hunted man and no longer able to personally direct or finance his worldwide empire of terror in its battle against the Great Satan.

But bin Laden had a huge ego. He wanted to make sure that even if others fought his battles, he still received credit. So he agreed to the partnership, with three pre-conditions: First, Bickley's organization should be called *al-Qaeda in America,* so that its successes could be credited to the worldwide movement bin Laden had founded. Second, Bickley and his fellow white supremacists should adopt Muslim code names to complete the camouflage. And third, Bickley's plan should be called Operation Saladin, in recognition of the great Muslim leader and warrior bin Laden considered a role model for defeating the Crusaders in 1187, recapturing Jerusalem, and uniting the Muslim world.

Despite his wariness that bin Laden was seeking to monopolize credit, Bickley readily assented to these terms, largely because he, too, had grandiose dreams of defeating a pesky band of crusaders called liberals, recapturing their Washington, DC citadel, and uniting white supremacists from South Africa to Europe under something akin to an Aryan Caliphate. For a Muslim code name, Bickley had chosen Ghazi, which means the Conqueror, and his organization was duly christened Al-Qaeda in America.

After a formal agreement was reached between bin Laden and Ghazi, Aziz had transferred $500 million into two bank accounts – one in Switzerland and the other in the Cayman Islands – for Ghazi to use in executing Operation Saladin. With part of the money Ghazi had recruited hundreds of bona fide Klansmen and neo-Nazis to run for local, state, and federal office as Republicans and Democrats – a rather easy thing to do at a time when Republicans and Democrats, enslaved to money, caring more about re-election than addressing the real needs of the American people, and the willing instruments and dupes of corporate lobbyists, were sounding so alike on a host of issues that Ralph Nader derisively called their two parties Tweedle-Dee and Tweedle-Dum.

Ghazi had personally trained these fifth columnists on how to effectively exploit the fears, insecurities, and xenophobia of the American people, engendered by the 9/11 terrorist attacks. Their deadly agenda was backed by a nationwide network of newspapers, television stations, think tanks, and radio talk shows owned by Aziz, and whose staple was liberal bashing, xenophobia, and fear mongering.

The campaigns of half of these fifth columnists, who were running for public offices as Democrats, were masterminded from al-Qaeda in America's Winston-Salem nerve center. The campaigns of the other half, who were running for public office as Republicans, were masterminded from the terror group's Arlington nerve center.

The brightest of these fifth columnists, Clarence Lynch, who also happened to be Aziz's son by a former actress and beauty queen from Louisiana, was masquerading as a Republican. Lynch had done such an excellent job exploiting the fears and insecurities of the American people, and bashing Ramsey as a big government, tax-

and-spend liberal whose opposition to the Iraq War gave comfort to al-Qaeda, that he was now holding a double digit lead in the race for governor of North Carolina.

"After he wins the governorship and gains the necessary experience as chief executive, Lynch will run for president in 2012," Aziz thought, recalling that four of the last five American presidents – Jimmy Carter, Ronald Reagan, Bill Clinton, and now George W. Bush – had been governors, and, more importantly, that every office in America, including the presidency, was now for sale to the highest bidder, thanks to the lack of meaningful campaign finance reform.

Aziz glanced at a silver-framed photo of Lynch – a telegenic and charismatic former talk show host turned politician – on the cover of the latest issue of *Newsweek*.

Could this man be America's next President? blared the headline.

Of course, and he'll be its greatest president ever. Greater even than Lincoln, Roosevelt, or Reagan, Aziz muttered to himself. He then opened a secret compartment in his attaché case, retrieved a letter, and brandished it. *And this is the reason why.*

Smiling, Aziz began reading the letter his father Otto had written him shortly before he committed suicide in 1972 in the study of his Egyptian villa, by blowing his head off with a 7.65-caliber Walther pistol. The weapon was similar to one Hitler had used to commit suicide in his Berlin bunker on April, 30, 1945, where he had presided over a disintegrating Third Reich as the Allies advanced from both East and West.

My Dearest Son,

I'm a dead man. A band of Jewish assassins is after me. They've somehow learned of my whereabouts and involvement in planning the Final Solution. But be assured that I won't let them take me alive and hang me, like they did Eichmann. I'm planning to kill myself, like my beloved Fuehrer did in Berlin. As my sole heir, I leave you my entire fortune. I know you are quite a playboy, and addicted to wine and women, but it is my fervent hope and prayer that you will use part of your inheritance to fulfill a duty I swore to my Fuehrer when we both realized that the end of the Third Reich was near.

I told him that I would dedicate my life, fortune, and sacred honor to getting revenge against America for entering the war and helping the Allies defeat Nazism. And what sweeter revenge than to transform America itself into a Fourth Reich! The tendencies are already there, my son, just as they were in Germany before Hitler came to power. But before Nazism can be reborn in America, liberalism, a Jewish inspired ideology, must be utterly destroyed as a political force, just as it was in Germany. Such a job obviously can't be done overnight or alone, so remember to have patience, and to enlist the help of groups that hate America and Jews, both at home and abroad.

I die in peace and without regret knowing that I've passed this important duty to you, my dear boy. On your shoulders rests the august responsibility of systematically destroying American Democracy and establishing upon its ruins a Fourth Reich that will indeed last a thousand years. Please don't disappoint me. Heil Hitler."

I won't, father, thought Aziz, wiping tears as he finished reading the letter. *After he wins the governorship of North Carolina your own grandson will, in a few short years, occupy the White House and transform America into the Fourth Reich.*

Aziz was reflecting on all this when his 30-something secretary, who was also a member of his harem, buzzed to say that Ghazi's limo had just arrived at the chateau. *But Ramsey stands in my son's way,* thought Aziz as he put away the letter. *I can't wait to hear how Ghazi plans to use Alison's baby to destroy his gubernatorial campaign.*

Chapter 12

Buck said he wanted a baby boy, an heir, Nancy thought as she walked through the sliding doors of Triad Regional Hospital. She had serious doubts that she would succeed in her high stakes mission of stealing a baby boy in broad daylight. But backing out was no option. She had told Buck that she already had the baby, so she had better have him by the time Buck arrived home tonight from his latest trucking trip.

Stay calm, Nancy told herself as her nervous eyes cast swift glances around the busy lobby and her callused fingers trembled slightly. A thin film of sweat dampened her brow and the strands of fake black hair nearest her face. She avoided making eye contact with anyone as she headed straight for the bank of silver-door elevators.

It was Sunday afternoon. The lobby was packed with visitors and florists delivering baskets of flowers, balloons, and get-well cards. No one noticed anything unusual about Nancy. She appeared to be just one of the many nurses employed by the busy hospital. She wore the all-white nursing assistant uniform she had worn when she temped at the hospital two years ago. Over her shoulder she carried a large, slightly worn, denim purse. She rode the packed elevator to the third floor. Everyone exited to the right, so she went left. She passed through the maternity ward, and then slowed as she neared the nursery. The blinds were open.

A new mother, wearing a blue bathrobe and white slippers, together with her proud husband, stood admiring their sleeping newborn through the glass. "Oh, look, honey!" the father said, grinning. "She's smiling in her sleep."

The mother said, "Look at her move her tiny little fingers."

Nancy paused, pretending to read a bulletin board, until the proud parents, their arms wrapped around each other, finished marveling at their private miracle and disappeared around the corner. Nearly two dozen babies had been born at Triad Regional Hospital since Friday – a new record. More were on the way that Sunday. Nurses, medical assistants, and obstetricians rushed back and forth behind the swinging doors to Nancy's left. She heard women scream behind half-opened doors as they mightily pushed those tiny bundles of life out of the comfortable security and liquid darkness of the womb into the blinding light of the world, with all its joys and heartaches.

"This one's a breech," she heard an obstetrician say.

"Breech!" a nurse shouted.

Word spread quickly among the medical staff. Nurses and assistants came running from every direction. Seconds later, a team of people in white uniforms rushed past Nancy pushing a woman on a gurney. The woman's sweat-covered face was a mask of agony. The sight of the woman reminded Nancy of her own miscarriage nine months ago after Buck, when she had denied having an affair with his supervisor, had kicked her in the stomach with his steel-toed boots. She shuddered at the thought.

With so much activity, Nancy was glad no one paid attention to her. No one noticed that she was the same woman who had visited the maternity ward twice in the past four weeks, inconspicuously observing the routines and staff, often from behind an open magazine in the visitor's lounge. In the midst of the chaos, Nancy returned to the nursery. She was so absorbed in her own thoughts that she didn't notice Eliot coming down the corridor, a jovial look on his face. The two bumped into each other.

"Oh, I'm so very sorry," Nancy said.

Eliot smiled. "No problem," he said and continued down the corridor.

*****

Eliot turned right, headed toward Alison's room at the end of the hallway. Half-way to the suite, his cell phone rang. Eliot glanced at the number; it was Ghazi. Eliot quickly ducked into the men's restroom, closed the door, and looked about. It had two stalls and two urinals and there was no one around. He turned on the water to drown his voice.

"Hullo," Eliot said with bated breath.

"This is Ghazi," said the caller. "How's the baby?"

"Fine. I just came from checking on him in the nursery."

"Where's Alison?"

"Back at the suite."

"Does she suspect anything?"

"No. Should I finally tell her the truth?"

"Not yet."

After hanging up, as he was making his way back to the suite to rejoin Alison, Eliot debated if he should ignore Ghazi's advice and finally tell her his long-held secret.

Nancy took a good look at the row of babies nearest the window. The one closest to the door had straight dark hair, just like Buck, a cute nose, alabaster skin and the bluest eyes. The label on the side of the clear plastic bassinet proclaimed, "I'm a Boy!" He was trying to suck on one of his tiny fists. She fell in love with him instantly.

"How cute," Nancy thought, moving closer to the window. Seeing two nurses coming by, she quickly moved away, then casually doubled back and passed the nursery a second time, furtively checking out the staff. In the special-needs nursery adjacent to the regular nursery, one nurse was bent over a preemie, adjusting a sun lamp. The little diapered lump of humanity moved its spindly legs and arms like a freshly hatched chick trying to shed the broken fragments of shell from its tiny wings. Its cry resembled the faint bleating of a lamb. Another nurse was diapering a three-pounder in an incubator.

The only staff member in the regular nursery was an African-American nurse who was bent over a desk and writing. Nancy had never seen her before. She was certain she must be new. Just then Nancy heard female voices coming toward her from an adjacent hallway. Nancy started walking briskly, pretending to be heading somewhere to perform an urgent task. Three white nursing assistants rounded the corner, passed Nancy with a quick hello, and entered the nursery. Nancy turned to watch.

"Feeding time already?" said the head nurse, looking up from her paperwork.

"Three o'clock," said the first nursing assistant.

"Okay," said the head nurse.

Careful not to be seen, Nancy watched from behind a medical supply rack as the nursing assistants grabbed three bassinettes and pushed them down the hall toward rooms where anxious mothers awaited their babies for those important first moments of bonding and feeding after the ordeal of birth.

One of the nurses in the special-needs nursery called for some help bathing a preemie. The head nurse set down her pen and disappeared from view between the swinging doors. *This is my chance*, Nancy thought as her brown eyes roved about.

She saw no surveillance cameras anywhere. The hospital chief had dismissed the idea of installing them as too expensive and wasteful. No one had ever stolen a baby from Triad Regional, and nationwide ONLY 23 cases of infant abduction had been reported in the last ten years. Nancy darted into the nursery through the open door, quickly grabbed the cart containing the baby boy she had been eyeing, and wheeled it out.

Now came the most difficult and dangerous part: getting past the nursing station.

What should I say if I get stopped?

The head nurse had her back turned and was talking to a nurse just arriving for duty. Looking straight ahead, Nancy thought she was home free when she heard the head nurse ask, "Has another one been called for?"

"Yes," said Nancy, trying hard to control her thumping heart. "Room 244." She kept her back to the nurse and spoke over her shoulder.

"You've got to keep an eye on these temps," the head nurse said in a low voice to the nurse coming on duty. "They don't know the routines." In a louder voice she addressed Nancy. "Be sure to check the mother's wristband before you give her the baby, hear. We don't want any mix-ups."

"Yes, Ma'am."

Breathing a sigh of relief, Nancy quickly pushed the cart down the hall and around another corner to the janitor's closet. She pushed the bassinet inside, pulled a white blanket from her purse, wrapped the baby in it, and then slowly opened the door. To her relief, the coast was clear. She knew this section of the ward had the least traffic.

She quietly shut the door and headed for the bank of elevators nearby.

The first elevator came. The doors slid open. It was full. *Don't push your way on. Don't act desperate. Stay calm.* As the doors slowly shut, the passengers all seemed to be staring at Nancy, some with smiles on their faces, others with stoic looks. *They know. They can tell.* Nancy glanced back at the swinging door through which she had just come. A nurse was heading her way. *Oh my God, she knows.*

"Another one going home?" the nurse asked.

"Yes," Nancy replied hastily, her face slightly averted.

"I'll be glad when this shift's over."

"Me too," Nancy said.

The nurse continued down the hall.

It seemed the next elevator would never come. Nancy feared someone from the nursery would burst out through the swinging doors, point at her and scream, "Kidnapper!" She contemplated going down the stairs, but was afraid that would be too obvious. No nurse would take a newborn down a dank and drafty cement stairwell.

Relax. This is your baby. God took it from your womb and put it into the womb of another woman for safekeeping. You're just picking up what's yours.

The second elevator came. Two visitors carrying huge bouquets of flowers disembarked. The rest of the passengers moved to the sides to create room. Nancy stepped in and pressed herself against the back wall, staring at the baby.

"Ground floor, please," she said without looking up.

Several women leaned over to take a look at the baby.

"How cute," said a silver-haired lady with a feathered hat, peering at the sleeping bundle from behind thick eyeglasses. "Is it a boy or girl?"

"It's a girl," Nancy heard herself saying. "She's the cutest thing on the ward and we hate to see her go, but her mother's been discharged."

To Nancy the elevator was taking ages to descend three floors. Each time the doors slid open, she expected to see a burly cop standing there, gun drawn, handcuffs ready. Finally the elevator reached the ground floor, its doors opened, and people streamed out. Outside the door, Nancy ran into Darlene and Ramsey, who were waiting to take the elevator to go see Alison and the baby and were carrying flowers and a teddy-bear. Nancy was in such a hurry to get to the side door that she bumped into Darlene.

"I'm sorry, ma'am," Nancy said.

Darlene smiled. "It's okay, may I take a look at the baby?"

"Sure."

Darlene took a peek and cooed at the sleeping baby, "How sweet. Boy or girl?"

"Boy. Her mother just checked out and is waiting in the car."

"Tell her she has a very beautiful baby," Darlene said.

"I will," said Nancy and then hurried toward the side door. Darlene and Ramsey climbed into the elevator and it left. Nancy reached the side door and grabbed its handle.

"Stop!" a deep male voice said, terrifying her. Nancy froze. She slowly turned and saw an African-American security guard in a beige uniform coming toward her. His expression was stern. A holstered gun banged heavily against his leg.

Nancy's instincts told her to drop the baby and run like hell.

Chapter 13

Alison grabbed the phone next to the bouquet of a dozen fresh red roses she had received that morning from Hunter. She slowly dialed the four-digit nursery extension. A nurse answered. "This is Alison Whitaker. Could you please bring my baby to Room 244?"

"Certainly. I'll have someone bring him to you right away."

"*I'm caught,* Nancy thought as the stern-faced black security guard strode toward her. *It's all over.* Nancy's heart was racing a mile a minute as she struggled to remain calm.

The guard stopped five feet from her. "That's an emergency exit, ma'am," he said. "Use the other side door, please." He pointed the way.

"Sorry," Nancy said, sighing heavily. "We've been so busy today I forgot which doors are which. The baby's mother's been discharged. She's waiting in the car."

"That's all right, ma'am," said the security guard, smiling. "A few other people have made the same mistake today. I've never seen the hospital this busy."

Nancy smiled nervously at the security guard, then quickly retraced her steps and went out the other side door. Once outside, in broad daylight, she headed straight for the brown Buick station wagon she had parked nearby to facilitate her getaway. She hurriedly placed the baby in the carrier on the floor of the backseat, and then covered him with a pale blue blanket. She rearranged the handbag and laundry basket on the backseat to keep anyone peering through the window from seeing the child.

Nancy drove slowly toward the booth where a bald-headed white attendant with a thick mustache stood collecting parking fees. She dug into her purse and was about to remove a five-dollar bill to pay the $1.50 fee when the attendant, spotting her nursing uniform, waved her past. *That was stupid of me*, Nancy thought as she pulled onto Main Street. *I should have remembered that the hospital staff park for free.*

Driving down Main, Nancy adjusted the rearview mirror and shifted in her seat so she could glimpse the baby, still fast asleep in the carrier "Hullo, Buck Junior," she cooed, "Your daddy will love you when he sees you tonight."

The baby still had not arrived when Eliot entered Alison's delivery suite, followed by Ramsey and Darlene. The latter was carrying a brown teddy bear.

"How are you, kiddo?" said Ramsey, kissing Alison on the cheek.

"I'm feeling much better, thanks. I'm waiting for the nurse to bring Dylan."

"You haven't seen him yet?" Darlene asked, surprised.

"No. He's been fast asleep in the nursery and I didn't want to wake him up until you got here. And I needed some rest. Delivery exhausted me."

"Poor thing," Darlene said. "Well, here's something to cheer you up." Darlene kissed Alison on the cheek, then handed her the teddy bear and balloon.

"Thanks. Please put them by the chair over there."

"Before he left for his meeting with Kessler Reggie ordered you a bouquet of yellow roses," said Ramsey. "Have they been delivered yet?"

"Yes. They were delivered a while ago," Alison said. "And they're very lovely."

Eliot kissed Alison on the cheek before taking a seat next to the bed. "My Dad and Mary Lou are also on their way here," he said.

"They're very proud of you, honey, really proud. This is their first grandchild, you know." Alison smiled as she remembered the note they had sent with their bouquet of red roses: *There's no greater honor and privilege for a woman than becoming a mother. And there's no greater gift to a child coming into this world than to have the love of both parents. Mary Lou and I are well aware of the difficulties in your marriage. But for the sake of the baby, we hope and pray that you and Eliot will resolve your differences and stay together.*

> *With the utmost love and respect,*
> *Theodore and Mary Lou."*

Suddenly a frantic-faced nursery employee in a pink uniform appeared at the door, glanced about the crowded suite, and then left without saying a word. Alison, Eliot, Darlene, and Ramsey exchanged puzzled glances. A second nurse from the nursery burst in and asked in a tremulous voice, "Isn't the baby with you, Mrs. Whitaker?"

"Why, no," Alison said. "I called for him about fifteen minutes ago."

The second nurse disappeared.

"What's going on?" Ramsey asked.

"I don't know," Alison said.

An alarm suddenly went off. It filled the sterile corridors with a high-pitched wail and flashing lights. "Have all the exit doors been sealed?" Alison heard a male voice shout frantically, then hurried footsteps and hushed but agitated voices whispering outside the door. "Don't just sit there," she said to Eliot, a feeling of panic rising within her. "Go see what's happening!" Before Eliot could move, the head nurse, a security guard, and Betty burst into the room.

"Mrs. Whitaker," the head nurse said in a voice laced with dread. "Didn't a nurse bring your baby boy to you half an hour ago?"

"No!" Alison screamed, leaping up from the bed. "My baby! Where's my baby!"

Darlene restrained her. "Calm down, honey," she said in a shaky voice. "There's obviously been some mistake."

"Give me back my baby!" Alison's voice trailed to a whimper. "I want my ba...."

While the head nurse and Darlene tried in vain to comfort Alison, security guards and medical staff raced up and down the halls, checking rooms and closets.

Eliot and Ramsey went out and rushed down the hall, trying to find out what had happened, talking to security guards, to doctors, to nurses, to anyone they bumped into. A few minutes later, both returned. Their faces were ashen.

"They found Dylan's empty cart in the janitor's closet," Eliot said dejectedly. "What does that mean?" Darlene stammered, clutching her mouth.

"It means our grandson has been kidnapped," Ramsey said.

Chapter 14

Now is the right time to confront Mama, thought Myron while watching CNN from the tastefully furnished living room of his mother's rent-controlled apartment overlooking St. Nicholas Park in New York City.

Mrs. Pearson had just accompanied the last of her dozen guests, who had come to celebrate her fifty-eighth birthday, downstairs. The guests were mostly members of her church and colleagues at the AIDS orphanage where she volunteered.

Myron glanced at his watch. It was 3:30 p.m. He was still watching TV when his mother returned. She was a slight woman with speckled gray hair and brown soulful eyes that, despite hinting at a life of hardship, still exuded that quiet dignity, resiliency, and faith typical of black women from the pre-Civil Rights era.

"Thanks for coming, son," she said, sitting next to him on the loose-pillow Brunswick sofa dominating the small living room. "I know you're very busy."

"I wish I could come see you more often," he said, muting the TV.

"I understand. I know you have a tough job. I only hope you can find time to relax, son. By the way, are you seeing someone?"

Myron shook his head. "Why do you ask?"

"Oh, just curious. It's been more than a year since you and Alison broke up."

Myron bit his lower lip. "I haven't stopped loving her, Mama."

Mrs. Pearson looked concerned. "But you must move on, son."

"How can I when you still haven't told me the real reason you pressured me to call off the wedding?" Myron said, looking his mother straight in the eye.

Discomfited by the question, Myron's mother rose and went to the kitchen. "What's the use of rehashing the past?" she said as she placed the leftover birthday cake in a Tupperware. "Alison is a happily married woman now. And according to the newspapers, she and her husband are expecting their first child."

"She's not happily married, Mama."

"How do you know?"

"I saw how she looked on her wedding day. There was sadness in her eyes. And her friend Chanel told me that on the day of the wedding, Alison almost didn't go through with the ceremony because she doesn't love Eliot."

Mrs. Pearson returned to the sofa. "Son, please forget about her," she implored, squeezing Myron's hand. "What's done cannot be undone. Move on with your life."

"I want to move on. But I can't unless I know the truth. Why didn't you want me to marry Alison?" His voice was insistent.

She let go of his hand and sighed deeply. "You're right, son. I didn't tell you the truth. And the reason I didn't is because of a deeply held secret."

Myron's heart started racing. "What secret?"

For the next hour Myron listened, spellbound, as his mother related a secret she had kept hidden for decades. Raised in one of the few land-owning black families in North Carolina, Ellen Pearson had grown up on her grandparents' three-hundred-acre farm in the Smokies, about fifty miles from Connemara, the house to which Lincoln's biographer, the poet Carl Sandburg, and his wife, Lillian, moved in 1945. As a child she had listened to Marian Anderson on the radio and dreamed of someday becoming an opera singer.

That idyllic life was shattered when she turned thirteen. While her father, an Army sergeant, was away in Europe fighting the Nazis in order to make the world safe for freedom and democracy, Ellen watched helplessly as her grandfather, the son of former slaves who had recently lost his wife to cancer, was dragged out of bed by a posse of Klansmen and lynched from a nearby sycamore tree for refusing to sell his farm to a local sheriff who coveted it. The posse, led by the sheriff, had then set fire to their home.

In the dead of night, Ellen Pearson, her brother Robert and their mother Monique had trudged their way up North. Shortly after arriving in New York City, where they stayed with her uncle in a cramped two-bedroom apartment in Jamaica, Queens, word reached Ellen that her beloved father had been killed during the invasion of Normandy. Her forty-one-year-old mother – having lost her home, husband, and father, all within six months – suffered a severe nervous breakdown and had to be institutionalized.

"Despite all the pain I've suffered at the hands of white people," said Mrs. Pearson, after a sip of water, "I still had no objection to your marrying Alison because I don't believe in guilt by association. It was only after the man who'd brought to justice the Klansmen who'd murdered your grandpa asked me to stop your wedding that I did."

"Who's the man?"

Mrs. Pearson paused a long moment then said slowly, "Alison's father."

Myron was thunderstruck. "Alison's father?"

Mrs. Pearson nodded.

"But how can that be? Alison said that her father approved of our plans to marry."

"That's not what his campaign manager said when he was over here."

"His campaign manager?"

"Yes. Ramsey sent his campaign manager to come and talk to me while you were away on the book tour. I believe his name is Reginald Hunter."

Myron shook his head in disbelief. "What exactly did Hunter say?"

"He said that he'd conducted several polls which show that a majority of whites in North Carolina wouldn't vote for Ramsey if his daughter married interracially. So Ramsey wanted me to talk you out of it. At first I was torn, son. I didn't want to hurt you, for I knew how much you loved Alison. I relented when Hunter reminded me that it was Ramsey who'd helped bring your grandpa's murderer to justice, and that because of his commitment to civil rights, if he were elected governor, he'd improve the lot of black people in North Carolina. Hunter also promised that as Governor Ramsey would help me reclaim your grandpa's land, which is now owned by a Klansman named Chandler."

"Why didn't you tell me all this before?"

"I didn't because Hunter asked me not to before he left," Mrs. Pearson said. "He didn't want word to get back to Alison and make her mad at her father."

Myron was stunned by the revelation.

"Something interesting happened before Hunter left," said Mrs. Pearson.

"What happened?"

"He almost fainted."

"Almost fainted?"

"Yes. It was when he saw the wedding photo of your uncle Robert and his white wife Jade that I keep on the mantelpiece," said Mrs. Pearson. "When I asked him what was wrong, he replied that your uncle's wife, who died in childbirth from an obstetrical hemorrhage, reminded him of someone he knew. He asked me questions about your Uncle Robert. I told him that was he was killed by a letter bomb. That's when he responded that he was mistaken about knowing your uncle's wife."

Myron was about to say something when he noticed an image on the muted TV that almost made his heart stop beating. It was Alison at a press conference. Myron turned up the volume. When he and his mother finished listening to coverage of the kidnapping of Alison's baby, Mrs. Pearson said, "Please son, move on with your life. Alison has enough problems on her hands already without your bringing back the past."

"I'll try to move on, Mama," Myron said. "But it won't be easy."

"I know, son," said Mrs. Pearson. "But it's the best thing for all concerned. In the meantime, I'll pray that Alison's baby is found unharmed."

While riding a yellow cab on the way to the airport to catch a shuttle flight to DC, Myron continued to be bothered by what his mother had revealed about Hunter's secret visit.

"Why would Ramsey send Hunter up to ask Mama to pressure

me to call off the wedding," Myron wondered, "while at the same time telling Alison that he had no objection to our getting married? And why would Hunter faint at seeing the photo of my uncle's white wife?"   Myron wished he could talk to Alison directly about the matter, but he knew that he couldn't, particularly now that her baby had been kidnapped.

"There's definitely more to Hunter than meets the eye," Myron thought as the 737 jet broke through a cloud cover on its way to landing at Reagan National Airport in Washington, DC. "I know who to call to find out more about him."

Chapter 15

Hunter and Kessler sat at opposite ends of a double pedestal cherry dining room table covered with an embroidered lace cloth. Above it hung an ornate silver chandelier. The table stood in the middle of a large, glass-walled room overlooking a rose garden, beyond which the Great Smokies, still shrouded in a hazy mist, were spread like folds of lavender velvet. The lunch fare was what you would expect to see at the table of one of the richest men in the world – it consisted of caviar, roast goose with apple chestnut stuffing, hot buttered rum, salad, and a Remy Martin Louis XIII Diamond Cognac. But the animated conversation between the two men was, to say the least, very strange.

"Bin Laden is not happy with the way you've done things, partner," said Kessler, pouring the cognac into two pear-shaped crystal snifters and handing one to Hunter.

"Why not?" retorted Hunter, a bit miffed.

"Oh, he thinks your political strategy won't work because you're too obsessed with getting revenge against Ramsey for what he did to you," Kessler said. "Also, he thinks that your military strategy won't work because it's been almost a year since Abdul's cell picked up the weapons, and they've yet to start any serious training."

"There's a reason for the delay," said Hunter. "My informant inside the FBI told me that a counter-insurgency unit has been assigned the task of infiltrating Abdul's cell to find out if there are any links between it and William Krar. Apparently during his search for weapons before he came to us, Abdul tried purchasing them from Krar."

Krar was an east-Texas man who, along with his common law wife, pleaded guilty to the possession of weapons of mass destruction after investigators found inside his home and storage facilities a sodium-cyanide bomb capable of killing thousands, more than a hundred explosives, including remote controlled bombs disguised as briefcases, half a million rounds of ammunition, dozens of illegal weapons, antidotes for nerve agents, and stacks of anti-Semitic, anti-black, and anti-government literature.

"How do you plan to deal with this wrinkle?" asked Kessler.

"Well, I still intend to pay Abdul's cell the stipend so they can quit their jobs. But instead of starting military training right away, I want them to become Klan buffoons."

"Klan buffoons?" said Kessler. "I don't understand."

"Well," Hunter said, "the Klan has been pretty marginalized since 9/11 because of the focus on Islamic Jihadists. I intend to have Abdul's men start wearing their robes, holding rallies and parades, and spouting the usual Klan claptrap. Such antics will not only fool the FBI into thinking that Abdul's cell is pretty harmless, but they'll help me gain even more control over Ramsey."

"How?"

"Ramsey hates the Klan with a passion," Hunter said. "And if he believes that the group is making a comeback in his beloved North Carolina, he'll be even more desperate to win. And that means the campaign will be more under my control."

"I see," said Kessler. "But are you sure he doesn't suspect anything?"

"How can he?" said Hunter. "After all I'm the miracle worker who brought him victory in the primary, convinced you to bankroll his campaign, and has promised to bring him victory in November, despite the odds. He doesn't have the slightest idea that I'm his worst enemy, and that I've been giving him bad advice and feeding him fake polling and focus group results. Had niggers not unexpectedly turned out in record numbers during the primary, he'd have lost big to our agent Douglas."

"Why did niggers stick with him after you made him repudiate liberalism?"

"Niggers are very loyal," Hunter said. "They remembered his anti-Klan crusade. Also, Darlene overruled my decision not to have Ramsey give that speech before the NAACP, which apparently galvanized the nigger vote."

"It sounds like Darlene is proving to be harder to dupe than Ramsey and Alison."

"She sure is," Hunter said. "It's the Jew in her. She's been wary of me since her husband hired me as his campaign manager. And she's such an unrepentant liberal she continues to think that Alison should have married that nigger Myron instead of Eliot. That's why I'm eager to hear what she has to say about me on the audio file headquarters just sent me," Hunter said, retrieving a laptop from his briefcase.

Having said that Hunter – aka Ghazi – powered his laptop and the audio file that Dawoud had e-mailed him began playing through Windows Media Player 11. Kessler – aka Aziz – leaned forward, eager to hear every word between Darlene and Ramsey, the one man who stood in the way of Hitler's godson becoming president and transforming America into a Fourth Reich allied with bin Laden's al-Qaeda.

As the yellow cab he was riding from JFK crawled along a congested Long Island Expressway toward Manhattan, Myron pulled out his cell phone and dialed his friend Isaac. He answered, but told Myron that he couldn't talk because he was at Holman's Maximum Security prison in Atmore, about to sit down for a very important meeting with Tommy Cone, the Klansman who was on death row.

Isaac promised to call back as soon as the meeting was over.

After listening to the audio file, Kessler chuckled. Leaning back in his cushy chair, he said, "I'm amazed how well you've managed to convince Ramsey to defend your integrity even as you plot his political demise. You're more cunning than Iago."

Hunter smiled. "I've carefully studied his psychological profile," he said. "He's more gullible than Othello. And my plan to get him to alienate his traditional base by repudiating liberalism and running as a conservative is working brilliantly."

"But you said niggers remain loyal to him," said Kessler, puffing on his cigar. "Won't they turn out in November, especially if you let him continue giving rousing pro-civil rights speeches like the one he gave at that National Association of Alligators, Coons, and Possums convention in Winston-Salem?"

Hunter sipped his cognac. "I'll make sure he doesn't. I also intend to use a group called Afro-Purists to neutralize the nigger vote in the general election."

"Who are they?"

"They're a black group whose separatist agenda has been gaining in popularity since the O.J. Simpson verdict revealed how deeply divided America is racially. But the group needs a charismatic leader who'll give it even more credibility. At the moment it's being led by a shrill mulatto woman named Queen Nefertari. Granted, she's been as relentless as a hound dog in her criticism of Ramsey as a paternalistic liberal. But still, her mulatto background makes her racial loyalty suspect in the eyes of darker niggers."

"Do you have a replacement in mind?"

"Yeah. A smooth-talking talk show host named Rayvon Turlington. Once I co-opt him, I intend to use him in a plan involving Alison to destroy Ramsey's campaign."

"What kind of plan?"

For the next fifteen minutes, Hunter meticulously outlined the plan he had code named Operation Mumbo-Jumbo.

Kessler roared with laughter. "Operation Mumbo-Jumbo is absolutely brilliant, partner. Now I understand why you schemed to get Alison to break up with Myron. But are you sure she won't find out the truth before Mumbo-Jumbo is executed?"

"Not if Myron's mother keeps her word."

"What if she breaks it?"

"Then the blame will fall entirely on Ramsey."

"I see." Kessler refilled his wine glass. "But there's a point I'm unclear about."

"What is it?"

"How will you get Rayvon to leave his job as host of an extremely popular talk show and become leader of an obscure group such as the Afro-Purists?"

Hunter grinned. "Simple. I've recently found out that he can't keep his dick out of women's panties, so I plan to do a little J. Edgar

Hoover trick on him."

The sun had dissipated most of the mist, uncovering a breathtaking panorama of verdant valleys, virgin forest, rolling pastures, waterfalls, and meandering streams that made the North Carolina Mountains one of the most scenic spots in America. Hunter rose to stretch his stiff legs by pacing up and down the balcony. Kessler, who looked trimmer after losing more than sixty pounds following quadruple bypass surgery, lit another cigar.

"By the way," he said, "while you go about destroying Ramsey's campaign, you don't have to worry about Tommy Cone. His execution date has finally been set."

Hunter's large ears perked up. "Really? When is it?"

"October 6th."

"How did you find out?"

"Through my contact in the governor's office," Kessler said between cigar puffs. "The new governor, a Democrat, is keeping his campaign promise to speed up executions. The news should be in the papers within a day or so."

Hunter rubbed his small hands in glee. "That's the best news I've heard since 9/11. So Cone, my final link with the past, will soon be dead."

Kessler puffed on his cigar. "I actually like Cone," he said, blowing a cloud of smoke. "I like people who remain loyal to an oath, even when their lives are at stake."

"I like him too," Hunter said. "But he knows too much. We can't afford the risk of having him around. Not with Operation Saladin at such a crucial stage."

"I agree. Well, may God have mercy on his faithful Klan soul."

"Amen. I'll drink to that."

Half an hour later a jovial Hunter was in his bullet-proof limo on his way back to High Point. It was almost 4:30 p.m. No longer fearful of being implicated in murder, now that he had learned that Cone was headed for the gas chamber, Hunter focused on the next phase of Operation Saladin. He reached into his leather briefcase and retrieved his small black book. He carefully studied the latest entry on Rayvon Turlington, which contained transcripts of calls he had made in the last 24 hours, and his daily schedule. Hunter noticed that Rayvon was having a date with Chanel that evening.

Good, he thought, recalling that he also had an entry on Alison's best friend. During the rest of the trip, Hunter reviewed both entries, searching for things to use in his J. Edgar Hoover-inspired plan to make Rayvon leader of the Afro-Purist movement.

Chanel is desperate for a man, thought Hunter. *And Rayvon is handsome and available. I wonder how their dinner will go, and what they'll do afterwards.*

Hunter retrieved his cell phone and called Dawoud.

"Did you arrange for Chanel's and Rayvon's dinner table to be wired?"

"Yes. I persuaded the waiter to place an infinity bug in the vase of flowers by telling her that I was from the FBI, and that Rayvon was a suspect in a top-secret investigation to uncover an al-Qaeda terrorist cell in Greensboro."

"Excellent. What about Chanel's bedroom?"

"The crew placed a hidden camera in the light fixture above the bed."

"Perfect."

Chapter 16

Chanel admired the bouquet of flowers in the middle of the table inside the Barn Dinner Theatre in Greensboro, where she and her date, Rayvon Turlington, were sitting watching a play. During a scene break, Chanel set her glass of Chablis between her plate and a flickering candle, then glanced admiringly across the table at Rayvon, a thirty-five-year-old former NBA player whose career was cut short by a knee injury. Rayvon, a native of Greensboro, was now host of *The Rayvon Turlington Show* on cable TV.

Chanel exhaled. *Lord, I sure hope Rayvon turns out to be Mr. Right*, she thought, as she took another sip of wine. *I'm ready to settle down. I'm not getting any younger.*

Rayvon was only the third man Chanel had dated since returning home from Atlanta a little over two years ago to nurse her mother back to health following breast cancer surgery. This was due in part to her role as caretaker, and to her maddening schedule as a TV anchor for the area's top-rated news program. But in the main it was because, like many professional black women, Chanel was having a hard time finding black men at her educational and income level who were ready for a serious, monogamous relationship.

Chanel's gaze returned to the brightly illuminated stage in the center of the theater. She and Rayvon were watching a stage production of *Guess Who's Coming to Dinner*. So far Chanel had found the play, put on by performers from the North Carolina School of the Arts, highly entertaining and informative about the challenges and subtleties of interracial love. Though the acting fell short of the tour-de-force performances in the 1967 Oscar-winning film version starring Spencer Tracy, Katherine Hepburn, Sidney Poitier and Katherine Houghton, the actors and actresses performing just five feet away from her had the advantage of immediacy and spontaneity.

The theater was a renovated barn with a platform stage that descended slowly, at the push of a button, from the ceiling to the floor once the buffet tables had been cleared. The Sunday evening crowd filled the small square tables arranged in tier fashion around the center stage.

Rayvon was so engrossed in the play that he didn't notice Chanel studying him. At six foot eight, he had a fashionable square haircut that glistened with Brylcreem, sexy brown eyes, dark- skin, broad shoulders, and several tattoos on his upper arms. During his short-lived NBA career, Rayvon had hobnobbed with movie stars and had often been seen at some of Hollywood's hottest parties, including one at the home of O. J. Simpson in Brentwood, before the former gridiron superstar was accused, and later found not guilty, of the double murder of Nicole Brown Simpson and Ronald Goldman.

The issue of race had mattered little to Rayvon while he was moving in such colorblind circles. But as host of a popular talk show devoted mostly to issues of black pride, black culture, black identity, black music, and black love, he had become passionately, and some would say, obsessively, Afrocentric.

On his show Rayvon never ceased gushing about the virtues and sacrifices of black women. *Ebony* had recently named Rayvon one of its top bachelors for 2004. The magazine had also interviewed him for a popular article in a forthcoming issue titled "Why I Love Black Women." Rayvon's quote, which was certain to elicit even more fan mail from swooning black women, had described them as "goddesses whose beauty, intelligence, strength, and wit are peerless, and who deserve to be pampered by the love of a real black man." Needless to say, Chanel had been extremely flattered when such a man had asked her out thirty minutes after they had met at a fund-raiser for the Urban League organized by the Triad Association of Black Media Professionals.

The play ended with the black groom and white bride happily sitting down to dinner with both sets of parents and an approving minister. While Chanel applauded, Rayvon simply rolled his big brown eyes and shook his head.

I have a feeling he doesn't like interracial couples, Chanel thought. As Rayvon raced along U.S. 421 in his brand new red BMW 318i convertible, he and Chanel fell to discussing the play, and then got onto the topic of whether blacks and whites could learn anything from interracial couples that would help them bridge the racial divide.

"A close friend of mine was once in a relationship with a black man," Chanel said, thinking of Alison and Myron. "She said it helped her to overcome a lot of stereotypes about black people, especially black men."

"Is that right?" Rayvon said.

"Yes. She said the relationship taught her the importance of honest communication. She said that blacks and whites don't often do that. They seldom talk *to* each other but always *about* each other. I must say I agree with her."

"Enemies have nothing to talk about, Chanel."

"Oh, come off it, Rayvon. Stop being a black separatist."

"I'm not. I'm simply pro-black," Rayvon said as the BMW came to a stop at a red light. "There's a big difference. Now if you want to meet a real black separatist, I'll introduce you to Queen Nefertari. I'm planning to have her as a guest on my show."

Chanel rolled her eyes. "Again? Hasn't she been on it five times already?"

"Eight times to be exact. The sister's very popular with my audience."

The red light turned green and Rayvon accelerated.

"What's the topic this time?"

"How integration has failed the black community."

"Don't you think some of Queen Nefertari's views on the subject are a bit too extreme?" asked Chanel, crossing her long legs – a move that didn't escape Rayvon's roving eye.

"Which ones?"

"Her claims that blacks shouldn't mix with whites because blacks are genetically superior. She calls us the sun people and whites the ice people."

Rayvon grinned. "Aren't we superior?"

"Of course not. There's good and bad in all races. And for your information, the main reason Queen Nefertari is so anti-white is because she desperately wants to be accepted as black, even though her mother is white."

"She's black as far as I'm concerned," said Rayvon as the BMW came to a stop at yet another red light on highway 68. "After all, white America says you're black even if you have just one drop of black blood."

"And she's a racist too."

Rayvon glared at Chanel. "No black can ever be racist."

"Why not?"

"Because we don't have the power. To be racist one has to have the power to enforce racism. So only white people can be racist because they control America politically, culturally, and economically."

The light turned green and Rayvon again accelerated. He loved speed.

"I don't buy that," Chanel said. "Anyone can be racist, including blacks."

"Loving your own isn't racist, Chanel. Don't you love your own people?"

"Of course I do. But not by denigrating others. And some of the things Queen Nefertari has written in *The Motherland* about interracial couples are sickening."

"But they're true," Rayvon said, switching lanes to pass a slow car.

"Come on," Chanel said, shaking her head so her dark Jerri curls bobbed. "What's true about saying that black men who sleep with white women are schizophrenics who are trying to get back at the white man for slavery? And that black women who go out with white men are masochists who just want to be raped by massa again?"

"If it's not true, what else would attract people who are so different?"

"Love, of course."

"Love? Don't make me laugh," Rayvon scoffed. "So-called interracial love is all about sex. Nothing more. Sex pure and simple. It's the jungle fever syndrome."

"Come on, Rayvon."

"I know what I'm talking about, okay," Rayvon said, his voice suddenly rising in anger as the BMW slowed due to thick traffic on highway 421. "My poor mother devoted her whole life to a man who then left her with six children for a white woman."

"I'm sorry to hear that."

"To be honest with you, black men who date or marry white women make me sick. What has the black woman done to be so insulted?"

"Well, love is supposed to know no color."

They were now driving past the Piedmont Triad International Airport. A USAir plane from Charlotte coming in to land passed directly above their heads.

"I entirely agree with Afro-Purists," Rayvon said after the plane had landed with a puff of smoke from its wheels. "The only way to improve race relations in America is to have blacks and whites completely separate. People should stick with their own kind. We need to protect the purity of the black race if it's to survive."

"Purity?" Chanel said, almost shouting. "Shoot. No one in America is pure, least of all African-Americans. We've got every type of blood you can name mixed up in us."

"You might be a case of mixed nuts, but I'm not," Rayvon said testily.

They fell silent. Chanel could tell she had touched a raw nerve. The tension was thick. The BMW came to a stop at a four-way intersection.

I wonder what Alison would think of Rayvon, Chanel thought. *It doesn't matter. I just blew it. There's no way he'll ask me out again, and that's fine with me. I'm not willing to stroke his ego. I'm not that desperate to get a man.*

The resolution emboldened Chanel to speak her mind. "What if some day you happen to fall in love with a white woman yourself? You're handsome. It could happen."

"I'm not a traitor."

"Are you saying you'd never marry a white woman, even if she were the perfect mate?" Chanel asked as the BMW drove past a strip mall.

"Never."

"Would you ever sleep with one?"

"Of course not! What do you take me for?"

Chanel had never seen a black man get this angry before over the topic of interracial love. On the contrary, she had found that black men were apt to be more understanding of such relationships than black women, presumably because more of them, especially athletes and entertainers, were involved in such relationships.

"Given how smart you're, I'm surprised by your naïveté when it comes to the issue of interracial relationships," Rayvon said, turning into an upscale condominium complex overlooking Oak Hollow Lake, whose surface shimmered in the sun.

Don't patronize me, Rayvon, Chanel felt like saying, but she held her tongue. This, after all, was the man of her dreams, despite his obvious shortcomings.

"Have you read Frantz Fanon's *Black Skin, White Masks*?"

"Yes. In a feminism class at Spelman."

"Do you remember a chapter called 'The Man of Color and the White Woman?'"

Chanel recalled the shocking chapter. "Yeah. It's the third chapter."

"I personally recommend it to all the brothers who, for some reason or another, find themselves addicted to white women," Rayvon said. "That chapter brilliantly lays out all the psychological reasons behind their addiction."

Chanel rolled her eyes and crossed her arms. "You men are *so* sick, you know that? I can't believe you use us women as pawns in your ego battles."

"The white man's to blame."

Chanel raised her hands. "Wait a minute. Where did that come from?"

"Whitey's the one who started the whole shit," Rayvon said. "If he hadn't raped black women during slavery, and castrated and lynched black men during Jim Crow, none of this interracial sex bullshit would be happening today."

As a seasoned journalist, Chanel wasn't surprised that Rayvon seemed willing to twist facts to suit his pet theory. *A lot of people do that. Instead of wrestling with complex issues, they latch on to simplistic explanations to support pre-conceived notions.*

Rayvon came to a stop in front of a Mediterranean-style condominium surrounded by huge willow trees and a well-kept garden. "Do you mind if I come up for a drink?" he said with a seductive smile as he purposefully rubbed her bare arm lightly.

Chanel hesitated, wondering what lay behind the request. *Will this lead to something?* "Well, I don't mind sharing a nightcap," she said.

As she was getting out, Rayvon stunned her by saying, "But don't get any big ideas about a serious relationship yet. I like you and all that, but I want no strings attached. Some sisters think I want to marry them just because I show them a good time."

"Well excuse *me*, Prince Rayvon," Chanel said angrily, her hand on the door handle. "It would certainly be an honor to let you make love to me, since you *must* be God's gift to women. But I'd rather spend the night cleaning my cat's litter box."

With that Chanel got out of the BMW and slammed the door. Rayvon, who had never been turned down before by a woman, gaped with a wounded ego at Chanel as she flounced self-assuredly toward her condo. Still fuming at being considered a one-night stand, Chanel found three messages on her answering machine. The first was from her mother, reminding her to stop by for dinner the next evening. The second was from Nelson, a local union organizer, thanking her for the positive story she had done on migrant workers, and asking if he could take her out to dinner sometime.

Just as Chanel was about to call Nelson back, the phone rang. It was her station manager. He wanted her to come to the studio immediately and anchor a late-breaking story about the kidnapping of a newborn from Triad Regional Hospital.

The remote farmhouse was dark and silent when Nancy arrived with Dylan Andrew Whitaker, who was now squalling from hunger. Cradling the newborn in one arm, Nancy walked into the kitchen and flipped on the lights. She removed the black wig, shook out her blond hair, and tossed the wig onto the counter. She opened the refrigerator and reached for a colorful Barney baby bottle she had prepared before she left for the hospital.

The tiny lips closed eagerly around the rubber nipple and the baby sucked greedily, his eyes squeezed shut, his tiny hands balled into fists.

Nancy smiled and spoke softly to him.

"Slow down, Buck Junior. My darling little one."

She lightly kissed the top of his pulsating head, and then sat down in the La-Z-Boy recliner to watch him feast. He kicked the soft white receiving blanket from around his legs and wiggled his tiny toes in the air.

It was then she noticed the small white ID bracelet around his ankle. It read "Alison Ramsey Whitaker, Baby Boy, May 16th, 12:34 a.m., nine pounds three ounces." She noted the coincidence that the mother's middle name matched the last name of her husband's employer, but the thought quickly passed. Her mind was preoccupied with her baby – the baby she was eager to show Buck when he returned tonight from his trucking trip – the baby she was certain would stop his philandering, abuse, and heavy drinking.

After a while the baby grew limp. His milky lips slipped from the bottle's nipple. He was fast asleep. She carried him down the hall to the nursery she had elaborately prepared and placed him gently in a white crib she had bought at a yard sale. The fresh-smelling teddy bear quilt and bumper pads had been laundered in Ivory Snow. A clown mobile singing ditties dangled over the sleeping baby. Johnson's Baby powder and newborn Pampers were neatly stacked under the changing table.

With a pair of sewing shears Nancy gently clipped and removed the ID bracelet. She went into the bathroom intending to flush it down the toilet but changed her mind. Instead she hid the bracelet inside a small white box containing a supply of chloral hydrate capsules, which she often took to help her fall asleep whenever Buck was late returning from a trucking trip. She placed the box with her sewing material on the upper shelf of the closet. She leaned over the crib and stared lovingly at the sleeping baby for a long time, watching his spontaneous, fleeting smiles curl his tiny lips.

"You sleep tight, Little Buck McGuire," she whispered. "Your daddy will be home soon. And he'll be very happy to see you."

She tiptoed out of the nursery and went to the living room, where she plopped down on the sofa, reached for the phone on the end table beside her, and executed the next phase of her plan by placing a call to Tennessee.

"Hi, Mom," Nancy said is a cheery voice.

"Nancy! Any news yet?"

"Yes. It's a baby boy."

Her mother shrieked with joy so loudly that Nancy had to hold the phone away from her ear.

"Are you calling from the hospital?"

"No, I'm home already."

"So soon?"

"They don't keep mothers long in the hospital any more. It's too darn expensive."

"Oh, you can say that again. I want to congratulate Buck. Put him on."

"He's not home yet. He's delivering furniture in Alabama."

"Nancy! Why didn't you call me? I would have driven right over there. It's only four hours."

"There was no time, Mom. The baby came in a hurry. But I'm fine."

Nancy's mother wanted to come over and be with her, but Nancy said it wouldn't be a good idea because Buck, who didn't see eye to eye with his mother-in-law because she was critical of his heavy drinking and womanizing, would soon be home. "But you can come over next time he's on a trucking trip."

Nancy's mother agreed.

As she hung up, Nancy heard her yell, "I'm a grandmother! Thank you, Lord!"Nancy's denial of her second miscarriage was so complete that she truly believed she had actually delivered a healthy baby boy. She had gained more than twenty pounds in the five months since her miscarriage two weeks after being beaten by Buck. Her gaining weight had convinced everyone, including Buck, that the baby had been growing well. Nancy had continued to wear maternity clothes and had complained frequently of prenatal aches and pains. Now she had her baby. After all, it was her due date.

The shock of Nancy's second miscarriage, and the stress she was under to hide it from her abusive husband, had led to a complete psychological breakdown. Though Nancy truly believed this was her baby, deep in her subconscious she remembered burying the dead fetus in the backyard one dark wintry afternoon when Buck was away. A psychiatrist, if she had seen one, would have diagnosed her problem as a dissociative disorder – psychogenic amnesia.

Feeling exhausted, Nancy picked up the remote and turned to News-8. A beautiful young woman with dark hair and tear-filled, sparkling brown eyes was sitting beside a man with caramel curly hair. She recalled bumping into the man in the corridor of the maternity ward. The man had his arm around the crying woman. In front of them were about a dozen microphones. It looked as if they were in some kind of hospital. Nancy turned up the volume.

"...And I just want to say to whoever took my baby, please, please bring him back!" the woman was saying. "I don't know who you are or why you did this, but I'll try to understand. Just return my Dylan safe and unharmed – please, I beg you."

For some reason Nancy felt a pang of remorse. But it quickly passed.

Chanel's face filled the TV screen.

"Alison and Eliot Whitaker last saw their baby in the delivery room of Triad Regional Hospital at approximately 10:30 this morning," she said. "The baby weighed nine pounds three ounces and has blue eyes and straight dark hair. Anyone with information about a baby fitting this description, please alert Crime Stoppers."

The camera panned out to include Chanel's co-anchor, Gary Shaw.

"The political ramifications of this tragedy are already being felt," Shaw said. "Since his grandson's kidnapping, Lawrence Ramsey, who's postponed the official start of his general election campaign to be by his daughter's side, has shot up ten points in a random poll conducted by the local radio station. There obviously is great sympathy for Ramsey, who barely won the primary because his last-minute conversion to conservatism alienated many in his traditional liberal base, without winning over Jessecrats. And until the baby is found, pundits predict that his standing in the polls will continue to rise."

The camera panned back to Chanel.

"The hospital announced today that a surveillance system will be installed in the hospital as early as tomorrow," she said. "Police are showing composite drawings to employees entering the hospital in an attempt to gather more information about the kidnapper. The drawing is based on a description given by two nurses and a security guard who claim they saw a dark-haired woman dressed in a white nursing uniform."

The screen showed an African-American security guard at the hospital being interviewed. A jolt of recognition made Nancy catch her breath. It was the same man who had stopped her from going out the emergency exit. *Will he remember me?*

"After the alarm sounded, doors to the hospital were sealed immediately, but a floor-by-floor search revealed no trace of the woman or baby," Chanel continued.

Gary Shaw said, "As many as two dozen police detectives have been assigned to the case. The FBI is working on a psychological profile of the kidnapper. Reginald Hunter, Lawrence Ramsey's campaign manager, who is also the godfather to the mother of the kidnapped baby, is offering $250,000 of his own money as a reward for information leading to the baby's recovery. Theodore Whitaker, the tobacco mogul and grandfather of the kidnapped baby, has added $250,000 to that reward."

The program turned to other news. Nancy switched off the set.

I'm no kidnapper, Nancy said to herself as she heard the baby fuss. *This is Buck's baby.* As she headed toward the baby's room at the end of the hallway, she thought, *He'll be so happy to see him that he won't leave me for another woman.*

Nancy's determination to save her marriage, whatever the cost to her physical or emotional well-being, had its roots in her childhood. Nancy was convinced that her mother did not fight hard enough to save her marriage to her coal-mining father. In the Appalachian mountains of Tennessee, where Nancy grew up, big families were the norm, partly because poverty claimed many children in their infancy. After she was born, her father had wanted more children, sons. When, for some reason, her mother couldn't conceive again, her father had begun womanizing. Later he had moved out of their aqua green-and-white trailer with its peeling paint, narrow corridors and small, dark, and musty rooms and started living with a large-breasted, platinum blond woman down the mountain who, it turned out, had secretly borne him twin sons.

A year after her father deserted them, Nancy's mother met and married Orville Mayberry, a smooth-talking, hard-drinking itinerant televangelist and former army chaplain with a penchant for gaudy three-piece suits and loud ties, who had just arrived in town to set up a revival ministry called "Let me Lead You to Jesus." The marriage had lasted only six months. Not only did Orville abscond with her mother's savings – at the time she worked as a seamstress at a textile mill – but during the brief marriage, unbeknownst to her mother, Orville had sexually molested Nancy, who was only twelve.

The next man her mother married, Lyston Floyd, a hard-drinking laid off mineworker, had continued the abuse, and would beat Nancy's mother whenever she tried to intervene. The abuse continued until Nancy ran away from home at fifteen. She stayed with various friends for some time, and eventually moved into a foster home in Winston-Salem run by a black woman named Mrs. Wilma Brown, who urged Nancy to finish school and convinced her to stop blaming herself for the abuse. After graduating from high school, Nancy had moved into a small apartment with Irma Higgins, a waitress at the Do-Drop-In Truck Stop. Irma had helped Nancy get a job as a waitress at the same place while she studied to be a nursing assistant at a local community college. And it was while Nancy was waitressing at the Do-Drop-In that she had met Buck, who at the time was gainfully employed, and hadn't yet joined the Klan.

Nancy had vowed never to follow in her mother's footsteps by losing a husband. And she was convinced that once Buck had the son that he had always wanted, he would stop drinking, philandering, and abusing her, and that they would be a happy family again. She couldn't wait for him to return from his trucking trip and see his blue-eyed baby boy.

Chapter 17

Shortly after nine, as dusk deepened into night, the semi truck Buck was driving crossed the Tennessee border into North Carolina. Though he was eager to get home to Nancy and the baby, Buck couldn't resist a quick stop at his favorite haunt. Around 10:30 p.m. his truck pulled into the crowded parking lot of the Do-Drop-In truck-stop on Interstate 40 near Statesville. Flashing neon lights in the large window, advertising Coors and Bud, made the shards of broken glass on the pavement shine red and yellow in the limpid darkness. As soon as Buck entered the greasy-smelling truck stop, Irma Higgins, its plump waitress, whose platinum blond hair was disheveled by hairnets and bobby pins always on the verge of slipping out, looked up.

Irma's heavily made-up face instantly brightened. "Well, look what the cat doggone dragged in," she cried, cocking her oval head seductively to the left as she lowered the sound of the blaring TV. Six grizzled truckers slumped over greasy hamburger platters and mugs of coffee, turned and gave Buck cursory looks as he perched himself onto a bar stool down the counter from them.

"Hey, Irma," Buck grunted. "Gimme a Miller."

"Sure." Irma pried open a bottle and set it before Buck, along with a tall glass.

"Did you hear the news?" she said, wiping the counter with a dirty rag.

"What news?" Buck asked, sipping his beer.

"Your boss's grandson has been kidnapped."

"You mean Lawrence Ramsey?"

"Yeah. He was snatched from Triad Regional Hospital this afternoon."

Buck almost yelled with joy. "Are you kidding me?"

"It's been all over TV. The baby's mama – her name is Alison, I think – was just on just as you walked in. She was begging for the kidnapper to return the child."

Buck smiled and thought, *Serves her right for tellin' her daddy to hire a nigger and make him my boss. I wish I knew who took the baby. I'd give them a reward. If I'd done it, I'd strangle the little brat just to get back at Ramsey.*

After draining his beer, Buck slapped some cash on the counter for Irma and left for his truck. He was about to jump behind the wheel when something stopped him. It was a car, a fiery red Beetle, driven by the last person he had expected to run into.

"Hey, Buck," said a top-heavy woman with long auburn hair and a tight black leather miniskirt. She parked the car, got out, and leaned on her open driver's door.

"Hi, Candy," Buck said. His heart started beating fast.

"Why don't you stop by and see me no more?" asked Candy with a coquettish wriggle of her large hips. "It ain't nice of you to neglect me like that."

"I've been busy."

"Too busy to stop by and say hi to your sweet little thing?"

Buck knew he should get into his truck and head home to be with Nancy and the baby, but then he remembered how Candy's long fire-engine red fingernails felt as they slid up and down his naked back. His lascivious eyes ogled her ample cleavage.

"I've been real lonely since you stopped coming to see me, honey," she said, seductively fingering the necklace pendant between her breasts.

The temptation was too much for Buck to bear. He was about to yield when he again thought of Nancy, and the promise he had made to be faithful to her now that she had born him a son. "I'm sorry," he said. "But I gotta get home. My wife just had a baby."

Candy knew what that meant. Their affair was indeed over. Though somewhat hurt, she didn't mind, because she had already found another sugar daddy.

Buck found Nancy in the living room, humming a lullaby to the baby, who had just finished feeding from a bottle. "Is that Buck Junior?" he asked, approaching Nancy on tip-toe.

Nancy nodded and smiled.

"T-t-that's my son?" he stammered in amazement, staring at the baby in wonder.

"Yes. Your very own."

"My own flesh and blood?"

"That's right."

Buck felt pride at having resisted Candy's temptation and coming straight home. *I'll never have another affair again,* he vowed silently. "I promise I'll take good care of you and Buck Junior," he said in a voice cracking with emotion. "I promise." He dropped to his knees beside the rocking chair and stared at Nancy and the baby reverently, as if they were the Madonna and infant Jesus. "I'm a daddy," he kept murmuring. "Thank God Almighty." Hearing a male voice, the baby turned restlessly and opened its small eyes.

"Ain't he handsome?" Nancy said.

"Skin as white as snow and eyes as blue as the sky," Buck said, smiling down at the baby. "He sure is cute. Can I hol' him?"

"Of course." As Nancy watched Buck cradle the child in his arms and coo at him, she knew that their marriage was back on solid ground, and she was glad she had given him the heir he had desperately wanted. *I'll take very good care of his son.*

The next morning, Buck was a very happy man as he drove to New South Fine Furniture. He not only had a son, but he no longer cared if he was fired, because he was due to start receiving that $10,000 a month stipend Ghazi had promised to give members of his cell so they could start preparing themselves to launch the military phase of Operation Saladin. As he was pulling the semi into the loading dock, Buck spotted his African-American boss, James Caldwell, hanging up the phone inside the office and heading straight toward him. Relishing a confrontation with his muscular supervisor, Buck immediately leaped out of the cab.

"Hey, chief," he said with a fake smile, using an address the racially sensitive James loathed because he thought it connoted images of a primitive Africa

"You're late again," Caldwell said severely.

"I am?" Buck said, feigning surprise.

"Two days late, to be exact."

"What'd you expect, chief? You sent me all over the goddamn country."

"You should've stuck to the schedule."

"I can't help it if I get delayed, chief."

"By what?"

"Traffic, bad weather, flat tires. And I've got to sleep too, you know, chief."

"Buck, I've heard enough of your excuses. You knew that I needed the truck for other deliveries. And you could have called to let me know that you'd be late."

"My cell phone was broken, chief."

"What about the public phone?"

"I had no change, chief."

Aware that Buck was needling him, Caldwell, barely able to contain his anger, said, "You know what, you're a good driver, but you're also irresponsible. Unless you –"

Buck's face reddened. "Who are you callin' an irresponsible, nigger?"

Caldwell was incensed. "What did you just call me?"

"A nigger, and there ain't nothin' you can do about it."

"YOU'RE FIRED!"

"FINE!" Buck said gleefully. "I'm sick and tired of workin' for niggers anyway."

"I hope I never lay eyes on you again," Caldwell said.

"You will," Buck said with a sneer as he stalked away. "I'll come back to haunt you, Caldwell. Just you wait. No nigger's gonna fire *me* and get away with it."

After being fired, Buck climbed into his pickup and headed home. He was so furious at Caldwell that he almost got into an accident at an intersection on Highway 68 with a dark blue Oldsmobile driven by a tall, broad-shouldered black man in a tweed jacket.

Muttering, "Watch it, nigger," Buck made a finger at the man who, absorbed in a cell phone conversation, apparently didn't notice the insult.

Buck was half-way home when his cell phone rang. It was Chandler.

"Can you come over to the compound immediately?" asked Chandler.

"Sure," Buck said. "What's going on?"

"It's about the FBI."

Chapter 18

The tall broad-shouldered black man in the tweed jacket turned off the cell phone, climbed out of the dark blue Oldsmobile and strode hurriedly toward the front door of the FBI field office in Greensboro. After looking about to make sure that no one was watching or approaching, he punched in his code and then peered into the retina scanner. Every eye has a unique pattern of blood vessels, and the scanner had stored in its memory the eye pattern of every employee at the office. The patterns matched.

The scanner automatically unlocked the door, and stored in its memory the time – 11:30 a.m. – and the name of FBI Special Agent in Charge Bruce Lindsey Evans. This was one of several security devices the FBI had installed at its field offices across the country since 9/11. Evans, clutching a fat leather briefcase in his right hand, headed straight for the conference room at the back of the building. A single parent, he had been trapped in heavy traffic on the way to dropping his seven-year-old son Jamel at school.

Evans was already ten minutes late for an important meeting with five resident agents from satellite offices across North Carolina. Upon entering the conference room, Evans found the five RAs, three men and two women, seated around a teak conference table, sipping food service-grade coffee out of Styrofoam cups, munching Krispie

Kreme glazed doughnuts, and making small talk. The six agents, the nucleus of an investigative unit that was now part of the Department of Homeland Security, considered themselves almost exiled. While their colleagues around the country were part of America's war on terror, with its focus on tracking down al-Qaeda sleeper cells, and carrying out electronic and physical surveillance of Muslim-Americans and Islamic groups, Evans and his agents had been assigned to investigate garden variety cases, including kidnappings and white supremacist groups that, in the wake of 9/11, were widely viewed as less of a menace to American society than jihadists.

"Let's begin, shall we?" Evans said after an exchange of greetings. He took off his tweed jacket, opened his briefcase, pulled out thick folders marked "Confidential," and handed them out to the agents. "The High Point police department, which, as you know, is taking the lead in the case, informed me on the way here that there hasn't been any significant development since Alison's baby was kidnapped. So we'll move on to the latest edition of *The Intelligence Report,* which is published by the Southern Poverty Law Center." Evans walked back to the head of the conference table and sat down. "As you can see, since the start of the Iraq War, there's been a dramatic increase in the number of hate crimes." Evans sipped his coffee. "A dozen black churches have been firebombed. On the back of one church, someone scrawled the words 'The Turner Diaries will liberate White America from ZOG [Zionist Occupational Government.]' *The Intelligence Report* has reason to believe that these bombings are part of an attempt by a group of white extremists, who've been marginalized since 9/11, to stage a comeback."

"Any idea which group might be responsible, sir?" asked Renee Millet, an African-American who had advanced quickly through the FBI ranks after BADGE, an organization representing black agents, threatened to file a class action suit on behalf of 230 agents who alleged discrimination by the Bureau. Millet had recently cracked a tough case involving the theft of sophisticated weapons and ammunition from Camp Lejuene.

"We don't know yet," Evans said. "But *The Intelligence Report* believes that the goal of these hate crimes may be to fan the flames of racial hatred as the election season heats up. Don't forget, ladies and gentlemen, that the *Turner Diaries* predicts there will be a race war that leads to the overthrow of the federal government."

"But the Turner Diaries is just racist fantasy, sir," said agent Arthur Blackmos, who was also African-American. A recent graduate from the FBI's training academy on the Quantico Marine Base, the thick-bearded Blackmos was brilliant at wiretapping, thanks to a long-time fascination with electronics and a computer science degree from North Carolina A & T in Greensboro, where he had been a member of the same fraternity as one of the university's most distinguished alumni, the Reverend Jesse Jackson.

"Blowing up a federal building in Oklahoma and killing one hundred and sixty-eight innocent people is not racist fantasy, Arthur," Evans countered. "And *The Turner Diaries* provided Timothy McVeigh with a blueprint for that terrorist act which, before 9/11, was the worst ever committed on American soil."

Blackmon's wide-set brown eyes looked skeptical.

"I see you don't believe me," Evans said. "Read aloud the summary on the Oklahoma City bombing and you'll see what I mean. It's at the bottom of page 12."

Blackmos, a bit flustered, fumbled to page 12. In a slightly shaky voice, he read the following:"*In the Turner Diaries a truck containing 'a little over 5,000 pounds' of fuel and ammonium nitrate fertilizer is detonated at 9:15 a.m. in front of FBI headquarters in Washington, DC. In Oklahoma City on April 19th, a truck containing approximately 4,400 pounds of fuel oil and ammonium nitrate fertilizer was detonated at 9:05 a.m. in front of the Alfred P. Murrah federal building that houses FBI and ATF agents.*" When he finished reading, Blackmos gave Evans a sheepish look.

"So, do you still consider the book a fantasy?" Evans asked.

"No, sir," Blackmos replied in a chastened voice.

"Always remember," Evans said, looking in turn at all five agents, "that the fantasy of madmen can easily become reality if conditions are ripe. Hitler proved that. He used his *Mein Kampf* fantasy to precipitate a world war and exterminate millions of innocent human beings. And on 9/11, Osama bin Laden's fantasy of a worldwide Islamic Jihad killed more than three thousand innocent human beings."

The agents looked down at their files, absorbing Evans's words in silence. Evans took a sip of water. "Now, let's move on to the third item in the file. As you can see, before 9/11 there were more than 800 militia groups operating across the country. Most of these groups were made up of survivalists and anti-government zealots. But scores of them harbored hardcore white supremacists, specifically former members of the UKA."

The United Klansmen of America, at one time the largest Klan organization in the States, had gone bankrupt in 1987 when a U.S. District judge in Alabama ordered it to pay an unprecedented $7 million settlement in a lawsuit brought by civil rights attorney Morris Dees, co-founder of the Southern Poverty Law Center, on behalf of Beulah Mae Donald, whose nineteen-year-old son, Michael, was abducted, beaten, and then lynched by two members of the UKA in Mobile, Alabama.

"Several of these white supremacist groups are listed in the latest *Intelligence Report*," Evans said. "Their names can be found on page three."

With a shuffling of papers, the agents turned to page three.

"But hasn't the FBI already infiltrated those militias?" asked Ruth Burkhart, a former music teacher of Arab descent who, after being laid off when the public school where she taught, strapped for funds, cut back on the Humanities, had joined the FBI. Ruth's specialty was infiltrating clandestine groups and recruiting informants.

"We have," Evans said. "But not all of them. We've only scratched the surface. Since 9/11 most of these groups have organized themselves into small, tight units called cells. The traditional military-style chain of command previously used by white supremacist groups was too easy to penetrate, as shown by the demise of the UKA."

"Sounds like they're following the ideas of *The Leaderless Resistance*," said Paul Lund, at forty-five the oldest of the agents and head of the SWAT team.

"Exactly," Evans said. "I see you've done your homework, Paul. *The Leaderless Resistance* advocates the use of the pyramid structure of command because one cell can be infiltrated without compromising the entire organization. Such secret cells are normally made up of between five and ten men who are skilled in explosives, sniper fire, sabotage, assassination, counterfeiting, and terrorism. There are several such tightly knit cells across the South. One of them, in the mountains of North Carolina, is headed by a former Green Beret named Johnny Chandler. You'll find his profile on page five."

"Johnny Chandler?" said Trevor Beckman, a veteran FBI agent who had worked alongside Evans on various cases involving members of the UKA, including the murder in 1967 of a liberal newspaper publisher and her assistant in Alabama. "Isn't he the son of Richard Chandler, the rabid segregationist who committed suicide in 1972?" "That's him all right," Evans said, impressed. "Trevor, can you give the rest of the group a brief description of the Richard Chandler case?"

Trevor, blond and with the build of a running back, cleared his bull throat and began speaking. "Richard Chandler was an influential member of the States Rights or Dixiecrat Party that splintered from the Democratic Party after President Harry Truman, at the urging of a group of liberals led by Hubert Humphrey of Minnesota, adopted a civil rights plank as part of his platform during the 1948 convention. In 1968, Chandler, who'd denounced the 1967 U.S. Supreme Court decision legalizing interracial marriages, was favored to win a seat to the U.S. Senate when Lawrence Ramsey, the anti-Klan crusader who's now running for governor, published a series of articles in his weekly paper, *The New South,* revealing that Chandler had fathered a child by his black maid. Because of the articles, Chandler was forced to drop out of the race. Ruined and humiliated by the scandal, Chandler blew his brains out with a double-barrel shotgun."

Evans took over the narrative. "His son Johnny was in the Army when all this happened. He served two tours in Vietnam and received a Purple Heart. Chandler is extremely intelligent. He has a college degree in History and speaks fluent German, Russian, and Afrikaans.

Evans explained why and how Chandler created a virtual empire of Klan dens across the South, fueled by his rage against interracial couples, and how he quit the army when his main Klan recruiter was convicted. He described how Chandler poured himself into white supremacist activities, such as publishing a bi-weekly newsletter called *Saving the White Race*; briefly hosting a right-wing radio talk show devoted to liberal-bashing, twice running for public office, and taking several trips to South Africa as an advisor to the AWB, a white supremacist group that had fiercely defended apartheid's anti-miscegenation pillars and was now clamoring for a whites-only homeland following black majority rule in 1994.

"After the 1995 Oklahoma City bombing, Chandler formed his own militia," he added, pausing to scan the faces of his rapt listeners.

"Since 9/11, Chandler and his fellow white supremacists have been lying low. But we do know that at one time he was scouring the country for weapons, and that he did try to buy some from William Krar, who's now behind bars. So part of our job is to find out what groups like Chandler's are up to. But Chandler's very smart. So far he's avoided giving us any excuse to go after him. And his group is very tightly knit. According to *The Intelligence Report*, Chandler spends most of his time using short wave radio to spew hatred against liberals, African-Americans, gays, and immigrants, and denouncing the Federal government. On weekends he leads his militia in survivalist training sessions at his compound in Asheville."

"But the First Amendment gives him the right to say what he pleases," said Renee, "and the Second Amendment gives him and his men the right to bear arms."

"That's true," Evans said. "But remember, 9/11 doesn't mean that the threat from internal terrorists is over. And given Chandler's history, I want to know what his militia is really up to. And our only hope of infiltrating his group may lie in the fact that two years ago Chandler married Anna Botha, a thirty-two-year-old South African woman who, according to *The Intelligence Report*, was connected with the AWB."

Evans paused and cleared his throat. "You'll find a summary of Anna's startling background on page seven," he said. "After you read it, I have no doubt that you'll agree that she holds the key to our finally infiltrating Chandler's militia."

The agents hurriedly flipped to page seven.

Evans continued. "The FBI also believes that Anna holds the key to a case about the double murder of a prominent civil rights newspaper publisher in Montgomery, Alabama, and her assistant during the third March on Selma in 1963. Tommy Cone confessed to the murder, but the FBI is convinced he had an accomplice."

Buck pulled his pickup behind several vehicles parked haphazardly across a bumpy lawn in front of a whitewashed double-story Greek revival farmhouse with a red barn in the backyard. The vehicles, all pickups, sported a variety of bumper stickers: "Liberals are Scum," "I'm proud to belong to the NAAWP, " "Guns Don't Kill, People Do," "I don't care how you do it up North," "Remember Ruby Ridge and Waco," "Smokers Rights," and "Long Live Southland."

Buck climbed out of the pickup, strode across the lawn, and knocked on the front door of the farmhouse. A lanky woman with a long sand-colored braid and green eyes that set off the paleness of her round face peeped timidly through the crack in the door without taking off the chain. She was holding a seven-month-old boy wearing a Huggies diaper and a Mickey Mouse shirt. His face was smudged with baby food, as was the copy of *People,* with Angelina Jolie on the cover, the woman had apparently been reading. Behind the woman two teenage daughters sat on a sagging sofa watching TV.

"Afternoon, Anna," Buck said.

Chandler's South African bride smiled and undid the chain. "Good afternoon Buck," she said with an Afrikaner accent. "They're waiting for you up at the cabin. I'm supposed to give you these." She handed him a set of keys. "The Jeep's behind the barn."

"Thanks." Buck grabbed the keys, sprinted toward the barn, hopped into a jeep painted with camouflage colors, and gunned it several times. Fifteen minutes later the jeep arrived at the remote cabin, partially hidden by a mass of vines and undergrowth. He bounded up the wooden front steps and rapped on the tattered screen door.

Chandler opened it. Upon entering, Buck looked about and noticed, in the dim light of the musty cabin, that all members of the cell, who ranged in age from thirty-nine to fifty-five, were present and sharing cans of beer. Thad, a freckle-faced, twice-divorced ex-marine who was an expert in germ warfare, was sitting on a sagging sofa next to Jimmy Ray, a short, squat former army sniper and the cell's second in command.   On another sofa near the TV sat a tall and lean former FBI agent named Bob, who specialized in counter-insurgency. Next to him sat Orville Mayberry, a rotund former army chaplain and itinerant evangelist with bushy eyebrows. All members of the cell had at one time or another belong to the United Klansmen of America.

"I didn't think you could get away from your job," said Chandler.

"I no longer have any," Buck replied.

"What happened?" asked Thad, handing Buck a can of beer.

"The nigger fired me," said Buck, sitting down.

"You don't say," said Bob. "What for?"

"For being two days late."

"Don't worry about the fucking job," Chandler said in a fatherly tone, his large arm wrapped around Buck's drooping shoulders. "Ghazi called me yesterday after he met with Aziz. Now that the political phase of Operation Saladin has been launched, he wants all of you to quit your jobs so we can start preparing ourselves as the Minutemen who'll launch its military phase as soon as Lynch is elected governor."

"If we quit our jobs," asked Bob, who was a contractor, "how will we live?"

"Ghazi plans to pay each of you a monthly stipend of $10,000," said Chandler.

The amount left the men stunned. They whooped with joy.

"But before we can start with military training," Chandler said, "Ghazi wants us to first throw an FBI unit that's been assigned to investigate us off our trail."

"How? " Buck asked.

"By pretending to be a harmless Klan militia," Chandler said. "Ghazi wants us to start wearing our Klan robes, marching in parades, denouncing niggers and Jews, and basically making fools of ourselves. He figures that such behavior will make the FBI think we're nothing but a bunch of buffoons. Terrorists don't engage in such behavior."

"I think I still have my old robes," said Buck.

So did the other members of the cell.

"Great," said Chandler, and then proceeded to outline their agenda as Klan buffoons.

They would be staging several Klan rallies and parades over the next couple of months, and engaging in outrageous stunts intended to generate media coverage. One such stunt would involve the disruption of the swearing-in ceremony for Greensboro's Truth and Reconciliation Commission (TRC), the first of its kind in the country. Modeled after South Africa's TRC, Greensboro's TRC was spawned by the November 3, 1979 Greensboro Massacre, in which Chandler took part, and was intended to address issues of racism, anti-Semitism, and poverty in order to heal and unite the community.

"Ghazi also wants us to disrupt several of Ramsey's campaign rallies," Chandler said, "and to prepare ourselves to appear on the Rayvon Turlington Show."

"You must be fucking kidding," cried Jimmy Ray. "Appear on a nigger show?"

"I'm serious," said Chandler. "Ghazi has a plan for us to be invited as guests."

PART II

Chapter 19

Despite the FBI and the local police devoting more manpower to the search for Alison's missing baby, he still hadn't been found after three months. Ironically, Dylan's disappearance did wonders for Ramsey's campaign. Voters who, before the baby was kidnapped, had had a negative view of Ramsey, no longer seemed to care that he was a liberal masquerading as a conservative, nor that he had flip-flopped so many times on key issues that he might as well have been running for the role of a trapeze artist in a circus.

Ramsey the flip-flopper had, according to an editorial in *USA Today*, become Ramsey the Teflon candidate. Not even denunciations by the Klan could stop Ramsey's ascendancy in the polls. All voters seemed to care about, it seemed, was the fate of Alison's cute missing baby – thanks largely to the mainstream media's obsession with sensational and sentimental stories now that it had prostituted its role as a government watchdog, and was into the business of entertaining the public the way gladiators used to do in Roman times. Several independent polls, including Gallup and Rasmussen, showed that the sympathy vote was largely responsible for Ramsey's whopping thirty-point lead over Lynch – with only eight weeks to go before the general election – despite Hunter's feverish but clandestine attempt to sabotage his campaign.

Notwithstanding her father's seemingly insurmountable lead in the polls, Alison was unhappy. Ever since Dylan had been kidnapped, her marriage to Eliot had deteriorated amid mutual recriminations. The couple, at Hunter's behest, had tried marriage counseling – to no avail. Their relationship had reached the point where the two knew that they were headed for divorce, especially now that both were convinced that the baby that could have saved their marriage was gone forever.

Eliot, ever the workaholic, buried his grief in company business, and Alison, ever the political addict, buried hers in her father's campaign, despite her disagreement with his strategy to run as a conservative. She regularly accompanied Ramsey and Darlene as they crisscrossed the Tar Heel state. Everywhere they went Alison was a huge hit. Thousands of women flocked to the rallies simply to see and touch her. After soliciting votes for her father, she would hear women eager to shake her hand make remarks like:

"I'm a proud Republican. I never thought I'd vote for a Democrat, but I plan to vote for Ramsey in November because of that missing little boy."

"I'm a proud independent. I don't agree with everything Ramsey stands for, but I plan to vote for him because of that missing little boy."

"I'm a proud Jessecrat. I haven't voted Democratic in years because I consider the party too liberal, but I'll vote for Ramsey because of that missing little boy."

At a rally in Wilmington, an elderly woman with snow white hair approached Alison following her remarks and said, "I'm going to vote for Ramsey because you're not like that Susan Smith who murdered her children and blamed it on a black man."

The statement jarred Alison, particularly its reference to a "black man." Not a day went by without Alison wondering how life would be if Myron hadn't jilted her. Deep inside, she knew that she still loved him, despite what had happened between the two of them. She also had a glimmer of suspicion that Dylan, despite his appearance at birth, might still be Myron's baby, because since his disappearance, she had read books on mixed babies, and had been surprised to learn that most of them looked white until their melanin appeared several months later, and their eyes changed to their natural color.

Her suspicions were reinforced by a recurring nightmare she had been having for weeks. In it, a white woman who had stolen Dylan from the hospital calls Alison and asks that they meet secretly in a thick forest. The woman, who wants no reward money, apologizes profusely for kidnapping the baby and causing Alison so much pain. She then states as her reason for returning Dylan the fact that he had turned out to be black, and she had wanted a white baby. Desperate to save her father's campaign, Alison, in her dream, smothers Dylan and secretly buries him in an unmarked grave in the dark forest.

"Can you believe the baby-killer said this?" cried Martha Louise, wife of a local minister, staring at the open page of the book she was holding in her lap.

"What did she say?" asked Lucille Briggs, the wife of a local banker.

Martha Louise adjusted the spectacles on her long nose and read, "'David, when I get out...if I get out of here, I hope that maybe we can get back together and have more kids.'" After reading the quote, she slammed the book shut in outrage.

"What a nerve!" cried Lucille, indignant.

The two matrons were attending a book club, which was meeting at Martha Louise's home in HeavensGate, a posh neighborhood in High Point. Darlene, a member of the club, was away on the campaign trail with Ramsey and couldn't attend. Several other members were also absent, having gone to the mountains to view the spectacular fall colors. The Book-of-the-Month, which Martha Louise had recommended the club read in order to gain insights into the mysterious disappearance of Alison's baby, was *Beyond All Reason: My Life with Susan Smith*, and its author was Susan's ex-husband, David Smith. The instant bestseller had hit the newsstand back in 1995, shortly after Susan Smith was convicted in Union, South Carolina, of murdering her two sons by rolling her Mazda Protégé into a lake and then claiming that they had been carjacked by a black man. Her false accusation had particularly incensed the American public because it had revived memories of a 1990 case involving Charles Stuart, a resident of Boston, who had shot his seven months pregnant wife to death in their car, and then told the police that a "black mugger in a jogging suit" had killed her for her jewelry.

"She had me totally convinced," said Rebecca Chase, a lawyer's wife, to the group of six women gathered in the living room, austerely furnished in the Shaker style. "I totally believed her when she said a black man had kidnapped three-year-old Michael and thirteen-month-old Alex. What with all those carjackings going on."

"I remember my heart went out to her when I saw her mopping up her tears on the *Today* show," said Martha Louise. "She was going on and on about how much she missed her kids and how much her heart ached. What an actress!"

"Let's not be too severe on Susan," cautioned Angela Weldon, the wife of an internist. Pro-choice, she was a friend of Darlene's and one of the few liberals in the book club. "After all, psychiatric evidence revealed that, while not insane, Susan suffered from a mental disorder that made her incapable of carrying out a complex murder plot."

"What mental disorder?" demanded Martha Louise. "I hope you're not excusing her abominable behavior because you're a feminist."

"I'm not excusing her behavior," Angela said. "I'm simply saying that women like her are sometimes victims too. And we have to make allowance for that."

Apparently sensing a looming confrontation between Angela and Martha Louise, Lucille, as was often the case during book club meetings, deftly attempted to shift the debate. "I heard an expert on *Oprah* say that kidnapped children are one hundred times more likely to be taken by friends, loved ones, or parents than by strangers."

"That's true," said Sandra. "I watch the show too."

"Speaking of kidnapping," Martha Louise said, "are there any new developments in the search for Ramsey's grandchild? It's been over three months since he was snatched from Triad Regional. Isn't it mighty strange that there's been no arrest yet?"

"My husband plays tennis with a police detective who's working on the case," said Sandra, the lawyer's wife with an hourglass figure. She then lowered her contralto voice to a funereal whisper. "They aren't supposed to discuss the case, so I really shouldn't be telling you this. But they're starting to suspect some monkey business."

"Really?" cried Lucille, leaning closer so she could catch every word.

"Well, of course," Judy said. "Just think of it. So far all the leads have turned out to be dead ends. Despite the fact that Ramsey's campaign manager has increased the reward money to $1 million, and old man Whitaker himself, not to be outdone in the search for his grandson, is offering $2 million. So that makes it $3 million altogether."

"That much money should have produced plenty of clues," said Martha Louise.

"And the police and the FBI have learned from the Susan Smith case not to rule out anyone," Judy said. "Not even the mother. And you can't ignore the fact that Ramsey, because he's so liberal, was behind in the polls when his grandson disappeared. Now he's thirty-five points ahead of Lynch. All because of the sympathy vote."

"Are you implying that Alison arranged to have her own baby kidnapped so her father could win an election?" Angela Weldon said indignantly.

"The detectives can't rule out that possibility," Judy said.

"Alison could never do such a thing," Sandra said.

"That's what everyone thought about Susan Smith," Martha Louise said.

"– And the police detective told my husband that new information has come in suggesting a possible motive for the kidnapping," Judy said.

"What information?" asked Angela.

"It has something to do with one of the men Alison was dating before she married Eliot," Judy said. "What raised their suspicion was how quickly Alison agreed to marry Eliot, despite the fact that the two of them are so incompatible politically."

"Is the man black?" Martha Louise said, gaping.

"The detective wouldn't say because the FBI has insisted that the information remain strictly confidential," Judy said. "But it's opened a whole new direction in the investigation. My husband says he wouldn't be surprised if the whole truth becomes known right before the election. And his feeling is that if it does, Ramsey's campaign for governor might be completely destroyed."

"Good heavens!" cried Martha Louise.

Chapter 20

Ramsey was riding so high in the polls because of the sympathy vote, and he felt so confident of victory, that he even ventured into what was considered enemy territory. With two and a half weeks to go before the election, he gave a speech on education reform (that Hunter had written) at a public high school in Monroe, the hometown of arch-conservative Jesse Helms. The speech, which borrowed copiously from George W. Bush's "No Child Left Behind," was so well received that Ramsey was interrupted by loud applause several times. After the speech, he slipped into the principal's office and made a call to Hunter, who was back at campaign headquarters in High Point.

"I just spoke before the most conservative voters you can imagine," Ramsey said, ecstatically. "They regard Jesse as their idol. Yet most say they plan to vote for me. I never thought I'd say this, but I believe I even have the conservative vote locked up."

"That's wonderful," Hunter said. "And is Alison there with you?"

"Yes. She's being mobbed on the stage by women offering her condolences."

"Well, keep the road show going and we'll have the election sewn up in no time."

"Thanks for everything, Reggie. Your strategy is brilliant."

"Don't mention it, old buddy."

Hunter was incensed and deeply-disturbed when he left campaign headquarters after talking to Ramsey on the phone. On the way to the parking lot, he muttered to himself, *If the sympathy vote continues to grow, the nigger-lover will win by a landslide because voters apparently don't care about his flip-flopping. I wonder who kidnapped the baby.*

While Hunter was riding in his limo, on the way to his condo, his car phone rang. It was Kessler, and he was fuming. "So what the hell do we do now?" he demanded. "Ramsey has a thirty-five point lead in the polls. We're headed for disaster. If Lynch doesn't win, it's the end of Operation Saladin."

Hunter tried to put a positive spin on things. "Don't worry, partner, he'll win. There's still two and a half weeks left before the election. That's an eternity in politics."

"But voters aren't interested in anything but that damn baby," Kessler bellowed. "And if it's not found, Ramsey will win by a landslide."

"Trust me, he won't."

"What makes you so sure?"

"Because I've already activated Plan C."

"What Plan C? You never told me about it."

"Well," Hunter said as the limo stopped at a red light, "I've begun feeding false information to the detectives working on the baby kidnapping case."

"What false information?"

"Well, in most kidnapping cases parents or close relatives are usually involved," said Hunter. "So I've begun insinuating that Alison might have orchestrated the kidnapping to hide a scandal that would have destroyed Ramsey's campaign."

"What scandal?"

"I plan to have our people start making anonymous phone calls to the police suggesting that Alison murdered her own baby because he was a mulatto."

"What makes you think the police will buy such a crazy story?"

"Because of a tape Dawoud just sent me. When you listen to it, you can hear Alison telling Chanel about a recurrent dream she has that her baby turns out to be Myron's. She dreams she has it kidnapped from the hospital after it's born and strangled to prevent the scandal from ruining Ramsey's campaign. So I intend to send, along with the tape, photos of Myron and Alison making love."

"How did you obtain such photos?" asked Kessler.

"They were taken by a hidden camera in Myron's New York apartment shortly before he and Alison broke up," Hunter said. "Once the photos and the tape are sent to the police, and our TV and radio talk show hosts start playing up the story, Ramsey's double-digit lead will evaporate, and Operation Saladin will be back on track."

"You're a genius, my friend."

"Thank you."

After hanging up, Hunter reached into his briefcase and removed Rayvon's file. As he was perusing its latest entry, a thought suddenly occurred to him that made him chuckle. He picked up the phone and dialed Dawoud.

"Is everything ready for the Rayvon operation?"

"Yes, sir. We installed the cameras yesterday. And she's coming tonight."

"Excellent."

Chapter 21

Rayvon stood behind the sliding glass door of his condo, anxiously peering between the slats in his vertical Levelor blinds into the limpid darkness. It was Saturday night and the parking lot of the apartment complex in Greensboro where he lived was packed with vehicles. He saw no sign of his female visitor yet. She always parked her little 2004 Nissan Sentra in the same spot whenever she came over to see him.

He returned inside and surveyed the condo to make sure everything was ready. The table was set for two and a savory, juicy rack of lamb was stewing in the oven. He peeked under the lids of the pots of wild rice and vegetables simmering on the stove. Everything looked delectable. A bottle of white Zinfandel was chilling in a bucket of ice. He checked the bedroom to make sure everything there looked romantic also. He had polished the large headboard mirror of his king-size waterbed and placed fragrant candles all over the room – on the dressers, the window sills, and the nightstand.

Spotting the pile of *Hustler* and *Penthouse* magazines, he quickly gathered them into his arms and shoved them under the bed. He returned to the mirror for the sixth time in the ten minutes since he had showered to make sure he was still looking good. He dabbed himself with his favorite cologne, one he believed drove women wild.   He practiced his different expressions: forceful, adoring, adamant, jovial, aloof.

The doorbell rang. He hurried to answer it. A tall, stunning blonde in her mid-twenties stood outside. Her long straight hair was parted in the middle and fell to her waist. She dressed the way she knew Rayvon wanted her to – vampish – in a black leather miniskirt, spike heels, and a low-cut top. She looked as though she had just walked straight off the cover of *Penthouse Magazine.*

Rayvon pulled her inside and quickly shut the door.

"Did anyone see you come up here?" he demanded uneasily.

"No."

"Are you sure?"

"I was very careful. I know you don't want anyone to know about us."

"You can never be too careful, you know," Rayvon whispered.

"What's the big deal anyway? So what if someone sees me?"

"Do you want to have me lynched?"

Startled, the blonde said, "Why, no, of course not, I–"

"Don't be so naïve about racism, Nell," Rayvon interrupted. "I know you can't help being ignorant about what it's like to be black in America because you're white. Racism runs deep in this society. It runs so deep that most white people don't even know they're racist." He looked at her and realized she hadn't the faintest idea what he was talking about, so he elaborated. "The white power structure is always trying to figure out ways to exterminate black men. It pours drugs and guns into black neighborhoods. It invented AIDS as a form of genocide. Black men in America are an endangered species."

"What's our love got to do with endangered species?" Nell asked innocently.

Rayvon cringed when he heard the words "our love. " Did this dumb blonde really think that he, Prince Rayvon, host of *Know Your Heritage* and the lover of black women, was in love with her? It made him want to burst out laughing. Instead of answering, he simply relaxed, stepped down from his soapbox, and looked her up and down. "You're looking mighty fine tonight, baby. Good enough to eat." He chuckled.

Nell smiled, glad to see they once again had safely skirted the issue of race. She wondered why Rayvon always lost his temper whenever anything even tangentially related to skin color came up.

Nell had been disowned by her Baptist parents for refusing to give up for adoption a baby fathered by a black football player she had dated while in high school. She supported herself and her four-year-old son by working as an aerobics instructor at a gym in downtown Greensboro. Before that, she had worked as a secretary for a real estate firm in Thomasville, whose owner had briefly dated her and, when he found out that she had a son by a black man, had fired her.

Despite her gorgeous looks, Nell, because she had chosen to have a child by a black man rather than abort it, was considered damaged goods by most white men. She therefore found herself pursued almost exclusively by black men, having apparently lost her membership in the white world. Rayvon had been her lover now for three months. He had met her at the gym, where he often worked out.

"So, what do you think, baby?" Rayvon said, gesturing to the table settings, the candles, and the chilled wine.

"It looks great."

Something on the couch caught Nell's attention. It was a copy of *Ebony*.

She reached for the glossy magazine. "Is this the issue in which you're mentioned as one of the thirty leaders of the future?"

"Yeah, that's it," he said.

"May I read it?"

"Sure. My picture is on page 88. But it's not the best."

She took the magazine and headed down the hall. As soon as Nell vanished inside the bathroom, Rayvon slid a CD into the CD player of his Pioneer megawatt stereo.

Nell returned, magazine in hand, smiling.

"What's made you so happy, baby? Surely not my picture."

"No. I've seen better ones of you. It's this article on black men and white women. It's the first balanced piece I've read about interracial relationships. I didn't know that all these famous black celebrities were married to white women."

"It's the wave of the future, baby."

The two sat down to eat. The sensuous voice of Luther Vandross and the fragrant smell of jasmine incense filled the room. After dining on lamb, wild rice, vegetables, and rich sauces, and after enjoying the wine and chocolate mousse dessert, Rayvon and Nell were giddy and complacent. They laughed and teased each other.

They slow-danced around the room, her head resting languidly on his broad shoulder. He started stroking her long platinum blonde hair from the top of her head to her waist, kissing her hard, and grinding his hips into hers to the beat of the music.

Suddenly Nell pulled away from Rayvon and looked him in the eye. "Rayvon?"

"Yeah, baby. What's the matter?"

"Do you love me?"

"Why do you ask?"

"Well, it's just that all the black men I've dated have only been interested in sleeping with me. And I hate that."

"Of course I adore you, honey."

"Then why are you always denouncing interracial relationships on your show?"

"That's simply an act, baby," Rayvon said, squeezing her bottom. "I'm colorblind. And I'm gonna marry you some day soon, even in the middle of a race war."

It was a line that always drew a highly erotic response from the dozens of white women he had used it on. During his college and brief NBA basketball career, women of all races had thrown themselves at him. Yet his preference had always been for white women, especially blondes. He couldn't remember how many women he had laid, but he was nowhere near the numbers quoted by some famous basketball stars.

Rayvon led Nell to the bedroom. It reeked of incense, and was lit only by candles. A king-size waterbed stood in the middle, surrounded by mirrors. Before putting on an X-rated show that included oral sex, Rayvon and Nell snorted Crystal meth, a highly-addictive central nervous system stimulant whose users often experience an increasing and urgent need for sex, and the capacity to engage in marathon sexual sessions.

Outside Rayvon's condo, next to Nell's Nissan Sentra, stood a dark blue Chevy van labeled "Triad Electricians: There When you Need Us." Inside the van, Fadi and Dawoud listened and watched Rayvon's and Nell's marathon X-rated performance. The images were being transmitted by a tiny, remote-controlled camera inconspicuously hidden inside the vent directly above the king-size water bed. The camera had been installed by two "electricians" who had been summoned to Rayvon's condo the day before when his power mysteriously went dead.

"That's the guy Ghazi wants to be the leader of the Afro-Purist movement," Dawoud asked, shaking his head. "Gimme a break."

"Yeah," Fadi said, his eyes glued to the color TV monitor. "Ghazi says he'll give the movement a lot of credibility."

They both laughed.

Chapter 22

While Rayvon was in bed with Nell, busy proving his loyalty to black women, Chanel was at The Queen of Sheba, a popular Ethiopian food restaurant on Martin Luther King Junior Boulevard, in an impoverished black section of Winston-Salem known as Happy Hills.

What a refreshing contrast from Rayvon, Chanel thought as she studied the medium tall, ruggedly handsome black man in a faded denim shirt, khakis, and work boots who was sitting across the table from her, talking about his life and work.

Nelson Wallace was a union organizer, as his father and grandfather had been. At thirty-four, he was eight years older than Chanel. The two had met when Chanel did a story on the decline of unions in North Carolina, a right to work state.

"I got into union work because of my father," Nelson said in his euphonious tenor, reaching for a piece of Sambousa, a baked triangular phyllo-dough pocket filled with spicy lentil stuffing. "He was a member of the Communist Party and used to take me along on some of his unionizing trips across the state."

"Was he by any chance involved in the 1979 Greensboro clash between the Communist Party and a group of Klansmen and Nazis?" asked Chanel as she began eating her Timatim Fitfit, an appetizer made from diced vine-ripened tomatoes, peppers, onions and crumpled injera tossed in a lemon and olive vinaigrette.

"He was among those shot," Nelson said. "Luckily he survived."

"I witnessed the massacre," Chanel said quietly.

Nelson was surprised. "You did?"

Chanel sipped from her glass of merlot. "Yes. I was home that Saturday morning with my brother when it happened. My mother was away at work. Our house was on the route taken by the caravan of cars and vans carrying the Klansmen and Nazis. My brother and I were standing by the window, and I saw the Klansmen and Nazis open the trunks and distribute rifles and handguns. After that first shot rang out and the demonstrators ran for cover, I saw the Klansmen and Nazis methodically go about pumping bullets into demonstrators as they lay helpless and writhing on the ground."

"But the police said it was a shootout."

Chanel shook her head vehemently. "It was no shootout. It was a massacre. I saw it with my own two eyes. The demonstrators didn't have a chance. I saw bleeding and dead bodies strewn on the ground. Those demonstrators were executed."

"I believe you," Nelson said. "Especially since only CWP and union leaders were shot. But as you know, only four of the forty white supremacists who carried out the massacre were ever brought to trial. And all four were acquitted by an all-white, all-Christian jury, which claimed that the Nazis and Klansmen had acted in self-defense."

"I know," Chanel said. She had been only eight and she had had nightmares weeks after the incident. "Let's talk about something else, if you don't mind," she said.

"Okay. Tell me more about yourself. How did you escape from the projects to become such an intelligent, gorgeous, and sophisticated woman?"

Chanel laughed and blushed. "Well, it's a long story."

"We have all evening," Nelson said, smiling.

He's so unpretentious, Chanel thought. *Unlike that jerk Rayvon.*

"If I tell you," Chanel said, "then you'll have to tell me why such an intelligent, handsome, and sophisticated man, who could have pursued any profession, chose such a thankless job as union organizing – in North Carolina, of all places?"

"It's a deal."

Chanel twisted one of her long braids. "Well, where do I begin? I have an older brother named David, who is currently serving in Afghanistan. My family moved to Greensboro from Rocky Mount when I was three. My mother never finished high school. Yet she was the best teacher I ever had. She taught me the most important lesson in life: survival. I never knew my father. I'm told he was a janitor. He abandoned the family shortly after I was born, so we moved around a lot. We came to Greensboro to live with my aunt until my mother could find a job. She finally found one as a maid in the homes of various prominent white families in the Triad. Despite her meager income, she raised my brother and me all by herself. She refused to accept a cent of government money."

"She sounds like a remarkable woman."

"She is," Chanel said, and then sipped her wine. "So, tell me about yourself."

"There isn't much to tell."

"Let me be the judge of that."

The waitress brought their entrees. Chanel had ordered Atikilt Wot, a vegetarian dish consisting of fresh string beans, long-cut carrots, and cabbage cooked in a sauce of olive oil seasoned with coriander, cumin, and garlic. Nelson had ordered Doro Tips, which was made from dice-cut chicken breast marinated with onions, olive oil, rosemary, jalapeno, and sautéed in kibe and a touch of Chardonnay.

"Well, I never went to college," Nelson said as they began eating, "But I was a straight-A student and valedictorian of my class at West Forsyth High School."

Chanel stopped eating and looked at Nelson. "Why didn't you go?"

"I wanted to finish the work my father had begun," Nelson said. "He died of a heart attack my senior year. From overwork."

"That was unselfish of you," Chanel said, deeply impressed.

"It wasn't, really. I believed in what my father was doing. I'd seen the terrible working and living conditions of the men and women, both black and white, whose blood, sweat, and tears built this country. I've been to the coal mines of Appalachia. I've seen the poultry farms and the textile mills. I've traveled with migrant workers. I've worked on tobacco fields and on hog farms. I've experienced firsthand the Dickensian working conditions that still exist for workers in many parts of this state. All this led me to conclude that the only thing that would give meaning to my life would be to insure that workers are treated as human beings. But I must admit it isn't easy work."

"I bet."

"I've been called all sorts of names and received all kinds of threats," Nelson said. "Twice I was shot at. But I'm committed to the struggle for economic justice. I'm committed to humanizing capitalism, if such a thing is possible with conservative ideologues in control of Congress and the White House, and hell bent on undoing the gains of the Great Society and enslaving workers to corporations."

Chanel knew of that commitment. It had earned Nelson the respect of thousands of workers and liberals across the state and the country.

"In all my years of union work, I've come to this conclusion," he said, growing more animated as he spoke about his life's devotion. "The best way to protect workers' rights in this state, or any other state for that matter, is to get black and white employees to unite. Politicians are good at pitting black and white workers against each other. You remember that infamous ad that got Jesse Helms re-elected in 1990?"

"Yes, I do,' Chanel said, recalling the commercial that many had called racist and believed was largely responsible for Helms retaining his U.S. Senate seat by a narrow 53% to 47% margin. The ad showed a close-up pair of white hands crumpling a rejection slip while the voice-over explains that the man had lost his job to a less qualified minority because of minority racial quotas supported by Harvey Gantt.

"My toughest job now is getting white workers not to fall into such traps," Nelson said. "They've got to see past race, especially in these times when companies are downsizing and exporting jobs to cheap labor markets overseas. They need to realize how much they have in common with minorities. If they can unite, they can better fight for a living wage and better health care and benefits."

"I can see why Ramsey asked you to join his campaign," Chanel said, after taking another bite. "How's that going?"

"Not too well, I'm afraid," Nelson said, wiping his mouth with a lace napkin. "It seems every time I come up with a good idea, that damn campaign manager of his or one of his cronies shoots it down.

Hunter was even against my idea to have Ramsey give a speech before the NAACP. He said that it would alienate white voters. Yet that speech was responsible for the high black voter turnout that won Ramsey the primary."

"It was one of his best speeches. People could tell that he was speaking from the heart when he said that the Civil Rights Movement was America's finest hour. So what made Ramsey go ahead and give the speech if Hunter was against it?"

"Darlene. She overruled Hunter. You know what? Hunter's been against me from day one. He didn't even want Ramsey to bring me on board because, he claims, the labor movement is dead. He's obsessed with turning Ramsey into a pseudo-Republican. I'm glad Darlene is around to go to bat for me on liberal issues."

"She's quite a strong woman," Chanel said.

"To tell you the truth, I'm really confused about Ramsey," Nelson said. "Why did a proud liberal like him hire a guy like Hunter as campaign manager?"

"They're childhood friends," said Chanel. "And Hunter has an amazing track record of getting Southern Democrats elected."

"Elected as what? DINO?"

"Well, you know how it is in the South. Democrats feel that if they don't ape Republicans they'll never win another election in America."

"Bullshit," Nelson said, then quickly added, "Pardon my French."

"No problem," Chanel said. "I know how strongly you feel about these issues."

"It's just that I hate it when people insist that the only way for Democrats to win elections is to betray their core principles," Nelson said, growing more animated. "I respect Lawrence Ramsey for his civil rights record and for standing up for workers' rights over the years. But I'm really bothered by his decision to run as a conservative."

"Couldn't that simply be a strategy to win?" Chanel said. "After all, how many Democrats are there today who publicly embrace the L word?"

"But voters aren't fooled," said Nelson. "Democrats who distance themselves from liberalism end up losing." He shook his head. "I tell you, that Hunter's got his claws dug deep into Ramsey. He controls everything – I mean everything. He and those cronies from his consulting firm even write every word in Ramsey's speeches."

"It's the rare politician who won't do whatever it takes to win. Both Republicans and Democrats pander to their audiences. Why should Ramsey be any different?"

"Because Ramsey's a leader, not a politician," said Nelson fervently. "He's always done what was right despite the political risks. To be honest with you, I'm not passionate in my support of Ramsey. But I'll do what I can to help him win because Lynch is nothing but a fascist. That's why I'll be going to that fund-raising dinner at the Braxton's next Saturday, even when I don't have a date. Do you mind being my date?"

"I'd love to."

"You mean it?"

"Why not?"

Nelson stared at the flickering candle. "Well, it's just that I've been turned down a few too many times by some of the educated sisters who look down on blue-collar men like me. I've never been to college. I don't drive a fancy BMW or a Mercedes. I don't own a condo. I don't make six figures. And I don't host a talk show."

"So you heard about Rayvon and me, huh?" said Chanel with a smile.

"Through the grapevine. But I'm glad you told him off."

"He's a jerk," Chanel said. "He thinks that just because he's a celebrity and the host of a popular talk show, women should kneel at his feet."

Nelson looked directly into Chanel's eyes and went on. "Well, I'm neither a celebrity nor a talk show host. I share a rented one-bedroom apartment with some ants, a couple of mice, and a black lab named Beer Breath. I drive a '92 Chevy with a hole in the floor, a dragging muffler, and a glove compartment that falls open every time I hit a bump. I drink an occasional glass of wine with dinner. I don't do drugs, I'm not gay or bi, and I'm HIV negative. But I do desperately want to kneel at your feet."

Chanel laughed. "Nelson, all those qualities make you the perfect man for me. I may have more education and earn more money, but I'm still a woman. All I care about is that you be proud of who you are, respect me, and never cheat."

Nelson was silent for a while, as if mulling something over. Then, in a soft voice, he said, "I have another confession to make."

"What about?"

Nelson self-consciously looked away from the table. He coughed. Chanel could tell that whatever was on his mind was making him extremely uncomfortable.

"I was previously engaged to a white woman."

"I knew that."

"You did?" Nelson said with a start.

"Yes. Her name is Kayla Rhoades. She's a union worker, went to Berkeley and her parents are very well-to-do and live in Asheville."

"How did you find out?"

Chanel smiled. "You're not the only one who does his homework."

Nelson smiled awkwardly. "That doesn't bother you?"

"Why should it?"

"Well, a lot of black women are bothered when I tell them that I was once engaged to a white woman. In fact, it's led some of them to break up with me."

"I'm not exactly a fan of interracial relationships," Chanel said. "But if your motives for falling in love with a white woman were pure, then that's fine with me."

"They were. I truly loved Kayla. But things just didn't work out."

"I personally wouldn't marry someone white."

"Why?"

"I don't think I'm prejudiced. It's just that emotionally it would be difficult for me. I try to judge people by the contents of their character, but I find it much easier to relate to black men than white or Asian or Hispanic men. But that's just my personal preference. I have nothing against interracial couples. In fact, my best friend Alison was once in a relationship with a black man, but it didn't work out."

"I appreciate your candor and fairness," Nelson said. "Especially because some people in the black community have even tried to use the fact that I was once engaged to a white woman to discredit me."

"Who?"

"Rayvon."

"Then why are you planning to appear on his show next week?"

"I'm never one to shy away from a fight."

"But can't you see it's a set-up? Queen Nefertari's supposed to be there too. And she and Rayvon are two peas in a pod when it comes to their views on integration. They insist the best solution to

America's racial problems is complete separation of the races."

"I know," Nelson said. "But there's going to be a third guest."

"Who?"

"The producers told me he's to remain a mystery until the day of the show."

"I don't like the smell of this."

"Maybe it will be Ramsey. Who knows?"

"Fat chance," Chanel said. "Not with Hunter as his campaign manager. Please don't go, Nelson. I care a lot about you. I don't want to see you hurt."

"I appreciate your concern, Chanel," Nelson said as he reached across the table and gently held Chanel's warm hand. "But integration is a fight I'll never back away from. America is *our* home also. Black people have struggled and sacrificed and shed blood for the right to be considered American citizens. We can't let misguided demagogues like Rayvon and Queen Nefertari lead us to a Fools' Paradise."

Chapter 23

Nancy propped seven-month-old Buck Junior in the white plastic baby tub and softly sponged him with warm water while humming the Sesame Street song "Rubber Ducky, you're so fine, I'm so glad you're mine." The baby's hair, once straight and light brown, had started to darken and curl. The baby's eyes, once sapphire blue, had darkened and then turned brown. The baby's skin, once paler than hers, had begun to turn a soft beige. The changes had occurred so gradually that Nancy had not paid much attention.

But now, looking at his beige skin juxtaposed against the magnolia whiteness of the tub, Nancy shuddered. Something strange was indeed happening to her child.

The door opened behind her and Buck walked in.

"Hey, hon'," Buck said, "I'm home. Is Buck Junior awake? I have a new game I'd like to teach him today." Since being fired from his job at New South Fine Furniture, Buck would leave home each morning after telling Nancy that he was going to look for work. In reality, he spent the day at Chandler's compound, engaging in military training.

"He's awake," Nancy said. "I've just been giving him a bath."

Buck came over to the bathtub. He took one look at the baby and his smile instantly vanished. "What the hell did you do to that child?"

"What do you mean?"

"Why did you leave him in the sun all day? Look at his skin."

Oh, my God, Nancy thought. *So there is something wrong with the baby.*

"Well," Nancy said in a slightly shaken voice, "I did take him for a long walk in the stroller yesterday."

"Woman, don't take my son outside, you hear?" Buck said, wagging a finger in her face. "That sun is damn hot. I don't want him turning into a nigger."

"I'll keep him inside from now on, Buck. I promise."

"You better," Buck said, then walked into the kitchen, yanked open the refrigerator, and took a can of Miller from the shelf. He opened it, took a few gulps, let out a huge belch, then wandered into the living room to watch TV. An object on the chair arrested his attention. It was a man's hat. Curious, he picked it up and examined it. It was a stylish London Fog tweed, and it was slightly damp. He smelled it.

"Nancy!" he roared. "You leave that baby and come out here this minute!"

"What is it, Buck?"

"Where'd this hat come from?"

"Oh, that's Mr. Caldwell's. He must've forgotten it."

Buck glared at her. "*Mister* Caldwell? That nigger fired me, and you can stand there and call him *Mister* Caldwell? What the hell was he doing in my house?"

Buck's face was red. Veins stood out on both sides of his neck.

"He stopped by wanting to talk to you," Nancy said.

Buck gave Nancy a suspicious look. "About what?"

"He says he's willing to give you your old job back if you promise to stick to your driving schedule. Market's coming up, he said, and they're expectin' lots of orders."

"He wants me back, huh? I'm never ever gonna work under no nigger again," Buck said, recalling that any day now he would be receiving his third $10,000 stipend. The first two he had squandered on liquor, prostitutes, and his latest hobby, gambling.

Buck took the hat outside, set it on the porch, unzipped his fly, and urinated into it. He stepped back into the house. "There," he tossed the wet hat at Nancy. "Now when your *Mister* Caldwell comes back for his hat, you make sure he puts it on, you hear?"

"Thanks for coming along," Alison said as the Cherokee she was driving ascended another steep hill along Highway 421, headed toward the Blue Ridge Mountains.

"I needed the break," Chanel said from the passenger's seat. "I've been working non-stop since the election season began."

The two best friends were on their first camping trip together since high school. With Eliot on a business trip to China and Russia to explore new markets for Whitaker Tobacco Inc., and the baby still not found, Alison felt she needed to get away from the big and lonely house, which reminded her of so much that had gone wrong with her life.

"By the way, congratulations on finally meeting your soul mate," Alison said.

"Thanks. Nelson is the most honest man I've ever met. And in this drought, girlfriend, I'm not about to let him go. I'm sick and tired of dates from hell."

"Well, I hope that if you two get hitched some day, your marriage will be happier than mine," Alison said, shifting the Cherokee into low as they climbed the final, winding stretch of Highway 421.

"So there's no hope of salvaging your marriage?"

Alison shook her head. "Ever since the baby was kidnapped, Eliot and I have been trading accusations about who's to blame for our loveless marriage. In the meantime, my love for Myron has only grown, despite what happened between us."

Alison fell silent. Chanel thought it best not to pursue the subject. Instead, the two friends enjoyed the scenery. Sometimes they would catch glimpses between the trees of ramshackle, windowless log cabins that had once been used for curing tobacco leaves but were now rotting beneath intricate webs of vines. They passed a farmer in bib overalls, sitting on a stump with his elbows on his knees, patiently waiting for passersby to stop and buy the jars of homemade jam, jelly, and honey lined up on the open tailgate of his ancient pickup truck. A deer, standing bug-eyed as if frozen, suddenly darted into the woods as they pulled onto the Blue Ridge Parkway and headed south.

The winding road, which led to Grandfather Mountain and provided them with a breathtaking view of serene and gently rolling pastures and the spectacular colors of autumn leaves, made Alison hum John Denver's "Country Road." Forty-five minutes later, they reached the entrance to the 4,000-acre wilderness area that is Grandfather Mountain. They paid the entrance fee and proceeded to drive up the serpentine road past the nature museum and animal habitats to the parking lot near the summit.

"Just look at that," Chanel cried, pointing to scores of tourists tottering across a mile-high suspension bridge, grasping the rails and screaming as if they actually thought they were about to tumble into the ravine.

"Let's get away from this tourist trap," Alison said, surveying the scene of the parking lot and gift shop, which were jammed with camera-toting tourists of all races and nationalities. Being in the mountains brought back memories of her last romantic weekend with Myron when they climbed Mount Washington in New Hampshire, the day after he had proposed to her. *Oh, Myron,* she thought. *I miss you so much. Why did you betray our love? Why did you force me to marry Eliot?*

Alison parked the Cherokee and she and Chanel unloaded their gear, pulled on their backpacks, and hit the trail. Both wore hiking boots, cut-off shorts, tank tops, and sunglasses, with bandannas as headbands. After twenty minutes of rigorous hiking, they reached the back country. Now the only people they saw were an occasional pair of serious hikers, or muscular rock climbers toting coiled ropes and carabineers.

"This is just what I needed," Alison said, climbing up a boulder.

"I knew being out in nature would do you good," Chanel said, following closely behind. "Remember what nature freaks we were at Wellington Academy?"

Alison grinned. She and Chanel had a way of sparking the free spirit in each other. At Wellington Academy they had been famous for their impromptu camping trips to the Smokies and the Outer Banks. Alison scrambled a steep boulder, searching for a tree root to grab or a crevice to wiggle her fingertips into to steady herself. The sun beat down on her tanned limbs and sweat trickled down her neck and face. *This is what makes me feel alive,* she thought, *not material things.*

An hour later Alison and Chanel emerged from the forest onto a broad slab of rock at the peak of the mountain. The Appalachian range spread out before them, like ripples of lavender silk. In each fold floated a layer of mist from low-lying clouds. Far below them they could see the mile-high suspension bridge, like a matchbox toy dotted with tourists the size of ants. A cool wind blew across the smooth rock face, drying the damp strands of hair that clung to their necks.

"You really pushed me," Chanel said, still breathing hard as she and Alison lay back on the smooth rock. Using their packs for pillows, they gazed up at the cloudless sky that resembled a blue china bowl.

"No way. You were the one pushing me, as always."

"We're strong."

"We're awesome."

Alison and Chanel laughed, then watched a hawk soar gracefully across the sky.

"That's a gorgeous chateau," Chanel said, pointing at a German-style chateau perched on a cliff, with a breathtaking view of the Smokies.

"That's one of the homes owned by Richard Kessler, the billionaire."

Chanel looked at Alison. "Kessler's supposed to be a recluse like Howard Hughes. I wanted to interview him after *Forbes* named him one of the richest men in America, but his lawyer told me that he never grants any interviews."

"Uncle Reggie has been inside," Alison said.

"Really?" said Chanel, surprised. "What took him there?"

"Business. He went to persuade Kessler to host a fundraiser for my dad."

"Did he succeed?"

"Hmmh. As a matter of fact, the fundraiser will be at the Sawtooth Center next Saturday night. It's supposed to be quite a grand affair."

"Your uncle Reggie sure is a miracle worker."

"That's why I like him so much," Alison said. "And he's been trying very hard to help me and Eliot overcome our differences. But they're irreconcilable, Chanel. You and my mom were right. The marriage was a terrible mistake."

"I knew from the start that you didn't really love him," Chanel said. "You were simply playing the role of savior, as you always do. You wanted to save him from the grip of his right-wing and domineering father. And to Eliot, you were the liberated woman his mother had adored. You were a sort of surrogate mother to him."

"I should have realized that Eliot was more like his father than he was willing to admit," Alison said. "But like you said, I wasn't thinking clearly. I was so hurt by Myron's betrayal that I wanted to bury the pain in a marriage that seemed perfect."

Alison and Chanel paused in their conversation and unpacked their lunch of tuna and fruit salad. As they began eating, Chanel said, "You know, I was quite surprised when I found out that Nelson was once engaged to a white woman."

"Really, and what happened?"

"She broke off the engagement."

"Why?"

"Apparently she couldn't deal with all the hostility directed at her, especially from black women," Chanel said. "She thought they'd consider her open-minded and accept her with open arms because of her relationship with a black man."

"I don't blame her," Alison said. "I thought the same thing. And, boy, was I surprised when many women started hating me for being with Myron."

"I think hate is too strong a word."

"It's true, Chanel. You should have seen the looks they gave me each time they saw us together. I remember this one time when I accompanied Myron to a performance by Miriam Makeba at the Apollo Theater. I got such cold stares I got up and left."

"But I don't hate you. You're my best friend."

"Sorry for stereotyping. I didn't mean you. I just mean some black women."

"I still think hate is too strong a word. 'Dislike' or 'resent' is more like it. We're not haters. Usually it's whites who truly hate mixed couples."

Chanel's right, Alison thought. *There's a difference between the violence of the Klan and the cold stares of black women.* "Okay then," Alison said, "let's use the word 'resent.' Why do so many black women resent me?"

"Every black woman is different. If a black woman resents you for dating a black man, you have to find out where she's coming from. What's her background? Is she a black separatist? Did she ever lose a boyfriend or husband to a white woman? Once you know that, add the problem facing most single black women."

"Which is?"

"Good black men are scarce. It's not easy for black women – especially professional ones like me – to find an educated, employed, good-looking, responsible black man to marry. I think there are ten black women for every black man in that category. It's like a drought. Rarely a week goes by when I don't hear one of my friends complain about seeing some black guy they had their eye on with some blonde."

"By the way, we're not all blondes," Alison said.

Chanel laughed. "Touché. Sorry for stereotyping."

"But seriously, if a black woman saw the man of her dreams with another black woman, would she be as upset?"

"She'd be a little jealous, but she'd get over it. But a white woman – forget it, girl. When black women see a black man – especially if he's educated and successful – with a white woman, they go wild inside. They take it as a personal affront. Some even get sick to their stomachs – I mean physically ill. And I know the feeling. I know what they're going through because I'm a black woman."

"I don't understand."

"You can't. There's too much history involved. It goes all the way back to slavery." Chanel sat up and reached for her flask of apple cider.

"Why would you feel betrayed?"

Chanel sighed. "Slavery isn't my favorite subject, Alison."

"If you'd rather not discuss it, I – "

"No, it's all right. I'll explain." Chanel sipped her apple cider. "During slavery," she began, "the white slave master and his sons could have a black woman any time they wanted. They owned us. They used us. The sons of well-to-do Southerners often had their first sexual encounter with black women. As a way of practicing, I guess. On the other hand, white men castrated and lynched black men for simply looking at a white woman. That's why I personally would never marry a white man."

Alison was stunned. "I didn't realize –" she began, then stopped, not knowing what to say. She felt she could only listen, only try to understand.

"And I don't think I'm racist," Chanel went on. "It's just that emotionally I couldn't deal with it. And I believe that a relationship cannot survive if both partners aren't emotionally honest."

"Of course you aren't racist," Alison said. "I know you. Not everyone who doesn't approve of interracial marriages is a racist. The racists are persons – black and white – who persecute interracial couples."

"That's the way I see it, too. And if I had a son – and I pray that God blesses Nelson and me with children someday despite the problems I've had with endometriosis – I'd prefer that he marry a black woman. If he told me he wanted to marry a white woman, it would hurt me deeply, though in the end I'd support and love him."

"Why would it hurt you?"

"Well, it would be the same as if he said, 'Mama, even though you took good care of me, nurtured me and taught me right from wrong, I don't appreciate you.'"

Alison was perplexed. "Why in the world would you think that?"

Chanel crossed her legs, yoga-style. "It's hard to explain. You see, the black woman has always been there for the black man. She's busted her ass to support him, to raise his children, to keep the black family together. If it weren't for the black woman, there'd be no black race. We're the ones who've been frowned on, stepped on, and spat on, and we're still plugging away, fighting to get and keep a good black man. And it hurts us when those same men slap us in the face by going out with a white woman – someone who can't possibly understand him or support him the way a black woman could."

"But why shouldn't a black man be free to make that choice? What if he falls in love with a woman for who she is and she just happens to have white skin?"

"Intellectually, I agree with you one hundred percent," Chanel said. "But I must be honest with you. There are many black men out there who go out with white women simply because they're white. To them, white women are a status symbol. There's a lot of that going on in professional sports and the entertainment industry. And many white women are with black men only because they've got money and fame."

"No one can accuse me of having wanted Myron for his money," Alison said. "When we met he didn't have a penny to his name and hadn't written any books. I liked him for his sensitivity, ideals, and commitment to making the world a better place."

"I know, girl," Chanel said. "You're one of the few white liberals I know who I can honestly say is truly colorblind."

"Thanks. But sometimes I think I'm naïve. I mean, just look at how racially polarized America is. Blacks and whites might as well be living on separate planets."

"That's why we need people like your dad in office," Chanel said. "He's one of the few white politicians I trust when it comes to race. He not only believes in Dr. King's dream of a colorblind society, but he's been willing to pay the political price for it."

Alison fell silent. *That's why I can't jeopardize Dad's chances of winning. I must find Dylan before the police do because if he's black, it will destroy Dad's campaign.*

"Did I hit a raw nerve?" Chanel asked. She knew Alison too well to think that her silence meant nothing. A couple of minutes passed as Alison pondered whether to tell Chanel her deeply guarded secret about Dylan's possibly being Myron's baby.

"What's the matter, girl?" Chanel asked, hugging her knees to her chest.

Tears welled in Alison's eyes. "There's a secret I've never told anyone. Not my parents, not Uncle Reggie. And I'm afraid it might destroy my father's campaign."

Chanel stared at Alison. "What is it?"

Alison coughed nervously. "There's a possibility that Dylan is not Eliot's baby."

"What? You must be joking."

Alison's face was grim. "I'm not."

"If Eliot isn't the father, who is?"

Alison was tongue-tied, but her silence gave her away.

"Oh, my God," Chanel gasped. "Myron?"

Alison nodded glumly.

"Are you sure?"

"I'm not one hundred percent sure. But there's a strong possibility."

"When did you find out?"

"Remember the day we went jogging around Oak Hollow Lake last fall? I was wearing white shorts, and you told me I was leaking."

Chanel thought a while, then said, "Yes. You and Myron had just broken up. I remember you were still deeply hurt and didn't want to talk about it."

"Myron and I had made love the day he proposed."

"Didn't you use any protection?"

"I normally use a diaphragm. But I was so happy at the news, so in love, so excited that we were finally going to get married that I forgot to wear it. Besides, I didn't mind having the child of the man I knew I was deeply in love with."

"Are you sure Eliot isn't the father?"

Alison nodded. "I'm almost one hundred percent sure. He and I have made love only three times since we got married. And every time I used a diaphragm and spermicide and insisted that he wear a condom. I didn't feel comfortable making love to a man I don't love, so I always came up with excuses."

"Then Dylan is Myron's son, girl. There's no two ways about it."

"That's why I've got to find him before the police or FBI do," Alison said. "What if his melanin has started to come in? Can you imagine the scandal it would cause if the press were to get wind of the story? I can just see the headlines. 'Daughter of Gubernatorial Candidate Conceives Mulatto Child Out of Wedlock.'"

'I hear you girl," Chanel said. "We better find that baby before it's too late."

Chapter 24

Rayvon, dressed in the resplendent robes of gold, green, and yellow popular with West African royalty, sat on a chair embroidered with Kente cloth, cordless mike in hand.

"Welcome to *The Rayvon Turlington Show*," he said in his well-rehearsed TV voice. "We're coming to you live from Studio Five in downtown Greensboro. Our topic today is about integration. My three guests are going to engage in a no holds-barred debate of this important issue, which has bedeviled America since we Africans were torn from our beloved motherland and brought to these alien shores as slaves more than two hundred years ago. When we come back, we'll meet our three special guests."

Two prompters signaled to the audience packed inside the huge semicircular studio that it was time to clap. The audience of two hundred consisted mostly of black men and women wearing the black robes of Afro-Purists. There was one cluster of five white men, who looked mighty uncomfortable surrounded by a sea of black militants.

Peter Feldman, a chubby-cheeked former Republican lobbyist with a squeaky-clean image, was the show's producer and station manager. He signaled a commercial break and Rayvon's guests were ushered onto the stage. The first to appear was Nelson Wallace, neatly dressed in a pair of gray slacks, a blazer, a white shirt, and a tie with a civil rights logo on it. Chanel had had a hard time persuading the down-to-earth Nelson to dress up for the show.

"Appearances are everything on TV, honey," she had said.

The second guest to appear was Queen Nefertari – a tall, slender, and intense woman with a straight nose, thin lips, and high yellow skin. She could easily have passed for white. She was decked out in Afro-Purist garb, including a black and gold headpiece. As she strutted onto the stage, enthusiastic cheering burst from the audience.

The appearance of the third guest, who was escorted by two beefy black security guards, elicited jeers and catcalls from the audience.

"I told you we were going to have a mystery guest," Rayvon said with an impish smile as the third guest, who was dressed in the Burgundy red robes of a Klan Titan, took his seat. "But please, let's be civil. No disrespect to any of my guests. I don't want this to turn into another Geraldo or Jerry Springer show. We are here to discuss a very important subject. That means we have to respect all points of views, no matter how obnoxious."

After Rayvon's three guests were seated and had been miked, Feldman signaled to Rayvon that they were about to come out of the commercial break.

Rayvon cleared his throat, glanced quickly at his notes, and then looked straight into camera one as he introduced his guests. "Nelson Wallace is a union organizer and chairman of the *Triad Interracial Alliance*, a group dedicated to building what it calls bridges of friendship and understanding between the races. Nelson is currently an advisor to Lawrence Ramsey, the Democratic candidate for Governor. Nelson's father was a member of the Communist Workers' Party that was involved in the bloody shootout with Klansmen and Nazis in Greensboro in 1979. Nelson credits his father with helping shape his conviction that integration, not separation, is the key to improving race relations."

Turning to Queen Nefertari, Rayvon said, "My second guest is Queen Nefertari, the gorgeous and outspoken leader of the North Carolina branch of the Afro-Purist movement. She's been a frequent guest on this show to discourse on such important topics as black beauty, the theft of black music by white artists, and black genetic superiority. She's the daughter of a white mother and black father, but has long since rejected her white part. She was born in Winston-

Salem but has lived most of her adult life in New York City. She recently moved back to North Carolina because, as she put it, the state has become a battleground for integration, which she adamantly opposes."

There were loud cheers and a standing ovation for Queen Nefertari.

"Our third guest, whose name is Johnny Chandler, has worn many hats in his long and interesting career," Rayvon said. "Since the 1970s he's been one of the South's best-known advocates of total segregation between the races. He's a highly-decorated Vietnam Veteran, has a Ph.D. in history, and speaks several languages. He's also the publisher of a newsletter called 'Saving the White Race.' He's thrice run for political office – once for governor as a Democrat, once for Congress as an Independent, and once for the U.S. Senate as a Republican."

Rayvon paused, turned, and retraced his steps. "Chandler believes that integration has not only failed, but that it is a defiance of God's will. America's problems, he says, can all be traced to integration, which is nothing but an attempt by liberals to destroy the cultures of both whites and blacks by producing a degenerate mulatto race. Chandler says that he supported the Million Man March, for he believed that black men needed to atone for their shortcomings as husbands, fathers, and boyfriends, and to accept responsibility for the future of their own communities rather than depend on government handouts and paternalistic liberals. He plans to organize a Million White Men March later this year, so that white men, too, can atone for their shortcomings, and take greater responsibility for the future and survival of the white race. Welcome to the show, ladies and gentlemen."

Rayvon shook hands with his guests. The prompter signaled to the audience to cheer. Feldman signaled to Rayvon that they were about to go to another commercial break. "When we return," Rayvon said into the camera, "we'll start talking to each of our interesting guests, in what promises to be one of the liveliest and most exciting discussions to date on the thorny issue of integration."

I hope the men keep their cool, Chandler thought as he spotted Orville, Bob, Thad, Buck, and Jimmy Ray in the audience, *despite being in enemy territory.*

The audience was again prompted to applaud heartily as the show returned from a commercial break. "Mr. Wallace," Rayvon began, standing in front of his guests. "I guess, in the interest of full disclosure and in fairness to you, I should make it clear to the audience that your support of integration has nothing to do with the fact that you were once engaged to a white woman. It's a matter of principle, am I right?"

Nelson realized that Rayvon was attempting to undermine his credibility with the mostly black audience. He was ready. "I live my life according to my beliefs, Rayvon. Unlike some who preach one thing in public and do another in private."

Rayvon's heart skipped a beat. For some reason he thought that Nelson was alluding to him. Trying hard not to sound nervous, he said, "What do you mean?"

"My relationship with a white woman was consistent with my beliefs that we should judge people by the contents of their character rather than by the color of their skin. In that context, a white woman is just as worthy of my love as a black woman."

"Black men who talk black and sleep white are suspect to me," Queen Nefertari interjected. "They absolutely have no right to speak for the black community."

Nelson looked straight at Queen Nefertari. "I made no claim of speaking for the black community," he said. "My views are my own, just as yours are. Neither of us can speak for the entire black community, which is very diverse. But I will say this: the black community owes more to integration than it does to separatism. The civil rights gains we've made in this country have been the result of blacks and whites standing shoulder to shoulder against injustice, under the brave and inspiring leadership of Dr. King."

"But Dr. King failed to take account of human nature, Mr. Wallace," Chandler interjected. "He didn't realize that the black and the white cultures are so different they can never melt into one, as liberals and their Uncle Toms want them to. If Dr. King were alive today, I bet you he'd be celebrating Kwanzaa instead of Christmas. Also, he'd be dressed like our honored host here, instead of like you, an imitation white man."

The audience laughed at this.

"If Dr. King were alive today," Nelson snapped. "He'd be wondering why a spook like you is still haunting America in the 21st century."

There was great laughter at this.

"I see Mr. Wallace is here to crack jokes rather than engage in a serious discussion of the issues," Chandler said.

"It's because he has nothing important to say, really," Queen Nefertari scoffed. "I take my cues on integration from Malcolm X, not Dr. King. The main goal of Dr. King's turn-the-other-cheek movement was not freedom and justice for black people. It was the insignificant right to use the same bathroom as crackers." The audience roared at this. Chandler's followers were visibly disconcerted at being referred to as crackers.

"On the other hand, the goal of Afro-Purists is black power, black pride, black dignity, and black unity," Queen Nefertari said emphatically. "And on that there can be no compromise, especially with liberals and their brainwashed Uncle Toms."

"Queen Nefertari is absolutely right," Chandler said. "I remember Brother Malcolm saying at one time that the true motive behind integration was to weaken the black community. He said, and I quote, 'When you got some coffee that's too black, which means it's too strong, what do you do? You integrate it with cream...But if you pour too much cream in it, you won't even know you ever had coffee. It used to be hot, it becomes cool. It used to be strong, it becomes weak. It used to wake you up, it puts you to sleep.'" To Chandler's surprise, the audience heartily applauded this statement.

"Can integration ever work in the U.S.?" Rayvon asked Nelson.

"Integration isn't a panacea, but it can work if certain ingredients are in place."

"What ingredients, Mr. Wallace?" asked Rayvon.

Nelson said, "Integration can work if there's trust and honest communication between the races, along with a willingness to compromise and cooperate for common goals. And these qualities are in very short supply in America."

"But Jews were the most integrated group in German society," Queen Nefertari said, "In fact, Germany was considered one of the most civilized nations of the world. The assimilation of Jews was so complete that many had changed their names, religion, noses and had even intermarried with non-Jews. And Jews were responsible for many of the great achievements in Germany, just as we African-Americans are in America. They were artists, Nobel laureates, composers, politicians, professors, and publishers of influential papers. But when Hitler came along and accused them of ruining German society, assimilation didn't save six million of them from the gas chambers. Why should African-Americans, whose history of persecution parallels that of the Jews, be deluded into becoming accomplices to their own genocide here in America?"

The audience went delirious with clapping. Even Chandler and his men clapped. *She's not a bad leader of niggers,* Chandler thought. *Pity she's a mongrel.*

"Queen Nefertari's observations about Jews are most profound," Chandler said. "They're the most incisive I've heard from anyone, black or white. Yes, Jews in Germany were the most integrated and assimilated non-Aryan group. In fact, they were so integrated and assimilated they controlled everything in Germany, just as they do in America. But because they were cut off from their roots, because they'd become aliens to themselves and traitors to their race, when the Nazi storm came, it swept them overboard. In other words, one might say that Jews caused their own Holocaust."

There was a gasp from the audience.

"Can you explain what you mean by that interesting observation?" Rayvon asked.

"I'd be glad to," Chandler said. "The truth of the matter is that if Jews hadn't been the blood-suckers that integration invariably made them, if they had not systematically corrupted German society with their liberalism, Marxism, Judaism, and Internationalism, then Hitler would have had no reason to put them in ghettoes." Chandler chose the word "ghetto" deliberately, for he wanted blacks to equate it with American ghettoes. "The Nuremberg Laws passed by the Reichstag in 1935 were nothing but an attempt by responsible German leaders to protect the Aryan race against Jews."

"Can you please explain to the audience what those laws entailed?" Rayvon asked with a solicitude that he didn't show toward Nelson.

"Sure," Chandler said. "They stripped Jews of German citizenship. They outlawed marriage and extra-marital relations between Jews and Aryans. And after their passage there were signs all over Germany announcing that Jews were not welcome at hotels, in trains, in stores, in schools and other public places. There was even a sign along one road that said: 'Drive Slowly! Sharp Curve! Jews 75 miles per hour.' That's how much integration had made Jews hated. By the way, Hitler clearly explains all this in his masterpiece, *Mein Kampf*. But, of course, no one took him seriously."

"Not only was Hitler not taken seriously," Rayvon observed with a sage look on his face, "but his detractors dismissed him as a raving demagogue. Just as they are dismissing Queen Nefertari here and her prophetic warnings about the various diabolical schemes white America is using to destroy the black race."

Queen Nefertari leaned forward. "I'm afraid that what happened to Jews in Nazi Germany has also begun happening to African-Americans in this very country," she declared. "There's irrefutable evidence proving that agents of the racist and imperialistic government of the United States are working overtime to exterminate black people. They tried it with slavery, they tried it with lynchings, and now they're trying it with AIDS and crack, which were invented in CIA labs as the ultimate genocide tools. And do you know what's preventing black people from realizing the bitter truth? I'll tell you. Liberals have hoodwinked us into believing that we're wanted in America, that we'll have justice if only we become assimilated into American society. In other words, if we become white. But we can never become white. Assimilation has done nothing but cut us off from our roots. It's made us strangers to ourselves and to each other. And most damaging of all, it's confused our men into abandoning black women for white women."

The audience's cheers were deafening.

"Queen Nefertari," Rayvon said, wrapping his arm around her. "That was most profound. Really profound. You've touched upon an issue which many of us believe lies at the heart of both black and white fears of integration: miscegenation. When we come back, we'll explore the controversial issue of interracial relationships. And before doing that, we'll show the audience two clips from Spike Lee's masterpiece, *Jungle Fever*."

The two clips, which were introduced by Stevie Wonder singing the theme song *Jungle Fever*, were the most controversial scenes in the movie. One showed a successful and married black executive humping a white secretary on a drafting table in his office after hours. The second clip was of the famous "war-council scene," which showed the adulterer's light-skinned black wife and her friends venting their frustration and rage against white women, who were seen as Circes out to snare successful black men.

"Many believe that those two clips tell the whole truth about interracial relationships," Rayvon said. "The first one shows that these abnormal liaisons are about sex. And the second clip proves that there's nothing more humiliating and infuriating to black women than to be left for a white woman. What do our guests think?"

"The most tragic thing about miscegenation," Chandler said, "is that it produces offspring who are neither black nor white, and therefore don't belong anywhere."

"I agree," Queen Nefertari said. "Children are our future. They are the carriers not only of our genes, but also of our culture and our identity. The worst crime any parent can commit, in my opinion, is to deprive a child of his or her identity. And that's precisely what race mixing does. The children of such unions are the most confused in the world. I should know. I'm a product of such an illicit relationship. My father, a successful African-American businessman, was snared by his white tramp of a secretary, who married him only for his money. After my father died when I was seven, rather mysteriously I must add, she abandoned me. Her family rejected me. If it hadn't been for my black grandmother, I don't know where I'd be today."

Queen Nefertari was overcome with emotions. "But because I was never taught anything about my true heritage," she continued with great difficulty, "for many years I didn't know who I was; where I belonged; or where the hell I was going. I was rejected by both the white and black communities. I was burdened with a terrible identity crisis. In the end, I was so filled with self-loathing and self-hatred I almost committed suicide."

Queen Nefertari wept at the end of this wrenching confession.

Rayvon, ever the compassionate host and lover of black women, again wrapped his right arm around Queen Nefertari. "It's all right, sister," he said softly. "It's all right." He glanced at his producer. "Let's go to a commercial break."

After the commercial break, Queen Nefertari appeared more composed and was able to explain her complex emotions. "Afro-Purists saved my life," she said. "They told me that despite my white skin, I was black, because of America's one-drop rule. They had me participate in this beautiful African ceremony that purged me of my whiteness and restored my heart, mind, and soul to their original black purity."

"Is that why you changed your name from Scarlett Clayborne to Queen Nefertari?" Rayvon asked, apparently conscious of his own pending name change.

"Yes. Scarlett Clayborne was nothing but a symbol of my degradation and brainwashing. Queen Nefertari, if your audience doesn't know, was the favorite wife of the great and powerful Egyptian king, Ramses II, who gave her enormous independent wealth and power and used to call her 'the one on whom the sun always shines.' After she died in 1225 BC, Ramses II built Queen Nefertari the most spectacular tomb in the Valley of the Queens, which is called the Sistine Chapel of Egypt."

There was tremendous applause for Queen Nefertari. Several black women in the audience wiped tears from their eyes. Even Chandler and his followers clapped.

"So you see, ladies and gentlemen, the true fruits of integration," Rayvon said. "It leads to nothing but tragedy. But maybe Mr. Wallace has a different take on the issue of race-mixing. Especially since he almost married a white woman."

"I'm sorry about what happened to Queen Nefertari," Nelson said. "She's obviously suffered great pain. But that doesn't excuse her irresponsible statements about interracial relationships. Integration and race-mixing are two different things. And the movie *Jungle Fever* is not about interracial relationships. It's about adultery. That black man had no business cheating on his wife with anyone, black or white."

"I see," Rayvon said, pursing his lips as he suddenly remembered Nell.

"And it's an absolute fallacy to claim that integration automatically leads to race mixing, and that the children of interracial couples are tragic mulattos," Nelson continued. "If anything, some of the best adjusted children I know are biracial and multicultural children. Why? Because they are brought up in families where differences are respected and celebrated. They are taught to have open minds. They're taught to regard people as human beings and to judge them as individuals. Most important, they aren't taught hatred as a family value."

"I see," Rayvon said. The audience was very still.

"And yes, I admit I was once engaged to a white woman," Nelson said. "I make no apologies for that. She was the best woman for me at the time. Just as the best woman for me at this time happens to be a black woman. And it's utter rubbish to allege that all interracial relationships are all about sex. If they were, they wouldn't last, given the tremendous pressure that society often brings to bear on such relationships. True, some interracial relationships are perverted, but so are some same-race relationships."

"I don't entirely blame black men for wanting to taste the forbidden fruit," Queen Nefertari said. "American society has brainwashed them into thinking that white is beautiful and black is ugly. There are over a million mixed marriages in the United States, and mostly because white women are nothing but temptresses."

"Can you elaborate, Queen Nefertari?" Rayvon asked, sensing in her statement a possible explanation for his own secret lust for white women.

But Queen Nefertari wasn't about to offer Rayvon a balm for his secret guilt. She was more interested in crucifying white women. "To tell you the truth," she said, "I just can't stand white girls who have nothing better to do than steal black men. And not just any black man, mind you. Oh, no. They always snare the best. The BEST. They leave us the ones who are in prison, on parole, on drugs, or gay."

"Right on," shouted several women in the audience.

"Why don't you date a white man for a change?" Nelson said. "There are certainly plenty of good white men around. And it might teach you to be tolerant."

"You won't catch me betraying my race," Queen Nefertari fumed. "Besides, what would I want with some skinny-lipped, pointy-nosed, flat-assed white boy? I want me a real man." The audience roared with laughter and clapped.

"I'm afraid we have to go to another commercial break," Rayvon said, seeing Feldman's signal. "But when we return, we'll get closing statements from our guests, and I'll give my own view on this very important subject."

As soon as the break was over, Rayvon gave Nelson the floor.

"All I can say to you, ladies and gentlemen," Nelson said, "Despite your jeers and name-calling, is that integration is the only game in town. America is our only home. We must learn to live together in peace and mutual respect, and, as Dr. King once said, to judge people not by the color of their skin, but by the content of their character."

"Integration has failed the black community," Queen Nefertari said. "It's failed because whites will never accept blacks as equals. They're scared stiff that if blacks and whites start mingling their blood and genes, then white people will always come out the losers. Mix black and white and black comes out. Never white. That's why America had Jim Crow; and that's why South Africa had apartheid. Black people are sick and tired of begging for acceptance from people who will never accept us. That's why I say, separation now, separation tomorrow, separation forever."

Queen Nefertari's battle-cry brought the crowd to its feet. Even Chandler and his men stood up and applauded vociferously. The cry, after all, was very familiar to them, bearing as it did an eerie familiarity to George Wallace's 1963 Inaugural speech in which he vowed to defy desegregation orders by liberal federal courts.

It was now Chandler's turn to deliver his peroration.

"Queen Nefertari and I are kindred spirits," Chandler said, "despite our obvious color differences. We both want the best for our people. I wholeheartedly agree with her when she says that integration has failed the black community. You can see its results all across America. It's failed because it's one more attempt at social engineering by those paternalistic liberals in Washington, who think that simply by mixing the races, everything will be honky-dory. I say that if blacks want separation, let them have it. They know what's best for their community, not some fat liberal bureaucrat with alligator shoes in Washington. I see nothing wrong in having blacks-only schools if that's what will improve the education of black children. Why should your children be forced onto buses that take them miles away from home to attend school with hostile whites?

"The same thing applies to blacks who want control of their own communities. Why shouldn't you have it? The Indians have their reservations and they're thriving on them. They're making a fortune on their casinos. I'll tell you the real reason why liberals keep insisting on integration. They want to deny you the opportunity to preserve and celebrate your unique heritage and the noble accomplishments of your race. They want to rob you of the chance to preserve the purity of your genes, which have produced so many famous African kings and queens. But if we let liberals, who are like Shakespeare's weird sisters, mix the races in some cauldron called a melting pot, your sense of pride and self-esteem will be lost in the hodgepodge. Your children won't know, as Queen Nefertari has so eloquently put it, whether they're black or white, where they come from, and where the hell they're going in this big and complicated world."

Incredibly, Chandler also received a standing ovation from black militants.

Finally, it was Rayvon's turn.

"My own personal view of integration, for what it's worth, is that, despite all its good intentions, it has clearly and manifestly failed. We saw the results in New Orleans after Hurricane Katrina hit. Integration has failed because it has lacked the full support of both blacks and whites. Why? Because blacks are proud of their distinct culture and community, and so are whites. Both groups fear that integration will lead to assimilation. Things they value most will disappear. Separatism, despite what its critics say, seems to me the most reasonable solution to an intractable and vexing problem. Its supporters, like myself, recognize that in order to thrive as black people, to instill in our children the kinds of values that will make them proud and productive citizens, we must build our communities up without any help from paternalistic liberals who, in the name of integration, only perpetuate the enslavement and alienation of black people."

Rayvon paused for a sip of water. "It is my hope that black separatists will become a factor in the upcoming gubernatorial election. Their agenda deserves to be heard and debated. To whites I say, it is in your best interest to support Afro-Purists, because their solution to the race problem is the only one that will give you the security you've been craving all along. I know that most of you secretly blame blacks for the rampant crime in America. So instead of speculating about aborting black babies, of constantly conspiring to keep blacks down, why don't you simply let my people go?"

There was tremendous applause from the audience for a show many believed would soon catapult Rayvon into the elite of talk show hosts, alongside Oprah, Dr. Phil, Jerry Springer, and Ellen Degeneres.

Hunter watched the show with Dawoud and Fadi inside the surveillance room. With Ramsey soaring in the polls, he now spent more time devising ways to sabotage his candidacy than accompanying him on the campaign trail.

"We'll see how long the fucking hypocrite will remain popular," Hunter said to Dawoud. "How's work on the tape coming along?"

"It's ready, sir," said Dawoud. "Should we send it out?"

"Not yet. We'll send it after the fund-raiser."

Chapter 25

Kessler's magnificent 126-foot, ocean-going, motor-sailor yacht named *Bismark*, which was powered by two 550-horsepower Baudouin engines, lazily cruised the warm, clear blue waters around Hilton Head Island. On its sunny teal deck sat Kessler and Hunter, smoking cigars and sipping wine as they waited for lunch to be served.

"Are you sure Clinton will be at the fund-raiser tonight?" said Kessler as he rubbed suntan lotion on his arms, legs and stomach. Seagulls hovered over the yacht, then screeched and flapped their wings as they flew on into the azure sky.

Hunter nodded. "I received word before I left this morning that he'll definitely show up. He may be a bit late, though." He squeezed suntan lotion onto his small hands.

"What brings him to North Carolina?"

"Apparently he's a great admirer of Ramsey's," Hunter said, rubbing the lotion onto his arms and legs. "They first met during a panel discussion on the future of race relations in America at an event called Renaissance Weekend, when Clinton was still governor. Ramsey told me that the event began right here on Hilton Head."

"I attended it once," Kessler said.

"You did?"

"Yeah. But I didn't like it. People there spoke too frankly for my taste."

A tall, slender brunette in a skimpy bikini, whose strings looked like they were about to snap from the weight of her grapefruit size breasts, brought Hunter and Kessler lunch. It consisted of roast goose with apple chestnut stuffing, hot buttered rum, oysters, and avocado salad. "Thank you, Elsa," Kessler said.

"You're welcome," Elsa said. "Would you like anything else?"

"I sure could use some dessert later," Kessler said, pinching her left buttock.

"Brigitte and I will be waiting for you below deck," Elsa said.

"Gorgeous, isn't she?" Kessler said, ogling Elsa as she wiggled her bottom on the way to the ladder leading to the lower deck. Her thong hid nothing.

"Sure is," Hunter said, and yet he felt no sexual emotion whatsoever. Such emotions had long died in him, replaced by a single one: revenge against liberals, specifically against Ramsey, for what happened to him more than thirty years ago.

Kessler and Hunter began eating.

"So what's the latest on Alison's baby?" asked Kessler. "The election is three weeks away and Ramsey's lead over Lynch keeps growing."

"The baby still hasn't been found," said Hunter. "But it doesn't matter."

"What do you mean it doesn't matter?" Kessler shot back. "If that fucking baby isn't found Ramsey will win by a landslide, and Operation Saladin will unravel."

"Not if I have anything to do with it," said Hunter. "Rayvon's show went better than expected for three reasons. First, Chandler's brilliant performance as a Klansman should throw the FBI off while enraging Ramsey so much that he'll give me even more control over the campaign's message. Second, Fadi and Dawoud have the tape of Rayvon ready, but the timing for its release has to be just right to expose him as a hypocrite so he can become leader of the Afro-Purists. And third, before I left I made sure that Alison comes under my powers even more after tonight's fund-raiser."

"What did you do?" asked Kessler, stuffing the oyster into his cupid mouth.

"Read these." Hunter handed Kessler two letters on pink

stationery.

Kessler quickly read the letters.

"Can you imagine," said Hunter, "Alison's humiliation and rage at Myron after she learns that he cancelled their wedding because of an addiction to prostitutes?"

"My God, this Myron is a fucking pervert," Kessler said.

"Not really," Hunter said. Again he flashed his cunning smile. "Those letters are forgeries. Myron never visited prostitutes during his book tour. But Alison doesn't know that and she'll believe anything. I got the idea from what Iago did with that handkerchief – a prized marriage present from Othello – he had his wife filch from Desdemona."

Kessler's eyes brightened. "I remember. Iago planted the handkerchief on Cassio, and then convinced the jealous Othello that Desdemona had given it to Cassio."

"And the insane nigger strangled Desdemona, thinking she was a whore, while all the time she was as innocent as a newborn babe. Having studied Alison's psychological profile, she'll act exactly like Othello, especially after she sees these pictures."

Hunter handed Kessler several photos he had retrieved from his briefcase.

Kessler ogled them. "Wow, how did you manage to get these?"

"They were easy to forge using Photoshop," said Hunter. "All I did was splice photos of Myron that Alison gave me, together with photos of nigger porn stars I found on the internet, to make computer-generated images of Myron having orgies in hotels during his book tour, after proposing to Alison. Like some of the tabloids do, you know."

Kessler clapped his hands. "You're a genius," he said.

"Operation Saladin is too important for me to be outwitted by niggers and nigger-lovers. But I have to be very careful around Myron. He's a smart one."

"What makes you say that?"

"I think he knows about that visit I paid his mother."

"What makes you think he knows?"

"He's been asking questions."

"What kind of questions?"

"Oh, where I grew up and how Ramsey came to know me."

"Who has he been asking these questions?"

"Nelson Wallace, the union organizer whose apartment I had Fadi and Dawoud bug after Ramsey hired him as an advisor."

"Do Myron and Nelson know each other?"

Hunter nodded. "They started corresponding shortly after Chanel gave Nelson a copy of Myron's book, *One Nation*, for his thirty-fourth birthday."

"What has Nelson told Myron?"

"The same story I told Ramsey and everyone else. That after graduating from the University of Alabama in 1968 I went into the Peace Corps, was posted to Egypt, where I remained for the next fifteen years because I'd fallen in love with the people and the culture. I then started an import-export business, which made me a millionaire, and then taught English Literature at the American University in Cairo. As a believer in Civil Rights, after my hero Jimmy Carter was elected President in 1976, I decided to return to the U.S. and go into politics with the mission of helping Democrats recapture the South."

"Brilliant cover," said Kessler. "But isn't there a danger that Myron might find out the truth if he keeps digging?"

"How can he?" Hunter said, confidently closing his day planner. "No one knows that as Ebenezer Bickley I was leader of the Fiery Cross. And thanks to the plastic surgeons you arranged for me, I'm now Reginald Hunter, one of the best political strategists in the country. Only Cone knows the truth and he thinks I died in a plane crash. And after the 'executors of my estate' sent him that rare gift as part of my so-called will, I'm told he wept tears of gratitude. No, partner, Cone won't betray the dear memory of a departed comrade. He'll carry my secret to the gas chamber."

Kessler wiped his mouth with an embroidered silk napkin. "I forgot to tell you, partner," he said, "but this morning I received a telegram from my contact within the governor's office in Alabama. Cone apparently has a new lawyer."

"A new lawyer?"

Kessler nodded. "And the lawyer has filed a last-minute clemency appeal with the governor, which may delay Cone's scheduled execution day after tomorrow."

"On what basis?"

"*The Montgomery Advertiser* says the lawyer doesn't believe Cone acted alone."

Hunter was thunderstruck. His face grew ashen.

"Has Cone talked?"

"No, he's remained loyal to his Klan oath," Kessler said. "And you're right, he'll never talk as long as he believes you died in a plane crash."

"Then there's no need to worry," Hunter said. "This is another one of those desperate last-minute appeals. Who's the lawyer?"

"You won't believe this," Kessler said. "He's the son of Nora Driessen, that Jewess who died with her nigger assistant when the Fiery Cross firebombed the offices of that liberal rag on the eve of the March on Washington in 1967."

"You must be kidding."

"I'm serious. His name is Isaac. Apparently since 2000 he's been traveling around the world investigating human rights abuses for Amnesty International. He's now back in Alabama representing death row inmates. And one of my spies said that he saw Isaac and Myron eating lunch at the Vintage Year restaurant in downtown Montgomery."

"Are you sure it was Myron?"

"I'm sure. Here's the photo my spy took." Kessler handed Hunter a black and white digital photo he had retrieved from his briefcase.

"That's Myron all right," Hunter said with a frown. "Alison told me that they attended Yale Law School together. But I wonder what he's doing in Montgomery."

"Maybe they were getting reacquainted," Kessler said.

Hunter scratched his head. "Maybe, and maybe not."

"You said that Myron will be at the fundraiser tonight?"

Hunter nodded. "He wants to talk to Ramsey and me about the campaign. But I have a feeling he wants to see Alison. But I bet you she won't want to have anything to do with him after she reads those letters and sees the photos."

Chapter 26

So this is why the fucking bastard dumped me, Alison thought with rage as she lay face down on the bed, her eyes red from crying. Two tear-stained letters were in front of her, along with a collection of very sexually explicit photos. Alison had read the letters more than a dozen times, but she couldn't bear to look at the photos. Once had been enough.

And to think that the whole time he was slipping that ring onto my finger, Alison thought as she fought back tears, *and saying I was the only one he'll ever love, he was carrying on with prostitutes behind my back.* Alison felt like bursting into tears again, but all her tears were gone. Only a deep ache remained in the pit of her stomach.

And the torture I've been putting myself through all these months, Alison thought as she rose from the bed and went to the bathroom for more Kleenex. *If I'd only known. And to think he's coming to the fundraiser tonight. I can't stand to even look at him.*

Alison had half a mind not to attend her father's fund-raiser that night. She didn't think she could control herself in front of a man she had once loved with all her heart, but who had betrayed her in the most intimate sense. She must talk to someone, the pain she felt was too deep to be dealt with alone. She thought of calling Eliot, who was still at his office, but decided against it. *I don't think I can go through with a confession right now.*

Alison thought of calling her mother. She was addressing a N.O.W. Regional conference in Chapel Hill. *The news would come as too much of a shock to her.*

She thought of calling her father, who was giving a speech on the environment at his alma mater, Davidson College. *I can't bear the thought of admitting that he'd been right to oppose the marriage in the first place.*

She thought of calling Chanel. *I can't trust her to be objective. She's been Myron's apologist since the breakup, and her boyfriend is a big fan of his.*

The only person left was Hunter. *He'll understand,* she thought, reaching for the phone. *Especially since he's been so concerned about saving my marriage. I wonder if he's back from the fundraising trip to Hilton Head he took this morning.*

Alison hurriedly dialed Hunter's cell phone number, which he had given her in case of an emergency. "Hi, Uncle Reggie," Alison said, trying hard not to burst out crying.

"What's wrong, my dear?" Hunter asked from the back seat of his bullet-proof limo as it left the Smith-Reynolds Airport in Winston-Salem. He had just flown in from Hilton Head Island in his Lear Jet. "Sounds like you've been crying."

"I have. For the last two hours."

Hunter feigned concern. "What happened? It's not the baby is it?"

"No. It's- it's-" Alison couldn't continue.

"What is it, dear? Do you want me to come over? I've just left the airport and I'm on Highway 52. I can be there in less than half an hour."

"No, I'll be fine, Uncle Reggie. I'm just terribly upset, that's all."

"Over what?"

"Over some letters and photos I received this morning."

"Letters and photos? From whom?"

"I don't know who sent them to me. They came without a return address."

Hunter smiled. "Really? What about them is upsetting you so much?"

Alison started sobbing.

"Calm down now, my dear," Hunter said, still smiling. He could imagine the raunchy photos and letters in Alison's possession, and secretly congratulated himself on having come up with the brilliant idea. Hunter reached into the small liquor cabinet built into the left side of the limo and poured himself a tot of brandy. He crossed his legs and settled deeper into the plush leather seat, thoroughly enjoying Alison's distress.

"The real reason Myron called off our wedding was because he was sleeping with prostitutes during his book tour. One of them is called Latisha."

"Prostitutes?" Hunter said, feigning the utmost surprise. "I don't believe it. Myron would never do such a thing. After all his professions of love for you?"

"He did. There's no doubt about that. These letters and photos are pretty graphic."

"I'm stunned, my dear. I thought the world of Myron. Whatever happened to honor among today's young men? Are you sure the letters are authentic?"

"They're authentic, Uncle Reggie," Alison said, gazing at the photos spread before her. "This is definitely Myron in the photos. And the poems he used to read to me apparently he also read to her. Remember the one I told you he loved reading to me?"

"Do you mean Elizabeth Browning's *How Do I love Thee?*"

"Yes. Apparently he loved reading it to Latisha also."

"It must have been his favorite line."

"And the things he said to her about me."

"What things dear?" Hunter asked, smiling.

"I can't possibly repeat them, Uncle Reggie."

"I understand." He paused, took another sip of his brandy, then said, "So, what do you plan to do, my dear? You're still coming to the fundraiser tonight, aren't you?"

"I don't think I can."

"I know how hurt you are, my dear," Hunter said. "But I know you're a strong woman. Please do come. It's important for your father. And President Clinton, your hero, will be there. You don't want to miss the opportunity to meet him, do you?"

"But Myron will also be there."

"Don't worry," Hunter said. "I'll be there too. And I'll do

everything I can to keep the double-crossing hypocrite away from my beloved godchild."

The Sawtooth Center for the Visual Arts on North Marshall Street in downtown Winston-Salem was a low red building with jagged gable windows that jutted up diagonally like the teeth of a saw. It housed galleries, weaving rooms, pottery studios, printing studios, wood-carving rooms and a darkroom. The large room upstairs had been set up for the elegant, invitation-only dinner. The centerpieces on each of the round tables were silver and gold-wrapped packages stacked artistically and overlaid with glittering ribbons.

Alison anxiously watched through the Center's glass doors as a steady stream of Mercedes, BMWs, Infinities, Jaguars, Lexuses, stretch limos, and Rolls-Royces pulled up to the curb. Elegantly dressed guests emerged from the vehicles, laughing and chatting.

She was standing at the entrance, next to Hunter, her mother, father, Eliot, Mary-Lou, and Theodore, greeting guests as they stepped in from the crisp October evening air. Alison looked absolutely gorgeous, having worked hard to whittle herself down to her pre-pregnancy weight of one hundred and twenty-two pounds. Her floor-length black velvet dress hugged her splendid figure and a set of her mother's heirloom jewels sparkled around her slender neck. Her dark shiny hair, arranged in loose curls, was swept up from her neck in a chignon. Despite her looks, Alison was in agony. *I don't know how I'll react when I see the bastard,* she thought as she forced herself to smile at each new arrival. *I'm so mad I could gouge out his eyes with my bare hands.*

"I've never voted for a Democrat in my life, but I'm voting for you," said a grinning banker with pudgy cheeks, pumping Ramsey's hand up and down.

"Thank you."

"I hear President Clinton might drop by tonight," Alison's born-again friend and one-time maid of honor Karen, whispered conspiratorially to Alison while her husband – a textile magnate and staunch conservative – chatted with Eliot. "Is that true?"

"The former President has a very busy schedule," Alison said diplomatically. "He's traveling across the South campaigning for various Democrats. But if he does show up tonight, it would be a great honor for my father."

"No doubt," Karen said. "I'd love to meet him, even though he's a Dem."

In preparation for a possible visit by the former President, who was still very popular among Democrats and independents eight years after leaving office, especially given the mess his successor Bush had made of things, a metal detector had been set up at the entrance. Secret service agents in dark suits and stoic faces were scattered throughout the spacious lobby and now and then they whispered into their sleeves.

Kessler arrived with his entourage of bodyguards. He was deeply tanned and wore a double-breasted, tapered Armani suit that flattered his paunch. He vigorously shook Ramsey's hand. "I see we're getting a good turnout – a very good turnout indeed."

"I really appreciate your support," Ramsey said.

"No trouble at all," said Kessler. "Even though I hate publicity, there's nothing I'd love more than to tell people that I helped elect the next great governor of our wonderful state. Is this lovely lady your daughter?" asked Kessler, looking at Alison.

"Yes. My one and only."

"Pleased to meet you, young lady," said Kessler, shaking Alison's hand.

"The pleasure is mine," said Alison.

"And this is my son-in-law, Eliot Whitaker," said Ramsey.

Kessler grinned as he shook Eliot's hand. "What a lovely pair you two make. You're exactly what the American family should look like. Beautiful, happy, and very much in love. I'm very sorry to hear about the baby. I hope he's found soon."

"Thank you," Alison said.

Ever the vigilant journalist, she was studying Kessler's features. Something about his satiated face made her feel uneasy. His eyes seemed to be stripping her naked.

It must be my imagination, Alison thought as Kessler moved on and began talking to Eliot's father. *My head is so full of those lewd photos that I'm projecting on everyone.*

Alison had been shaking hands for God knows how long when she heard Eliot say, "I'm hungry. Do you want me to get you anything, honey?"

"Yes, please," Alison replied, though she wasn't hungry. She simply wanted to be nice to Eliot, to make up to him for having treated him so badly during all those months she had been foolishly yearning for the perfidious Myron.

"I'll get you something."

"Thank you, honey."

Eliot headed toward a long table laden with appetizers in the gallery. North Carolina's elite examined the works of art that would be auctioned later in the evening while they waited their turn for melon cocktail, herbed bread, lamb meatballs, spicy chicken wings, and Edam dip. A bartender served mixed drinks and wine in the adjacent corner. Little girls in frilly dresses with ribbons in their hair wandered through the crowd selling the balloons that bobbed over their heads for $1000 apiece. Each balloon contained a number that could only be retrieved by popping the balloon. The numbers could then be used to get one of the elegantly wrapped gifts in the table displays.

Alison's heart skipped a beat when she heard a siren, and then saw a stream of police cars turn into Marshall Street. The police cars led a procession of three long black limousines, which pulled up to the curb, followed by several more cars. A secret service agent opened the back door of the middle limo and President Clinton climbed out.

Alison sucked in her breath. She had never met him in person. A crowd of onlookers immediately formed around the President, though secret service agents kept them behind the wooden barricades. The President shook as many outstretched hands as possible, and occasionally stopped to chat with an awed onlooker as he made his way to the entrance to the Center. *He's much taller in person*, Alison thought, as Clinton came up the stairs. *And quite gregarious.* The former President, who looked slimmer since his heart surgery, hugged Ramsey, slapped him on the back, and joked with him about the rigors of the campaign trail and the challenges of being a Southern governor.

"And you must be Alison," Clinton said warmly, looking directly into her face. "The one with a mission to afflict the comfortable and comfort the afflicted."

Speechless, all Alison could do was nod. *My God, he even knows the reason I went into journalism.*

"I enjoyed some of the articles you wrote for *Street News*."

"You've read them, Mr. President?" Alison was astonished.

"I used to read the paper on my way to my foundation's office,"

Clinton said. "I'm concerned about the plight of the homeless, and wanted to find out what they really think. I must say I share many of your observations about their plight."

Alison wanted to say something but she was tongue-tied.

"And by the way," the President went on. "I'm deeply saddened to hear that your baby hasn't been found yet. And Hillary is too."

He really means it. Alison managed a hoarse, "Thank you, Mr. President."

"I hope Chief Evans has been quite helpful," the President said.

Alison was stunned. *How does he know Chief Evans,* she wondered.

As if reading her mind, Clinton answered her question. "Chief Evans and I are good friends," he said. "He's originally from my hometown. As a matter of fact he and I went to high school together. And I was a year behind him at Georgetown."

How in the world does he remember all these minute details about people? Alison wondered, awestruck. Her eyes followed Clinton as he moved on down the line, shaking hands, and stopping to chat to strangers as if they were bosom buddies. *If Monica Lewinsky hadn't happened,* Alison thought, *Clinton would have easily been remembered as the best American president since FDR. And, who knows, Gore might be president and there would have been no Iraq War. What a costly affair.*

"Hi, Alison," a familiar voice jarred her from her reverie.

Alison felt suddenly faint as she saw Myron standing before her.

"How are you?" he said, shaking hands awkwardly.

"I'm fine," she said coolly. She abruptly pulled her hand away from his. All she could think about were Latisha's steamy letters. The contents of one particular letter were so deeply painful they were branded in her memory. *"The honky bitch was quite a fool to think you'd marry her simply because you gave her a ring. But all liberal honky bitches are like that. She wanted you only as a trophy, as proof that she isn't a racist. She can never understand you – emotionally, spiritually and sexually – like a black woman can. If only she knew that each time you were reading her a poem, each time you were fucking her, you were thinking of me, comparing her to me, your black princess. I'm glad you came to your senses and ditched her, my black prince. Now we can enjoy pleasuring each other without restraint, and without worrying about that frigid honky bitch.*

Yours always and forever, Latisha."

Recalling these words so overwhelmed Alison with rage that she wanted to scream at Myron, "What are you doing here, you fucking hypocrite?" Fortunately, Hunter suddenly appeared. "Well, well, well," he said, "if it isn't Myron Pearson."

"You look great in that tux, Uncle Reggie," Alison said, relieved.

"I chose this style especially for you, my dear. It's a Pierre Cardin."

Hunter winked at her, and then turned to Myron.

"I'm glad you stopped by," he said, shaking his hand coldly. "But I'm afraid I don't have the time to talk to you. I hope you don't take offense when I say that with Ramsey thirty points ahead of Lynch, we don't need LUPA's help. Thanks anyway."

Eliot came back with a platter of food, which he handed to Alison.

"By the way, have you met Alison's husband?" Hunter asked.

"No, I haven't," Myron said awkwardly, shaking hands with Eliot.

Hunter spotted Kessler in the middle of the room.

"Please excuse me," he said, and went over to him.

"If you'll excuse me," Myron said, and went outside.

Shortly thereafter, Chanel appeared, dressed in a flowing emerald gown. Nelson was right beside her in a black tux with a white bow-tie, which became him rather well.

"You look great," Chanel said, hugging Alison. "Hi, Eliot. How are you?"

"Fine, you look lovely."

"Thanks. This is my fiancé, Nelson Wallace."

"Hi," Eliot said, shaking his hand. "I've heard a lot about you. I read a story in the *Winston-Salem Journal* the other day about how you didn't think it was in the best interest of workers at Whitaker Tobacco to unionize because – " As Eliot and Nelson started talking, Chanel whispered into Alison's ear, "I've got to talk to you, girlfriend."

"Excuse us, guys, we're going to the ladies room," Alison said. "We'll be right back." As they made their way through the crowd, Chanel squeezed Alison's arm.

"Guess who I saw standing outside!" Chanel said.

"Who?" said Alison.

"Myron!"

"I just spoke to him," said Alison, coldly.

"You have? How did it go?"

"Eliot's my husband, you know."

"Of course I know that," said Chanel. "But you've been so looking forward to seeing Myron. Remember what you said during our hiking trip?"

"That was foolish talk. Now I know where my loyalty lies. It lies with people who aren't hypocrites and don't betray me. From now on I want nothing to do with Myron."

"Whoa, wait a minute, girl," Chanel said, taken aback. "What's going on?"

Alison told her about the package she had received that morning and its contents.

Chanel was horrified. "I can't believe this." she shook her head. "There must be some mistake. Myron sleeping with prostitutes? I'm going out to talk to him about it."

Alison grabbed Chanel by the arm and pulled her back. "No, don't! It's over between him and me. He's got Latisha now. And I'm Eliot's wife."

"But what if he's the father of your baby?"

Alison's eyes flashed. "Why do you have to ask such complicated questions?" she demanded. "You did it right before my wedding. Now you're doing it again."

"I still wish you had listened to me and not walked down that aisle to marry a man you don't love," Chanel said. "Then you wouldn't be in this mess."

Alison was about to say something when a familiar voice made her turn.

"Ladies, what's all the bickering about?" Hunter asked, walking toward them, a concerned look on his face. "Anything I can help resolve?"

"Oh, Uncle Reggie," Alison said, a bit embarrassed. "We weren't bickering. Chanel and I were just talking about the missing baby." Befuddled by Alison's changed demeanor, Chanel excused herself and stepped outside to talk to Myron.

Chapter 27

I wonder why Alison is behaving so strangely, Myron thought as he stood outside the entrance to the Sawtooth Center, cell phone in hand. *I wish she'd given me a chance to tell her what Isaac has found out about Hunter.*

"Hi, Myron," a female voice said.

Myron looked up and saw Chanel.

"Hi, Chanel."

"Too crowded for you in there?"

"Yeah. I also needed to make a call. But before I do, can you do me a favor?"

"Sure."

"I know that Alison is a married woman now," Myron said, "and that it would be awkward for me to talk to her. But I need to warn her about something very important. But for some reason, she hates the very sight of me. I don't know why."

"I do," Chanel said, buttoning her coat against the nippy cold. "And I came out here to talk to you about that. But first, what is the warning about?"

Myron hesitated a moment, and then said, "It's about Hunter, her father's campaign manager. But please promise you won't tell Alison until I say so. The information is potentially explosive. But it still needs to be verified."

Chanel had a puzzled look on her face. "I give you my word I won't tell her."

Myron told a stunned Chanel what Isaac had uncovered about Hunter.

As soon as Chanel stepped outside, Hunter wrapped an arm around Alison's shoulder. "I know it must be hard to know Myron's in the same building with you, my dear," he said, "but you've behaved splendidly, my dear, splendidly."

"I still can't believe he'd do such a thing."

"I can't either. But you saw the pictures and the letters."

Alison started crying.

"Oh, you poor thing. Would you like me to drive you home?"

"No, thanks." She straightened and wiped her eyes. "I'll be okay."

"Alison, I hope you don't mind my saying this," Hunter said. "But you're still fairly young, despite being a married woman. There are a lot of things you don't understand about men. Men like Myron are a dime a dozen. And it has nothing to do with skin color, mind you. Both white and black men of his kind behave the same way. They see a pretty face and they go for it. They have no sense of commitment, honor, or responsibility. They have a sense of entitlement. They grab what they want, use it, and then discard it. It hurts me to tell you this, but that's exactly what he's done with you."

"I guess you're right," she said softly.

"I know that Eliot hasn't been the perfect husband," Hunter said, "and that you've had your share of differences. But what married couple doesn't? Marriage is never perfect. It's something that requires constant work. It also requires compromises from time to time, and honest communication. I'm confident that once Dylan is found he'll bring you and Eliot closer together. That's why I'm doing the best I can to locate him. You'll be happy to know that I've just increased my portion of the reward to $1 million."

Alison gasped. "One million dollars?"

"Yes. This morning. That's how much I care about your well-being, my dear."

"Thank you, Uncle Reggie."

Hunter kissed her on the cheek. "You're welcome, my dear. It's the least I can do for my godchild. But please promise me that you'll do your part to make the marriage work? I've talked to Eliot and he's pledged to do his part."

"I'll try."

"That's my girl," Hunter said. "Now let's rejoin your father and the President. This is a big night, Alison. I estimate that when it's over, thanks to Mr. Kessler, your father's campaign will have raised well over two million dollars."

"Thanks for all you've done for the campaign, Uncle Reggie," Alison said.

"It's my pleasure, my dear," Hunter said. "And don't forget there's only two weeks to go before Election Day. With your father enjoying his biggest lead ever over Lynch – thirty-five points according to the latest Gallup poll – only a miracle can prevent him from becoming the next governor of North Carolina. And he'll owe his victory to you. One can't put a price on the sacrifices you've made to help him beat the odds."

Listening to Hunter, Alison felt her strength renewed. *Uncle Reggie is right,* she thought as they headed toward the gallery to join the dinner guests already seated and listening to former President Clinton at the podium deliver a ringing endorsement of the Ramsey campaign. *From my pain and misery has come a lot of good. But there's only one problem, and a very serious one at that. What if Dylan turns out to be Myron's child?*

Aboard his flight to DC, Myron thought, *If there's a link between Ebenezer Bickley and Hunter, as Isaac believes there is, then Ramsey's campaign is in deep trouble.*

"Why are you so mad at Myron?" Chanel asked Alison, who was sitting across a square, oak table on the balcony of the Market Square Restaurant in downtown High Point. It was three days after the fundraiser and Chanel had asked her to lunch.

Alison gave Chanel a sharp look. "Let's not talk about that hypocrite, okay?"

Chanel laughed. "You're still in love him, aren't you?"

Tears formed in Alison's eyes. She was silent for a long while. Finally, she bit her lower lip and said, "Yes. I still love him. I've never stopped loving him. That's why what he's done hurts so much. And I don't know what to do. I'm so confused."

"I understand how you feel, girl," Chanel said, reaching across the table and taking Alison by the hand. "That's why I'm here. I want to help you. But I can't unless you're willing to listen to me instead of being angry and defensive."

"I'm listening."

"The first thing I'd do if I were you, is to tell Eliot about Myron."

Alison stared at Chanel. "Are you crazy? He'll go ballistic."

"But he's got to know. Either you tell him, or the media will tell him. And you know what happens when the media breaks a story."

"Why does the media have to find out?"

"Have you forgotten about Dylan? What if he's found and turns out to be Myron's baby? The media will have a field day exploiting the fact that he's mixed. His little brown face will be plastered everywhere – on TV, in tabloids, on the front page of newspapers. How would that make Eliot feel? You've got to tell him, girlfriend."

"I see what you mean," Alison said. "I'll do so as soon as possible."

"So what is it you wanted to tell me?" Eliot asked.

He and Alison were sitting on a picnic table at a park overlooking Oak Hollow Lake, the day after Alison's lunch with Chanel. They had just finished a three-mile run. Eliot, after being warned during his annual check-up that his blood pressure was high and that he was courting a heart attack, was trying to get back into shape.

"It's about the baby," Alison began, playing with one of two paper cups beside a tall bottle of Perrier water, which they had shared.

Eliot grew tense. He found their conversations about the kidnapping irritating and futile. They always ended up shouting accusations at each other, blaming each other as if it had been within their power to prevent the kidnapping.

"Look, I've been keeping in constant touch with Chief Evans and the police," Eliot said. "If there were anything, anything at all, that could be done to get our child back, it's being done. There's nothing more to talk about."

"Yes, there is." She said it so firmly that Eliot studied her face with a puzzled expression. Gazing out across the shimmering water she said, with a calmness that surprised her: "Dylan may not be your child."

"Could you repeat that? I don't think I heard you right."

"You might not be Dylan's father."

Eliot stared at her in horror. "You mean you cheated on me?"

"No. I didn't say that."

"Then how in the world could Dylan not be my son?"

"There's a possibility he was conceived shortly before we were married because I was set to marry another man three weeks before I married you."

Eliot was so stunned he couldn't utter a word.

Having begun, Alison felt compelled to confess the whole truth. "Do you remember how cool I was toward you on our honeymoon? I knew that I shouldn't be getting married so soon after breaking up with someone I had deeply loved. As a matter of fact, I almost bolted from the church on our wedding day. That's how torn I felt. And that's why I've been so reluctant to make love during our entire marriage."

Eliot started pacing up and down, his fists shoved into his Adidas sweat pants. He kicked a clod of dirt, trying hard to control his temper. So tell me," he demanded. "When the hell did you realize the baby might not be mine?"

"As soon as I found out I was pregnant."

"Why the hell didn't you tell me then?" he shouted.

"I was afraid to because of my dad's campaign."

"Bullshit!" He pounded the picnic table with his fist. The bottle and cups jumped. "You were planning to pass off another man's child as mine, weren't you?"

"No! Like I said, the baby might be yours. I decided to wait until it was born. I thought I'd be able to tell from his appearance whether or not he was yours."

"That's the most fucking illogical statement I've ever heard," Eliot snapped. "How the hell were you going to tell?"

Alison paused a long time. Finally, with a calmness that surprised even her, she said, "Because the man I was involved with is black."

Eliot's eyes widened, his jaw dropped. He looked like a man who had been struck by a freight train. "Did you say he's black?"

"Yes."

"Black as in black?"

"Yes."

"You slept with a black man?"

"Are you deaf?" Alison shouted. "And stop looking at me like that."

"Like what?"

"Like I've got some kind of loathsome disease."

"For all I know, you do!"

Overcome with rage, Eliot grabbed the empty Perrier bottle and slammed it against the cement floor of the picnic shelter. It smashed into tiny pieces that flew outward in every direction. Flying shards of glass struck Alison's legs and arms and made her wince. Alison had never seen Eliot so angry. She clambered over a picnic chair and backed away from him, uncertain what he might do next.

"How many black men did you sleep with?" Eliot demanded. "Huh? How many? Twenty? Thirty? Fifty? One hundred?"

"How dare you talk to me like that!" Alison shouted. "What do you take me for?"

"A slut."

"That's not true."

Eliot was so furious he didn't know what to do. He wrung his hands. He stared into empty space. He paced back and forth, muttering curses.

"Was he a good FUCK, huh?" Eliot said mockingly. "Did he do it to you all night? Was his cock two feet long?"

Alison realized that Eliot was feeling threatened. He obviously believed in the Myth of the Black Male Sex Machine and was afraid he didn't measure up.

"Eliot, we'll talk about this once you've calmed down, okay?" Alison said. "I'm going home."

"Good riddance."

She headed for the shiny black Cherokee in the parking lot up the hill, overlooking a row of clay tennis courts, climbed in, and then drove home.

On the way, she picked up her cell phone and called Chanel.

"I told him, like you suggested," Alison said.

"What happened?"

"He snapped." Alison told Chanel everything that had transpired.

"Let me talk to him," Chanel said. "Where is he?"

"I don't know," Alison said. "Some of the things he said made me so mad that I left him at the park. He must be walking home by now."

*****

Chanel quickly climbed into her fire-engine red Porsche and drove straight to Oak Hollow Lake. She cruised slowly down Oakview Road, and then around the lake looking for Eliot. She saw him ahead on the right, walking on a red clay footpath, head bowed. She pulled up beside him and lowered the car's window.

"Get in," she said.

Eliot kept walking, his jaw firmly set.

"Alison told me what happened. Get in and let's talk."

"There's nothing to talk about."

"Yes, there is. Come on, get in. I'll drive you home. You've got at least three more miles to go and it's hot." Reluctantly Eliot got into the Porsche and Chanel sped up. The cool breeze from the air conditioner quickly dried Eliot's sweat.

"The color of Alison's former boyfriend isn't the issue, Eliot," Chanel said.

"How do you know?"

"Because I know you. You aren't a bigot. Let's face it. You've just received the biggest shock of your life. The baby you thought was yours might not be."

"You're right," Eliot said, sighing. "My reaction is partly because I had a strong feeling all along that the baby was not mine."

"What do you mean?"

"Can you keep a secret?"

"Sure."

Eliot looked at Chanel for a long time. Then he blurted out, "I'm gay."

Chanel stopped the car dead in the middle of the street, as if she had just suffered a heart attack. She quickly pulled to the side. "What did you just say?" she stammered.

"I said I'm gay."

"You're kidding me."

"I'm not. I came out my freshman year of college."

"Does Alison know?"

"No one knows except Hunter."

"Hunter. How did he find out?"

"He caught me at a gay bar in Greensboro one night a year and a half ago," Eliot said. "I was there with my partner, Peter, who's a painter. He always travels with me whenever I go on trips abroad because that's the only way we can be safe."

"What was Hunter doing at a gay bar?"

"He said he'd just been hired as Ramsey's campaign manager," Eliot said, "and that he was doing research into issues that were going to be key in the 2006 midterm elections. He said Gay Rights was going to be one of them."

Chanel smiled.

"What's so funny?"

"Oh, nothing."

"Anyway, he asked me if my father knew that I was gay. When I replied that he didn't, and that if he ever found out, he would disinherit me, Hunter recommended that I hide the fact by getting married. And he suggested Alison."

"He did?"

"Yes. He said he could arrange it. I was skeptical at first. But when he arranged for Alison and I to have dinner and she agreed to marry me, I was in awe of him."

For a while Chanel considered these stunning revelations. Finally, she said, "So if you're gay, why were you so mad at Alison?"

"It was just an act. After all, she knows me as straight, and it would have been strange, would it not, if I hadn't reacted angrily. Also Hunter, who knew that I was a liberal, said that I had to act like a conservative to convince my dad that I wasn't gay."

"I see."

"So who's the guy who might be Dylan's father?"

"His name is Myron Pearson."

"The one I met at the fundraiser?"

"Yes."

"Does Myron still love Alison?"

Now that Eliot had admitted to being gay, Chanel knew that telling him the truth wouldn't hurt him. "Yes," she said. "Myron has never stopped loving Alison. In fact, the day of your wedding last fall, she almost bolted from Duke Chapel. But she knew that if she did, and the press found out that the reason she didn't marry you was because she was in love with a black man, her father's campaign would be destroyed."

Eliot sighed. "You know, I've sensed for a long time that Alison was keeping something from me, just as she must have sensed I was keeping something from her. It began on our honeymoon. She had this faraway look in her eyes all the time, as if she was remembering someone. And she was reluctant for us to make love. I didn't mind it, though I pretended to. From then on our marriage went downhill." They rode in silence for a few minutes, then Eliot said, "Does Myron know that he might be Dylan's father?"

"He doesn't," Chanel said. "Since she married you, despite her love for Myron, Alison hasn't had any contact with him. That's how seriously she took her vows."

"Shouldn't he be told? Just in case?"

"That's a good idea," Chanel said. "I'll give him a call."

"Should I finally tell Alison that I'm gay?"

"Not yet," Chanel said. "Furniture Market is coming up and Alison will be quite busy helping her Mom. Also, Myron's friend Isaac has been digging into Hunter's background for some time and wants us to keep things quiet until his investigation is done. He has a feeling what he finds out may affect Ramsey's campaign."

"Okay," Eliot said. "I also need your advice on something?"

"What?"

"Hunter told me that the Rayvon Turlington show wants Alison and me to appear to discuss the baby," Eliot said. "Do you think we should accept?"

"I wouldn't if I were you."

"Why not? Hunter said it might help us locate Dylan."

"I doubt that very much," Chanel said. "Unless you and Alison are willing to reveal on the show that your marriage is a sham, and that Dylan might be mixed."

"I see what you mean," Eliot said.

Chapter 28

Peter Feldman, the executive producer of *The Rayvon Turlington Show*, received a special delivery package via UPS one Thursday afternoon. It arrived when he was putting on his brown London Fog overcoat to leave early for the day. Feldman was a very happy man. Since the show on integration five weeks ago, the ratings of Rayvon's Afrocentric talk show had skyrocketed, as had advertising revenues. Syndication negotiations with several major distributors were already under way, and Rayvon had already been approached by agents from New York firms dangling lucrative book and movie deals.

Rayvon was the pride of the Piedmont black community, and Feldman, a conservative who believed in racial pride, self-reliance, responsibility, and family values, especially when they increased the bottom line and pacified him for having once opposed integration, felt very proud to have made his contribution to racial progress. Also, negotiations with Rayvon over a long-term contract were going smoothly, despite Rayvon's insisting that he was worth much more than Feldman was offering.

The package Feldman received was wrapped neatly in plain brown paper. It had no return address. Curious, Feldman set down his Samsonite briefcase and opened the package. Inside he found a video cassette labeled: *The Truth about Rayvon.* Puzzled, Feldman popped it into his briefcase and hurried home, eager to keep a dinner date with his wife to celebrate the phenomenal success of *The Rayvon Turlington Show.*

The ranch-style house in Jamestown was empty when Feldman arrived. His wife had taken their four-year-old son and six-year-old daughter to soccer practice and had left a note saying she would be back in time for them to go out to their favorite Italian restaurant. Since he had about half an hour to kill, Feldman kicked off his Rockport shoes, loosened his woven cotton tie with the logo of his alma mater, Wake Forest University, pushed the videocassette into the slot in the VCR, and sat down in a recliner in his living room to watch. His beady eyes grew into saucers when he saw his ticket to fame and fortune smoking meth and having oral sex with a naked blonde. He watched the entire tape from start to finish, three times, pausing at certain crucial scenes, and then snapped off the TV in horror, disgust, and outrage.

"The fucking hypocritical bastard," Feldman swore out aloud. He reached for the package, wondering if there was any accompanying note. Sure enough, an unsigned note, which had escaped Feldman's attention, was at the bottom of the envelope containing the tape. It read: "You have twenty-four hours to fire the bastard, Mr. Feldman. After that time, this tape, which is but the tip of the iceberg, will make headlines nationwide."

A livid Feldman instantly reached for the phone.

Rayvon was grooming himself for a night out to celebrate the success of his show when the phone rang. He was wearing a suit made of Kente cloth and looked in every way the African prince he fancied himself to be. He answered on the first ring with a "Yo," thinking it was his date, Queen Nefertari. The two were going to see *Othello*, which was showing at the High Point Theater. Queen Nefertari was planning to critique the play in the upcoming issue of *The Motherland,* and Rayvon wanted to see it because he was still in search of further psychological insights into why he loved sleeping with white women.

"Rayvon, this is Feldman."

"Hey, Peter," said Rayvon in a breezy tone. "What's up? Have you come to your senses and realized the reasonableness of my terms?"

"I *have* come to my senses, Rayvon."

"Good. Then you can have me for another year. Beyond that I can't commit."

"The station doesn't even need you for one minute, Rayvon."

"What are you saying?"

"You heard what I said," Feldman said. "You're fired."

"Pardon me?" Rayvon said, stunned.

"My station is not a haven for hypocrites."

"Hypocrites?" Rayon fumed. "Are you calling me a hypocrite, you fucking racist? I've sensed for a long time that you were nothing but a paternalistic, condescending closet racist who thinks that I'm one of those shuffling, step-n-fetchit slaves back on massa's plantation! You're badly mistaken, Feldman. I know who I am."

"Do you?" Feldman said sarcastically.

"Yes. I'm a descendant of the proud Mangetu tribe of Africa and I won't take any crap from the white power structure that can't deal with strong black men. I don't need you, a member of the white power establishment, to validate my identity and heritage."

"Who do you need, Rayvon? A white woman?"

"What?"

"Read *The National Inquirer.*"

Feldman hung up.

The sensational photos of Rayvon smoking meth and having oral sex with a blonde appeared the next day in a special edition of *The National Inquirer*. They caused a sensation around North Carolina and across the nation. The photos were appropriately censored because they were too explicit, but there was no mistaking who was doing what to whom. Along with the front-cover picture of Rayvon on his knees in front of a naked Nell, there was a ten-page spread of more salacious photos inside.

The headline read: "Famed Lover of Black Women Finally Reveals His True Preference." The accompanying article read:

"Rayvon Turlington, host of *The Rayvon Turlington Show*, North Carolina's most popular Afrocentric program, which was on the verge of national syndication, was caught in a red-hot tryst with a white aerobics instructor named Nell Harmon. Turlington, a former NBA player well-known for his strong condemnation of black athletes and entertainers who date or marry white women, was caught in the very act he so vociferously denounced in others. Turlington had repeatedly charged that black men in relationships with white women were disrespecting black womanhood. He even went so far as to call them traitors to their race. Who's the traitor now?"

Hunter had sent the tapes not only to Feldman and *The National Inquirer*, but also to dozens of TV and radio stations, newspapers, and magazines across the U.S., which had a field day with the scandal. The public had grown tired of politics and war news and was hungering for titillating stories about race-mixing scandals à la the O.J. Simpson trial.

Dozens of reporters staked out Rayvon's condo.

"What's your response to the pictures?" a journalist for a British tabloid screamed at Rayvon as he got out of his BMW and hurried to his condo, surrounded by two Afro-Purist bodyguards with stern faces, bow ties, dark suits, and shades.

"I was set up by the system, man," Rayvon said angrily. "I don't even know the girl. The white power structure is out to destroy black leaders like me. Just like the FBI tried to destroy black leaders like Dr. King with manufactured sex scandals."

"But the photos are real, Rayon, and they show you were an eager participant," said a correspondent for *Der Spiegel*.

"I was drugged, man. I had no control over what I was doing."

"Did you say you were drugged?" asked a journalist for a French magazine.

"Yes. You guys don't know the insidious nature of racism in this country. The woman was an FBI agent. The FBI does this kind of thing all the time to black leaders it wants to discredit. Black men are an endangered species."

Rayvon disappeared inside the condo, leaving reporters scratching their heads and goatees, wondering what in the world the FBI and endangered species had to do with Rayvon's sexual preferences. But it was the season for bizarre conspiracy theories. Even the venerable *New York Times* had recently reported in one of its editorials that over a quarter of African-Americans believed that AIDS was part of a white conspiracy to commit genocide against blacks. As for the tabloids, conspiracy theories were their staple. The week before, *The Globe* had reported that the U.S. Congress was secretly controlled by Martians in cahoots with Nazi zombies.

But the black community around North Carolina, even though it knew that the FBI and the White Power Structure were capable of anything and had previously done many underhanded things to discredit black leaders, surprised pundits and skeptics this time. The groundswell of knee-jerk support that Rayvon had expected didn't materialize.

A statewide Mason-Dixon poll conducted shortly after the scandal broke showed that the majority of black North Carolinians did not believe Rayvon had been set up. Even more startling was the fact that the poll revealed that, for the first time, blacks no longer bought the argument that blacks should support black leaders simply because they are black, regardless of their guilt or innocence.

The mainstream press hailed this as a remarkable departure from how the black community had reacted in cases such as the ones involving O. J., Marion Barry and other black leaders and celebrities accused of crimes. African-American women, in particular, were Rayvon's harshest critics. They felt insulted, deceived, and betrayed. Their unanimous opinion was that Rayvon had indeed been caught with his pants down. Not surprisingly, the only group of blacks to rally to Rayvon's side were the Afro-Purists, led by a defiant Queen Nefertari. She urged the black community to support one of its own out of racial loyalty, regardless whether he was guilty or not.

"We must stick together!" she said. "Or else the white power structure will destroy us through its divide-and-conquer tactics."

But the black community didn't buy such an argument.

After he was fired, Rayvon publicly repudiated what he called his "slave name." As Shaka Zulu, he was initiated into the mysteries of Afro-Purism. Given his charisma and rage – especially the latter – he soon became the black separatist group's most militant and popular leader to date, as Hunter had predicted. As was often the case with discredited blacks who blamed their problems on the white power establishment, Rayvon was a big hit on the college lecture circuit, and was booked solid with lectures for Black History Month. He crisscrossed the country passionately preaching the message that integration had failed the black community, that blacks would get no justice in America, that those blacks who supported integration were Uncle Toms, and that the U.S. Congress should pay African-Americans reparations so they could either set up their own independent state or return to the Motherland.

"Afro-Purists," Rayvon always vowed at the end of his canned speeches, "will be a force to be reckoned with in the upcoming Governor's election in North Carolina."

Chapter 29

The week Rayvon's sex scandal broke coincided with the start of the fall International Home Furnishings Market, when furniture connoisseurs from all over the world descended on High Point to sample the latest in furniture lines displayed in over 2,200 exhibits housed in more than 150 buildings, covering approximately 7 million square feet. The furniture market was big business: Americans alone spent $14 billion each year on furniture, and there were over 4,800 furniture companies in the country, employing more than 280,000 people. One of those companies, New South Fine Furniture Gallery, had 200 employees and more than $5 million in gross annual revenues.

With her husband proving to be the quintessential Teflon candidate and seemingly poised to become the next governor of North Carolina, Darlene took time out of her busy campaign schedule to devote herself to showcasing the newest furniture line manufactured by New South Fine Furniture.

The family-owned furniture company was a perennial favorite among buyers, mainly because Darlene, with Alison's help, had designed a much-sought-after line of eclectic furniture that combined the avant-garde with the traditional.

"Maybe we should cluster those brass lamps together on that

antique table," Darlene told Alison. Market was already half-over and Darlene was still rearranging. The showroom occupied four thousand square feet on the green concourse of the IHFC building on East Commerce Street and was brimming with buyers from across the world.

"Mom, everything looks fine just the way it is. You did a great job of designing the room settings. Orders are already pouring in. The buyers from Bloomingdale's and Macy's bought a whole slew of case goods. It's the best market we've had since the 1995."

"Oh, all right," Darlene said. "I'll let it go. But I definitely need to lower that painting over the black leather sofa. There's too much of a gap."

Alison rolled her eyes. "Mom, just relax. The people who pay attention to wall art are in the accessories wing."

"Where's Caldwell?"

"He's out trying to find more drivers. We've been swamped with orders."

A group of Japanese businessmen in dark blue suits brushed by Alison's shoulder on their way into the showroom. Alison stepped aside and checked her watch.

"I'd better get back to greeting customers," she said, noticing that it was already 4:30 p.m. "I need to leave early today. I'm helping Chanel with her engagement party."

"Where is it?"

"At Noble's Grille in Winston-Salem. Will you be okay?"

"Sure. I hope Caldwell finds more drivers."

Unable to find experienced drivers, Caldwell decided to try one more time to entice Buck to come back to work, despite the acrimonious way they had parted. Caldwell was prepared to give him a hefty raise. *If he proves reliable, I might even recommend him for a promotion,* Caldwell thought as he pulled into the driveway of Buck's remote farm house. Nancy, who had just finished showering, answered the door wearing a loose house dress and fuzzy slippers. Her blond hair was up in curlers and some strands had come loose and hung in spirals beside her pale cheeks.

"Sorry, Mr. Caldwell," she said. "Buck's not home."

"Do you expect him any time soon?"

"I really couldn't say."

"By the way, congratulations," Caldwell said, catching sight of a baby swinging in a battery-operated Gerry swing in the far corner of the living room. "Boy or girl?"

"Boy. Buck Junior."

"Well, tell Buck to give me a call if he's interested in his old job."

"I don't think he wants it back."

"Has he found another?"

"Yes," Nancy lied.

"Well, I won't bother him again. Goodbye."

Caldwell started down the front steps, then stopped and turned. "Did I by any chance leave my hat the last time I was here?"

Nancy hesitated before replying. She remembered that Buck had urinated in it. But she had washed it and it was hanging in the back of the house.

"It got kind of wet and I had to hang it to dry. I'll go fetch it."

"Thanks."

Nancy made her way to the back of the house, leaving Caldwell standing by the door. The minute she left, the baby started bawling. Caldwell went over to the swing. The baby had been in deep shadow and his features were hard to see from the front door. Caldwell stepped back in surprise at seeing the baby up close. He had no doubt the child was mixed. As Caldwell scrutinized its features, wondering how in the world Buck and Nancy could have conceived a mixed-race child, Nancy returned with the hat. Her jaw dropped when she saw Caldwell at the swing.

"Don't touch that baby!" she screamed.

Caldwell turned, startled, and faced Nancy. Her face was pale.

"I just thought I'd try to quiet him, ma'am."

"He don't need no quieting. I'm his mother. Now here's your hat. Please leave."

"Sorry, ma'am," a bewildered Caldwell said as he took back his hat. "I meant no offense with the baby."

"And please don't come back."

"Okay, ma'am."

Caldwell left, still wondering about the unusual-looking baby. He wanted to do some further investigation into the matter, but happening to glance at his watch, he realized that he would be late for the theater with his date.

*****

"Boy, niggers sure are hypocrites," said Thad as he and his comrades filed into the musty cabin after three hours in the woods practicing escape and evasion tactics. "Who would've thought that nigger talk show host who claimed to be such a lover of black women would be caught in bed with a white chick?"

"All black men lust after white chicks," said Jimmy Ray. "I know because of the looks my ex used to get whenever we walked past a bunch of niggers."

"That's why we needed those anti-miscegenation laws that were overturned by the liberal Supreme Court," said Thad, who along with Orville, Jimmy Ray, and Buck were standing by a grimy sink, wiping the charcoal off their faces with pieces of rags.

"And if I remember right, Ramsey fought for their repeal," said Bob.

Chandler, who knew of Hunter's plan to bring about Rayvon's downfall, smiled and said, "What happened to that nigger talk show host is perfect for the cause."

"How so, Peter?" asked Thad, wiping his hands with a filthy rag.

"With him as leader of the Afro-Purists," Chandler explained, "there's a greater chance that the nigger vote will be split in the general election."

"But will that be enough to defeat Ramsey?" asked Thad, as he retrieved his AK-47 from the row lined up against the wall. "He's still thirty points ahead of Lynch."

"You know, I'm beginning to suspect that Ramsey may have pulled this kidnapping stunt in order to win votes," said Orville, picking up a copy of a magazine from the pile on the bookshelf. "Remember that Lynch was ahead in the polls when the damn baby disappeared."

Jimmy Ray, Thad, Bob, and Buck nodded in agreement. "I bet you they have that baby set up somewhere nice as you please, bein' taken care of by a bunch of mammies," Buck said, lighting a Marlboro.

"I wouldn't be surprised," said Orville. "Ever since the baby was kidnapped, voters are no longer listening to Lynch's charges that Ramsey's a phony liberal."

"Jesus H. Christ," cried Bob. "Listen to what this race-mixing rag says." He waved the copy of *Interrace* magazine he had been perusing.

"What's got you so worked up, Bob?" inquired Orville.

"It's this pack of lies by the author of some race-mixing propaganda book called *Sweeter Juice*. It suggests that if you mix black and white you get something sweeter, better. The author was interviewed by someone named Jamoo."

"Who the hell would name their child that?" scoffed Thad.

"Niggers," Buck said. "They're all hung up on African names."

"Anyway," Bob went on excitedly, "this author claims there's no such thing as racial purity. Listen to this. 'I have been called Egyptian, Italian, Jewish, French, Iranian, Armenian, Syrian, Spanish, Portuguese, Greek, black, Peola, nigger, high yellow, and bright. I am an American anomaly. I am an American ideal. I am an American nightmare. I am Martin Luther King's dream. I am the new America."

"She sure is Martin Luther's dream," Chandler said. "She sounds so mixed up."

"But that's not all," Bob said, growing even more animated. "She goes on to claim she's done research into the issue of race and has discovered that 95 percent of white people in America have African heritage."

"She's stark-raving mad," cried Jimmy Ray. "I don't have nigger blood in me."

The rest of the gang made similar professions of the purity of their lineage.

"There's more," Orville said, growing animated. "She claims that eight-five percent of Africans have European heritage. This means that niggers aren't a different species, like the Bible says. They're our own cousins."

"Our cousins my foot," snapped Jimmy Ray. "Who publishes that rag? Jews? Only Jews could invent such an outrageous lie. Just like they invented the Holocaust."

"The publishers are a bunch of race mixers," said Chandler, who subscribed to the magazine as part of keeping himself informed about race-mixing news and statistics.

"Obviously they get their money secretly from Jews," Thad said. "Jews are behind every conspiracy to do in the white race in America."

Orville returned to reading the rest of the story. "But I agree with the author in this," he said. "America is getting browner, tanner, and yellower every day."

"She's right about that," Chandler said. "That's why I can't wait for Operation Saladin to succeed. Ghazi has promised to give me the same duties and powers in the new America that Himmler had in Nazi Germany. My department will be charged with rounding up of Jews, homosexuals, Mexicans, niggers, mongrels, and various other mud people and placing them in concentration camps. I'll also be responsible for getting rid of any white persons with as much as an ounce of nigger blood."

Buck, who had been unusually silent throughout this enlightening debate on racial purity began, was quietly thinking: *I hope Nancy has no nigger blood in her family. That baby of hers sure has been getting darker every day.*

I don't know what I'd do if that baby of hers turns out to be a mongrel, Buck muttered as he drove his pickup home from Chandler's compound after the meeting. Two and a half hours later he arrived at the farmhouse and found Nancy in the living room. The baby was asleep in his swing and she was lying on the couch dozing. Buck stood before the swing staring at the child.

"Shit," Buck muttered. "He *is* a fucking mongrel."

At the sound of Buck's voice, Nancy's eyes fluttered open.

"Oh, hi hon'," she said sleepily. "Welcome home. How was your day?"

Buck ignored the question. Eyes aflame with rage, he approached Nancy. "You haven't been keeping any secrets from me, have you?" he demanded icily.

Nancy sat up, sensing his bad mood.

"What do you mean?"

"Do you have any nigger blood in your family?"

"Not that I know of."

"Well then, that there baby ain't mine," he said firmly. "I've been watching him, and I'm sure of it now. He keeps getting darker and darker every day. And his nose and hair ain't white no more. That there baby's a half-breed. And I demand to know why."

Nancy was speechless, having run out of excuses.

"You haven't been fornicating with niggers, have you?" said Buck, glaring at her.

"No, Buck. I haven't. Honest."

"Then why isn't that baby white?"

"I don't know."

"Liar!" He slapped her hard across the face. "Now out with the truth! Why isn't that baby white if it's mine?"

"I'm telling you the truth."

"I bet you was fornicatin' with some filthy nigger whenever I was out of town," Buck said, wagging a finger in her face. "Now tell me the truth. Who's the nigger?"

"Honest, Buck, I ain't slept with a nigger."

"Then why'd you give birth to a mongrel?"

Nancy made no reply.

"You're nothing but a dirty, lowdown, nigger-loving whore." He spat on her. "If you don't confess, I'll kill you."

Nancy covered her face with her hands and let out a frightened whimper, expecting another blow. Instead Buck, whose sense of smell was particularly sharp, sniffed the air. "What's that strange smell?" he asked.

"What smell?"

"I smell cologne. Someone's been here."

"Nobody's been here," Nancy said, afraid to tell him about Caldwell's visit. Buck's eyes darted around the room suspiciously, searching for a stray article of clothing, a forgotten comb or wallet or tie – anything to confirm his growing suspicion that the cologne belonged to Nancy's nigger lover.

"Where's that hat?" Buck demanded.

"What hat?"

"You know damn well what hat. That nigger Caldwell's hat."

"I threw it away."

"Why?"

"It stunk."

"When?"

"This morning. I threw it in the garbage can."

"Go get it."

"The garbage men picked it up already."

"That's a lie!" Buck said triumphantly. "I saw that hat hangin' on the clothesline just yesterday. And the garbage collectors came three days ago!"

Nancy opened her mouth to speak, but her throat was choked with fear. The baby awoke and started crying.

"So I was right! You've been sleepin' with that nigger Caldwell!"

"No!" Nancy cried. "He came here again looking for you."

"What for?"

"He's short of drivers because of furniture market. He wanted to know if you wanted your old job back. I told him you was away and gave him back his hat. I swear it's the truth, Buck!"

"If it's the truth then why did you tell me you threw the hat away?"

Nancy said nothing.

"You're fucking lying," Buck shouted. "I know the real reason that nigger was here while I was away. He came to see his mongrel." He pointed at the baby.

"No!"

"Then why does the nigger keep comin' here when I'm not home? I've already told him a million times that I ain't never gonna work under no nigger again."

"He says you're one of the best drivers."

"You're lyin'! I bet he came to get another piece of white meat!"

"No! That's not true!"

"I'm gonna kill that nigger! But first," he said, creeping toward her, "I'm gonna take care of you, you filthy nigger-loving hag."

He punched her so hard in the face she flipped backward over the couch and onto the floor. Blood from her lower lip dripped onto the linoleum. He kicked her in the face.

"That's for starters!" Buck fumed. "I'll be back to trash you some more. But first I'm gonna take care of that nigger!" he stalked out the door, slamming it behind him.

The baby wailed hysterically.

Chapter 30

At half past eleven that night, Caldwell left the High Point Theater inside the IHFC building on Commerce Avenue, after seeing a production of *Othello*. It had been another sold-out, superb performance by the North Carolina Shakespeare Festival, one of the finest regional theaters in the country, which was headquartered in the city. Ramsey gave his employees tickets to the series of performances each year, from October through December. Caldwell, a bachelor, always snatched up several tickets and took dates, but the woman who was supposed to have been his date that night had cancelled at the last minute because she was bedridden with the 'flu.

As Caldwell headed down Main Street, the image of Nancy and the baby came to mind again. He suddenly realized what had been bothering him: Nancy's baby, despite its brown skin, bore an uncanny resemblance to Alison in other respects as well: the triangular shape of the face and the high cheekbones. Could Nancy's baby be Alison's kidnapped child? But Alison was married to Eliot, her baby was supposed to be white.

Caldwell turned left on Lexington, deep in thought. Then he had it: someone had been darkening the baby's skin methodically with sunless tanning lotion to hide its identity. Of course. He had seen such kidnapping stories on Reality TV.

Caldwell was only a few blocks from Lawrence Ramsey's house in Emerywood, but it was now a quarter to ten and he didn't want to create a scene. A neighbor might spot him walking up the Ramsey's brick pathway and call the police to report a prowler. It had happened to him before. Spotting the green and yellow illuminated sign of a BP station on the corner of Lexington and Main Street, he took a left turn, pulled past the pumps, and parked in front of the pay phone outside the convenience store. He paged quickly through his address book until he found Ramsey's home number.

Rebecca Jones, the Ramseys' live-in maid, answered the phone.

"Hello, Rebecca. This is James Caldwell. I'm trying to reach Alison."

"Hi, Caldwell," Rebecca said, recognizing the voice. "Alison's out tonight."

"When do you expect her back?"

"I don't know. Is it urgent?"

"I'm afraid so."

"I can give you her cell phone number. She's at Noble's Grille."

Fadi knew Caldwell's voice. He had it in the audio file, along with all the voice samples of people who had been in contact with Ramsey since the bugs were planted in his home. He wondered what Caldwell was calling about. He didn't think it was serious but, since Ramsey squeaked through the primary, Hunter had said that every call had to be closely monitored and relayed to him. So Fadi summoned Dawoud and asked him to try to reach Hunter. Dawoud went to the huge tracking map on the wall. He saw a blinking light on the city of Raleigh, and next to it the letter G, indicating Ghazi's location.

"Hi, James," Alison said amid the noise of Noble's Grille restaurant on Knollwood Road just off I-40. She was in a little booth by the corner. "What can I do for you?"

"I'm sorry for interrupting your dinner, but it's urgent. Do you have a minute?"

"Sure."

"I'm calling about the kidnapped baby."

Alison stopped breathing and gripped the cell phone more tightly. "Dylan? Do you know where he is?"

"I'm not exactly sure it's him. I just have a hunch. The baby I saw resembles you in some ways but not in others." Caldwell described the features of the baby boy he had seen at Buck's home, and Nancy's strange behavior.

Alison closed her eyes and pressed the phone to her chest. She felt certain the baby was hers. If it was, then Myron was the father after all.

"Hello? Are you there?" Caldwell asked.

"Listen, James. Don't tell anybody about this, okay? Don't call Crime Stoppers, the police, the media, or anyone. Not even my dad. I want to be the first to check out the story. Now tell me exactly where Buck and Nancy McGuire live and how to get there."

"I wouldn't go out there alone if I were you," Caldwell said. "Especially at night. Their house is pretty isolated and Buck's a real redneck. Let me take you out there first thing tomorrow morning."

"All right. What time?"

"I'll pick you up around quarter to eight. How's that suit you?"

"It suits me fine. And remember I'm staying at my parents' while Eliot's away on a business trip. And thank you very much, James."

Alison stepped back into the restaurant and went up to the table where Chanel and Nelson sat, surrounded by a dozen or so of their close friends, who were laughing and chatting. "I need to talk to you," Alison whispered into Chanel's ear. "It's urgent."

The cargo van carrying Buck, Jimmy Ray, Orville, Bob, and Thad drove up a narrow gravel road in the dark until it came to a mailbox marked "Caldwell."

"This is it," Buck said.

Thad turned off the headlights and the van cruised slowly around the bend. He parked it in deep shadows on a side-street.

"I love you guys for helping me do this," Buck said clipping a magazine into his Glock pistol. He then put on a black ski mask and gloves.

"You know we'd never sit back knowing that a fucking nigger raped your wife," Jimmy Ray said.

"Chandler said the job gotta be perfect," Bob said.

"It'll be perfect all right," Buck said as Buck put on a black ski masks and gloves."I don't see any lights," Jimmy Ray said. "You think the nigger's asleep?"

"Probably," Buck said. I heard him tell his nigger brother one time that he liked going to bed early."

"How are you gonna lure him outside?" asked Thad.

"I'll knock," Buck said. "And when he opens the door, I'll let him have it."

As Buck was talking, a car approached with its lights on. The men ducked. The car, a Chevy Camaro, belonged to Caldwell.

Caldwell was still thinking about his phone call to Alison when his Chevy Camaro pulled up to the carport. He turned off his lights and engine. He stepped from the car and headed toward the side door. As he reached into his pocket for his house key, he did not see Buck until he was upon him.

"What the hell?" Caldwell stammered. That was all he had time to say.

Buck shot him four times, twice in the head, and twice in the chest as he went down with a thud. Buck ran back into the van and it sped away, leaving Caldwell sprawling on his driveway in a pool of blood – dead.

Buck arrived home around two in the morning. Before parting, he and the boys had shared a bottle of Jack Daniels to celebrate Caldwell's murder. He was weaving slightly as he made his way down the hall to the bedroom. Nancy was sound asleep. The baby, who had finally figured out the difference between day and night, was fast asleep in his crib, his tiny arm wrapped around a teddy bear twice his size. As Buck, gun in hand, groped for the bed in the dark, he knocked over the lamp on his nightstand.

Nancy awoke with a start and switched on the lights.

"Your nigger lover is dead," Buck said, pointing the gun at Nancy. "Now it's your turn to join him in hell. Along with that nigger baby in the next room."

Nancy was horrorstruck. "You murdered Caldwell?"

"No white man ever murders a nigger. I executed him."

"Please, Buck, don't hurt the little baby!"

"He ain't mine."

"That's true. He ain't yours."

Buck grinned demonically. "So, the truth comes out at last."

"But it's not what you think, Buck. I knew you wanted a baby real bad. I had a third miscarriage and I was afraid to tell you. I thought you'd beat me again, or leave me. I took that baby from the hospital on my due date. I had no idea it was Lawrence Ramsey's grandchild. I swear I didn't. Honest to God it's the truth."

Buck stared at Nancy, uncomprehending.

"What are you blabbering about, woman?"

"That baby in the next room. I took him from Triad Regional hospital. He ain't mine. His real mother is Lawrence Ramsey's daughter, Alison."

"Stop lyin', woman," Buck said angrily, waving the gun. "How can Alison have a mongrel baby when her husband is white? Do I look stupid?"

"I swear it's the truth!"

"Bullshit. You're just tryin' to protect your little nigger baby!"

He pointed the gun at Nancy's head.

"Wait, Buck! I can prove it!"

"Prove it? How?"

"I have evidence."

"Show me."

Nancy, wearing only a skimpy blue nightie, jumped out of bed and ran into the nursery. Buck followed her and watched as she reached under the pile of clothes on the top shelf, retrieved the baby's hospital ID and several other items.

"What's this?" Buck asked as Nancy handed him one of the items.

"That was around the baby's ankle. It's the ID bracelet they put on babies at the hospital after they're born. It's to identify them. Read it."

Buck squinted to make out the small words as he read: "Alison Ramsey Whitaker, Boy, 9 pounds 3 ounces, Triad Regional Hospital."

"This is the blanket he was wrapped in. And here's a photo I took of him the day I brought him home. I used the Polaroid Instamatic you bought me for Christmas."

Buck scrutinized the photo. "Yeah, that's what he used to look like when he was white." Buck was silent for several minutes. Then the truth dawned on him. He stormed out of the room, grinning. Nancy ran to the nursery to guard the crib.

But Buck walked past the crib, out the house and climbed into his pickup.

"Where are you going?" Nancy asked as the pickup roared away.

*****

Inside the cabin, Chandler, Thad, Jimmy Ray, Bob, and Orville were incredulous as they listened to Buck's fantastic story about how Nancy had kidnapped Ramsey's baby. They were all still somewhat sleepy. It was about three-thirty in the morning.

"So you mean you killed that nigger for no reason?" Orville asked.

Buck shrugged. "Guess so."

"That's one less uppity nigger to worry about," Jimmy Ray said. "And remember, Buck, he fired you."

"That's right," Buck said.

"But if Nancy really did kidnap Ramsey's grandbaby," Thad said, "and Alison is married to a white man, then how come she gave birth to a nigger baby?"

Chandler furrowed his broad brow in thought. "There's only one explanation," he said brightly. "Alison cheated on her husband with a nigger."

"Looks that way to me," Orville said. "There's no other way to explain it. And she's the kind of liberal white whore to do such a thing."

A sparkle in his green eyes, Chandler said: "God Almighty, this is perfect!"

"What's perfect?" Bob asked.

"Why, don't you see?" Chandler said. "We've got Ramsey's grandson, and he's a mongrel. He's generated a lot of sympathy for Ramsey because the good white people of North Carolina all along were assuming that a poor little white baby had been cruelly taken from its white parents. That's why Ramsey has that huge lead over Lynch. But we now have the perfect weapon with which to destroy the scalawag's campaign."

"What do you mean?" Thad asked.

"All we have to do is to contact Ghazi and tell him about the mongrel," Chandler said. "In fact, let me run down to the bunker and call him on the secure phone."

The men helped Chandler move the heavy bookcase, behind which was a secret door leading down a flight of stairs to the bunker underneath the cabin.

*****

Hunter was in his condo overlooking Oak Hollow Lake when Dawoud reached him.

"Abdul just called," he said, using Chandler's code name. "He says he has explosive information that could destroy Ramsey's campaign. Should I put him through?"

"Is he using the secure line?"

"Yes."

"Put him through."

After speaking to Ghazi for almost twenty minutes, Chandler rejoined his men. His face was beaming. "Buck, you've just saved Operation Saladin. Ghazi wants you to go fetch the mongrel and bring him here. Along with proof that he's indeed Alison's baby."

Buck grinned. "No problem."

Chapter 31

Alison stepped out of the shower and dried her long lean body with a thick soft towel. The baby had left only fine, barely visible stretch marks on her stomach, which was already toned down from doing a hundred sit-ups and leg-lifts each morning.

She glanced at her watch. It was 7:39 a.m. Caldwell would be by to pick her up any minute and they would stop by Chanel's apartment to pick her up, too. She slipped down the hall to her room and dressed quickly in denim shorts and a sleeveless white shirt from Ross. While combing her long brunette hair, she heard, from the floor below, the sound of rushing footsteps and unfamiliar male voices mingled with her father's voice.

She snuck to the head of the stairs and listened. Three men, two wearing police uniforms, were standing in the foyer talking to her father. She recognized the first one, Officer Gary Tomlinson. He had questioned her about the kidnapping. The black man with wavy dark hair and a neatly-trimmed goatee was FBI chief Bruce Evans. She didn't know the third, also a black man, but from his dark suit and stern face he looked like an FBI agent. Her father was dressed in a dark-blue suit, ready for another full day of campaigning. Today his hectic schedule called for appearances in Charlotte, Gastonia, and an evening speech at Lenoir-Rhyne College in Hickory.

"The murdered man was identified as one of your employees," Chief Evans was saying. "James Caldwell."

Alison gasped.

"Caldwell? Murdered?" Ramsey said in disbelief. "By whom?"

"We have no suspects at the moment," Detective Tomlinson said. "He was found shot four times in the driveway of his house around 11p.m. last night."

Horrified, Alison covered her open mouth with her hands to avoid screaming. She was still on the top step, out of view. She considered rushing down and telling Chief Evans that Caldwell had called her shortly before he was killed, but she decided against it. *He'll want to know why Caldwell called*, Alison thought. *And I dare not let it be known that Dylan's mixed. Oh, God, I wonder if my baby's still alive.*

Alison quietly closed the door of her bedroom. *I must let Chanel know.*

Alison waited until her father and the police and FBI were gone, then she got into her Cherokee and raced over to Chanel's apartment.

"James Caldwell's been murdered," Alison said with bated breath. She was standing inside Chanel's living room, which was tastefully furnished with African art.

"Murdered!" Chanel said, horrified.

"Yes. The cops and the FBI were just at my parents' home."

"Oh, my God. What are we going to do now?"

"We must go to the farmhouse. I have to see that baby."

"Alone? Are you crazy? We can't go out there alone."

"Why not?"

"Because whoever killed Caldwell might be waiting for us."

"I'm going by myself then," Alison said stubbornly. "I have to see that baby."

"Okay, okay, just calm down," Chanel said. "Let's not be too reckless now. We have to do this right. Do you know anyone with a gun?"

"Eliot has one."

"Can you get it?"

"I think I can."

"Good."

As the two friends headed toward Alison's Cherokee, Chanel

said, "And have I got shocking news for you too, girl."

"Shocking news?" Alison asked, as she opened the door to her Jeep.

"Yes. It's about your so-called Uncle Reggie."

Hunter and Ramsey were alone in the back room of campaign head-quarters.

"So you say Caldwell has been murdered?" asked Hunter, feigning surprise.

"Yes," replied Ramsey, still distraught over the news of his supervisor's death. "The police and the FBI were over at my place just a little over an hour ago,"

"I'm really sorry, Lawrence," Hunter said. "Do they know who did it?"

"They have no suspect. It was a professional job."

"Where's Alison?"

"I left her at home."

"And Darlene?"

"She's at the company breaking the news to the workers. I plan to join her as soon as I'm done with the Guilford College speech. I wish I could postpone it, Reggie. I don't feel like doing anything today. Caldwell was more than a supervisor. He was a friend."

"I understand," Hunter said after a sip of cranberry juice. "But it's important that you give the speech. Caldwell's murder is bound to inflame racial tensions and that's the last thing the campaign needs with only ten days to go. Given your civil rights record, you are the only candidate who can credibly appeal for racial calm."

"That's a great idea."

"You're telling me that Uncle Reggie was never in the Peace Corps?" Alison said, visibly shocked. The two were just driving past Wall Mart on 311, headed north toward Nancy's farmhouse. Alison had gotten the address from the phone book. "You must be kidding."

"I'm not kidding," Chanel said seriously. "Myron called me late last night."

"How did he find out?"

"Through the Peace Corps. He checked their files. No Reginald Hunter was ever posted to Colombia or to anywhere by the Peace Corps."

Stunned, Alison reached for a can of orange juice on the dashboard and took a sip. "What made Myron suspicious?" she asked.

"Apparently your Uncle Reggie paid his mother a visit."

"Uncle Reggie visited Myron's mother?" Alison cried, almost rear-ending a Ford Taurus ahead of her, which had suddenly stopped at a red light. "When?"

"Last August, while Myron was away on his book tour. Your uncle Reggie told Myron's mother that if Myron married you, the resulting scandal over your interracial marriage would destroy your dad's campaign. "

Reeling, Alison said, "I don't believe it! You must be kidding. "

"I wish I were. I didn't believe it either. But now it all makes sense."

"What makes sense?"

"What Eliot told me the day you told him about the baby."

"What did he tell you?"

"I hope you're ready for this, girl," Chanel said.

"I'm ready."

"Eliot is gay."

"What!"

As the Cherokee cruised along Highway 311, Chanel proceeded to tell Alison about Eliot's confession, about Hunter catching him at a gay bar, about why Myron's mother had pressured him to call off the wedding, and about the sinister role Hunter had played in inducing Eliot to marry Alison to hide the fact that he was gay.

It took Alison several minutes to get over the shock, but at last she was able to say something. "Poor Eliot," she said with a sigh. "Now I understand why he was trying so hard to put on a conservative façade and to please his father."

The Cherokee took the Kernersville exit off 311, and then made a right turn at the top of the ramp.

"But why did Uncle Reggie do all this?" Alison asked.

"I have no idea, girl," Chanel said. "He's your Uncle Reggie. And if I were you, I'd start probing into his background without raising his suspicions. You used to be one heck of an investigative journalist. You know how it works. Myron is already doing some investigating of his own and will let me know if anything turns up."

"I feel terrible the way I treated Myron," Alison said. Suddenly she thought of something. "But what about his sleeping with a prostitute named Latisha during his book tour – do you mean to tell me that the letters and photos are forgeries?"

"I wouldn't be surprised if Hunter had something to do with them," said Chanel.

"How fucking gullible could I be," Alison said. "All the time I was confiding in him about my love for Myron, he was plotting to tear us apart. But why?"

Before Chanel could answer, she cried, "There's the farmhouse."

Alison drove closer to the house, whose blinds were drawn. The two of them got out of the Cherokee. Alison led the way. "Remember, we're here to do a story," she said.

"Okay."

"And keep your finger on the trigger," Alison said.

"Don't worry, girl. Remember I have a brother who's in Iraq."

Alison knocked on the front door. No one answered. She tried the knob. It was locked. Alison managed to pry open the sliding glass door in the back.

"Chanel! This way!"

They entered. The place was a mess. It was obvious there had been some sort of a struggle. A standing lamp was knocked over. A chair was on its side. In the nursery baby clothes were scattered around as if someone had grabbed and packed handfuls of them in haste, dropping some in the process.

"We're too late," Chanel said.

"Let's look around."

Even in broad daylight the old farmhouse was quite dark. The floorboards squeaked eerily as they walked about, searching through closets, looking in drawers.

In one of the drawers Alison found a stack of papers.

"Hey, take a look at all this," she said in amazement.

"What is it?"

"Klan and Nazi literature. Tons of it."

"You mean your baby's in the hands of the Klan?" Chanel gasped.

"Listen to this," Alison said, reading from one of the newsletters the lead article titled "Saving the White Race": *White women are the foundation of the Aryan race. If they listen to liberals and feminists who tell them that careers are more important than bearing children, the race is doomed. But there's something worse than not bearing children at all. The greatest sin white women can commit is to give birth to mongrels, whose polluted blood threatens the survival of the White Race. Such women are whores, scum, and traitors to their race. They and their half-breed offspring deserve to die.*

Alison looked up from the newsletter. Her face was colorless. She and Chanel stared at each other. "We have to find my baby," Alison said. "Before it's too late."

Buck, an AK-47 slung over his shoulder, climbed the wooden stairs and unlocked a creaky door leading to an upstairs room inside the musty cabin. As soon as he walked in, he noticed that Nancy was awake and feeding the baby from a Mickey Mouse bottle.

"Why did you bring us to this strange place?" Nancy asked.

"Ghazi's orders."

"Who's Ghazi?"

"He's an American Patriot. He's gonna cleanse America of liberals, niggers, mongrels, Jews, and nigger-lovers so we can be a white Christian nation again."

"He ain't goin' to harm the baby, is he?" she asked, clutching the baby more tightly to her breast.

"Depends on his granddaddy. If Ramsey does what we want him to do, he'll get his mongrel back. If he doesn't, I'll personally strangle the little shrimp."

Nancy's eyes darted about the room and came to rest on the small window.

"Don't think about escaping," Buck said. "You'll be guarded twenty-four hours a day. By me. And I won't hesitate to shoot you if you interfere with our plans."

"How'd you get mixed up with these people, Buck?" Nancy asked. "I thought you said you were working for the Department of Homeland Security."

"That was just a cover," Buck said. "I couldn't just sit around on my damn ass and watch niggers take away white people's jobs, pollute our schools and neighborhoods and liberals destroy America, could I? So I joined up with people who wanted to do something about it. There's gonna be a race war in America, and we're ready."

Nancy shook her head. "I don't like all this one bit."

"I don't care what you like. I'm the man. I'm supposed to protect the interests of my own race. And that mongrel there's goin' to help us do that."

Chapter 32

Hunter climbed out of his limo and entered Dana Auditorium on the campus of Guilford College just as Ramsey concluded his speech on racial healing, which was sponsored by the Greensboro Truth and Reconciliation Commission. Ramsey was milling around chatting and posing for photos with students, professors, and members of the community, when Hunter approached and whispered in his ear, "May I see you alone for a minute?"

"Sure. I've been wondering where you were."

"I had to make a quick trip downtown."

Ramsey excused himself and followed Hunter into one of the auditorium's back rooms. Hunter closed the door.

"Please sit down," he said. "You don't want to hear this standing up."

Bewildered, Ramsey sat down on a brown sofa. "What is it?"

"Your grandchild has been found."

"Found?" Ramsey looked puzzled, then thrilled. "Thank God!" he cried.

"Not too fast. He's been found all right –"

"Yes?"

"But he's..." Hunter looked tearful and swallowed hard. "But he's dead."

"D-d-dead?"

"Yes!"

"No!" Ramsey screamed.

"I'm very sorry."

For several minutes Ramsey didn't say a word. He simply sat there on the sofa, staring on the floor, a blank expression on his face. He buried his head in his hands. Hunter went over to Ramsey and put his arm around his shoulder.

"I'm really sorry," Hunter said. "I know how this double tragedy must make you feel. First it was Caldwell. And now it's your poor grandchild."

Ramsey composed himself and asked, in a voice quivering with emotion, "Where did the police find him?"

"The police didn't find him. I did."

"You did?"

"Yes. Ever since he was kidnapped I've been working around the clock to locate the poor child," Hunter said. "One of the private detectives I hired finally tracked him down to the black section of Greensboro notorious for its gangs and crack houses. I just returned from a secret meeting with his kidnappers."

"You went alone?"

"Yes. "

"That took some courage."

"Those were their conditions," Hunter said. "And you know how much I care about Alison. I didn't want to do anything to make matters worse. When I got there, they provided me with proof that they had indeed kidnapped and murdered him."

"What proof?"

Hunter reached inside his briefcase and withdrew a hermetically sealed plastic bag containing the baby's ID bracelet and a photo of the baby taken the day he was kidnapped. "Do you recognize these?" he said, handing the bag to Ramsey.

Ramsey took the bag, hurriedly opened it, and scrutinized the items. His face grew pale when he read the bracelet."Who are the kidnappers?"

"Afro-Purists. Apparently their leader arranged for one of his girlfriends to kidnap your grandson, with the intent of using him as a bargaining chip."

"But the police say a white woman kidnapped my grandson."

"Yes. That was their leader's white girlfriend."

"White girlfriend? But I thought Afro-Purists were against race-mixing."

"I did too. But apparently I was wrong."

"How did little Dylan die?"

"Brace yourself, Lawrence. This ain't gonna sound pretty."

"I can bear anything."

"He was strangled."

"Strangled!" Ramsey cried in horror. He again buried his face in his hands. "My God! My God!" he sobbed piteously.

Squirm, nigger-lover, Hunter said under his breath as he watched the helpless Ramsey. *Now you know how I felt when Abigail left me for a nigger because of you.*

"Apparently the Afro-Purists are nothing but a satanic cult," Hunter said. "They worship an African god called Mumbo-Jumbo. Their high-priest, a light-skinned mulatto who calls herself Queen Nefertari, told them that Mumbo-Jumbo wanted the blood of a white child if he's to grant them their wish of preventing you from becoming governor. That's when they came up with the plan to kidnap Dylan from the hospital. But then their plan went awry, which then led them to strangle him."

"Went awry?" Ramsey said, he was now pacing aimlessly around the small room.

"Yes. Dylan turned out not to be a suitable sacrifice to Mumbo-Jumbo."

"What do you mean?"

"He wasn't white."

"Dylan wasn't white?" Ramsey said with surprise. "What are you talking about?"

"Lawrence, your grandson was a mulatto."

"A mulatto? Are you mad?" Ramsey, who had been standing, now staggered back into the sofa, as if struck by an invisible iron fist.

"I wish I were."

"How can it be?" Ramsey said hoarsely. "Alison's married to Eliot. And the baby's white in this photo you just showed me."

"But he's not white in this one," Hunter said as he reached into his inner jacket pocket and removed the second photograph.Ramsey leapt from the sofa as if he had been shot from a cannon and snatched the photo from Hunter's hand.

"My God! Dylan *is* a mulatto!"

As Ramsey stared in horror at the photograph, Hunter studied him with a smirk on his face. *Squirm, nigger-lover, squirm*, he said to himself. *When I'm done with you, you'll wish you'd never been born.*

"Haven't you heard of melanin?" Hunter asked. "It's what gives us our color. Because the baby was mixed, his melanin took some time to appear. The baby looked white at birth, but over the next several months his melanin apparently came in."

Ramsey scrutinized the photo. The baby looked tanned, but he still resembled Alison. "So what do the Afro-Purists want in return for my poor grandson's corpse?"

"Three million dollars."

"Three million!"

"Yes. And that's not all. They want you to repudiate integration."

"Repudiate integration?"

"Yes. They claim that integration has weakened the black community and ruined the black family. And they blame liberals like you for it."

"But most blacks support integration," Ramsey said.

"Not the Afro-Purists. And they're dead serious about using your grandson's corpse to destroy your campaign if you don't comply with their demands."

"How will they do that?"

"They've concocted a fantastic cover-up story."

"What kind of story?"

"They plan to call a press conference two days before the election, at which Rayvon, their new leader, will tell the world that after Alison revealed that the baby she was carrying might be Myron's, you secretly approached Afro-Purists and struck a deal with them. You were down in the polls and feared that a scandal involving a mixed grandchild would destroy your campaign. In return for distancing yourself from liberalism, you arranged with Afro-Purists to kidnap Alison's baby from the hospital as soon as he was born. If the baby turned out to be Eliot's, you wanted Afro-Purists to keep him so that his disappearance could generate a sympathy vote, and return him after the election. But if he turned out to be Myron's, you wanted them to strangle him."

"That's preposterous! This Rayvon is mad."

"He certainly is," Hunter said. "But there's method in his madness, don't you think? Particularly because he plans to tell the press that he carried out his part of the bargain, but that you reneged on yours because of the comfortable lead you were enjoying in the polls. You then decided to blackmail him in return."

"Me blackmail him?"

"Yes. Rayvon plans to tell the press that you secretly set him up with that blonde, and then videotaped him. You then showed him the videotape and demanded Dylan's corpse, and when he refused to give it to you, you sent the tape to his producer."

Ramsey was in utter shock. He ran his hand through his hair in a helpless gesture.

"The black-mailing swine," Ramsey said as he reached for the phone. "I'll call the police. They'll know how to deal with the psychopathic scoundrel."

Hunter put out his hand to stop Ramsey. "I wouldn't do that if I were you. I agree that Rayvon is nothing but a psychopath. But you don't have to destroy your own campaign by calling the police. If you follow my advice, we can outmaneuver the Afro-Purists and still preserve your lead in the polls. Don't forget there's only ten days to go before voters elect you the next governor of North Carolina."

"What should I do?"

"First, under no circumstances should you breathe a word of this to anyone, understand?" Hunter said. "Not even to Alison and Darlene. Second, I want you to have the $3 million ransom ready by the end of the week. Then I'll personally contact the Afro-Purists to set up a secret meeting."

"Thanks, Reggie."

"Don't mention it."

Chapter 33

Tears welled up in Ramsey's eyes and his voice cracked as he was about to speak. He found it impossible to look into the eyes of his daughter Alison, who had just emerged from a heated indoor swimming pool after swimming laps for half an hour, something she did every afternoon as part of a fitness regimen that included jogging. Ramsey and Darlene had just arrived and Eliot was away in South America on a business trip.

The warmth from the golden glow of a gas fireplace in a nearby corner was in sharp contrast to the late October chill, and the horror of the news that Ramsey was about to impart. Luckily for Alison, the swimming pool area of her sprawling thirty-room mansion was the only area Hunter's operatives hadn't bugged.

"What's the matter with dad, Mom?" Alison asked, joining her parents, who were sitting around a rectangular cedar table with four chairs.

"I don't know," Darlene said. "He simply picked me up at the company and said we should go for a drive. In the car he uttered not a word. And we came straight here."

"I know I shouldn't be telling this to you or to anyone," Ramsey began in an anguished voice. "But I can't hold the secret any longer. It's killing me. I need to share it with people I love. I don't care if it destroys my campaign, as I'm sure it will."

Darlene and Alison exchanged puzzled looks.

"If what destroys your campaign, Dad?" asked Alison, reaching for a jug filled with iced water. She poured it into three tumblers and handed them out to her parents.

"What are you talking about, Lawrence?" Darlene asked, apprehensive.

Ramsey looked at his daughter, who was sitting down on one of the four chairs. "I have awful news for you, Alison," he said. "Horrible news. Tragic news."

"Is it about the baby?" Alison asked.

Ramsey nodded solemnly. "Yes. He's been found."

"Found?" asked Alison. Her heart skipped a beat.

"Yes," Ramsey said. "And he's dead."

Darlene let out a scream and covered her face with her hands.

"Dead?" Alison asked with little trace of emotion in her voice. "Says who?"

"Your Uncle Reggie." Ramsey went on to relate his entire discussion with Hunter earlier that afternoon. He ended by showing his wife and daughter the photographs of Dylan and the ID bracelet he wore the day he was kidnapped. Alison and Darlene stared long and hard at the baby's photos. One photo showed a white infant with straight hair and the other a brown five-month-old baby with nappy hair.

"Are these photos of the same child?" Darlene asked. "The face is the same, but the color and the hair are..." Her voice trailed off.

"That's the way melanin works, mom," Alison said calmly. "It comes in slowly in biracial children. The photo proves what I've suspected for a long time. Myron, not Eliot, is Dylan's father."

"But how..."

"Dylan must have been conceived the weekend I flew up to New York to tell Myron that dad had given us his blessing. That was three weeks before I married Eliot."

"My God," was all Darlene could utter as she rose abruptly, walked to the edge of the pool, and stared blankly at its placid surface.

Ramsey followed her and wrapped his arms around her. "Take it easy, honey."

Darlene gave Ramsey an anguished look. "Our grandchild is

dead, Lawrence. How can I take it easy? I never got to touch him. To tell him that I loved him."

"I don't believe Dylan's dead," Alison said. Her mind had been working all the while she was studying the photo. Her parents turned and faced her. She was at the table, busy scrutinizing the photos of her baby.

"What makes you say that, dear?" Darlene asked.

Alison looked up. "It's a hunch I have."

"Well, your Uncle Reggie received the news from a very reliable source, honey," Ramsey said. "And you can't deny those are the baby's items."

"What was the source?" Alison asked.

"The kidnappers themselves."

"Who are they?"

"Afro-Purists."

"Afro-Purists?"

"Yes."

"Uncle Reggie told you that?" Alison asked.

"Yes."

"And he's sure it's the Afro-Purists who kidnapped Dylan?"

"Yes. One of the private detectives your godfather hired to work on the case found that out. He also arranged for Reggie to meet secretly with a representative of the kidnappers, who are demanding a $3 million ransom for the return of Dylan's corpse."

Alison thought for a long while. "Where's Uncle Reggie now?"

"I left him at campaign headquarters. We're supposed to leave this evening for Raleigh to meet with Democratic Party leaders to plan strategy for the final week of the campaign. I didn't tell him I was coming here. He expressly forbade that I do."

"Why?" asked Alison.

"He feared that word might leak out to the press and destroy my campaign."

Alison put down the photos she had been holding. "Dad, how well do you know Uncle Reggie? I know you two grew up together, but that was a long time ago."

"I thought he told you the story."

"He did. But I want to hear it from you."

"Well, after his family left our farm in Eastern Carolina we lost touch. That was back in 1954. The next time I heard about him was when he started making waves as a political consultant around 1994, the year the Republicans took over both houses of Congress for the first time since 1952. Hunter had just opened a big consulting firm in Texas, which also has offices in all the Southern states, including North Carolina. Its goal was to help Democrats retake the South. We were reunited, so to speak, in May of 2002, when, because of his impressive record, I hired him as my campaign manager for the open gubernatorial seat in 2004."

"Did you ask Uncle Reggie what he was doing before he became a political consultant?" Alison asked in a casual tone.

"Yes. He told me that after graduating from the University of Alabama at Tuscaloosa in 1963, he went into the Peace Corps. He was stationed in Colombia, South America, helping in various agricultural programs and teaching English at the local high school, his majors at the University. After his two-year posting in Colombia, he signed up for another two years. This time he was posted to Egypt, where he stayed and taught English at the University of Cairo and also went into the export-import business. He must've been quite good, for he became a multimillionaire by the age of 35. Then he sold his business to return to the States when he realized that the Democratic Party was under attack for its Great Society programs, one of which was the Peace Corps. He told me that he decided to become a political consultant because he wanted to help the party rehabilitate itself and make a comeback, especially in the South."

"Did you ever check out his story?"

Ramsey was taken aback. "Check out his story? Why? He's my childhood friend, Alison. And your godfather. He wouldn't lie to me, would he?"

Alison didn't reply. For several moments she was deep in thought. "Do you remember what made Uncle Reggie and his family leave grandpa's farm?" she asked.

"I certainly do," Ramsey said after taking a sip of water for his dry throat. "It was shortly after we busted the Klan together."

"Busted the Klan?"

"Yes. Reggie and I had just spent one of those long, hot, and muggy summer days swimming, fishing, and hunting for small game on the farm. It was evening and we were walking back home, arguing about the implications of Black Monday."

"What's Black Monday?" Alison asked.

"May 17, 1954, honey," Darlene said. "The day the Supreme Court ruled that segregated schools were unconstitutional. I remember it well because on that day my parents had invited their friends for dinner at their West Side apartment. Several of the guests were Holocaust survivors, and the dinner conversation was dominated by comparisons between Jim Crow and the Nuremberg Laws and the need for Jews to join the fight for Civil Rights. I remember being so deeply affected by what the adults were saying that I later told my mother that when I grew up, I would fight for civil rights."

Ramsey smiled at Darlene, mindful that she had done just that, and that her decision to obey her conscience was what ultimately brought them together.

"While your mother was being converted to the civil rights cause," Ramsey said, "there was mass hysteria across the South because of the Supreme Court decision. The Klan took advantage of the decision to intimidate black people. As Reggie and I were walking, we stumbled upon a group of eight hooded Klansmen holding an open-air meeting in a clearing deep in the woods. They were apparently plotting how to drive black workers off the farm, so only white workers would remain."

"Your grandpa was a rarity among tobacco farmers in the South during the 1950s," Darlene said. "He was a product of the Great Depression and grew up working alongside blacks on his family's cotton fields. Despite his anti-Semitism, he was a big supporter of Roosevelt's New Deal programs and a champion of labor and land-reform."

"Jobs at dad's 500-acre farm, one of the largest in the county, were coveted because workers were given more than a fair wage," Ramsey said proudly. "After working several years, they became part owners of the farm."

"So what happened when you stumbled upon the Klansmen?" Alison said. As a journalist, she was aware of people's tendency to digress when speaking. But such digression often yielded valuable information. It was the trained journalist who knew when to steer the interview back to its central focus.

"'Lawrence,' Reggie whispered as we watched the Klansmen through a cluster of pine trees. 'You run back and get help. I'll stay here and keep an eye on them.'"

"And did you?"

"Yes. Since Reggie had a clubfoot, I ran the mile back to the farmhouse."

"Uncle Reggie had a clubfoot?"

"Yes. But I wasn't supposed to let you or Darlene know this."

"Why?" Darlene asked.

"Because Reggie is very conscious of his former deformities, my dear."

"Deformities?"

"Yes. He used to look very different when he was young."

"How different?" Alison asked.

"Well, he not only had a clubfoot," Ramsey said, "But he also had a broad, flaring nose and thick lips, which led many to think he was colored."

"You mean to tell me Reggie has had plastic surgery?" asked Darlene.

"Radical plastic surgery, my dear. The doctors who worked on him while he was in South America performed wonders. As a teenager he was so ugly kids used to constantly make fun of him. I was practically his only friend."

Alison was stunned. Her Uncle Reggie used to be deformed?

"That was also why he changed his name," said Ramsey.

"I didn't know he changed his name," said Darlene.

"He changed it while he was abroad," Ramsey said. "He used to be called Ebenezer Bickley. Apparently he wanted a complete break with his past."

"I thought there was something strange about Hunter from the beginning," Darlene observed. "But I didn't know it was that strange."

"So what happened when you got home after leaving Uncle Reggie to keep an eye on the Klansmen?" Alison asked, steering the discussion back to the original issue.

"When I got back," Ramsey said, "I found your grandfather on the porch, talking to Peter, his black foreman, about plans to hire more workers following his acquisition of more farmland. 'Dad! Dad!' I called breathlessly as I flew up the steps. 'There's a group of Klansmen in the woods. They're planning to harm your colored workers.'"

Alison and Darlene smiled at Ramsey's attempt at dramatizing his childhood recollection. He was pretty good, actually. "'Where are they?' Dad asked," Ramsey said. "I hurriedly explained where I'd left Reggie keeping an eye on the six Klansmen. 'You stay here with your mother,' your grandpa said as he and Peter gathered a posse of eight men armed with rifles. I protested, but Grandpa stood firm, saying that the Klansmen were dangerous. 'Don't worry, we'll bring Ebenezer back safely,' he said reassuringly."

"And did he?" asked Alison.

"Yes. He was true to his word," Ramsey said. "Reggie returned unharmed and excitedly told me how at the arrival of the posse the Klansmen had fled in all directions and how your grandpa, on horseback, had chased their leader into a swamp. After the Klan was busted that night, it never again reared its hooded head in Craven County."

"Quite a story," Darlene said. "I wonder why you've never told it to me before."

"Like I said, honey, Reggie asked me not to reveal details of his past to anyone in part because he wanted to make a clean break with it," Ramsey said.

Alison thought a long while. "Dad, will you do me a favor?" she said presently. "Don't pay the ransom."

"Don't pay the ransom?" Ramsey said. "But the Afro-Purists have poor Dylan's corpse, honey. And they plan to use it to destroy my campaign."

"I know. But please don't pay it. At least not yet. There's something I want to investigate first."

"Investigate what, honey?" asked Ramsey.

"I can't tell you what it is right now."

Ramsey looked dubious.

"Please trust me, Dad. You know I've never let you down."

"Okay, how much time do you need?"

"Seven days."

"Seven days. But that leaves only four days before the election."

"I know,' Alison said. "But this is very important. The viability of your campaign may hinge on the results of my investigation."

"All right."

"Thanks," said Alison." And I want you to also do me this favor. Don't let Uncle Reggie know you've told Mom and me about the baby. Instead, tell him you're having trouble raising the money and will need at least a week."

"Okay."

"Another thing," Alison added with a solemn look on her face, "I wouldn't discuss anything important in his presence if I were you."

"Come on, hon', take another bite," Nancy said, smiling. She brought the baby spoon, full of pureed pears, to Dylan's lips. He clapped his little hands together, and then swatted the spoon away. The pear mush ended up on Nancy's lap.

"Here comes another one," she said, aiming for his laughing mouth.

She got the spoon inside before he could close it, but then he tricked her. He blew bubbles into the spoon and the pear mush splattered all over his little sailboat bib and chubby brown arms. The next spoonful he knocked onto the tray before him and started smearing it around with both hands, squealing with delight and making cooing noises.

"All right, you win."

Nancy closed the jar, put it back in the cooler, and cleaned up the mess. She set Dylan on the floor and propped him up with pillows to help him sit. He sat wavering for a few seconds, and then keeled over. She tried to make him sit up again, but he was still too floppy. She picked him up and kissed his soft cheek.

"You just like to be held, that's all."

As she was cuddling him and nuzzling her nose against his tiny ear, she heard approaching footsteps. Buck yanked open the door to the upstairs room and peered inside.

"Why are you always touching that mongrel?" he snarled. "Leave him be."

Nancy quickly set him down among the pillows.

"You might catch one of them nigger diseases, like sickle cell anemia," Buck said. "I brought our spiritual leader. He wants to take a look at the mongrel."

"Why?" Nancy asked, instinctively reaching for Dylan.

"Ghazi, our leader, just told us that as soon as we receive the ransom money," Buck said, "we should strangle the little shrimp and send it to its granddaddy in a plastic bag. And Reverend Orville Mayberry here wants to give it its last rights."

Nancy looked up and, recognizing in Orville Mayberry the itinerant televangelist who had molested her when she was fifteen, she instantly fainted.

The morning after the chilling talk with her father about Dylan, Alison drove south on Highway 85, picked up Route 601 in Kannapolis and bore down south toward the South Carolina border. She felt confident she would find answers to the nagging questions about Hunter in his hometown of Monroe, which he had left more than forty years ago.

Her first stop was Monroe High School on Lancaster Avenue. It was made up of several modern buildings which obscured the impact of the original schoolhouse Hunter had taken classes in. It was an imposing neoclassical, Revival-style, two-story rectangular building fronted by a monumental portico. In the school's library she found a shelf lined with old yearbooks. Aware that Hunter was two years younger than her father, she calculated the year he had graduated. She was shocked at the photo of Hunter in the 1960 volume. *My God, is this how he used to look?* Alison found it hard to believe that the figure with the protruding teeth, and thick glasses over a flaring, bulbous nose was the Hunter she knew. *Pretty damn good plastic surgery,* she thought.

Alison took her reporter's notebook out of her purse and started jotting down the names of some of Hunter's classmates, particularly those who appeared in candid photos with him. Noticing that there were only a few such photos, Alison concluded that Hunter must have been something of a loner. *No wonder*, Alison thought. *Who would want someone this ugly for a friend?* To her surprise, she did notice that Hunter was in the high school band as a tuba player. And there was also a strange photo of Hunter standing next to a gorgeous, full-figured blonde with magnolia skin, jade almond-shaped eyes, and an aquiline nose.

There was no caption under the photo, but it might as well have been called Beauty and the Beast. *She reminds me of someone I know*, Alison thought, scrutinizing the blonde's picture. *But who?* She wracked her brains but couldn't place the face.

From the school library Alison next went to the public library. She found the librarian, a middle-aged woman with thick glasses, very helpful. "Oh yes, I do remember Ebenezer Bickley," said the librarian. "I remember him quite well. He used to come to the library a lot. It was sad what happened to him though."

"What happened?"

"Oh, he died in a plane crash in Colombia, while serving in the Peace Corps."

Alison was shocked. But she tried very hard not to show it.

"When did he die?"

"There was a story about the incident in the paper. I believe it was in 1979."

"Do you still have the paper?"

"Sure. It's on microfiche."

Alison was stunned by the headline of the story, which was on Page 2.

Ebenezer Bickley, a former Monroe High School star student, Tuba player and Peace Corps volunteer, died in a plane crash in the jungles of Colombia. The plane was on its way from Bogotá to Medellin to deliver medical supplies to a remote native village when it disappeared from radar. It is believed to have crashed into a mountainside. But the wreckage was never found because of the thick, impenetrable jungle.

Alison was stumped by the story. *Why would Hunter fake his own death? What about his past did he so desperately want to forget that he went to the extent of weaving an elaborate story of deception and lies?* Alison went across the street to a pay phone. She started searching for the names of Hunter's classmates in the Monroe phonebook. She found only a handful. She called each number, posing as a freelance journalist who was doing a story on the Peace Corps for the *New York Times* Sunday magazine, and was profiling some of its distinguished alumni. Ebenezer had been one of the Corps' best volunteers before his untimely death. Surely there would be someone willing to talk about the hometown boy who, despite his infirmities, had acquired a fame of a different sort from that of another famous Monroe native son, U.S. Senator Jesse Helms.

William Burke had been in the band with Ebenezer, where he had played the tenor saxophone. He now owned a bowling alley and video arcade in town. He was also a member at the Monroe Country Club, which Alison had passed while driving on Highway 601. Sure, Burke was willing to say a few words about his old buddy, Ebenezer.

Burke gave Alison directions to his Greek Revival home, which was a couple blocks away from The Lady of Lourdes Catholic

Church. She found him sitting on a porch swing smoking a cigar. He was a large man with a loud voice and heavy jowl. After brief introductions, Alison took a seat next to him. Burke's demure wife bustled in and out of the house, supplying them with iced tea and warm sweet potato pie.

"So when did you and Ebenezer become friends?" Alison asked.

"Soon after his family moved here," said Burke. "I believe he was in sixth grade. They came from some small town down East."

"You mean in the eastern part of the state?"

"Yeah. I can't remember the name of the town. Ebenezer told me his family had to leave in an awful big hurry."

"Did he say why?"

"At first he was reluctant to talk about the matter. Then one day he and I were watching a Klan parade downtown. When I excitedly told him that my uncle who lived out in the county belonged to the Klan, Ebenezer looked at me with surprise and said, 'Are you proud of that?'"

"What did you say?"

"I said, 'Sure I'm proud. The Klan is mighty respected by most white folks because it's fighting to protect the Southern way of life from Communists and Yankee integrationists.' That's when Ebenezer's face lit up and he told me the story of his own father having been a Klan Grand Wizard, and that his family was forced to leave the farm down east after he was discovered. From that day on Ebenezer and I became close buddies because both of us had relatives in the Klan."

"Interesting," Alison said, without looking up from her notebook. She was trying hard to mask her astonishment at this new twist. Now it all made sense. The Klan ringleader her granddaddy had chased into the swamp was none other than Hunter's father. That's why her father wasn't told. It would've hurt him deeply to discover the truth: that his dear friend's father was a Klansman.

"What sort of man was Ebenezer's father?"

"Oh, he was your typical redneck," Burke said. "He couldn't read or write. And of course he hated colored people, Jews, and Catholics."

"What kind of work did he do?"

"He was a janitor."

"And his mother?"

"She too was illiterate. She worked as a maid and was often depressed. Used to drink and swear a lot too."

"How did Ebenezer became such a good student with such parents?" Alison asked.

Burke paused and smiled.

"What's so amusing?" Alison asked.

"Well, he fell in love. It was a real shocker to everybody, given how he looked, you know. Students used to make fun of him, saying that he had Negro blood. Not too many girls, to say the least, wanted to go out with someone with a clubfoot."

"Who was the girl?"

"Abigail Chambers. One of the prettiest and smartest girls at Monroe High."

Abigail! Could it be her picture in the yearbook?

As Burke laughed at the memory and took another drag on his cigar, Alison was feverishly jotting down everything, despite the shock she felt over the revelations.

"So Ebenezer fell in love," Alison said slowly, feigning mild interest.

"That's right," said Burke, who apparently was very eager to talk. "The change that came over him you won't believe. He used to be a D student. He started getting As. He joined the high school band and became a maestro at tuba-playing. He was the best member of the debating society. Everybody knew it was because of Abigail."

"Were they truly in love?"

"Ebenezer was. But Abigail loved him more like a brother. She was a Quaker, you know, so she had a great deal of compassion for people who were persecuted or made fun of. I remember some students calling the two of them Quasimodo and Esmeralda, from the Victor Hugo movie about the deaf bell-ringer. What's its name?"

"The Hunchback of Notre Dame."

"Yeah, that's the one," he said, laughing.

"What made Ebenezer think that his relationship with Abigail was more than platonic?" asked Alison.

"By what she did."

"What did she do?"

"Well, her junior year Abigail was voted homecoming queen," Burke said. "And guess who escorted her to the prom?"

"Ebenezer?"

Burke nodded. "Can you believe it? The most beautiful girl ignoring all the jocks on campus to dance with a dweeb with a clubfoot." Burke chuckled at the memory.

"Well, true beauty often lies on the inside."

"I guess so."

"What happened after the prom?"

"Well, Ebenezer now lived only for Abigail. She was his angel. He worshipped the ground she walked on. He applied to the best universities because of her. She constantly told him that he could be whatever he wanted to be despite his looks. Ebenezer surprised everybody when he won a full scholarship to the University of Alabama at Tuscaloosa. Before he left, he told Abigail that if he ever got married, she would be the woman he'd marry and no one else."

"What did Abigail say to that?"

"Well, she wasn't into hurting anyone, so she simply smiled. As I said, she considered Ebenezer a brother. She was an orphan, you know."

"An orphan?"

"Yes. Her parents were killed in an automobile accident in Philadelphia where they were teaching at a mixed Quaker school. The only relatives Abigail had left in the world were her Baptist aunt and uncle who lived in Monroe. She moved down here when she was twelve. In many ways she was more of a Northerner than a Southerner."

"What do you mean?"

"Well, she was always calling the War Between the States the Civil War. She also insisted that Jim Crow, which Southerners considered a normal way of life, was wrong."

"And what did Ebenezer think of that?"

"That was the only thing about Abigail that made him really mad. But he blamed it on the fact that Abigail was a Quaker, and that she subscribed to a paper which most white folks around here hated. He thought that the longer she lived in the South, and became familiar with our way of life, the sooner she'd outgrow such foolish thinking."

"What was the paper?"

"Oh, it was called *The New South*. People hated it because it was pro-integration."

Alison was stunned. *Dad's newspaper*. But again she deftly hid her emotions. "Did Abigail outgrow her foolish thinking?" she said in an even voice.

Burke's smile vanished. He stubbed out his cigar and flicked it over the railing into the Rhododendron bushes. "Have you ever heard of the Kissing Case?" he asked.

"No."

"Well, it involved two Negro boys, ages eight and nine, who were charged with trying to kiss a seven-year-old white girl," said Burke. "Now that was a mighty serious crime back then, so the judge sentenced the two Negro boys to reform school."

"Reform school?"

"Yes. It was better than being lynched, wasn't it?"

"I guess so."

"Anyway, the Negroes made a big fuss about the sentence. Their rebel-rousing leader was head of the local NAACP and had ties with agitators in New York. He invited his gang of white and black Communists and Freedom Riders from New York to protest the decision. They protested right in front of our beautiful courthouse."

Alison had driven past the courthouse on Ramsey Street.

"What does the Kissing Case have to do with Abigail?"

"Plenty. The day the protests ended and the Freedom Riders and Communists left, Abigail mysteriously disappeared," Burke said. "The whole town was frantic. Search parties were dispatched in ever-widening circles around the town, led by bloodhounds with their snuffling noses to the ground. Night came, then day, then a second long night. Impromptu prayer meetings were held to pray for Abigail's safe return. Her aunt and uncle, who were convinced she'd been kidnapped by the Northern agitators, were swamped with calls of sympathy, and pledges of constant prayer for her safe return."

"What had happened to her?"

"The worst," Burke said. "On the third day Abigail shocked everyone by calling from New York. She said that she was safe and sound, had rejoined the church of her parents, and intended to go teach at a Negro school in Harlem."

"What was wrong with that? Maybe she wasn't too happy living in the South."

"What was wrong?" Burke blurted out. "Everything. Apparently Abigail was also in love with one of the protesters. He was a Quaker, like Abigail, and a graduate of Swarthmore College, like her father and mother were."

"So she'd found a soul mate?"

"A soul mate!" said Burke, almost screaming. "Hardly. According to most white people she'd committed the worst sin a white woman could commit."

"What do you mean?"

"Well, this educated and apparently well-spoken Quaker was a Negro."

Alison could feel her heart begin to pound. Her cheeks grew hot.

"It was such a shock to everybody, of course," Burke said. "And what was even more shocking was when Abigail told her distraught aunt and uncle that she was as devoted to the cause of civil rights as her fiancé was, and that together they hoped some day to return to the South and help the region wean itself of its horrid, racist ways. It done broke their poor hearts. They felt so humiliated and betrayed."

Burke paused and sipped his drink. He continued. "Yes, she was a Quaker and had been partial to Negroes and all that, but race mixing was quite something else. Stories began circulating that the Negro had drugged her, and carried her off, kicking and screaming, to New York where she was forced at gunpoint to place that phone call."

"But of course that wasn't true," Alison said.

"Unfortunately it wasn't," Burke said with resignation. "People couldn't understand how she could commit such an abomination. She could have had any boy she wanted. She could have even had Ebenezer for all they cared. But a Negro. No way. Gradually, however, people began believing it. They called Abigail all sorts of horrid names, and pointed to her as a warning that raising a girl to believe in racial equality and integration could lead to a fate worse than death."

For the first time Alison could picture Abigail. Here was this sensitive young woman, a Quaker like herself, lost amid a sea of hypocrites who professed to be good Christians and yet couldn't accept the most fundamental tenet of their faith: loving their fellow human beings. Most of them presumably frowned on Quakerism, because of its association with the Underground Railroad, and called Jews "Christ killers," even though Christ himself was a Jew and had been crucified by the Romans.

Most likely Abigail, finding inspiration and solace from the liberal pages of *The New South*, had steadfastly adhered to her Quaker beliefs. Outwardly she may have seemed to conform to the mores and traditions of the South. She presumably wore white gloves and fine dresses every Sunday when she went to church with her Fundamentalist aunt and uncle. But the seeds of Quakerism had already taken deep root within her.

Abigail must have felt an instantaneous soul-to-soul connection to the Quaker leader, despite his color, just as Alison had felt when she first heard Myron, during a reading from his book on liberalism, telling listeners that empathy and compassion were their best weapons against hatred and intolerance. Abigail must have believed in that Inward Light which was central to Quakerism, which informed her reason and taught her that humanity is one, and that blacks deserved the same freedom and equality as whites because they too were children of the Almighty.

And to think that she lived back in the 1950s. What courage. Alison thought.

"So how did Ebenezer take the news?" Alison asked.

"He was devastated," Burke said. "I was the one who broke the news to him in a letter I wrote to him at the University of Alabama. There's no doubt that he never did get over the fact that the only woman he had ever loved and had placed on a pedestal, could've rejected him for a Negro. He felt so ashamed and humiliated that he never again set foot in Monroe. Even when his parents died in an accidental fire in 1966, he never came for the funeral. The next thing I heard about him was the story in the local paper that he had died in a plane crash in South America. Nobody really mourned for him. They had long forgotten him. It had been over 30 years since he left."

As Alison drove back home, she kept thinking about Abigail as she revolved in her mind the incredible story she had heard from Burke. *Who does she remind me of?* Alison thought. *I could swear that I've seen that face before.*

Buck awoke with a start from the rocking chair on the porch of the cabin. In his hand he found an empty bottle of Jake Daniels. He stood up and hurled the bottle into the woods, swearing at himself for having fallen asleep when he was supposed to be on guard duty. He remembered that Nancy had fainted at learning that the baby was to be killed. *She's become very attached to that mongrel,* he thought. After reviving, Nancy had complained about not feeling well and had gone to sleep. *I better go investigate if she's awake.*

Buck bent over to pick up his AK-47, and then went over to check the doors and windows. They were still locked and no glass was broken. He opened the door a crack to make sure Nancy was inside. She was up, mopping the kitchen floor while the baby lay on his back in a basket, batting at clown figurines on the mobile over his head.

"So you're finally awake?"

"Yes," she said weakly.

"I told you not to become too attached to that there mongrel."

Nancy said nothing.

"What time is it?" Buck demanded.

"Ten o'clock."

"Shit! I was supposed to call Orville at nine."

"Is he coming back here?" Nancy said. There was dread in her voice.

"Not today," Buck said. "But he's offered to take up guard duty day after tomorrow. Don't worry, though, he won't be the one to kill the mongrel. I will have that pleasure." Buck felt his belt for his cellular phone. It was gone.

"Where's my phone?"

"I haven't seen it," Nancy said without looking up from her mopping.

"I know I had it." He paused. "Didn't I?"

"I don't remember seeing you with it. Maybe you left it at the farmhouse."

Buck bolted the door from the outside and hopped into the jeep. He roared down the mountain in the direction of the farmhouse, leaving a cloud of pale red dust sparkling in the sunshine. As soon as the jeep was out of sight, Nancy reached under the baby and retrieved Buck's cellular phone and his small phone book. She paged quickly through the book. *I must get out of here before that bastard who abused me comes back,* she thought. *I wonder how Buck got mixed up with him?*

As she was leafing through Buck's phone book, not knowing what she was looking for, she was stopped by an entry on the last page. It read "Reginald Hunter - Ramsey's campaign manager" and provided a phone number. Just below the name Reginald Hunter Buck had written, in parentheses beside it, the name: "Ghazi." Nancy recalled seeing Ramsey's campaign manager many times being interviewed on TV, and he seemed such a nice man. But what a strange nickname he had – Ghazi.

He should be able to tell me how to reach Alison, Nancy thought. She quickly dialed Hunter's cell phone number.

Hunter answered his cell phone on the second ring. He was at campaign headquarters, preparing to leave for the airport to join Ramsey on the campaign trail in Wilmington.

"Hello," Nancy said breathlessly. "Is this Mr. Hunter?"

"Yes."

"I need to speak to Alison Ramsey. Is she there?"

"What's this about?" Hunter said warily.

"I'm calling about her baby."

"What about her baby? Who is this?"

Nancy sensed the suspicion in Hunter's voice and her instincts told her that she had better play it safe, lest she be detected as the kidnapper. "I'm an old friend of Alison's from college," she said. "I heard the terrible news about her baby being kidnapped. I just wanted to call and express my sympathies. We've been out of touch for years."

"Oh, I see," Hunter said, relaxing. He was in a hurry to catch his plane, so why not give the poor woman Alison's number. "All right, do you have a pen?"

Nancy wrote down the number then thanked Hunter. After she hung up, she immediately dialed Alison's number, all the time staring out the window, fearful that Buck might come back any minute.

Alison was lying on a chaise next to the crescent-shaped indoor swimming pool, having just swum laps for half an hour to relieve stress. She was now studying the notes she had compiled following her visit to Monroe and her conversation with Burke when the phone rang. She heard an unfamiliar, frightened female voice at the other end.

"Alison Whitaker?"

"Yes."

"This is Nancy."

"Nancy who?"

"Nancy McGuire. The woman who took your baby."

Alison's heart skipped a beat. She hastily grabbed a pen and a notepad.

"Where are you calling from?"

"I don't know. The baby and I were brought here in the middle of the night. We are in a cabin somewhere in the Smoky Mountains."

"Dylan's with you?"

"Yes. He's right here with me."

"Thank God." Alison closed her eyes and muttered a prayer. Part of her had believed that Dylan was still alive, but there had been moments of doubt. "How is he?"

"I've been taking good care of him. I know you must hate me for taking him from the hospital, and I don't blame you. But I simply had to call you. I need your help. I'm afraid his life's in danger. They mean to harm him."

"Who's they?"

"My husband and some crazy Klansmen he's hooked up with," Nancy said. "They're holding him and me hostage."

"Can you give me a description of the place where you're being held?"

"I don't know where it is," Nancy said. "I'm never been allowed outside except after dark. All I know it's about two and a half hours from our farmhouse. I made sure to check the watch when Buck started driving."

"Is your husband the same Buck who used to work for my father?"

"Yes."

"By the way, how did you get my number?"

"Your dad's campaign manager gave it to me."

"Hunter gave you my number?"

"Yes. He sounded suspicious. So I lied and said I was your long-lost friend."

Alison smiled and thanked God for the lucky break.

"And where did you get Hunter's number?"

"It was in Buck's little phone book. Next to it was the name Ghazi." Nancy gasped. "Oh, no. I hear the jeep. Buck's coming back. I've got to go."

The phone went dead.

Chapter 34

"Has Lynch already been told about the mongrel?" Hunter asked.

"Yes," Kessler said. "He's eager, as I am, for details on how you plan to use it to destroy Ramsey's campaign. I'm on my way to meet with him."

The two white supremacists and masterminds behind Operation Saladin were inside one of Kessler's luxury jets, a custom built Boeing 737, which was parked outside a hanger in the general aviation section of Triad International Airport. Kessler was en route to Raleigh. It was almost 6 p.m. and flashes of lightning appeared between the tall, dark, and puffy clouds, followed by the ominous roll of thunder as a storm raged.

"Here's the plan," Hunter said, leaning over the table. "Ramsey informed me this afternoon that he'll have the money ready by Friday. In the meantime, I intend to make available to the detectives investigating the kidnapping the most sensational political scandal of the century. It's going to be bigger than Watergate, partner."

"What's the story line?"

"Kinky sex, kidnapping, blackmailing, drugs, and murder," Hunter said. "I've arranged for Rayvon to come to a secret meeting with Ramsey expecting to receive a $3 million bribe. In the meantime, Ramsey will come expecting to be given his grandson's dead body after he pays the ransom. Unbeknownst to both, the police and the FBI will be waiting after I tip them about the secret meeting. So both Ramsey and Rayvon will be arrested as co-conspirators in the kidnapping and murder of little Dylan."

Kessler's eyebrows shot up. "As co-conspirators?"

"Yes. Inside the trunk of Rayvon's car I plan to have Abdul put the strangled corpse of Ramsey's grandson. Inside Ramsey's there'll be the video of Rayvon with the blonde, and various electronics devices and manuals on how to make secret videotapes."

"I see," Kessler said brightly. "The police will then arrest Ramsey as a blackmailer and Rayvon as the killer."

"That's the plan. Which should result in a Lynch landslide, don't you think?"

"I see no reason why not."

"And after Lynch is inaugurated Governor," Hunter said, "We'll be ready to launch the final phase of Operation Saladin."

"You're peerless, partner," Kessler said, raising his brandy glass for a toast. "Not even Machiavelli, Richard III, and Iago combined can match your cunning."

Hunter raised his also. "Like I've said, partner, I'm determined to finally get my revenge for the pain and humiliation I suffered when Abigail ran off with that nigger because of Ramsey. And there's no sweeter revenge than that of using his nigger-loving daughter Alison to destroy his campaign as part of launching Operation Saladin."

Alison arrived at the Birmingham airport, rented a Honda Civic hybrid, and drove directly to the University of Alabama at Tuscaloosa, Hunter's alma mater. En route, she thought about her conversation with Nancy. *How did Hunter's name end up in Buck's phone book? Could he be responsible for the Dylan's kidnapping? If so, what was the motive?*

Part of her found it hard still to believe that her godfather, the man she had lovingly called "Uncle Reggie," could turn out to be her and her father's worst enemy.*That's why I simply couldn't tell dad or mom the truth*, Alison thought. *They'd never believe me. I need more evidence than the word of a kidnapper.*

The 900-acre university campus was located east of the city center of Tuscaloosa, a word that means "Black Warrior" in Choctaw. As she drove along University Boulevard, Alison passed huge white-pillared mansions built in the early 1800s when cotton was king. Despite the ante-bellum buildings, the city had a youthful feel because of the university. A variety of department stores and fashionable shops lined the Boulevard. As she neared the campus she saw throngs of students of all races milling about, walking up and down the sidewalks and entering buildings.

I wonder how integrated it was when Hunter was here.

The original university buildings had been built in 1831, the year the university was founded, but most of those were destroyed in 1865 by Union troops. Gorgas House and the president's mansion were among the only original buildings that survived the Federal fires of April 4, 1865.

Alison parked beside the Main Library and got out. She went straight to the reserved section of the library, where she found old course catalogues. She searched for the name of the head librarian in 1960-61, Hunter's freshman year. After a few minutes of searching she found it: Mrs. Mary Ann Wentworth.

The local phone book listed several Wentworths. None of them Mary Ann.

"Excuse me," Alison said to a man behind a desk in the library's back room. He was dressed in a blue shirt and red bow-tie and wore round spectacles.

The man looked up. "May I help you?" he asked with a pleasant smile.

"I'm looking for Mrs. Mary Ann Wentworth. She was the head librarian here 44 years ago. Does the name ring a bell?"

"Are you a relative?"

"No. But I need to talk to her. It's important."

"Yes, I know Mrs. Wentworth," the man said. "She was still working here part-time when I joined the staff. She retired about five years ago."

"Do you happen to know where I can find her?"

"Well, I believe she might still live in town. Here, let me check my files. We should have her address here somewhere."

Half an hour later Alison was seated in Mrs. Wentworth's parlor, a neat, airy front room of a three-bedroom bungalow near Bryce Hospital. It had cream wallpaper and was tastefully furnished with antique pieces. Family photos covered the mantle above the fireplace. Old black-and-white photographs of historic Tuscaloosa decorated the wall over a table holding a black manual typewriter. A complete set of *Great Books* and *Harvard Classics* filled a walnut bookcase near the large bay window with lace curtains.

Mrs. Wentworth was seventy-five, silver-haired, and moved rather stiffly with the help of a cane, the result of rheumatoid arthritis. Her only child, a daughter, was an aspiring actress in Hollywood. Her husband had died in Normandy during World War II.

"Would you like some sugar with your tea, dear?" Mrs. Wentworth asked.

"Yes, please."

Alison accepted the cup and stirred it with the antique silver spoon. Mrs. Wentworth was apparently delighted to have someone listen to her relive memories of a bygone era. She talked on and on about how different the university was back when she was head librarian. Alison tried to cut short her rambling without being rude. "Mrs. Wentworth, I wonder if you remember a student named Ebenezer Bickley. His friends say he was very studious, so I thought you might've seen him around the library."

Mrs. Wentworth paused, and then shook her head slowly. "That's an unusual name. But I'm afraid it doesn't ring a bell, my dear. In the forty years I've been at the library I've met hundreds of studious students."

"Perhaps his face might be familiar." Alison handed Mrs. Wentworth the Monroe yearbook, and pointed to Hunter's senior picture.

Mrs. Wentworth put on her thick reading glasses and scrutinized the picture a full minute. "Ah, yes," she said finally, with a sigh of recognition. "I remember him. His picture was in the obituary pages several years ago."

"Obituary pages?"

"Yes. Apparently he died in a plane crash in South America in 1979 while on the way to delivering medical supplies to a remote native village."

So Hunter had reason to hide his identity in Tuscaloosa too.

"When he was a student here, did you ever meet him?"

"Yes. He used to come to the library all the time."

"Did you ever talk to him?"

"Not much," Mrs. Wentworth said. "He always kept to himself. Struck me as a rather shy, sensitive, and introspective young man. I remember he was very much into the Civil War and Reconstruction. The reason I remember that is because he surprised me one day by asking for a book few people cared to read."

"Do you remember its name?"

"Certainly," Mrs. Wentworth said, as she slowly sipped her tea. "It was the only copy the library had left. We originally had ten copies but over the years nine disappeared. It was one of the most inflammatory books ever written about the aftermath of Reconstruction. It was called *The Clansman*, by Thomas Dixon."

"I've read the book," Alison said.

"You have?" Mrs. Wentworth said with surprise.

"Yes," Alison said. "For my history course at Brown University. I was working on a paper on why North and South have such differing interpretations of slavery, the Civil War, Reconstruction, and its aftermath. Its contents infuriated me, I must say, particularly its fixation on the issue of rape. But I read the book to understand the nature of its profound influence on so many generations of Southerners."

"I can never understand why a minister of a gospel about love could have written such a hateful and un-Christian book," said Mrs. Wentworth, shaking her head.

"I don't know either," said Alison, recalling that Dixon wasn't just another redneck preacher. Born in 1864 into an aristocratic Southern family, Dixon had studied law and history at John Hopkins University, where he was a classmate of President Woodrow Wilson. Eager for converts beyond his native South, Dixon had journeyed north, to Boston and New York, where his fiery sermons about "creeping Negroidism" and white Christian supremacy had found a receptive audience among Yankees steeped in racial pseudoscience. Dixon proved such a hit that he spent nine years mesmerizing worshippers at New York's Twenty-third Street Baptist Church, where one of his admirers, John D. Rockerfeller, even offered to pay half the expense of building him his own cathedral in downtown Manhattan. But Dixon declined the offer, preferring instead to reach an even larger audience by penning race-baiting novels of such virulence that one of them, *The Clansman*, became the basis of the epic *Birth of a Nation*, the largest grossing film of the silent era, which, on February 18, 1915, was shown in the East Room of the White House, to President Wilson, his daughters, and members of his cabinet and their families. After the viewing, an impressed and appreciative President Wilson said the following about a film that was to lead to the second revival of the Klan: "It is like writing history with lighting. My only regret is that it's all terribly true."

Aware of Hunter's paternal ties with the Klan, Alison asked, "Do you know if there was an active Klavern around campus when Ebenezer was a student?"

"Sure there was Klan activity around campus," Mrs. Wentworth said. "Remember this was 1961. Most people were opposed to integration. The Klan was constantly holding noisy rallies and marches around the campus. There was a showing of *Birth of a Nation* just about every night. It played to large and enthusiastic crowds, and proved to be the Klan's most effective recruiting tool."

Having seen D. W. Griffith's powerful epic, Alison wasn't surprised. It not only glorified the Klan, but the film gave the impression that joining the group was the most patriotic thing a Southerner could do. Its most powerful scene was aimed at fueling white fears of miscegenation. It showed a hysterical Little Sister leaping from a cliff to her death on the jagged rocks below, rather than be ravished by Gus, the free black from the North who, squat like an ape and foaming with lust, had chased her to her doom.

Mrs. Wentworth took a sip of tea. She then looked at Alison. "Young lady," she said, "I hope you don't find this question inelegant, but why are you asking all this?"

"I'm sorry. I should've explained. The estate of Ebenezer Bickley has commissioned me to write his biography. He had quite a remarkable life before his tragic death. And apparently his years at Tuscaloosa were quite formative."

"I see," Mrs. Wentworth said. "Well, the only thing I can fault Ebenezer Bickley for is that after graduating he went to work as an editor for one of those trashy papers which were very popular with segregationists and the Klan."

"Really?"

"Yes. The paper was called *The Cause*. I remember it because it employed that rascal Tommy Cone as its delivery man."

"Who's Tommy Cone?"

"Oh, he's one of those social misfits the Good Lord has seen fit to bless the Christian folks of Alabama with for clinging so long to such a benevolent institution as Jim Crow," said Mrs. Wentworth after sipping her tea.

Alison laughed. She could think of several misfits her own North Carolina was blessed with for similar acts of benevolence toward blacks and the poor.

"He was one of the most notorious Klansmen in Tuscaloosa," Mrs. Wentworth went on. "He was about 6'7" and wore size 13 shoes. He supposedly had a high IQ, even though he never finished high school. He was something of a poet, too."

"What kind of poetry did he write?"

"Mostly about the Civil War."

"What made him notorious? Surely not his poetry."

"No. He committed double murder."

"Really?"

Mrs. Wentworth suddenly looked at her watch. "Oh dear," she cried. "I forgot I have a bridge game in about an hour. Do you mind if I go call my friends to tell them that I'll be a trifle late?"

"No, not at all," Alison said gratefully.

Mrs. Wentworth stood up and with some difficulty and using a cane, walked to her bedroom. Alison heard her talking on the phone but couldn't make out what she was saying. Minutes later she returned, all radiant. "Well, that's taken care of," she said. "They know not to start without me because I'm the best player of the lot."

Alison smiled.

"Now where was I?" said Mrs. Wentworth, resuming her seat.

"You were talking about Tommy Cone committing double murder."

"Ah, yes. In 1965, shortly after the March on Montgomery, he bombed a pro-civil rights paper in Selma," Mrs. Wentworth said. "The bomb killed its publisher, Mrs. Nora Driessen, a fifty-two year old Jewish woman who was very outspoken about many things, and her assistant, a nice Negro young man who went to college up North because our own liberal-minded ones wouldn't admit him."

Alison smiled. She liked Mrs. Wentworth's irony. "Did Cone act alone?"

"He sure did," Mrs. Wentworth said. "Anyway that's what he said in his boastful and rambling confession. He claimed that though race mixers deserved to die for violating God's law, he wasn't aware there were people in there when he planted the dynamite. Of course our all-white, all-wise, and all-Christian jury acquitted him."

"Acquitted him?"

"Sure, honey," Mrs. Wentworth said. "Remember this was the Deep South during Jim Crow. Those who murdered so-called Communists and race mixers were regarded as heroes, not villains. They were honored with parades, instead of being sent to the electric chair. And Nora, as she liked to be called, was quite a Communist by Southern standards. She had an unconventional marriage. She and her husband, Samuel Driessen, were quite in love and yet lived in separate homes. And many of Nora's friends were Negroes. And Samuel was a prominent gynecologist who was known as the Butcher of Tuscaloosa because he wasn't hypocritical enough to hide the fact that he performed abortions for indigent Negro farm workers who more often than not were raped by white men. Nora and Samuel had a son, Isaac, whom they sent to schools up North."

Mrs. Wentworth paused to sip her tea.

"And Nora's mother, Ruth, who started the paper around the turn of the century, was one of the women who led the fight demanding that Congress ratify the 19th Amendment. I'm told she even dared publish Mary Wollstonecraft's *A Vindication of the Rights of Woman* in support of the amendment."

"Wow," Alison said, deeply impressed. "She certainly was ahead of her time."

"More than that," said Mrs. Wentworth. "She was one of the few Southerners to denounce the compromise reached in order to get the amendment ratified."

"You mean the denial of the vote to black women so as to make the amendment palatable to Southern states?"

"Yes. And the irony is that her daughter Nora was killed for defending the character of another courageous woman who was also ahead of her time and dared stand up for what was right."

"Who's that?"

"Viola Liuzzo. She's a Detroit woman who was shot by three Klansmen for riding in a car with a black man during the march from Selma to Montgomery."

"I remember her story."

"Nora's paper was very outspoken in Viola's defense," said Mrs. Wentworth. "Especially after the Klan began spreading those vicious lies about her being a prostitute and all that. On the other hand the paper that Ebenezer edited led the charge in maligning her until, that is, Nora and her Negro assistant were murdered."

"Then what happened?"

"The paper folded and Ebenezer left town," said Mrs. Wentworth. "This was before Cone's second trial began, at which he was found guilty."

"What year was that?"

"I believe it was 1968."

"What had changed to lead to a conviction the second time around?"

"Several things," said Mrs. Wentworth. "President Johnson had signed the Voting Rights Act into law, for one. And the Klan had begun to lose its allure as many white Southerners reluctantly made their peace with the new order. Most important, however, was the fact that blacks began registering to vote in record numbers, with the result that politics in the South were never the same."

"What happened to Cone?" Alison asked.

"He was sentenced to death by the second jury, which, thank God, had a majority of blacks and women on it," Mrs. Wentworth said. "And I'm proud to say I was one of the jurors."

"Really?"

"Yes. And I read in the paper the other day the wonderful news that Cone is to be executed in ten days time," said Mrs. Wentworth. "But his new lawyer has appealed to the Governor for clemency."

"Who's his lawyer?"

Mrs. Wentworth shook her head. "His lawyer is none other than Nora Driessen's only child, Isaac."

"What?"

"Yes. Nora's own son is defending his mother's murderer."

Alison was stunned. "Where can I find Isaac?"

"He has an office at the Southern Poverty Law Center," said Mrs. Wentworth.

Chapter 35

"Have you raised the money?" Hunter asked.

"Yes," Ramsey replied. "It's being transferred from a New York bank. I should have it ready by late afternoon tomorrow."

"Good. I'll contact the kidnappers and set up a meeting."

"Thanks, Reggie," Ramsey said.

"Don't mention it," said Hunter.

The two were alone in the back room of campaign headquarters.

"Reggie, have you heard those rumors going around? " Ramsey asked.

"I've heard them," Hunter said. "It's awful."

"I wonder who could've started them," Ramsey said, shaking his head.

"My feeling is that it's that Klan group headed by Chandler; remember him?" Hunter said. "You helped bring his father to justice, so he's seeking revenge."

"The bastard," Ramsey said. "But what enrages me even more is that people would even give credence to the scurrilous lies he's peddling on his radio show."

"People will believe anything in the heat of an election campaign, Lawrence," said Hunter. "That's why negative campaigning is so effective."

"Can I recover from this, Reggie?" Since the rumors had started two days before, the Ramsey campaign was in free fall. Ramsey's thirty-point lead had shrunk to a mere three points, well within the five percent margin of error.

"I think you can once the ransom is paid."

"But what about the fact that Dylan was born out of wedlock and is mixed?"

"I must admit that's a tricky one," said Hunter. "My suggestion is that you, Darlene, and Alison hold a joint press conference after we retrieve the corpse and come clean. Truth is the best defense in times like these. Do you know where Alison is?"

"She's gone hiking for several days," said Ramsey. "She said she needed the break. She's been under a great deal of stress. Her marriage is falling apart."

"I'm sorry to hear that," said Hunter. "Can she be reached?"

"No. There's no phone where she's gone. And I'm glad of that. I don't know how she'd react to all these rumors. But she promised to call before she heads back home."

"Let me know when she does."

"I will."

"In the meantime, no talking to the media until we retrieve the baby's corpse," Hunter said. "I'll handle everything. Also, don't let anyone know where you're going after we have the ransom money ready."

"Not even Darlene?" Ramsey asked.

"Not even Darlene," Hunter said, and then a moment later, he added, "On second thoughts, she can come along to give you moral support when the corpse is handed over."

"If Alison is back home, can she also come along?" asked Ramsey.

"Certainly. After all, she's the mother of the poor baby."

"I really appreciate this, Reggie. I don't know how to repay you."

"Your friendship is payment enough, ol' buddy."

"So you're interested in talking to my mother's killer," Isaac said with a smile that made his periwinkle eyes twinkle behind his pewter-color glasses.

"Yes. It's very urgent," Alison said.

Alison was sitting across from Isaac in a small, book-lined

office at the Southern Poverty Law Center on Washington Avenue in Montgomery. The plaza in front of the Center was decorated with a Civil Rights Memorial, designed by Maya Lin, the artist who designed the Vietnam War Memorial. Inscribed on the curved black granite wall on the back edge of the memorial, which records milestones in the civil rights struggle and honors those who had died in the cause for racial justice in America, is the following line from Dr. King's 1963 "I Have A Dream" speech:

Until Justice Rolls Down Like Waters
and Righteousness Like a Mighty Stream

The Center had relocated from the original building on Hull Street, which Klan arsonists had torched the night of July 28, 1983, apparently anxious to destroy its priceless collection of data on hate groups. The data had survived, and included thousands of Klan photographs, reels of videotapes of white supremacy activity, and a computer backup disk containing the names of thousands of Klan and neo-Nazi members, along with politicians with known ties to white supremacist groups.

"Why do you want to talk to Tommy Cone?"

"It's a long story," Alison said hesitatingly, not knowing where to begin. "And I don't have much time. What I have to say may sound very bizarre."

"The Cone case is already bizarre enough, as you may be aware," Isaac said, smiling. "I'm the last person in the world you'd expect to be his lawyer."

"And I'm the last person in the world you'd expect to have a Klansman for a godfather," said Alison without missing a beat.

Isaac raised his eyebrows in surprise. "What did you just say?"

"The reason I desperately want to talk to Cone," Alison said, "is because I suspect that my godfather, who is also dad's campaign manager, is a Klansman, and that Tommy Cone might know something about him."

"You're joking, right?" Isaac said, tapping the edge of his cluttered desk with a sharpened pencil.

"I wish I were."

"But isn't your father Lawrence Ramsey, the famous anti-Klan crusader?"

"I know it sounds insane."

"Who's this Klansman who's running his campaign?"

Alison reached into her briefcase and removed the yearbook photo of Hunter.

"His name is Reginald Hunter. This is what he looked like before he had radical plastic surgery," she said. "As a Klansman he was known as Ebenezer Bickley."

Isaac looked up. "Did you say Ebenezer Bickley?"

Alison nodded.

"Can you wait here a minute?" Isaac said excitedly, rising from his chair. "I need to retrieve an important file down the hall. I'll be back. This is very, very interesting."

Isaac left. While Alison waited she kept thinking? *God, I sure hope I'm right.* She started perusing a copy of Morris Dees' book *Gathering Storm: America's Militia Threat*, which was lying on the coffee table. She read the blurbs on the back, from such luminaries as author Leon Uris, Abraham Foxman, national director of the anti-Defamation League, author Kurt Vonnegut Jr., and Rabbi Marvin Hier, dean of the Simon Wiesenthal Center. But it was Jimmy Carter's which deeply disturbed her:

This chilling story of America's private armies is not fiction. The danger of violent domestic conflict is all too real, as Morris Dees warns in this riveting wake-up call...

Suddenly Alison heard a knock on the door.

"Come in," she said.

The door opened. She raised her eyes expecting to see Isaac walk in with the file. Instead she saw someone she thought was an apparition.

"Myron!" she exclaimed.

"Hi, Alison."

"What-are-you doing here?" Alison stammered.

"I'm here on the same errand as you're. To find out who Hunter really is."

"Forgive me," Isaac said half apologetically. He was standing behind Myron. "But I wanted this to be a surprise reunion."

"Some surprise," Alison said. "It's the shock of my life."

"I bet," said a third voice.

Alison noticed that the speaker was someone standing behind Isaac.

"Alison," Myron said, as he introduced the speaker. "This is Morris Dees."

Alison looked at the tall, handsome man in a brown suit and tie. He had curly blonde hair, slightly large ears, and an infectious smile.

"Pleasure to finally meet you, Mr. Dees," Alison said as the two shook hands. "I've heard a lot about you from my dad."

"The pleasure's mine, Alison," Dees said. "I've heard a lot about you, too. From this courageous young man," he pointed at Myron. "Hopefully we'll have more time to talk later. But we have urgent business to attend to regarding Hunter. We've been investigating him for some time. Tell him what you told us, Myron."

"Hunter was the instigator of our breakup," Myron said. "Two days after I left to start my book tour, he paid my mother a secret visit."

"A secret visit?" said Alison, shocked.

"Yes," said Myron. "He expressly asked my mother not to tell me about it."

"To tell you what?"

"He claimed that your father had sent him to persuade my mother to pressure me not to go through with the wedding," said Myron. "He said that he'd conducted a poll showing that our marriage would destroy your dad's chances of becoming governor because a lot of white voters in North Carolina were opposed to interracial marriages. My mother, who believes that your dad, because of his pro-civil rights record, will improve the plight of blacks in her home state, reluctantly agreed."

Myron paused, took a sip from his bottled water, and then continued, "When I returned from the book tour she asked me to call off the wedding. At first I resisted because I didn't want to hurt you. But she persisted in begging me and I finally gave in, particularly when I reflected on the stakes if your father were to lose because of us. But our breakup left me depressed and riddled with guilt. Also I had a strong feeling that my mother was prejudiced. So I confronted her. That's when she finally told me about Hunter's secret visit. I then began investigating your godfather. I enlisted Isaac's help. As it turned out, he too had been on Hunter's trail ever since his mother died."

"That's partly why I went to South America, and then to Egypt," Isaac said. "I was tracking down Ebenezer Bickley. And when you called half an hour ago and said that you were in town and wanted to talk to me about Tommy Cone, I couldn't believe the coincidence. Particularly because we had already come up with plenty of circumstantial evidence linking Hunter with Cone. You provided us with the smoking gun."

"We think that Cone can be made to confirm that Ebenezer Bickley and Hunter are one and the same person," Myron said. "Despite the oath he took as a Klansman."

"And these photos and information you dug up about Hunter, along with what we already have on him, will be of great help in doing that," Dees said.

"What are we waiting for?" Alison said excitedly. "Let's go talk to Cone. Where is he being held?"

"At the Holman maximum security prison in Atmore," Isaac said.

"You and Isaac should go together," Dees said. "Myron and I will stay behind working on another part of the plan not only to bring Hunter to justice, but to possibly save the country from the greatest internal terrorism threat it's ever faced."

Chapter 36

Death row inmates at Holman are in their cells 24/7. For 45 minutes a day they're allowed outside, weather permitting, or they are taken to the gym, for exercise. They shower once every other day. They eat three meals a day, in their cells – breakfast between 2 and 3 a.m., lunch between 9 and 10 a.m., and dinner between 2 and 3 p.m. Normal sleep is almost impossible, as the guards wake inmates up as often as every fifteen minutes to check on them. This is the monotonous life Tommy Cone had known for thirty-nine years because of several rounds of appeals which kept him from the electric chair: thrice to the Court of Criminal Appeals, thrice the State Supreme Court, and once to the U.S. Supreme Court.

When Alison and Isaac came to see him, they found no other lawyers speaking to clients, so they had the entire conference room to themselves. A guard was posted outside the door. A slab of thick glass separated Cone from Alison and Isaac. Cone wore an orange prison uniform – a plain V-neck shirt with drawstring pants. His head was shaven, his dark eyes prominent. Life in prison had aged him beyond his fifty-nine years. His pale face was riddled with pockmarks and he had a diagonal scar across his left cheek. He wore the bored, blank expression of total resignation and hopelessness.

"I've brought someone who has interesting news about what

your friend Ebenezer Bickley has been up to since he returned to America," Isaac said casually.

The expression on the face of Tommy Cone was galvanic. But realizing that he was giving himself away, he sharply retorted, with a nervous laugh, "Huh, who said I had a friend named Ebenezer Bickley?"

"Didn't you use to boast that you had a friend who'll soon get you out of here?"

"That friend is dead. And his name wasn't Ebenezer Bickley."

"How did he die?" Alison asked.

"Plane crash, if that means anything to you."

"Is this your friend who died in the plane crash?" Isaac showed Cone a photo of Hunter taken while he was editor of *The Cause.*

"What if it's him?"

"What if I told you that this man here is not dead," Alison said. "But as alive as you are behind that thick plate of glass."

"I'd say you were mad."

"So you did know Ebenezer?" Isaac said.

"What if I did?"

"Do you know anything about reconstructive plastic surgery?" Alison said.

"Yes. I've read something about it," said Cone. "I've done nothing but read since I was locked up in this shithole. I'm now a walking encyclopedia."

"Do you know that done well it can totally change the appearance of a person?"

"Yes."

"What do you remember most about Ebenezer?"

"His thick lips, protruding teeth and colored nose."

"Okay, look very carefully at these following pictures," Alison said.

She then pulled out several recent photos of Hunter.

"Look very carefully," Alison said.

After scrutinizing the photos for several minutes, Cone said, "Forgeries."

"So you agree there's some resemblance between Ebenezer and this man?"

"Forgers can do anything."

"And maybe it's also a forgery that Ebenezer's now a

multimillionaire."

"A multimillionaire. Huh," Cone laughed. "If he's a millionaire then I'm about to walk out of Holman a free man. Shoot. Ebenezer was as poor as a church mouse when he died. That's why that fat cat in that picture can't be him."

"What makes you believe that?" Alison asked.

"Because I'm the sole beneficiary of Ebenezer's will."

"His will?" asked Alison.

"Yes. And the only thing he left me were a tuba and his most prized possession."

"What was that?" asked Alison.

"A book of poems."

"Do you have the book?"

"Yes, I carry it with me all the time," Cone said. "It's a reminder of my dear friend Ebenezer. I've even asked the authorities to bury it with me after I'm fried."

"Do you have the book with you?" Alison asked.

Cone nodded.

"May I take a look at it? I like poetry too."

Cone looked at her dubiously.

"Please."

Cone reached into his pocket and removed a small, leather-bound anthology of *The Greatest Poems in the English Language*. "It's one of only two copies," he said proudly. "The other copy Ebenezer had with him when he died."

Alison recognized the book at once. It was identical to the copy Hunter had given her. Only, Cone's copy had the initial *E* on the cover in calligraphy.

"Thanks," Alison said. "What does the E stand for?"

"Ebenezer, of course."

"You say there are only two copies of the book left?" Alison said.

"Yes."

"How do you know there aren't other copies?"

"Because Ebenezer told me that he had both copies specially bound and engraved. I was with him when he picked them up at the print shop in Montgomery. And according to his will, the second copy was with him when he died in the plane crash."

"Did the other book have the initial A on it?"

Cone looked stupefied. "How the devil do you know that?"

Alison ignored the question. "And did he mean to give it to a girl named Abigail Chambers? But before he could do that Abigail ran off with a black man?"

Cone's face resembled that of a man who was being throttled. Alison calmly reached into her purse and removed a leather-bound anthology of *The Greatest Love Poems in the English Language.* It was exactly identical to the one Cone was holding in his hands. She held it up against the thick plate glass for Cone to see.

"Where the hell did you get that?" Cone yelled, leaping from his chair.

"From Ebenezer. He gave it to me last year as a wedding present."

The Klan oath Tommy Cone had taken in the basement of the offices of *The Cause* two weeks before civil rights activists from across the country converged on Selma for the now famous march, during which Sheriff Jim Clark's mounted posse had used tear gas, clubs, and whips on peaceful demonstrators, had been administered by none other than Reginald Hunter, aka Ebenezer Bickley, leader of one of the most violent Klan groups ever to terrorize the Deep South.

Cone had joined the group after Ebenezer, through his clarion *The Cause,* had called on all red-blooded, Christian, patriotic, Anglo-Saxon men to defend Alabama, God, and Country against a Jewish-led invasion of whores, punks, scum, degenerates, kooks, atheists, perverts, and communists from the North. The oath read as follows:

I most solemnly swear that I will forever keep sacredly secret all my knowledge of the acts and proceedings of the Ku Klux Klan.

I most sacredly vow and most positively swear that I will die before I ever give evidence against any member of the Ku Klux Klan.

I most sacredly vow and most positively swear that I will never yield to bribery, flattery, threats, passion, punishment, persecution, or any other enticement whatever coming from or offered by any person or persons, male or female, for the purpose of obtaining from me any secret or secret information of the Ku Klux Klan. I will die rather than divulge the same, so help me God.

When he learned that the man who had administered the oath, the man whom he had protected by taking responsibility for murders he had committed, was alive, well, and rich, Cone repudiated the oath with relish. What made Cone especially bitter was the fact that despite his enormous wealth, Hunter hadn't even deigned to get him decent legal counsel. Instead, he had left his fate in the hands of overworked lawyers from the death penalty resource centers, which in Alabama were the sole providers of attorneys for indigent inmates facing the death penalty.

In spilling the beans on Hunter, Cone went even further. He told how Hunter had organized the group of four men who accosted Reverend James Reeb, a Unitarian minister from Boston, on March 9, and clubbed him into a coma with lead pipes. Reeb died two days later. Cone also revealed that shortly before Hunter fled to South America, he had mailed a letter bomb to one Charles Pearson, Abigail's husband, a law professor at Swarthmore. The bomb blew up in his face and killed him instantly.

But the most damning piece of evidence was the revelation by Cone that the Kessler Group had financed a great deal of the Klan violence against the Civil Rights Movement, and that when Hunter fled the States, he had linked up with Richard Kessler in South America, where the latter at the time had the headquarters of his vast empire. It was Kessler who had facilitated Hunter's escape, first to South Africa and later to Egypt, where he had undergone elaborate plastic surgery before returning to the United States in the fall of 1992.

By the time Cone was done ratting, three hours after Isaac and Alison had come to see him, Cone knew that even if he went to the electric chair, he wouldn't go alone. He would take Hunter, and possibly Kessler, with him. Definitely the double-crossing Hunter. Isaac assured him that his sworn affidavit of who had really committed the murders and why, if it turned out to be true, could win him clemency from the Governor.

"I knew there was more to Hunter than met the eye," Myron said, as he, Alison, and Isaac sat around a conference table in one of the spacious offices at the Center. "But I didn't know he was the swine who murdered my uncle."

"And my mother," Isaac said.

"And he's threatened to kill our son, Myron," Alison said.

Myron looked at her, stunned. "Our son?"

Alison held Myron's hand. "Yes, our son, Myron. Dylan is mixed. Apparently he was conceived that night I flew up to New York to tell you that my father had agreed to bless our wedding. Before I came down here, the woman who kidnapped him from the hospital nursery called and said that Dylan is being held somewhere in the mountains of North Carolina, and that he will be killed by a group of Klansmen linked to Hunter."

Myron was at a loss for words. His eyes blazed with anger.

Dees walked in from an adjacent room where he had been on the phone. "She's right, Myron," he said with a somber face. "I just finished talking to FBI Chief Evans in North Carolina. His SWAT Team has information that Dylan is still alive and is being held at a remote mountain cabin west of Asheville by a right-wing Klan militia led by Richard's son, Johnny Chandler. Not only that, but Chief Evans has also confirmed that Hunter has provided weapons and ammunition, including WMD, to Chandler's militia as part of igniting a Great Revolution that's outlined in *The Turner Diaries*."

"Jesus Christ," said Myron.

Alison frowned. "What's *The Turner Diaries*?"

Isaac spoke. "*The Turner Diaries* is a racist, anti-Semitic, and homophobic book that's considered the Bible of the right-wing militia movement. In the book a white private guerilla army wages war against a liberal federal government after passage by Congress of the Cohen Act legislating miscegenation. Following the war, the guerilla army exterminates all non-whites, Jews, gays, liberals, and white women married to Jews and blacks as prelude to transforming America into a fascist Aryan nation."

"Surely that can't happen in America," Alison said.

"It sure can," Isaac said. "All that fascism needs to take root is demagogues to stoke people's insecurities and fears, rational or irrational, and to find convenient scapegoats. Don't forget that people thought Hitler couldn't come to power in Germany. But he did. And his racial and militarist theories were derived from *Mein Kampf*, a book many dismissed as the ravings of a madman."

"*The Turner Diaries'* theories have already inspired several terrorist acts," Dees said. "Timothy McVeigh used the book as a blueprint for the Oklahoma City bombing. And in the 1980s, a white supremacist group in the Pacific Northwest calling itself The Order robbed banks, counterfeited currency, and bombed movie theaters and synagogues, in the hope of igniting the Great Revolution. The Order was finally infiltrated by the FBI and its members brought to justice after they murdered Alan Berg, an outspoken Jewish talk show host. Chief Evans believes that Chandler's ambition was to pick up where the Order left off, and to use the war on terror as a cover. He also believes that Hunter may have provided him the funds to purchase weapons and ammunition because a race war would serve his interests too, which are to destroy your father for what he's done, and to see America run by white supremacists who would cleanse America racially. So before you return to North Carolina, we must come up with a plan to save not only your child's life and your father's campaign, but also the future of our Democracy and way of life."

"Who provided Chief Evans with all this insider information about Chandler and his militia?" asked Alison.

"Chandler's wife, Anna," Isaac said.

Alison was stunned.

Isaac explained. "Anna is an Afrikaner from South Africa. Her brother used to belong to a white extremist group called the AWB, whose goal was to establish a whites-only homeland. She saw how hatred wreaked havoc on her people, and she didn't want any part of it. She came to America as an *au pair*. She overstayed her visa, met Chandler on the internet, and was taken by him. What she didn't realize was that he was a white supremacist who was determined to start a race war and overthrow the U.S. government. When she found that out, she contacted the FBI, who gave her instructions."

"Good luck, honey," Myron said to Alison as he hugged her. Isaac and Dees looked on.

"This is the final boarding call for U.S. Airways Flight 235 to Greensboro," the voice came over the loudspeaker system at the Montgomery Airport.

"I hope our plan goes well," Alison said to the three men.

"It all depends on you," Dees said.

Once the 737 had reached its cruising altitude of 37,000 feet, Alison removed the phone in the back of the seat in front of her, ran her Visa credit card through the slot, and dialed her parents' phone number. "Hi, mom," she said.

Darlene sounded panicked. "Alison, thank God. Where are you?"

"I just left Asheville. I should be home in another two hours."

The FBI told Dees that Hunter may have bugged the phone,

so I better be careful what I say, Alison thought. "How are things going?" she asked.

"All hell's broken loose, Alison."

"What do you mean?"

"We've been besieged by the media," said Darlene. "The street is swarming with trucks with satellite dishes. Reporters want to talk to you about the baby. I told them you're not here but they don't believe me. They just won't leave us alone. They're trying to follow up on some outrageous rumors the Klan started."

"What rumor?"

"They say that you, Lawrence, and I conspired to murder the baby in order to win the election. Your father has had to cancel the rest of his campaign schedule. He's holed up at campaign headquarters with Reggie and his advisors, figuring out what to do. His standing in the polls has plummeted. The campaign is self-destructing."

"Oh, my God!" Alison cried.

Fadi and Dawoud smiled as they listened to Alison talking to Darlene. The two white supremacists were inside the surveillance room in Winston-Salem.

"Alison doesn't know the reception Ghazi has arranged for her," Fadi said.

Chapter 37

Reporters mobbed Alison the moment she stepped off the plane at the Triad International Airport. But as a journalist, she was prepared for the reception, for she knew the unsavory tactics often employed by some members of her profession who, in their eagerness to get a scoop, didn't care about trampling on the humanity or feelings of their subjects.

"Did you murder your own baby?" one journalist shouted.

"Of course not," Alison said firmly.

"What race is your baby?" shouted another.

She ignored that one and headed straight for the parking lot. Like bloodhounds, the reporters chased after her. They shoved microphones, note pads, and video cameras into her face. One even blocked her way with a video camera. She went around him. More questions came in rapid fire fashion. "Is your marriage to Eliot over?"

"Did you and your father have the baby killed because it was mixed?"

"Did you do it in order to win the election?"

"Where did you hide the body?"

"Do you know who the baby's father is?"

"Was this a ritual murder?"

"Is it true that Rayvon's the father?"

The media hounded her all the way to her Cherokee. She got into the driver's seat, rolled down the window and, with perfect equanimity, she said, "I'll answer all your questions at a press conference tomorrow at the Embassy Suites."

Two hours before the noon press conference Alison held a meeting in Suite 129 of the Embassy Suite just off I-40. Present were her parents, Hunter, Eliot, Chanel, Theodore and his wife Mary-Lou, FBI Chief Bruce Evans, his assistant, Ray Millet, and two police officers. Eliot had arrived at the last minute, having flown nonstop from Rio in Brazil after hearing of the scandal on TV. CNN, Fox News, and various other television stations, together with various national and local newspapers, including *USA Today*, were full of speculation about Alison's pending press conference and rumors that Ramsey planned to do the unprecedented: withdraw from the race with only five days to go.

"With the exception of Eliot, Chanel, and Chief Evans, whom I talked to yesterday, all of you are probably wondering what I'm going to say," Alison said to the group gathered before her. She looked serious and professional in a maroon business suit with brass buttons. "Reserve judgment until you hear everything."

"We're listening," Ramsey said nervously, no doubt because the latest polls showed him twenty points behind Lynch. His campaign was imploding and he knew it. He was praying for a miracle. He had the ransom money ready, and he and Hunter had already arranged a meeting with the kidnappers for that afternoon.

"Incredible as it may sound," Alison said, "what I'm about to tell you is the truth surrounding my baby's kidnapping."

Mary Lou and Theodore exchanged glances. Hunter's eyes were riveted on Alison. Evans secretly signaled to Millet and the two police officers and they started moving toward the doors. "You, Uncle Reggie," Alison said, pointing directly at Hunter, "are an unrepentant Klansman and the mastermind behind a plot to have my baby murdered."

Mouths gaped. Darlene gasped. Even the usually imperturbable Theodore was visibly shaken. Hunter looked indignant. "How dare you accuse me of such a thing!" he said, glaring at Alison. "You must be stark-raving mad."

"Alison!" Ramsey said angrily. "Is this some kind of joke?"

"It's not a joke, Dad," Alison said. "Uncle Reggie was head of the Fiery Cross, one of the most violent Klan groups in Alabama in the '60s. He joined the group his sophomore year at the University of Alabama in Tuscaloosa, shortly after he heard the news that Abigail, the woman he adored, had fallen in love with a black man and had joined the Civil Rights Movement. That black man was Myron's uncle, Charles. When he heard that Abigail had died during childbirth in 1962, Hunter vowed revenge against liberals, whom he blamed for the Civil Rights Movement and Abigail's death."

The room was as silent as a tomb.

Alison went on. "Two years after Abigail's death, Hunter, who by now was Grand Wizard, mailed Myron's uncle, who was a professor of American history at Swarthmore College, a letter bomb that killed him instantly."

There were more gasps. Hunter's brow started to sweat.

"And throughout the 1960s, the Fiery Cross was responsible for the bombing of dozens of churches, synagogues, and businesses belonging to those who were part of or sympathetic to the civil rights movement. And in 1965 Hunter planted the dynamite that blew up the offices of *The Liberator*, a pro-civil rights paper in Selma. The blast killed Nora Driessen and James Cook, her black assistant, who were upstairs working late on a story related to the march. Cone, who was the lookout man, became the fall guy. At his first trial, he was acquitted by an all-white jury. Thanks to the 1965 Civil Rights Act, juries across the South became mixed and, at his second trial in 1968, Cone was convicted of first-degree murder. Shortly after his conviction, Hunter, with the help of the billionaire Richard Kessler, fled the country. First to Colombia, South America, and later to Cairo, Egypt, where he underwent elaborate plastic surgery."

While Alison was speaking, Hunter's face turned as white as a sheet.

"Alison, are you accusing Reggie of murder?" Ramsey said.

"Of more than murder. I'm accusing him of being a drug-dealer, and of providing weapons and ammunition to Chandler's militia, whose goal is to overthrow the U.S. government, kill all blacks, Jews and liberals, and transform America into a fascist, whites-only nation. And the woman who kidnapped Dylan from the hospital after he was born is currently being held hostage at Chandler's compound in the Smoky Mountains."

"Do you know for a fact that Dylan is still alive?" asked Ramsey.

Alison nodded. "In an ironic act of fate, it was Uncle Reggie who gave the woman my number after her husband told her Hunter wanted Dylan murdered, so that his corpse could be used to blackmail Dad and destroy his campaign."

"You're all mad!" Hunter shouted desperately. "I don't know anything about murders, drugs, kidnapping, and corpses. This is a clear case of mistaken identity."

"I happen to have a photo of you as Grand Wizard Hunter," Alison said, reaching into her brown satchel. "Or shall I call you by your true name, Ebenezer Bickley? Here he is, in full regalia, administering the Klan oath to a group of new recruits," she added, handing the photo to her father. "It was taken before he had radical cosmetic surgery."

Ramsey took one look at the picture and said, "That's definitely Reggie."

"That old thing?" Hunter said dismissively. "It was taken at a Halloween party. My friends and I hated the Klan so we dressed up that way to mock them. Ask your father. He'll tell you how much I despise the Klan."

"It's true, Alison," Ramsey said. "When we were kids, Reggie and I helped thwart a plan by the Klan to terrorize black workers. I told you about that, didn't I?"

"I'm glad you brought that up, Dad," Alison said. "Do you remember Hunter and his family leaving the farm rather suddenly?"

"Yes. My father told me that they wanted to start a new life in Monroe."

"No doubt," Alison said. "After all, Hunter's father was the ring leader of the Klan group you stumbled upon in the woods. Apparently Grandpa didn't want to hurt your feelings by telling you that your best friend's father was a Klansman. So he allowed the Bickleys to leave under false pretenses."

Ramsey shook his head in disbelief. "These are incredible allegations you're making, Alison. Do you have conclusive proof?"

"They're incredible but true, Lawrence," Eliot said. "The proof is in the folders Chanel is holding. Alison shared everything with me last night. And then I remembered how this creep" – he disdainfully pointed a finger at Hunter – "manipulated me into getting back together with Alison after he learned that I was gay."

"You are what?" cried Theodore, stunned.

"I'm gay, Dad," Eliot said. "I wanted to tell you all along, but knowing how much of a conservative you are, I thought you'd disown me."

Mary, who was normally taciturn, spoke. "How could your own father disown you, Eliot? You are his flesh and blood. The Cheneys, despite being staunch conservatives, didn't disown their daughter."

Tears filled Theodore's eyes. "Your mother is right, son. I'm a proud conservative, but I could never disown you for being true to the way God made you. But how did this creep" – Theodore pointed at Hunter – "find out you were a homosexual?"

"He saw me and my partner at a gay bar in Greensboro," Eliot said. "He said he was doing research on the issue. He warned me that if you found out, you'd disinherit me. So he suggested that I marry Alison to cover up the fact. He even arranged for me to pick her up at the airport after her breakup with Myron."

"He did?" Darlene asked in astonishment.

"Yes," said Theodore angrily. "When he came to my office and asked me to support your candidacy, Lawrence, I was quite surprised. I asked him why, since you and I didn't see eye to eye on the issues. He told me that it would help greatly because you had repudiated liberalism and were now a conservative."

"The bastard," Ramsey said.

"Please hand everyone the files, Chanel," Alison said.

Chanel began distributing the folders.

"And Chief Evans also has a fascinating story to tell about Richard Kessler, Hunter's partner in crime," Alison went on. "Please proceed Chief, and I'll fill in the gaps where necessary."

"With pleasure," Evans said. "Richard's father, Otto Von Kessler was a Nazi."

The room gasped.

"A Nazi?" Darlene cried.

"Yes," Chief Evans said. "And not just any Nazi. He was among the industrialists who helped bankroll Hitler's rise to power."

"Oh, my God!" Darlene said, trembling with rage. "Reggie was cavorting with Nazis when he well knew that my relatives had died in Hitler's concentration camps. I could kill you with my bare hands, you swine!"

Darlene advanced toward Hunter, who shrank into a corner. Ramsey, eyes blazing, wrapped his arms around Darlene. "Please proceed, Chief."

Evans took a sip of bottled water before continuing. "In the 1930s Otto became the driving force behind the formation of the Bund in the U.S. to propagandize the Nazi cause," he said. "Despite his American citizenship, he remained very close friends with Hitler. In fact they shared the same birthday, April 20, 1889. Hitler had been best man at Otto's wedding to an opera singer. Otto's son Richard was born on November 9, 1924, in Birmingham, Alabama, three months after his parents relocated to America. And records obtained from Germany show that Hitler was his godfather." Evans paused to let the statement sink in. "Because of Otto's influence within the Klan through ownership of *The Cause*," he continued, "he tried bringing about a merger between the Bund and the Klan. He also secretly backed Charles Lindbergh's attempts to have America sign a neutrality pact with Hitler, and helped arrange for Hermann Goering, founder of the Gestapo, to award the legendary aviator a Nazi medal of honor that he refused to disavow even after Hitler's concentration camps were exposed. Also, there's evidence that Otto may have been involved in the coup d'état attempt by big money interests against President Franklin Roosevelt. The plot was exposed by Major General Smedley Darlington Butler, an outspoken opponent of nascent fascism in America."

"And when President Roosevelt was preparing to run for a fourth term," Alison inserted, "Otto secretly funded efforts by the Klan to turn Southern Democrats away from the party. An amateur artist, he even designed a cartoon that first ran in *The Cause*, which has Roosevelt saying to Eleanor: 'You kiss the niggers and I'll kiss the Jews, and we'll stay in the White House as long as we choose.' When the Bund became a target of FBI and Congressional scrutiny after America entered the war," Chief Evans said. "Otto quietly moved his family to Colombia, and then to Egypt. However, he retained his American citizenship, and even sent his son Richard to American schools, despite continuing his 'patriotic duty' on behalf of the Fatherland."

Evans cleared his throat and took up the narrative again.

"In 1939, Otto scoured the jungles of Bolivia, Colombia, and Peru for deadly poisons for Hitler's scientists, who used them in concocting the Final Solution against the Jews," he said. "While there, Otto stumbled upon the *Erythroxylum coca* plants, which members of the Incan Empire had chewed for centuries to obtain euphoria, stimulation, and alertness. So he purchased vast tracts of land in South America to cultivate the coca plant using native peons. But after Hitler's dream of a thousand-year Reich failed, Otto relocated to Egypt, where he linked up with former Nazis who'd found sanctuary there."

"Meanwhile," Alison said, "Richard was having a wonderful time at the University of Alabama at Tuscaloosa. He was known as something of a playboy, accustomed to giving huge parties that turned into orgies. His debauched lifestyle infuriated his father. Otto had hoped to groom his son to someday run for president of the United States. But all that Richard apparently cared about was having a good time. And his extravagant lifestyle became easy to finance when, ten years after his father's death, cocaine started replacing marijuana as the drug of choice in the West. Richard recognized the windfall he was heir to. He linked up with a relatively small cocaine smuggling ring that was under the control of exiled Cuban criminal organizations based in Miami. They provided the carriers, or mules, and the distribution network. He provided the coca paste which was then refined in kitchen laboratories in Colombia, before being smuggled into the States. Their joint operation became known as *The Organization*. It quickly grew into the largest drug-trafficking ring in South America."

"*The Organization* preceded the Medellin and Cali Cartels by almost a decade," Evans said. "It therefore reaped billions with its sale of cocaine to the U.S., Europe, and Japan during the '60s and '70s. Kessler was smart enough to get out of the business before the 'Cocaine Wars' erupted. Shortly before the 1979 energy crisis, he got into the oil business and later, following the First Gulf War, he helped Saddam siphon billions from the U.N. Oil for Food program.

"Kessler's net worth is estimated at $40 billion," Alison said. "He owns banks, hotels, a charter airline, newspapers, radio and TV stations, a publishing house, restaurants, sports teams, a fleet of luxury jets and yachts, and casinos across the Americas, Africa, the Middle East, and Europe. Most ominous, he's the financier of one of the most powerful political action committees in the country. Known as *American Renewal Through Strength and Values*, or ARTSAV, the PAC annually spends tens of millions of dollars to influence the defeat of politicians of either party Kessler considers too liberal, and the election of those who openly repudiated liberalism."

While everyone was absorbed in what Alison and Evans were saying, Hunter furtively unbuttoned his single-breasted woolen jacket and whipped out a .45-caliber pistol. "Enough of this bullshit," he said, cocking the gun with a click.

Everyone froze and stared down the barrel of Hunter's gun.

"You two," he said, waiving the pistol at the officers. "Unbuckle your guns and put them on that table right there. And you two, niggers," he pointed the guns at Millet and Evans, "remove those guns under your coats. Make it snappy." He watched warily as they obeyed his command. "Now, everybody get to that corner of the room. Pronto. Any false move and you're dead. I've killed before and I won't hesitate to kill again."

Everyone obeyed.

"Reggie, what's the meaning of this?" said Ramsey. "Please put away the gun."

"Shut up, you fucking traitor!"

"Traitor!"

"Yes," Hunter said. "You're a Judas and a disgrace to your race. You, come over here." Hunter signaled to Darlene with the gun. Trembling, Darlene hesitated.

"Do as he says, mom," Alison said.

Darlene inched toward Hunter.

Hunter grabbed her roughly. "I want you to dial campaign headquarters and ask for my chief-of-staff." Darlene did as she was told. She handed the phone to Hunter, who took it with his left hand. The gun in the right hand was pointed at Darlene's temple. "This is

Ghazi. The game's up. I want you to shred all the evidence, gather the troops together, and meet me at the Triad International Airport in exactly one hour. I'm about to call Aziz to have him come pick us up." Hunter put down the phone and turned to Darlene. "Now I want you to dial another number and hand me the phone." Darlene punched in the numbers as Hunter recited them.

"Is that Kessler's number?" Alison said. "Is he Aziz?"

"Shut up, nigger-lover, or I'll blow your brains out."

Alison shut up.

Still keeping his gun aimed at Darlene's head, Hunter grabbed the phone with his free hand. "Partner, this is Ghazi," he said. "The game's up. The troops and I need a quick getaway. Can you pick us up at the Greensboro International airport in about an hour? Bring Aryan-Force One instead of the smaller plane. We all must clear out. Don't forget to shred everything connected to Operation Saladin." Hunter smiled as he replaced the receiver. "Now we just wait here a little while until it's time for me and a couple of hostages to take a quick trip to the airport. So everybody relax."

Chapter 38

Hunter still had the gun pressed to Darlene's temple when the phone rang. She could feel its cold steel muzzle digging into her skull. She tried not to think about how tenuous and precarious her hold on life was.

"Pick it up and hand it to me," Hunter said.

Darlene reached for the phone and handed it to Hunter.

"Richard?" Hunter said.

"Yeah, it's me, partner," Kessler said. "I've just arrived at the Greensboro airport. Aryan-Force One is parked next to the USAir terminal. The others have already arrived and are on board. We're waiting for you."

Hunter grinned. "Great. See you shortly."

He turned to Darlene. "Call the front desk. Tell the valet to bring your Lexus to the front." Turning to the rest of the group, he said, "Darlene is coming with me to the airport as insurance. If anybody attempts to stop me, she dies."

Ramsey stepped forward. "Reggie, leave Darlene alone. Take me instead. This is between you and me."

Alison stepped forward. "No, dad, it's between him and me."

Hunter studied Alison thoughtfully. Keeping the gun to Darlene's temple, he said, smiling, "All right, nigger-lover. You'll drive me to the airport. We two have a lot to talk about."

Hunter shoved Darlene away from him and grabbed Alison. Now it was Alison's temple the gun was pressed against.

"Let her go!" Darlene cried as Ramsey embraced her.

The phone rang again. It was the valet reporting that the Lexus was outside the entrance. Taking Alison, the gun still pointed at her temple, Hunter slowly backed toward the door. Alison prayed he wouldn't trip and fire accidentally.

"Hunter, you won't get away with this," Evans said.

Hunter grinned. "Wanna bet? Once Kessler and I are out of the country, you Fibbies won't be able to lay your paws on us. And we'll be back to finish the job."

"Where will you go?" asked Evans.

"There are plenty of countries that will gladly give us asylum. Iran, North Korea for instance. They will find our knowledge, expertise, and resources very useful."

The hallway was packed with reporters who apparently had overheard the commotion. They struggled to get a good shot of Hunter and his hostage. "Out of the way!" Hunter shouted, waiving the gun at them. Instantly, like the Red Sea parting at the behest of Moses, the crowd of reporters broke into two phalanxes. Television cameras rolled and camera bulbs flashed as Hunter and Alison made their way down the hall toward the elevators.

The hostage drama was being carried live by CNN, Fox News, and the other major networks. Hunter shoved Alison into the empty paneled elevator, still clutching the gun in his sweaty hand and pressing it hard against her head. The reporters scrambled down the stairs after them. Hunter looked out the window of the elevator and saw that the atrium was packed with journalists and the balconies with horrified onlookers. Once the elevator reached the ground floor, Hunter shoved Alison out first. Once more, the sea of reporters parted to let them through. Hunter and Alison crossed the elegant lobby and exited through its automatic glass doors. Her parents' black Lexus LS 430 was waiting for them with the keys in the ignition, engine still running. The temperature was a chill 49 degrees, and the air was slightly damp from a brief morning shower. The sky was a clear cobalt blue. The winding driveway in front of the hotel was lined with police cars.

Stern-faced police officers stared at Alison and Hunter through mirrored sunglasses. "If any of you as much as twitch a muscle, she dies," Hunter said, pressing the barrel of the gun hard against her temple. The police backed away. Alison slid behind the wheel of the Lexus. Hunter got in beside her, the gun still aimed at her head. The Lexus pulled out of the hotel driveway and within minutes was on U.S. 68, headed for the airport. Squad cars followed them at a safe distance. The scene was eerily reminiscent of the surreal O. J. Bronco Chase on a Los Angeles freeway. Several news helicopters flew overhead. Alison's eyes remained fixed on the road. Hunter studied her profile.

"What a pity your parents' liberalism turned you into a prostitute," he said.

Burning with anger at the insult, Alison clenched her teeth and gripped the leather steering wheel harder. She tried ignoring Hunter and focusing on the road.

"Why did you prostitute yourself to an overheated nigger ram?" Hunter said. "Was it to prove you aren't racist? We're all racists, baby, that's why we have to stick together. The survival of the white race, and the future of white power in America, is at stake, unless white women breed."

"Women are more than breeding machines, Hunter," Alison said.

"That's where you liberals are wrong," Hunter said. "A woman's place is in the home, taking care of her children while the husband provides as head of the family. That's why Viola Luizzo found little sympathy after she was murdered by the Klan. People wanted to know what she was doing in Selma, hundreds of miles away from her five children and husband."

Alison recalled the tragic but inspiring story of how Viola, spurred by her Unitarian beliefs in social justice, had left her home and family in Detroit to join the civil rights struggle in the South shortly after watching newscasts of five hundred peaceful and prayerful marchers in Selma being attacked by Alabama state troopers with billy clubs and gas grenades, only to be executed by a bullet to the head when Klansmen attacked the green Oldsmobile she was riding in.

"Viola was obeying her conscience, Hunter," Alison said. "Something you obviously don't have."

"I beg to differ," Hunter said. "I was there. I wrote those stories which the Klan, and even J. Edgar Hoover himself, circulated, saying that Viola had gone down to Selma in order to sleep with niggers. The civil rights movement was nothing but a veritable orgy. And white women were its chief whores."

"You're sick!"

"No, you're the sick one, baby," Hunter said. "You're the one with jungle fever. You'd rather swing on vines with black apes than settle down with a proper white gentleman. You aren't like Little Sister, who chose death rather than be ravaged by a nigger with yellow teeth, foaming thick lips, and the odor of an animal. I can understand why, though. You're a product of one of those Northern liberal colleges where, under the guise of a multicultural education, white women are being taught that they have a duty to get themselves nigger husbands, to prove they're not prejudiced. Go ahead and get your O. J.s, and you'll all end up like Nicole."

"You know nothing about love," Alison shot back angrily. "You're obsessed with race because being white is the only thing you ever had going for you."

"Okay, Miss Shrink. Psychoanalyze me."

"And you're obsessed with Abigail."

"There you're right," Hunter said. "She had no right to reject me for a nigger. And if she hadn't read that liberal rag your father published to promote race mixing, she would never have committed such an abomination. Take a right here," Hunter said, pointing to a side road that led to the general aviation section of the sprawling airport.

Alison took a sharp right and drove toward a lot filled with private planes. Once they were on the tarmac, Hunter pointed out Kessler's Boeing 747, which was parked alone at the far end of the terminal. About a hundred yards away from the giant plane was a squadron of about twenty police cars.

"Did you forge those photos and letters from Myron?" Alison asked.

"Yes."

"You're sick, Hunter, you know that?"

Before Hunter could respond, the chief of police's voice boomed over a loudspeaker. "Hunter, you're all set to go. We won't stop you if you don't harm the girl." Hunter flicked open his cell phone and punched in a number. "Hey, partner. I'm coming aboard with a hostage."

"I know," said Kessler. "I can see you through the window. All the troops are here and we're all set to go. Don't worry about the cops. As long as we got Ramsey's daughter as a hostage, they won't touch us."

"Good." Hunter shoved Alison out of the car in front of him and held her around the neck. Again she felt the bone-chilling sensation of the muzzle of a gun pressing against her temple. When they reached the jumbo jet, Hunter turned around and ascended the steps backwards, pulling Alison up with him step by step. On the top step he paused in the doorway of the plane and scanned the sea of police cars to make sure he saw no drawn guns or movement.

"Okay, nigger-lover," he said. "We're off to the land of the magic carpet."

I hope this works, Alison thought as she lunged at Hunter and knocked him into the plane. Instantly about a dozen armed FBI agents rushed forward and grabbed him.

"What the hell?" Hunter exclaimed, a look of shock frozen on his face.

"Welcome aboard, Hunter," Myron said.

Bewildered, Hunter looked about him. Richard Kessler sat hunched in the back row between two burly agents, his hands in cold metal cuffs that chafed against his thick sunburned wrists. Behind him stood Dees and Isaac. Hunter saw Kessler's harem, along with his entire Nazi staff, both those who had infiltrated Ramsey's campaign and those from headquarters, including Fadi and Dawoud.

Except for the harem, they were all in handcuffs and looked quite bewildered.

A despondent Kessler looked up. "She made them come after me first, old buddy," he said, flicking his bullet-shaped head in Alison's direction. "And all the time that I was talking to you on the phone, they had a gun pointed at my head."

Hunter glared at Alison as two FBI agents slapped handcuffs on him. "Where are you taking us?" he demanded.

"To the electric chair," said Alison.

Dees turned to Alison.

"Congratulations, Alison. You did an excellent job. We didn't think your plan would work. But that was a stroke of genius when you said we should get Kessler first. Unfortunately, by the time we reached him, he'd already shredded the documents on Operation Saladin. All we know is that Hunter provided Chandler's militia with money to build an underground bunker and enough weapons and ammunition to start a race war. Chandler and his men were supposed to start military training after the general election. So the priority now is to rescue your baby from the militia's compound, mindful that Chandler and his men are ruthless killers who are prepared to die for their cause."

Chandler hung up the phone inside the cabin. His haggard face looked grave. Buck, Orville, Jimmy Ray, Thad, and Bob stood dejectedly around him, watching his red-rimmed and puffy eyes scan their faces. Nancy was locked up in an upstairs room.

"It's true, Aryan Warriors," Chandler said gloomily. "Ghazi and Aziz were arrested this afternoon. And I just got tipped that ZOG plans to raid this compound on the pretense that they gotta rescue the little mongrel."

"What should we do?" Buck asked in an unsteady voice.

"Orville, guard Nancy and the mongrel," Chandler said. "Buck, take the jeep and go get Tina and the children. Jimmy Ray and Bob, come with me to the bunker. We're going to prepare fortifications. If the FBI attempts to storm the cabin, the way they did the Branch Davidians compound in Waco, then blood will flow. This is our Alamo."

Chapter 39

Clarence Lynch, who escaped arrest only because Kessler and his operatives had destroyed all the documents proving that he was Hitler's godson and part of Operation Saladin, stood at a podium overlooking a sea of eager-faced supporters at an outdoor rally at the Dixie Classic Fairgrounds in Winston-Salem.

The mostly white crowd waved red, white, and blue placards reading: "Reverse Roe V Wade," "Abolish Affirmative Action," "Scrap Welfare." The multitude chanted "We want Lynch." He waited until the roar had died down, and then resumed speaking.

"I'm here to address those false rumors being spread by the liberal media now that Ramsey's campaign is imploding. Yes, I did briefly join the Klan my freshman year at college. But I joined because I was frustrated about the rampant discrimination being suffered by white people simply because of the color of their skin. And ours was not a violent Klavern. We never lynched anyone. We simply held meetings in the basement of one of the local churches to discuss the plight of white people in America. And from time to time we marched in parades denouncing affirmative action, gay rights, and abortion."

Most in the audience nodded their heads; despite the fact that they weren't part of the Klan, they too, were against affirmative action, gay rights, and abortion.

"And I quit the Klan after realizing that the best way to fight liberalism's attempts to destroy traditional American values was by joining the political system. Liberals are hypocritical in condemning me when they've lionized Senator Robert Byrd of West Virginia, who has publicly admitted that he too once belonged to the Klan."

The crowd started chanting, "Liberals are hypocrites!"

"I promise that if you elect me your governor in four days," Lynch went on. "I'll sign an executive order abolishing affirmative action, welfare, quotas, set-asides, and forced busing. I'll work tirelessly to protect the life of the unborn. I'll build more prisons and enforce the death penalty. I'll never yield an inch in the fight to preserve the sanctity of marriage, which God said can only be between a man and a woman."

At this the crowd went wild. "We want Lynch! We want Lynch!"

Smiling, Lynch continued. "Another issue I'll fight against is forced integration. If blacks want to live by themselves, let them do so. This is, after all, a free country! They have a right to their own culture, schools, and communities, just like Native Americans! The misguided liberal experiment of forced integration has failed. It has failed because it was in defiance of human nature! After all, birds of a feather flock together."

This part of the speech brought the thick crowd to its feet. As people cheered loudly and waved placards and banners condemning forced integration, Lynch smiled and wiped the sweat from his brow with a white handkerchief.

"And to prove that what I'm saying is not racist," he shouted, "that it's a view held by many black people, who are tired of integration and are finally coming out and saying it, I want to introduce to you my newest allies and supporters, leaders of the North Carolina Chapter of the Afro-Purists, the true voice of black people in this country. Here to stand shoulder to shoulder with us are Queen Nefertari and Shaka Zulu. Aren't those lovely African names, ladies and gentlemen?" Lynch beckoned to Queen Nefertari and Shaka Zulu, who proudly ascended the stage, decked out in resplendent African garb.

"Thank you," Shaka Zulu said into the microphone, pleased by the polite applause from the confused audience. "In case any of you have never heard of the Afro-Purists," he began, "we represent the descendants of African royalty who were brought to America against their will, in chains, and now want to return to the motherland."

At the mention of "return to the motherland," the tepid enthusiasm of the white crowd became warmer. Shaka Zulu was a nigger they could do business with.

"Most blacks in America are fed up with integration," Shaka Zulu continued. "They're as proud of their culture as any other group of people are. We Afro-Purists believe that the races were meant to remain separate, that race mixing is against the laws of nature. Blacks and whites are different. Each is irreparably harmed when its blood is mingled with that of the other to produce a race which is neither black nor white."

Hearing this, many in the crowd began shouting, "Power to Afro-Purists!" in part because they were secretly against miscegenation, but had kept the attitude hidden behind a veneer of tolerance from fear of being called racist.

Shaka Zulu stood to the side of the walnut podium and it was Queen Nefertari's turn at the mike. "Thank you for inviting us, Clarence," she said, looking at Hitler's godson. "My remarks will be brief. I'm here to talk about why it's in the interest of white people to pay black people reparations for slavery and help us return to Africa, our ancestral home. First, let me make one thing clear. What I have to say may not be politically correct. But this is not the time for code words and doublespeak. I'm going to say the truth as you and I feel it in our hearts. The reason why most whites are opposed to race mixing is simply this: whenever you mix black and white, you get black. Never white."

At this a sizeable portion of the crowd gasped, most likely out of shock at having their latent fears expressed so succinctly by – of all people – a black person.

"White blood and genes are inferior because blacks are the sun people," Queen Nefertari continued. "They are warm and spontaneous in expressing their feelings. On the other hand, whites are cold and unemotional because they are the ice people. And everyone knows that the sun melts ice."

The audience grew quiet. It instinctively knew this was serious stuff. Queen Nefertari had dissected the American Dilemma. The reason why blacks and whites were seemingly doomed to remain eternal enemies, was because sun melts ice. And for its own survival, the ice will do anything to prevent the sun from melting it.

Queen Nefertari went on, "Now my friends, I ask you this: Do you want to see the white race wiped out by integration and its inevitable consequence – race mixing?"

"NO!" the crowd roared in reply. The roar was remarkably unanimous.

"And because we the sun people are humane, caring, and understanding," Queen Nefertari said in a voice full of sweetness and compassion, "we have no desire to exterminate you. Unlike what you've sought to do to us in the past. Shaka Zulu and I are here to offer you a helping hand, not a handout. We're here to pledge that we'll do our utmost to help elect Clarence Lynch, because he's the only candidate in the whole of the United States who openly opposes forced integration."

"Down with forced integration!" the cry went up. For two full minutes the chant continued vociferously. "Down with forced integration."

When it finally died down, Shaka Zulu again grabbed the mike. "To underscore what my sister here has said, we are joining forces with the Lynch campaign out of self-interest. Like you all, we love only our own. And because we love our own we don't want blacks to be deceived into committing racial suicide by supporting integration and race mixing. Integration has failed. Now is the time for separation. I therefore draw a line in the sand and toss the gauntlet before the feet of liberal tyranny and declare, 'Separation now, separation tomorrow and separation forever!'"

The cry was picked up with unusual gusto. It reminded those in the audience who were old enough to have witnessed the turbulence of the Civil Rights Movement, of Governor George Wallace's famous battle-cry against federally mandated integration: "Segregation now, segregation tomorrow and segregation forever!"

It was comforting indeed for whites to hear similar words from the lips of a black man. They went a long way toward assuaging whites of the guilt they often felt for segregating themselves from blacks. That white guilt made them feel they were doing something wrong, un-American, un-Christian. Now everything was crystal clear. Blacks wanted the same thing as whites: segregation. Then who was to blame for the deep animosities that existed between blacks and whites, when the two races had so much in common?

There could be only one answer: liberals. Liberals with their failed policies of social engineering, policies which were in defiance of human nature and God's law.

Queen Nefertari and Shaka Zulu each held up one of Lynch's hands in a sign of unity. "Vote for Lynch, a true American leader!" Queen Nefertari said.

"If blacks and whites stand united," Shaka Zulu said, "we can defeat Ramsey, the high priest of liberalism in the South. After we do, our movement will change America."

"Down with liberals! Down with Ramsey!" went the shouts as *Dixie*, mingled with the rhythmic beating of African tom-tom drums, blared from loudspeakers, and balloons went up from the midst of the now delirious crowd.

Chapter 40

The war council for the defense of liberalism met in the living room of the home of Darlene and Lawrence Ramsey, which had been debugged by the FBI after Hunter had confessed to bugging it, before he and Kessler were carted away to prison to await trial. The council included Myron, Alison, Chanel, Eliot, and Nelson, who were sitting in a semicircle in the middle of the room, and Darlene and Ramsey, who were sitting side by side on a floral loveseat. Everyone was armed with legal pads, pens, and BlackBerrys.

"So you're recommending that I totally revamp my whole campaign with only three days to go?" Ramsey said, his tie loosened, sleeves folded, and elbows on his knees. He was addressing Myron, who had taken a leave of absence from LUPA to manage Ramsey's campaign.

"I know it's risky," Myron said. "But it's the best strategy to adopt at this point."

"You've nothing to lose, Lawrence," Nelson said.

"Why do you say that?" asked Ramsey.

"Because you can only win if you stand up for what you believe," Nelson replied.

"He's right, Lawrence," Myron said. "Chanel and I have thoroughly analyzed the makeup of those who voted for you during the Democratic primary."

"And it's not the bogus numbers that Hunter was feeding you," Chanel said, who'd conducted the polls and the focus groups.

"The majority of those who voted for you were conservative Democrats," Myron said. "You've lost the support of Independents, moderates, and liberals. Your core constituency. They stayed away from the polls because they perceived you as having abandoned what was so admirable about your candidacy: principled, progressive leadership. These voters don't care about labels. What they care about is character."

"And you need them in the general election, Dad," Alison said.

"Yes," Myron said. "You have to rebuild and consolidate your base and then work hard to get the margin of victory."

"But is there enough time for Lawrence to do all that?" Darlene asked. "The election is in three days."

"A lot of elections have been won or lost in the last few days," Myron said, looking at Darlene. "The important thing is that Lawrence give voters something to vote for." He turned his attention from Darlene to Lawrence. "Up to this point you've been playing it safe – too safe. That's not being a leader. That's being a politician."

"Remember I told you that, Lawrence," Darlene said.

"The American people respect a leader, Lawrence," Eliot said. "Reagan was a leader. That's why people supported him even when they didn't agree with everything he said. The same goes for the Senator Jesse Helms."

"Eliot's right, Dad," Alison said. "Voters seldom go to the polls if they feel they're voting for the lesser of two evils. As I said, you must give them something to vote for. You must prove to them that you're not an empty vessel into which political consultants have poured meaning gleaned from focus groups and polls."

"That's exactly how I started feeling after Reggie began insidiously working on me to run as a conservative," Ramsey said.

"But you have ideas and principles," Myron said with passion. "You have a vision for this state. You just need to articulate it as clearly and as honestly as you can to the voters. It can be done, Lawrence. Besides, what do you have to lose."

"You're right, Myron," Ramsey said. "Everything you've all said makes sense. I'm ready to give it my best shot. But where do we begin?"

Myron was ready for that question.

"First, I'd recommend you hold a press conference right away," Myron said. "It's bound to get a great deal of coverage. The aim of the press conference would be to reintroduce the principled, pragmatic, progressive, and respected leader that the voters of this state know you to be."

"But hasn't Hunter tainted Lawrence's image in the public's mind?" Darlene asked.

"To a degree he has," Myron admitted. "The only antidote for that is for Lawrence to come clean. There's nothing more cleansing than truth."

"Especially in politics," Nelson said. "I'd say most voters in North Carolina aren't exactly fans of Jesse Helms. But nevertheless many vote for him time and again because he has strong opinions and he's not afraid to voice and defend them. That's why people say, 'When you vote for Jesse, you know exactly what you're getting.'"

"They said the same thing about Ronald Reagan," Eliot said.

"In other words, Dad," said Alison, "to regain the trust of voters, you must stand up proudly as a liberal, something few Democrats have done. You need to let people know exactly what they're getting when they cast their vote for you."

"Especially because your liberalism is not of the knee-jerk type," Myron said. "In the past, you haven't hesitated to criticize liberalism's excesses, and to call on the party to reform itself and adapt to changing times."

"I've always felt comfortable being myself," Ramsey said. "That's why this whole conservative charade had left me so befuddled."

"Which is exactly the way Hunter wanted you to be so he could easily manipulate you," Alison said. "And manipulate you he did. Big time."

"The best way to regain the trust of voters is to candidly admit your mistakes," Myron said. "To err is human. And voters are human too. They do forgive."

"But how will I ever convince them to vote for a man who let a Klansman and a Nazi run his campaign? They'd probably think I'm a darn fool."

"Not after you tell them everything that happened," Myron said. "Explain how Hunter planned your political downfall. Then explain to voters that the old Ramsey is the real Ramsey, and walk them through your life to prove that you've always stood for what you thought was right regardless of the consequences."

"But what I stand for isn't popular today. There's been a Republican Revolution. People seem to want a selfish, greedy, insular, divided, individualistic, ruthlessly competitive, and uncaring America run by corporate elites. I believe in social, racial, and economic justice. In tolerance, humanity, and community. I believe in an America where everyone, regardless of race, sex, creed, religion, or sexual orientation, feels needed, wanted, included, valued, and is proud to be American."

Alison slowly shook her head. "Dad, you have to do something that Democrats should've done a long time ago but haven't. And the consequences of their cowardice, confusion, prevarication, and inaction have been disastrous."

"What's that, dear?"

"Defend the enormous good that liberalism has accomplished for Americans with as much passion as Republicans have defended the meager accomplishments of their bankrupt ideology. Show voters that they literally owe their lives , liberty, and pursuit of happiness to liberalism rather than conservatism. Ask them what sort of country America would be without the progress liberalism has wrought."

"Alison's right," Chanel said.

"They'll never buy that," Ramsey said.

"Yes, they will. Provided you present the facts with conviction and without apology," Darlene said. "Remember that your friends Wofford, Ann Richards, and Mario Cuomo ran as proud liberals."

"And lost," Ramsey quickly added.

"But they lost with their integrity intact," Nelson said. "Which, my dad used to say, is a victory in itself, for what profiteth it for a man to win the whole world but lose his soul. If the Democratic Party loses its soul, it's finished."

"Principles are important in politics, Lawrence," Myron said. "And that's the big difference between Democrats and Republicans. The latter sticks to their guns, no matter what. When the GOP was in the political wilderness after the Goldwater defeat in 1964, it didn't give up its principles. On the contrary, it began spreading them through think tanks and grassroots-based groups across the country. As a result, in 1980, Ronald Reagan was able to use those ideas to help the GOP regain power by masterfully defining liberalism in the worst terms. Remember his speech in Neshoba County on states' rights?"

"All right," Ramsey said. "So we come up with a few good speeches that I can be proud of. Then what?"

"Then we'll barnstorm the state," Myron said, "concentrating on those key districts where support for you in the past has been strongest."

Ramsey nodded, looking pleased. "I like it."

"Sounds good to me, too," Darlene said.

Alison and Myron glanced at each other. She squeezed his hand.

Ramsey cleared his throat and said, "You guys are a godsend. You're my war council. You've renewed my spirit. I had almost given up hope of winning after the scandal broke. Let's go give them hell."

Everyone clapped and said, "Way to go, Lawrence!"

Alison stood up. "Chanel and I will leave the campaign to you guys. We are expected at the airport at three."

"By whom?" Darlene asked.

"Chief Evans. He's taking us to Fort Bragg by military helicopter. The raid on Chandler's compound to rescue Dylan will be launched from there."

Alison and Chanel sat on a hard wooden bench in a spare room at Fort Bragg. Through the small window they could see the airfield lined with about a dozen green and black Army helicopters with no markings. Around the Formica table sat two military officers, two ATF agents, and four FBI agents, including Chief Evans.

"Here's the layout of Chandler's compound from information Anna gave us," said Chief Evans. He unrolled a large white piece of paper and spread it on the table.

Everyone crowded around the table to take a better look at the large drawing on it.

"As you can see, the bunker's located directly underneath the cabin. It's approximately 1,200 square feet and made of concrete. It has five rooms. This room here is the communications center. It contains a printing press, two Panasonic faxes, three Packard Bell computers, a Xerox copy machine, and a counterfeiting machine. The largest room, which is right here in the center, is the sleeping quarters. It's lined with twenty-four military-style bunk beds. The third room, over here to the left, is a combination kitchen and laundry room. It's fully equipped with modern appliances, including a large stocked pantry and refrigerator. This room here is the lecture and meeting hall. It's equipped with a sophisticated sound system and has two 40-inch Mitsubishi plasma TV sets which receive their own feed from a small RCA satellite dish mounted inconspicuously on the side of the mountain."

"Where are the weapons?" asked ATF agent Gerald Tyler.

"Over here," Evans said, moving his finger down a narrow corridor and onto a diagram of the fifth and last room. "To the left is a lab with equipment and ingredients for manufacturing. Next to the lab is a larger room stocked with enough weapons to equip a small private army. Washington feels that the presence of these illegal weapons provides us with the perfect excuse for raiding the compound."

Alison had listened intently to all this. "I hope you all remember that my baby's in there," she said. "So let's not have a repeat of the Waco disaster."

"We're aware of that," Evans said. "That's why this is such a delicate mission. I can assure you this won't be another Waco disaster. We've learned from our mistakes. Trust me. Even if Chandler turns out to be another David Karesh, we're determined to get as many people out alive as we can. That's why we've assembled a top-notch SWAT team and hostage rescue squad."

"Who exactly are these people?" Alison asked.

"We've known for some time that the militia movement had been infiltrated by an organization which was bent on overthrowing the U.S. government," Evans said. "We just didn't know who these people were, because they were so hard to distinguish from ordinary militias. But after the raids on the other compounds, we've been able to come up with a psychological profile of its members. All of them are former members of white extremist groups such as the Klan, Aryan Nation, Skinheads, and Christian Identity. They believe in a Jewish conspiracy to rule the world. They feel betrayed by a government that they see as bending over backwards to please blacks, Jews, immigrants, gays, and feminists. They feel something has gone terribly wrong in this country. And finally, they share the common belief that Jews masterminded the civil rights movement, that integration and liberalism are to blame for America's problems, and that if blacks, Jews, and liberals were exterminated, America would become a paradise for whites."

The phone rang.

Banks answered it, and then handed it to Chief Evans. After a brief exchange, Chief Evans hung up and turned to Alison and Chanel.

"That was Attorney General Alberto Gonzales," Evans said. "The President has given us the go-ahead to raid the compound at dawn."

The crowd began gathering at the Dean Smith auditorium on the campus of UNC Chapel Hill two hours before Lawrence Ramsey was scheduled to appear. By the time his motorcade arrived from the Raleigh-Durham airport on this, the last leg of his whirlwind tour of the state, the auditorium was filled to capacity, as for a Carolina-Duke basketball game. The crowd was estimated at over 75,000 by the campus police. It included not only students, but also members of the community, old and young, from all over the state.

In just two days Ramsey had been to all eleven districts of the state, even making appearances in what was considered enemy territory. But Ramsey was not conceding a single vote. He wanted to be Governor of all North Carolinians.

Though exhausted both physically and mentally, Ramsey seemed to gain new strength as he ascended the podium and looked out at the sea of faces remarkable for their diversity, a sharp contrast from the white crowds which flocked to Lynch's speeches. Ramsey's audiences were truly representative of North Carolina and of the country.

High above Ramsey, on the rafters, hung student-made banners proclaiming "Unity Is Strength," and "One Nation."

Myron, Darlene, Eliot, Nelson, and about half a dozen of Ramsey's haggard-looking staff and advisors sat on several chairs in the front row, along with leaders of the state Democratic Party. Ramsey marveled at the size and enthusiasm of the crowd. Myron was glad to see so many TV cameras, including local affiliates of the four major networks plus C-Span and CNN. Even Fox News was there. It meant that this important speech, on which hinged Ramsey's candidacy, and which he had personally written – a rarity among politicians – would receive unprecedented media coverage.

"My fellow North Carolinians," Ramsey began. Ramsey's voice, though slightly hoarse, still carried. "It's been a long and exhausting three days. I've hardly slept or rested much. But it's been exhilarating. And this, the last speech I'm going to give before you all head for the polls tomorrow, is different from other speeches I've given in the past. In the past, I've always told you what I was going to do if elected. This time, I'm going to tell you what I stand for."

Ramsey paused to take a sip of bottled water.

"I know I disappointed most of you during the primary by running as a Republican clone. I deeply regret that. But by pretending to be something I was not, I didn't fool any of you. You weren't prepared to vote for someone who didn't have the guts to stand up for what he believed, even if the chips were down. And the chips are down for Democrats this election year, my friends, given how Republicans have manipulated the Iraq War. But that's not reason for us to abandon our principles and our convictions. That's not reason for us to shamelessly do anything and everything to win."

A hush fell over the crowd. This was obviously no ordinary stump speech.

"A politician without principles is like a body without a soul," Ramsey continued. "By running as an imitation Republican I was being a fraud. But I wasn't being a fraud of my own volition. I was under a spell. A spell cast by the machinations of someone in whom I had reposed complete trust because I considered him a friend and advisor. That's what handlers will do to you, ladies and gentlemen, so beware."

The audience laughed.

"I'm talking about that Klansman and Nazi you've all heard about, Reginald Hunter," Ramsey continued. "But I refuse to play the blame game. Hunter wouldn't have succeeded in duping me if I'd been faithful and true, if I hadn't been willing to say and do anything to get elected. But I told myself that since it was almost an article of faith among politicians to do whatever it took to win and sleep no worse for it, I could do the same. Yes, at first my conscience was outraged. But I pacified it with rationalizations and excuses. I comforted myself with the thought that history has shown that voters often remember what politicians did while in office, not how they got there.

"What I now realize is that Hunter succeeded in manipulating me precisely because I was being a politician and not a leader. There's a world of a difference between the two. A leader does and says what is right, not what will get him or her elected. A leader welcomes defeat, if victory means the violation of principle, integrity, and honor. A leader doesn't pander or flatter or trim or form opinions according to consultants, pundits, polls, and focus groups. A leader has to risk being misunderstood and vilified even, and a leader sometimes has to walk where angels fear to tread."

Ramsey paused and took another sip of water. Incredibly, no one in the vast audience even coughed, so riveted were people on Ramsey's words.

"As I stand before you today, in the waning hours of the campaign, I want you to know that I *will not* be a politician. I *will not* play it safe. I *will not* follow polls and pundits at the expense of what I believe in. I know that in doing that I may lose. But if I lose, I'll have lost with my principles and honor intact, which, in a way, is a victory far greater, because what profiteth it for a man to gain the whole world but lose his soul?"

The crowd seemed under a spell. Never in the history of modern politics had the words of a politician contained so much passion, candor, and soul.

"Which is the true Ramsey, and what does he believe in? I will tell you. I'm that proud Tar Heel who stood on principle and openly opposed and fought against Jim Crow at a time when the majority of citizens supported that inhuman system. In 1976 I ran for the legislature on a platform to integrate our schools at a time when most politicians stood in defiance of the Brown vs. Board of Education ruling. I lost that election. Many told me I could have easily won had I not gone against the wishes of the majority. I said then, and I say now, the majority is not always right."

Ramsey paused again, this time to wipe his brow, which was dripping with sweat.

"I'm the same Ramsey who, at a time when radio commentators and newspaper columnists routinely criticized the NAACP as communist-inspired, became its member. Mine was among the first businesses in North Carolina to completely integrate its work force. Yes, I was called names and the Klan threatened to put me out of business. But I believed in Dr. King's Dream of an integrated and fair America. I marched with him in Selma, where I met my dear wife Darlene. Again I was told that marrying a Jew would damage my future and career – even my own parents told me that – but that didn't stop me from marrying the best friend I ever had. And I became as ardent an opponent of anti-Semitism as I was of racism because I knew that both were twin heads of the same Hydra. Racism, anti-Semitism, homophobia, Islamophobia, and the various prejudices which bedevil our country only corrode the soul. They make us less worthy of being human. We must recognize, despite our differences, that we share a common humanity and a common destiny. Before we were black and white, gay and straight, Jew and Gentile, we were all human, created in the image of a loving, non-prejudiced God. And America is the better if we celebrate our diversity. It is our strength. It is the bulwark of our Democracy. It is what has made us the hope and the envy of the world."

The crowd was riveted. "Having defied the Klan and its death threats, having risked everything for what I believed, having been unafraid to stand alone, if need be, in defense of what was right, fair, and good about North Carolina and about America, I come to you today, my fellow citizens, to tell you that even in these dispiriting days when liberalism is in disfavor, when we no longer seem to care about racial justice, community, and the state of our collective soul, when we're daily being told by Republicans that liberals have ruined America, and that rugged individualism will make everything right, I stand up and declare for all the world to hear: I AM A LIBERAL, AND PROUD TO BE ONE."

The people could no longer contain their pent-up emotions. As if prompted by the cue of a conductor, the crowd spontaneously burst into thunderous applause, which lasted a full twenty minutes. After the applause died down, Ramsey continued, much energized:

"I know that embracing the liberal label may cost me the election. Liberal is now a dirty word. It's regarded by many as a political kiss of death. But I'd rather run the risk of losing than deny who I truly am, a liberal at the core. And by liberal I mean someone who seeks to preserve what is good in society, while reforming what is bad, in order to create a more progressive, stable, and harmonious whole. You know what, we Democrats are partly to blame for liberalism having become a dirty word. We've let Republicans define what liberalism is. And predictably, they've defined it narrowly to suit their own ends. It's time someone stood up in defense of one of the noblest political traditions ever known to man. Yes, liberals have made their share of mistakes. Yes, liberalism has had its excesses.

But what other great political tradition hasn't? And I'll be darned if I'm going to let the proud legacy of liberalism be maligned with impunity by people who owe their life, liberty, and pursuit of happiness to its great achievements."

Ramsey paused, wiped the dripping sweat off his brow, and took a sip of water. The crowd had again fallen eerily silent. It had been a long time since they had heard a Democrat admit to being a proud liberal. They had been accustomed to hearing and seeing many a Democratic politician cower, run, retreat, and prevaricate at being described as a liberal. Many in the audience thought they were dreaming when they heard Ramsey defend liberalism with as much passion as Republicans defended conservatism, rather than deny, Peter-like, that he had ever been a follower of the creed.

"My fellow Americans, I ask you this: where would America be without Liberalism? If our Founding Fathers had opted for a conservative Revolution, there would have been no Declaration of Independence, and we'd still all be vassals of England. If Roosevelt had not believed in the liberal ideals of putting people to work, there would've been no New Deal to dig us out of the Great Depression. Without Truman's liberal ideals there would have been no integration of the military, and no affirmative action through the G.I. Bill, which provided veterans and their offspring with a start in life. And without liberalism there would've been no Medicare, Medicaid, or Social Security; no Civil Rights movement to abolish America's apartheid; no Women's Rights; no Gay Rights; no OSHA to protect workers or the FDA to protect consumers; no EPA to protect our water, air and precious environment; no WIC and Head Start to insure that the children of the poor aren't stunted in their growth; no highway beautification programs and support for the arts and the national parks. The list goes on and on.

"So I ask you, my friends, why be ashamed of such a noble tradition of securing the well-being and protecting the interests of average Americans, who otherwise would be left to the mercy of the greed, selfishness, and ruthlessness of a capitalist system untempered by human and community concerns? Why be ashamed, I ask, of having fought for what is right and good about America – freedom, justice, fairness, and equal opportunity for all? Why be ashamed to fight for a national industrial policy that will rebuild America's manufacturing base – the backbone of our prosperity, economic greatness and high standard of living? Why be ashamed to stand up against those who want to keep exporting American jobs to the Chinas of the world, under the guise of free trade and the specious claim that the world is flat? The world is round, my friends. Everyone knows that. And it would be wrong, illogical, un-American and immoral for me not to proudly fight for the middle class. No democracy, no matter how powerful its army, can survive for long without the support of the people. World War Three has already begun, my fellow Americans. It is an economic war. And only liberalism can win it for America, by inspiring us to recapture our glory days, when we vanquished the Great Depression and Jim Crow on the way to becoming the first nation on earth to put a man on the moon."

The crowd was now delirious. They cheered and they stomped their feet. They were invigorated. They were born again. They knew they had found a true leader.

Ramsey came to the grand finale of a speech that came from his heart's core, a speech that was the summation of everything for which he had lived, worked, and sacrificed. "With Roosevelt, Truman, Kennedy, and Johnson for heroes, why should I not stand up, alone if need be, proudly in defense of the liberal gains these courageous Democrats have achieved for the American people, especially when their attackers are arrogant, right-wing ideologues who believe they have a God-given mandate to tear down the sacred temple of American egalitarian Democracy, which has taken centuries of toil, blood, and sacrifice to erect, and replace it with God knows what? I shall not retreat. I shall not prevaricate. I shall not hide. I am a liberal, and I'm proud of it. Thank you, God bless you, and God bless these United States of America."

Journalists were later to report that they had never heard such thunderous applause for a political speech before, nor witnessed such energy and enthusiasm among supporters for a candidate. The speech made the headlines of every major paper and TV station around the state, and was the lead story on the national news as well.

USA Today titled its story: "Liberalism: The Comeback Kid."

Chapter 41

Clarence Lynch, like Ramsey, was crisscrossing the state in a final push for votes. Mostly right-wingers flocked to his rallies, especially after the state Republican Party – petrified that Lynch's extremism, and the revelations that he had once belonged to the Klan, might taint the party and its slate of candidates – had quietly distanced itself from him.

But Lynch's support wasn't all right-wing. He found allies within the black community. Afro-Purists were able to assemble a crowd of several hundred in a vacant lot outside its headquarters in a rundown section of Greensboro, notorious for its crack houses. The Afro-Purists had originally wanted the speech held at NC A&T University, because of its prominence as a historically black institution once attended by Jesse Jackson, but the threat of massive demonstrations led to a last-minute change of venue.

At first Lynch was against giving the speech, fearing for his safety, but his handlers persuaded him of its importance. "I know you're terrified of drive-by shootings and all that," said one of his advisors. "But it's imperative that you give at least one speech on their turf. It'll give niggers the perception that you're on their side. And you need their vote neutralized in order to win."

Lynch stood on the steps of a boarded-up crack house, megaphone in hand. From time to time he glanced nervously around. He was somewhat reassured by the fact that Queen Nefertari and Shaka Zulu were with him, along with a phalanx of police officers who kept the demonstrators at bay. The demonstrators outnumbered Lynch's black supporters by a margin of ten to one.

"When I am elected governor," Lynch began, "one of the first things I'll do is petition the state legislature to pay reparations to the descendants of slaves."

The crowd cheered. Across the street from the empty lot, behind police barricades, the large crowd of protesters shouted, "Once a Klansman always a Klansman," and "Let's lynch Lynch!"

Ignoring the demonstrators, Lynch continued. "So I ask you in all fairness, how can you help elect a white man who lets his own daughter get pregnant, out of wedlock, by a fine African-American man she has no business being with in the first place, because he should belong to a black woman? Myron Pearson should be ashamed of himself! Why chase after a white woman where there are literally thousands of beautiful black princesses who'll stand by him as only a strong black woman can? Doesn't he know about the shortage of eligible black males?"

"That's right!" a dozen or so women shouted.

Queen Nefertari smiled. She had written a great portion of Lynch's speech.

"I know why he didn't marry a black woman. He wants to be white. And since the civil rights movement liberals have encouraged this sort of irresponsible behavior by black men. If you elect Ramsey, the liberal with a capital L, you'll be committing genocide. More of your men will leave you for white women. And without men your race will die. So my friends, if you vote for me, I'll do everything in my power to save you from extermination. If need be, I'll bring back the anti-miscegenation laws of this state, which Ramsey the liberal helped repeal. After all, the majority of black and white Americans are against mixing the races."

He was interrupted by loud applause and more shouts of, "That's right!"

Lynch looked over at Queen Nefertari and winked at her. She smiled encouragingly. At the end of his speech a few minutes later, Lynch, the Klansman, Nazi, and godson of Hitler, received a standing ovation, and was led off the stage like the savior of the black community he professed himself to be.

Darkness was rapidly setting in. Nancy ran down the slippery, rocky trail and then paused, breathless, listening for the sound of footsteps chasing her. There were none. But she knew that it was only a matter of time before they found out she was missing, and came after her. And she was at a disadvantage in that she didn't know the terrain.

She was now about a mile away from the cabin. Determined to put as much distance between herself and her pursuers as possible, she pushed on. But the thick forest and waning moon made the darkness dense and deep.

Twice she stumbled and nearly fell on top of the baby. In a clearing of soft pine needles, she spread out the thin blanket she had packed in her backpack. After giving Dylan a bottle of formula and rocking him to sleep, she gently placed his limp and languid body on the blanket and lay down beside him.

She tried to relax but could not sleep. All she could envision was Buck's red face, contorted in anger, when he discovered she was missing and what she did to Orville. The thought of Buck coming after her with a gun made Nancy tremble. She remained alert and wary for hours, then, intoxicated by the fresh mountain air after so many stressful days in captivity, she finally drifted off to sleep.

A fleet of twelve black helicopters flew in formation from Fort Bragg toward the Smoky Mountains of North Carolina. From the lead chopper's window the mountains looked to Alison like a spool of green silk that had been casually dropped on the ground, where it unfurled in smooth folds. As darkness fled, the first rosy light of dawn tinged the Blue Ridge Parkway as it snaked along the ridge like a meandering silver ribbon.

Chief Evans sat next to the pilot, watching the map of the terrain change on the computer screen before him and glancing down to scan the mountains.

Alison and Chanel were buckled into the seats behind him.

"The compound is on the eastern slope of the mountains," Chief Evans said. "Let's swing around to the South and make our approach from the western side. That way we'll take them by surprise."

"This is it, girl," Chanel said. "Are you ready?"

"As ready as I'll ever be," Alison said. "I just want to feel Dylan in my arms again, safe and sound."

A call came in from ground control. Evans grabbed the speaker and pressed a button on its side. "Go ahead, ground control."

"This is SWAT team commander Paul Lund," said someone with a rich baritone. "There seems to be something wrong at the compound, sir."

"What do you mean?"

"Several of Chandler's men are tramping through the woods around the bunker," said Lund. "They're heavily armed and are scoping out the woods with flashlights."

"I wonder what lured them out of the bunker," said Chief Evans.

"They seem to be looking for someone," Lund replied.

"Nancy escaped!" Alison cried.

"Lund, I have the baby's mother here," Chief Evans said. "She thinks the woman who kidnapped her baby – her name is Nancy - might have escaped. Use extreme caution. I want no gunfire. Where are you?"

"I'm parked in the woods, about half a mile from the compound."

"Keep alert and let me know if you see anything else. In the meantime inform your ground forces not to do anything until we arrive. This is going to be one hell of a delicate operation. We don't want any repeats of Ruby Ridge or Waco."

"Understood."

Nancy awoke abruptly at the sound of male voices. She sat bolt upright, disoriented, wondering where she was and how she had gotten there. Beams of yellow light flashed between the trees, growing closer. In an instant she recollected everything. She scooped up Dylan, who was still fast asleep, and grabbed the blanket and backpack to prevent her pursuers from finding them. She hurried through the woods. Pale dawn light was infiltrating the tall trees, making it easier to see the trail and avoid the rocks and roots that had tripped her so often during the night.

Dylan felt like a fifteen-pound rag doll in her arms. The bouncing and jostling gradually awakened him, and he stretched and yawned and looked up at Nancy, blinking sleepily, a questioning look in his eyes.

*****

Hearing the snapping of twigs ahead of him, Buck hurried toward the sounds. In the beam of his flashlight he caught a glimpse of Nancy scampering down into a ravine. The thin blanket trailed her like a fluttering veil.

"Nancy!" Buck bellowed. "You get your demented ass back here right now!"

Nancy disappeared behind a copse of wild magnolia trees. Buck caught a glimpse of the baby's small face. "Come back, woman! Or I'll shoot!"

There was no sign of Nancy. Buck fired a shot into the magnolias just to give her a scare. The shot echoed up and down the thickly wooded ravine.

Buck turned and shouted to the others, who had fanned out in search of Nancy. "Jimmy Ray! Orville! Bob! Over here! I've found her! And she's got the mongrel!"

The armed Klansmen, dressed in combat fatigues, were already running in the direction of the gunshot. Buck raced down the trail after Nancy, gripping his AK-47 with both hands. Nancy could hear Buck shouting after her as she ran.

"What the hell do you think you're doin', you stupid bitch?" she heard him shout. "Do you want to get yourself killed? Come back here!" Nancy stumbled and slid down a scree of loose rock on her side. Red clay dust filled her nostrils and coated her face and hair. Dylan sneezed and started to cry. When she landed at the bottom, rocks from above continued to tumble down the slope, bouncing and spinning out of control. Nancy covered Dylan with her head and held up her arms to block the blows as the rocks pounded her arms and back.

"Nancy! Where the hell are you?" she heard Buck shout. His voice came from directly above her. When the rock slide stopped, she made a dash for cover. She hurdled a stream and clambered between two boulders.

"There you are!" Buck cried.

A bullet whizzed past Nancy's head and ricocheted off the boulder to her left. Her foot stuck in a crevice between two rocks. She fell forward but her foot remained fast. Her ankle twisted. She heard something snap inside it. Intense pain shot up her leg. She cried out. She landed with a thud on the dusty red earth. Fortunately her elbow hit the ground first, protecting the baby. She lay there, gasping for breath, looking through her tangled blond hair at Dylan, who wailed helplessly.

"I can't move," she whispered to him. "My leg. Maybe I can crawl. Yes, I'll crawl. We'll hide. That's what we'll do. Oh, come on, baby. Don't cry. Don't cry. Shhh. Shhhh. Please. Hush."

As Nancy pulled herself and the crying baby with one arm toward a thick tangle of underbrush and vines, she heard a noise above her like a great beating of wings. She looked up and saw a fleet of twelve black and green helicopters roar over the mountain ridge from west to east, directly above her head. Her heart swelled with hope. "I pray to God your momma is in one of those flying machines," Nancy whispered to Dylan.

"Nancy!" Buck bellowed from the top of the rock slide. "I can hear that mongrel shrieking all the way up here! You might as well give it up! Them choppers can't save you now!"

Chandler and Orville stopped dead in their tracks when they heard the helicopters. They watched them fly overhead. "No markings," Chandler said ominously. "Just like I said. The army of the New World Order dictatorship has finally come for us. It's the Book of Revelation come to life here and now."

Chandler clutched his AK-47 more tightly in his sweaty palm. "But they ain't gonna take us without a fight. God is on our side."

"I think they're headed for the bunker," Orville said nervously, seeing the helicopters descend beyond the trees.

"Who's guarding it?"

"No one. Unless someone gave up their search for Nancy and headed back."

"Come on," Chandler said. "Get Thad and Bob on the cellular phone. We need to get hold of those rocket-propelled grenade launchers and Stinger missiles."

Alison and Chanel donned the bullet proof vests handed them by Chief Evans.

"Those were gunshots," Chief Evans said to the pilot. "Let's not waste any more time circling. Land this thing in that clearing down there, as close to the bunker as possible."

"But it's too dangerous, sir. They might fire at us."

"Land the damn thing, okay?"

"Okay."

"I think I saw someone down in that ravine we just passed over," Alison said.

"I saw them too," Chanel said.

Alison closed her eyes. "Please let Dylan be all right," she murmured to herself.

The black helicopter slowly descended into a meadow surrounded by rocky bluffs. The cabin over the bunker was now in full view. A man with a rifle quickly withdrew inside and closed the door.

Alison and Chanel jumped down from the helicopter even while the blades were still whirling. The eleven other Commando helicopters landed all around them and armed SWAT team members dressed in black jumpsuits with ATF and FBI logos on them leaped out. The wind from the helicopters whipped Alison's dark hair across her face. The roar of the engines and the beating of the chopper's blades were deafening.

Alison started running in the direction of the gunshots, but Chief Evans grabbed her by the arm.

"Not so fast!" he shouted over the roar. "You and Chanel get back inside the chopper. You're staying here!"

"No! I'm going to the ravine!" Alison shouted.

"You're staying here!" Chief Evans insisted. "It's not safe."

"I don't care!" Alison shouted in order to be heard above the noise. "My baby's down there. I'm going down there!"

Chief Evans studied her solemn face. He could see clearly that this was one determined young woman who would never be persuaded to stay behind.

"All right," he said reluctantly. "I'll send Lund and four other agents down with you. And take this."

He handed her a gun. "Do you know how to use it?"

"I haven't fired a gun in my life. I just pull this trigger, right?"

"It's not that simple."

He took twenty seconds to give her a few pointers.

"Remember, stay behind the men," Chief Evans said. He turned and barked instructions to the commandos leaping out of the other helicopters.

Alison seized the moment to start running down the footpath that disappeared into the dense copse of trees.

"Stop her!" Chief Evans shouted.

It was too late. Alison was gone. Evans ordered Lund and four others to follow her. Alison descended the rocky trail, leaping from rock to rock with the same finesse she had learned from running down the rocky trails from the peaks of the Presidential mountains in New Hampshire.

Buck slid down the bumpy pile of rocks on the seat of his pants, complaining about his "poor ass" under his breath and holding his AK-47 up in the air with one hand. When he reached the bottom of the ravine he headed toward the two boulders behind which he had seen Nancy disappear. He studied the bullet hole in the side of the rock, then scanned the thick ferns and underbrush with the trained eye of a hunter.

"Nancy, I know you're around here somewhere. It's just a matter of time before that mongrel lets out another cry. Give yourself up and you won't get hurt."

ATF and FBI agents surrounded the cabin above the underground bunker.

"John Chandler!" Chief Evans called through a bullhorn. "If you're in there, I have a message for you. We don't want anyone to get hurt. We want this thing to end peacefully. We aren't here to create another Waco."

Chief Evans and the agents watched the door. Nothing happened.

"If we get no response, we'll have to come in!" Evans said through the bullhorn.

Still no response.

"Okay, guys," Chief Evans said, "We're going in. We'll storm this bunker exactly the way I explained back at Fort Bragg."

As Chief Evans and the agents moved toward the cabin, Orville and Chandler rushed out of the nearby woods, firing from the hip with their AK-47s.

Alison reached the top of the rock slide, panting and glistening with sweat despite the early November chill. Lund and the four agents Chief Evans had sent after her were far behind. She looked in every direction, wondering how Nancy could have gotten down from here into the ravine. The only way down was straight down the rocks. It looked more treacherous than the Chemin Des Dames trail in the

White Mountains.

Suddenly she felt something glide around her bare ankle. She looked down and saw a huge copperhead snake wrapped around her foot.

She froze.

Its black forked tongue darted in and out of its flat triangular head. Alison did not dare breathe. After what seemed an eternity – it was only two minutes – it slowly slithered away. Its cold body sent chills down Alison's spine. As soon as her ankle was free of the snake Alison moved away, inadvertently striking a rock with her foot. It hurtled and bounced down the rock slide.

Buck heard it and turned. He emerged from between the two boulders and looked up. He quickly ducked his head behind the boulder as Alison fired. Alison got down on her hands and knees, crawled to the edge of the bluff, and aimed her gun at the spot where Buck had disappeared behind the rocks.

"You're at the end of your rope, Buck McGuire," Alison shouted. "You're gonna hang for what you did to Caldwell!"

Alison gripped the gun more tightly and looked around for the snake.

"You brought the Fibbies with you, didn't you?" Buck shouted, still shielded by rock. "You nigger-loving Jewess."

"Shut up, you fucking Nazi bastard! Where's my baby?"

"I don't have your goddamn mongrel!" Buck shouted.

"Then where is he?"

"He'll be dead in a split second if you don't get those Fibbies to back off and do what Chandler says!"

"Give me my baby first!"

While Alison and Buck shouted at each other, their voices echoing up and down the ravine, Nancy limped out of her hiding place under a thick cluster of ferns. The baby, sucking contentedly on his pacifier, was bound tightly to her back with the blanket.

Nancy crept up behind Buck. She picked up a sharp and heavy rock the size of a football. She hoisted it high up in the air. Buck heard a noise behind him and whirled around. Nancy brought the rock crashing on his forehead. Buck let out a scream. Bright red blood gushed from a gash in his wide forehead and ran down his face. But incredibly, he remained standing. His eyes bulged with rage.

"You fuckin' bitch!" he shouted.

He smashed Nancy across the face with the butt of his AK-47. She stumbled backwards and landed on her bottom. The baby screamed, letting the pacifier fall.

Hearing the baby's cry, Alison grabbed her gun and slid hurriedly down the rock slide. Nancy backed away from Buck on all fours like a crab. Her heart pounded wildly. He loomed over her, his face contorted with maniacal rage.

"A bullet is too good for you!" he screamed. "I'll kill you with my bare hands!"

He fell on top of her and gripped her neck with both hands. He squeezed with all his might. She choked and gagged, struggling to breathe. His blood dripped onto her reddening face. She fought vigorously at first, and then her body softened and stopped fighting. His angry red face floated above her, just as it had in her dream. Then everything went dark.

Chief Evans felt the searing pain in his leg and realized he had been hit.

"Hit the ground!" he shouted to his men.

Some agents ran for the trees, others fell flat on their stomachs. Orville dove behind a boulder and took cautious shots from behind it. He was about to put a second bullet into Chief Evans when an ATF agent jumped him from behind and wrestled the rifle from his hand.

Chandler, sheltered by a tree, kept firing. Bullets whizzed back and forth across the fifty yards separating the edge of the forest and the cabin.

"Orville!" Chandler shouted. "Where the hell are you?"

When he got no answer Chandler cursed. Determined to make it to the underground bunker, he made a dash for the cabin, blazing a path with bullets.

"You Jew-loving, nigger-loving Communists!" he screamed as he ran Rambo-like across the field. "I'll blast the fucking heads off every one of you!"

He stopped when he reached the spot where Evans lay clutching his leg, his gun on the ground beyond reach. He was crawling toward it. Chandler aimed his gun at Evans's forehead. "Tell your men to back off or you're dead meat!" Chandler shouted.

*****

Alison stopped four yards from where Buck was strangling Nancy. She aimed the gun at the back of his head with both hands and shouted, "Let go of her or die!"

Buck glanced at her over his shoulder, then burst out laughing. He let go of Nancy, who lay limp and unmoving on the ground. Baby Dylan was trapped beneath her and screaming at the top of his tiny but mighty lungs.

Buck stood up and faced Alison. "Look at you, trembling like a leaf," he said. "I bet you don't know a thing about firin' a gun."

He walked boldly toward Alison as if she had no gun at all.

"Stay back or I'll shoot!" she screamed.

"Sure you will."

He kept coming. She backed away, still aiming the gun at his head.

"Okay, you asked for it!" she cried. Alison closed her eyes and willed herself to pull the trigger. Buck knocked the gun from her hand just as it went off. The shot went into the ground. He grabbed her roughly by the arm and threw her down.

"You sorry little nigger-lover," he sneered. "You're gonna get what you deserve."

Alison tried to crawl away from him, but he lunged at her.

A gunshot rang out. She screamed.

Buck turned, his face a mask of disbelief.

"I'll be damned," he muttered, as he landed with a heavy thud beside Alison.

She shrank away from him, but he did not move. She shoved him with her foot. He was dead. Looking up, she saw Nancy holding Buck's smoldering AK-47, her face impassive.

Chandler looked around, panting breathlessly.

The FBI and ATF agents surrounding him stared at him, frozen, not daring to make a move. Silence reigned for a long minute.

Then a single shot rang out. A bullet caught Chandler in the back, made him spin around, and sent him toppling to the ground beside Chief Evans.

"You...are going to...destroy our race..." he gasped, trying to focus his eyes on Chief Evans. The FBI and ATF commandos turned around and saw Anna, Chandler's wife, standing by the cabin door, rifle in hand.

"I just had to do it," she muttered. "For the sake of my children."

"Are there any more people inside there?" the wounded Evans asked.

"Yeah. Thad and Bob are in there. But they won't give you any trouble. They're all locked up in the laundry room. I told them to hide there while I went to get help. They don't know I'm working for you. Here's the key."

"Great job," Chief Evans said.

Six SWAT team members stormed into the cabin and quickly made their way to the bunker below, where they arrested Thad and Bob without any resistance.

"You should've waited for us," Lund said to Alison as soon as he and the other agents reached her and Nancy. "You could've been killed, you know."

Alison made no reply. Her eyes were fixed on the crying baby in her arms. She kissed the baby and held him tightly, pressing his tiny head to her heart.

"My baby, my Dylan," she said softly as tears of joy streamed down her cheeks. "It's been so long." She thought back to the last time she had seen him, minutes after he had left the comfort of her womb. Dylan seemed to recognize his mother's voice and her familiar heartbeat. He grew quiet.

"No pulse," Lund said. He was leaning over Buck, pressing his fingertips to his carotid artery. The other agents were with Nancy. She looked haggard and pale. Buck's gnarled hands had left red imprints on her neck. She was glad to be alive. If Buck had choked her a minute longer she would have been dead.

Lund stood up, unclipped the walkie-talkie from his belt, and spoke to a pilot in one of the helicopters up in the meadow by the bunker. "We're down here in the ravine, next to a rockslide. We have one stiff to be picked up...Yes, we've recovered the infant. He's with his mother. He looks okay, but he'll need to be examined at the hospital."

He switched it off and turned to Alison. "A chopper is on its way. Hey, are you all right?"

Alison turned to him, still smiling down at Dylan through her tears, and nodded vigorously. "How could I not be all right?" she asked. "I have my baby back."

Chapter 42

The phone rang just as Ramsey and Myron were about to step into Ramsey's Lexus, parked in the driveway. They were on their way to the airport for a noon rally in Asheville, before heading for Charlotte, and then on to Raleigh. Election Day was less than twenty-four hours away.

"Myron! Lawrence!" Darlene called from the front door. "It's Alison!"

Myron and Ramsey froze with their hands on the car doors.

"She has the baby!" Darlene said.

Myron and Ramsey exchanged astonished glances, then raced back into the house.

Myron reached the phone first. "Darling, are you all right?"

"I'm fine," she said above the noise of the whirring helicopter blades.

"And Dylan?"

"He's right here in my arms."

"Is he okay?"

"I think so. He's going to be examined by a pediatrician shortly."

"Where are you?"

"At Chandler's hideout. We're about to rush Nancy to the hospital in Asheville."

"Is she okay?"

"Her wounds are serious," Alison said. "But she's tough. I think she'll make it."

"Thank God," Myron said with a sigh. "Listen, I'll meet you at the hospital. Your father and I were just on our way to Asheville when you called. He's doing great, by the way. Overnight polls show that voters are listening. But we still have a long way to go."

"Thanks for helping him, Myron."

"It's an honor to finally manage the campaign of a proud liberal. Where's Chanel?"

"Back at the bunker. She's reporting live from the scene for Channel-8."

An hour and a half later Myron and Alison were standing in a sterile hospital ward in Asheville, their arms around each other as they proudly watched their baby being examined.

"It's remarkable," the pediatrician said, removing her stethoscope and looking up at them. "He's in quite good shape despite all the trauma he's endured since birth."

"You found no problems?" Alison asked, amazed.

"Well, he does have a deep chest cold," said the pediatrician. "Probably from the dampness of the cabin. Some over-the-counter cough suppressant should be enough to help him get over that. He also has some slight bruising to his rib cage, most likely from being trapped underneath Nancy McGuire."

"Anything else we should be aware of?" Myron asked.

"No, other than that he's fit as a fiddle," said the pediatrician with a smile. "His length and weight are normal, just where they should be for a ten-month-old baby. I think Nancy must have taken excellent care of him. You're lucky. Most of the kidnapped children I've seen over the years as a doctor have been in terrible shape. You can take him home as soon as I sign these discharge papers."

Alison and Myron embraced each other, and then smiled down at Dylan, who flapped his little arms, kicked his tiny feet into the air, and squealed with delight.

Alison and Myron, the latter proudly carrying Dylan in his arms, walked down the hall to the intensive care unit. They found a plump nurse with dark hair attending to Nancy on a high rolling bed. She had been undressed and cleaned up. She now lay still in a hospital gown beneath a white cotton sheet and blanket. A bag of clear glucose fluid dripped into a vein in the back of her hand through an IV. The red marks on her neck left by Buck's fingers had turned to black and blue bruises. The heartbeat monitor at her bedside beeped steadily, though weakly. The green lines jumped with each beat. Alison picked up Nancy's right hand and squeezed it. Myron placed his hand on Alison's shoulder.

"Nancy, it's Alison," she said. "Can you hear me?"

Her eyes opened slowly.

"Listen, I want you to know that I forgive you for taking my baby," Alison said. "You must have had your reasons, and whatever they were, I hope you can someday explain it all to me. But for now, I'd just like to thank you for taking such good care of him. And thanks for risking your own life to save him."

"I...I'm sorry," Nancy said through parched lips. Her voice was hoarse, barely audible. Her eyes fluttered open. She looked dazed and sleepy. "I was so afraid Buck would be angry. I miscarried twice. The first time he beat me. I was so scared."

"It's all right," Alison said gently. "I understand. But Buck won't hurt you anymore."

"I know," Nancy said quietly. Her chin trembled and a tear rolled from her eye.

"What happened to Orville?" Nancy asked weakly.

"Who?"

"Orville. He was sort of fat and with bushy eyebrows."

"He was killed along with Chandler."

"Thank God," Nancy muttered.

"How did you escape?" Alison asked.

"By drugging Orville."

"Drugging Orville?" Alison asked, perplexed.

Nancy smiled. "Well, I sort of knew Orville from a long time ago."

"You did?"

"Yes. He came to our town shortly after my father left my mother. He was a traveling evangelist and my mother, who was tormented by guilt over her failed marriage, sort of came under his spell. He was real smooth. Within weeks they were married. I was thirteen. Orville began sexually abusing me."

"The bastard," Alison said.

"The abuse continued until he'd succeeded in stealing my mother's life savings," Nancy went on. "So the day after I was brought to the compound, you can imagine my shock when Buck brought Orville over to see your baby. I was so shocked to see him I fainted. Buck thought it was because of what he'd told me about plans to kill the baby. But no, it was from seeing my abuser again."

"I can understand," Alison said.

It was evident that Nancy was having a hard time talking. But it seemed like she wanted to talk, to unburden her soul, to make amends. "So when Orville was sent to fetch me the day of the raid, he told me that he missed me," Nancy said. "He said I should give him a quickie or else he'd tell Buck that I was a temptress and had seduced him. I said sure, I'd give him a quickie. Knowing that he loved to drink, I told him I had a bottle of Buck's liquor with me. His eyes lit up. I got the Jack Daniels from under the bed and gave it to him. He drank, and within minutes was snoring."

"Snoring?"

"Yes. Chloral hydrate," said Nancy, smiling wanly. "Got a supply when I used to temp at Triad Regional. Used it to fall asleep because I'd often be so worried whenever Buck was late returning from work, for I knew he was with other women."

"You loved Buck, didn't you?" Alison said.

She nodded.

"Even though he beat you and almost killed you?"

"He was a good man until he joined up with the Klan," she whispered.

On the morning of the election, a paperboy wheeled his bicycle through Emerywood and tossed a copy of the Triad's liberal newspaper, *The News Enterprise Journal*, onto the Ramseys' driveway. Darlene stepped outside in her striped bathrobe and pale pink slippers to get it. She pulled it out of its damp plastic wrapper and stared with admiration at the large color photo that almost filled up the entire front page.

It was a picture of Alison and Myron leaving the Asheville hospital together with their arms around each other, looking radiant and very much in love. Even Dylan, who was cradled in his mother's arms, was grinning. It was the first publicized photo of the baby. There they were, all three of them – black, white, and brown – in full color. And what most affected Darlene was that the photo showed them as a family, which was a far cry from the countless depictions of interracial couples in the media, which invariably excluded the children, as if to reinforce the stereotype that interracial relationships were abnormal, and had nothing to do with the desire to love, nurture, and raise families.

Darlene knew that the photo could be interpreted as breathtakingly beautiful or shockingly offensive, depending on the viewer's perspective and opinions on race.

The caption read: *Happy parents reunited with their kidnapped baby.*

The front-page article, for which Alison and Myron had been interviewed in Asheville, detailed the couple's relationship in moving terms. It described how convicted felon Reginald Hunter, using Iago-like tactics, had torn them apart just when they were planning their wedding. It quoted Eliot Whitaker as saying he felt no bitterness toward Alison, planned to give her a speedy divorce so that he and his partner, Jonathan, could get married and move to Washington, DC, where both planned to take up jobs with The Log Cabin Republicans, a federated gay and lesbian political organization whose constituency supported the Republican Party and advocated for lesbian, gay, bisexual, and transgender rights. Eliot wished her and Myron all the happiness in the world, because they belonged together, and invited them to attend his wedding with Jonathan. The article further explained that Alison and Myron planned to get married as soon as her marriage to Eliot was formally annulled.

Another front-page article described Lawrence Ramsey as a "courageous leader who is risking defeat by changing strategies at the last minute to defend his principles."

It detailed how Hunter had set out to destroy Ramsey politically because of the grudge he bore him for events that happened over 30 years ago. It also detailed, step by step, the methodical way Hunter went about sabotaging Ramsey's campaign. The article also gently reprimanded Ramsey for providing Hunter with an opening, by his desperation to win at all cost, and warned other politicians to remember that winning wasn't the only thing, and that the best ground to stand on politically is that of principle.

The article ended this way: "Today's election provides North

Carolinians with a unique opportunity to prove to the rest of the world that their state is truly the most progressive in the South, or that its reputation as backwards is thoroughly deserved."

The exclusive article, which went immediately on the wire service, had been picked up by papers across the state and the country, and millions were reading the story at the same time Darlene was. Darlene excitedly hurried toward the house to share the story with Ramsey, Alison, and Myron. But before she reached the front door, a second paperboy peddled by and tossed *The Tea-Party Clarion*, the Triad's conservative newspaper, which was owned by the now-imprisoned Kessler. Ramsey subscribed to both, just to compare the different slants they put on the same stories.

Darlene pulled the newspaper from its plastic wrapper and was surprised to see the same color photo of Alison, Myron, and Dylan on the front page.

The caption read: "Alison Ramsey, her lover, and their illegitimate baby reunited."

Darlene gasped when she read the headline of the lead article – "Doomsday for Ramsey: Race-Mixing Daughter Dashes His Chances for Governorship."

The article cited skewed polling data which showed that the majority of Americans oppose interracial unions. It professed that the children of such marriages suffered terribly, caught between the two separate and hostile worlds of black and white.

Darlene angrily skimmed other front-page articles accusing Ramsey of being "more slick than slick Willy," and that his switching his political message so late in the game was an act of desperation by an unprincipled liberal. The paper's editorial page accused "big-government, tax and spend liberals like Ramsey" and their misguided social experiments for worsening race relations and morally corrupting America.

"When will liberals finally accept the undeniable fact that no amount of social engineering can overcome human nature?" The editorial concluded.

Another color photo showed Hitler's godson, Clarence Lynch, campaigning vigorously in redneck country. The article next to it called Lynch, "Someone who's not afraid to tell it like it is," and drew lavish comparisons between him and Jesse Helms as politicians you either love or hate. "Lynch is one of the few politicians who's always upfront with voters. He was among the first politicians to openly defend white people's rights, even at the risk of being called racist. He was the one who spoke out against affirmative action, quotas, set-asides, reverse discrimination, and welfare, at a time when no one dared touch the politically sensitive issues. He was called out of touch with the mainstream of American voters, and now history has proven him right and his detractors wrong. Affirmative action, crime, and welfare are now front and center in major races across the country. When they go to the polls today North Carolina voters will have the historic opportunity to choose between the bold and visionary leadership of Lynch, and the cowardly and opportunistic liberalism of Ramsey. And we predict that this race is harbinger of the titanic struggle between conservatism and liberalism, to see which ideology will shape America's destiny in the 21st century."

The article asked voters not to hold Lynch's Klan past against him "because many Southerners have Klan skeletons in their closets whether they publicly admit it or not. "After all," the article concluded, "a Klan past did not stop Senator Robert Byrd from becoming a distinguished Democratic Party leader, and Hugo Black from becoming an effective liberal justice on the U.S. Supreme Court."

Darlene ran into the house clutching both papers.

Alison anxiously watched the returns on a large projection TV screen in a ballroom of the Radisson. Ramsey had chosen the spot of his primary victory for his election-night campaign headquarters. The crowd in the ornate ballroom was totally different. It was packed with progressives of all races, and was truly representative of the marvelous diversity of North Carolina and of the country. Festive, upbeat tunes played over the loudspeaker. But alas, the mood in the room was somber, bleak.

Ramsey was losing. Dylan was fast asleep on Alison's back, wearing a red, white and blue baseball cap with a photo of Ramsey stitched to the front of it. His cheek rested on the blue padded frame of the baby carrier. Myron adjusted his little arms so they did not dangle limply over the edge.

"It doesn't look good," Alison said.

"Anything can happen," Myron said.

"But 85 percent of the precincts have reported, and Lynch is ahead of your dad by three points," Chanel said.

"Well, even if we lose," Nelson said. "We did the best we could."

"Yes, no one will fault us for that," Darlene said.

"We're not conceding defeat yet," Myron said. "I still believe that North Carolina is a progressive state."

"I do too," Alison said. "But let's face facts."

"You never know which way the last fifteen percent of the precincts will go," Myron said.

"But they're mostly in conservative strongholds," Alison said gloomily. "That's Lynch's vote."

Myron said nothing. He too realized that a miracle was needed if Ramsey was to pull it off.

Alison looked over at her father, who was glued to the TV screen, listening to the comments of the media's political gurus in Washington and New York. CNN's Anderson Cooper announced that Clarence Lynch was now ahead by five points and was gearing up to give a victory speech. Ramsey looked crestfallen.

"I hate to feel this way," Alison said to Myron, "but I believe I ruined my father's chances to win."

Myron looked at her and frowned. "How?" he said defensively. "By falling in love with me?"

"No, no, no," she said resignedly. "It's not your fault. It's not my fault. No one can fault us for believing that people are more than their skin color. What I regret is that we Americans are so steeped in hatred we've ceased to be human."

Lynch was jubilant that he was about to be elected Governor of the State of North Carolina. Exit polls showed him holding a commanding lead in many of the state's counties. He couldn't wait for the polls to close at 8 p.m. Thanks to Hunter having destroyed the incriminating files, Operation Saladin could still be launched without his father and Hunter, who were about to go on trial on sedition, drug-trafficking, and murder charges. They were being kept at Holman Prison in Alabama, Hunter in the same cell previously occupied by Tommy Cone, whose sentence had been commuted to life by the Governor. Lynch's campaign headquarters rocked with upbeat country music. Queen Nefertari and Shaka Zulu couldn't contain their glee as Lynch's staffers started handing out plastic champagne glasses filled with fresh bubbly.

"It seems that, once again, race has played a major role in North Carolina," a political pundit told Larry King. "For months Lawrence Ramsey had been well ahead of former Klansman Clarence Lynch. But tonight it appears that hatred and fear-mongering have triumphed. Ramsey simply could not overcome the negative publicity he received when his kidnapped grandson turned out to be fathered by a black man not married to his daughter Alison. This race was a litmus test of whether interracial relationships are now considered part of our traditional values. The answer appears to be a resounding, 'No!'"

Queen Nefertari and Shaka Zulu smiled at each other and slapped a high-five.

Lynch's wife, wearing a red, white, and blue square-dancing skirt that flared out like a bell, jumped up onto a long conference table and started dancing. The ecstatic crowd roared and clapped in rhythm as she did some North Carolina mountain clogging.

"Come on, Clarence!" she cried, reaching toward him. "Come join me!"

Lynch clambered awkwardly onto the table and whirled her around a few times so that her skirt spun about her waist like a top and her red-and-white striped bloomers showed. The crowd roared its approval. Lynch and his wife laughed and kept up the frenzied pace."Lynch!" "Lynch!" "Lynch!" the crowd chanted.

Everyone was so wrapped up in the clogging couple that no one noticed when the final tally in the North Carolina governor's race came in fifteen minutes later.

"Myron, I think something's happening," Alison said, pointing toward the TV screen.

Myron looked up.

"Ladies and gentlemen, we reported earlier that exit polls projected a Lynch victory," Larry King said with amazement. "We were wrong. With 100 precincts reporting, the final results in that North Carolina's gubernatorial race show Democrat Lawrence Ramsey at 51 percent, and former Klansman Clarence Lynch at 49 percent. A political miracle has occurred, ladies and gentlemen. A liberal Democrat has won a statewide election in a state that was considered part of the solid South."

Alison screamed excitedly. "DAD WON! DAD WON!"

Myron gaped, and then his face broke into a broad grin. He threw back his head, thrust his fist into the air, and shouted, "YESSSSS!"

Darlene clapped and hopped up and down. She threw her arms around Ramsey and they spun around. Nelson, Eliot, and Chanel embraced, as did various advisors and campaign workers. Ramsey stopped spinning and shouted over to Myron. "We did it, Myron! We did it!" Myron gave him the thumbs-up. Ramsey ran over, and gave Myron a bear hug. "Thanks," he said, tearing. "You don't know what this victory means to me. Because of your steadfast love for my daughter, I was able to regain my most precious possession – my reputation as a proud liberal who's unafraid to defend his principles even when the chips are down. Welcome to the family – dear son-in-law."

"Thanks," Myron said, fighting back his own tears.

Turning to his daughter, Ramsey said, "Alison, never let go of him."

"I don't intend to," Alison said. "Unless, of course, he decides not to run for President by the time he's eligible in 2016."

They burst out laughing. Myron and Alison embraced and kissed amid a snowstorm of red, white, and blue confetti. Dylan awoke. With his soft, knobby fist he clutched a fistful of his mother's long silky hair and watched the dancing confetti with wonder in his large and innocent brown eyes.

Author's Note

This story was inspired by my conviction that liberalism is one of the best ideologies in human history but has been so maligned by conservatives in America that it is now considered one of the worst. It is my hope that liberals everywhere will proudly defend their creed, and use it to create a better world for all, regardless of color, nationality, race, religion, social class, gender or sexual orientation.

Acknowledgements

It took years to write *The Proud Liberal*. The journey was exhilarating and inspiring, even when I dealt with numerous false starts and the proverbial writer's block. Along the way, I learned a great deal about the strength, weaknesses and challenges of democracy, and about the way it is practiced in the United States, my adopted homeland for more than two decades. I also learned what makes America, despite her mistakes, truly one of the best places in the world to live and work. Her ideals of freedom, justice and equal opportunity are second to none. *The Proud Liberal* is an attempt to humanize those ideals and to remind myself and others of the sacrifices made by countless heroes and heroines, sung and unsung, to achieve and preserve them for posterity. I believe these ideals must be defended at all cost, particularly in a post 9/11 world, against all those, within and without, who preach and practice hatred and dehumanize others.

During the writing of *The Proud Liberal*, I sought the advice of countless people. They gave it generously and it proved priceless in helping me shape, focus and complicate a simple story that turned into one I feel proud to have written. I thank everyone who helped from the bottom of my heart, especially the following, without whom the book would have remained a mere twinkle in a writer's eye.

My dearest friend, wife and best and indefatigable critic, Gail.

My beloved sisters, Diana and Linah, for your valuable input and edits.

Anita Cohen and my mother-in-law, Deborah Scott Stewart, for your unbounded generosity of spirit and exceptional editing skills.

Steve Peterson, for your genius in creating unique and provocative book jackets, and for your patience in laying out the book and incorporating edits.

My mother, Magdalene, for always inspiring me with your unconditional love and humanity.

Our three children – Bianca, Nathan and Stanley Arthur – for challenging me, with your talent, hard work and empathy, to fight for a world for which proud liberals of all ages and nations have valiantly fought – a world in which our common humanity is cherished, freedom is the breath of the human soul, and differences are celebrated as the lifeblood of vibrant and progressive societies.